RIDERS OF FIRE

BOOK ONE

EILEEN MUELLER

RIDERS OF FIRE
BOOK ONE

EILEEN MUELLER

Dragon Hero, Riders of Fire © Eileen Mueller, 2018
Typesetting © Phantom Feather Press, 2018, American English
Cover Art by Christian Bentulan © Eileen Mueller, 2018
Dragons' Realm Map by Ava Fairhall © Eileen Mueller, 2018
Logo by Geoff Popham, © Phantom Feather Press, 2014
Paperback NZ Edition: 9780995115200
Paperback ISBN KDP 9781728754642

Phantom Feather Press
29 Laura Ave, Brooklyn, Wellington 6021, New Zealand
PhantomFeatherPress@gmail.com
PhantomFeatherPress.Wordpress.com

PHANTOM FEATHER PRESS

DEDICATION

For my mother, who encouraged me to dream,
and my father, who taught me to plan.
And for my children—keep riding dragons
your whole lives long.

LUSH VALLEY

The scrape of a blade sliding from its scabbard cut through the hum of the market square. Ezaara dropped her herb basket. Spinning, she drew her sword.

Tomaaz. Wasn't it enough that he'd beaten her last time? And the time before? Of course not—today he had an audience. Sensing a fight, people backed toward stalls of plaited-onion wreaths, wood carvings and hats, clearing a ring around Tomaaz and Ezaara. On the far side of the marketplace, painted scarves fluttered in the breeze.

Tomaaz lunged.

Ezaara blocked his blow, then feinted. In a flurry of strokes, he drove her backward toward an apple cart. Typical. Quick to attack, he loved to corner his opponents.

"Take five to one for Tomaaz," Lofty yelled. The clink of coppers sealed bets. Folk always favored her brother.

Ezaara whirled as his blade whistled past her face, the whisper of its passage kissing her cheek. That was close, too close. She ducked as he lunged again, then she danced out of reach, saved by her footwork. They fought their way past brightly-patterned bolts of cloth. Tomaaz thrust to her right. Dodging, she bumped the table and the bolts went flying.

"Hey, my cloth," yelled Old Bill as Ezaara leaped over the bolts and Tomaaz gave chase.

Ezaara faced her brother. Perhaps she could distract him. "Seen any pretty girls today?" she taunted, thrusting under his guard. "Look, there's one behind you."

His blade answered for him. He was stronger. And faster. She blocked him, arm aching from the impact. Tomaaz's sword sliced dangerously near. He was so sure he could beat her. Slowing her steps as if she was tiring, Ezaara pretended to stumble, landing on one knee. "Ow!"

Tomaaz faltered. "Ezaara, are you all right?"

Driving her sword under his arm, Ezaara tapped his shirt. "I did it!" she cried, leaping to her feet. "I beat you."

A chorus of cheers erupted from the onlookers. Lofty called, "Go, Ezaara!"

A man yelled, "Lucky she's not a tharuk, Tomaaz, or you'd be dead meat."

A chill skittered down Ezaara's spine. Thankfully there were no tharuks in Lush Valley.

"Aagh, beaten," Tomaaz groaned. Sheathing his sword, he wiped the sweat from his brow.

Ezaara met his green eyes squarely. "You chose to fight me here."

Around them, coppers changed hands. Suddenly, Lofty was there. He pulled her close and kissed her, right on the mouth, mooshing his lips against hers. The crowd *oohed*. Ezaara shoved him away. Old Bill put a pile of grimy coppers into Lofty's hand. Lofty punched his fist in the air.

How dare he! Her first kiss—some shrotty smooch, for a bet? Ezaara's cheeks burned. Half the village had been gawking. She snatched up her basket. Market was only a few days each moon—a nice change from healing people with Ma—but Lofty had just ruined it.

A bellow rang out. "Is that those twins again?" Klaus strode through the scattering crowd. A head taller than most, and as wide as a draft horse, he was the settlement's arbitrator.

Lofty slipped away. The coward.

"Tomaaz. Ezaara." Klaus put his hands on his hips.

Some villagers, pretending to be busy, glanced their way. Others stared outright.

"It's my fault." Tomaaz squared his shoulders. "I challenged her."

"In the middle of the marketplace?" Klaus glared. "You could have taken out a littling's eye."

Whoops, she hadn't thought of littlings. Ezaara held up her sword. "Our tips were corked and the blades aren't sharpened."

Klaus examined Ezaara's sword with his thumb and finger. "In any case, you shouldn't have—"

"She tricked Tomaaz," Old Bill, the traveling merchant, called, "fighting sneaky, like a dragon rider."

As low as a dragon rider? Why was Bill mentioning dragons? Especially in front of Klaus. Was he trying to get her into trouble?

Klaus spun on Bill. "I only let you trade here if you keep our rules. If I hear you mention those filthy winged killers and their stinking riders again, you'll be acquainting yourself with our jail."

Old Bill glared at Ezaara. She shivered. He gave her the creeps.

Klaus pointed a blunt finger at Tomaaz. "No fighting in the marketplace."

"Sorry, sir, it won't happen again," Tomaaz replied.

Ezaara mumbled her apologies too.

"They knocked over my cloth," Old Bill protested.

"Help Bill to tidy up." Klaus threw a last glare at them and went back to his leatherwork.

Old Bill rubbed his hands together. "So, kissed by Lofty, eh?"

Ezaara wrinkled her nose at his fetid breath. The sooner they were finished, the better.

Tomaaz stared at Bill in disgust. "I can't believe you put Lofty up to that. I mean, he's liked her for ages, and now he's blown it. There's no way my sister's going to like him back now."

Ezaara rolled her eyes. "Would you two stop talking about me as if I'm not here?"

Tomaaz continued as if she hadn't spoken. "Come on, Bill, you should've bet Lofty a silver."

Men! Ezaara punched his arm. "Come on, let's get this cleaned up." She picked up a roll of green cloth and dumped it on Old Bill's trestle table. "Good morning, Lovina." Would she answer today?

No, as usual, Bill's daughter, Lovina, ignored her, staring at the ground, lank hair covering her face.

Tomaaz threw most of the bolts on the table, then wandered off.

Ezaara held the last bolt for a moment, rubbing the sea-blue cloth. She'd been admiring it earlier. She'd never seen the sea, but if it was anything like the rippling pattern of blues flowing across this fabric …. She sighed, placing it on the table. Maybe one day she'd see the real ocean.

Old Bill leaned over the stand, his gnarled hand plucking at Ezaara's sleeve like a roach clinging to a table cloth. "You'll like this." He opened his jerkin and pulled out a scrap of black cloth covered in vivid patterns. "Look." It was beautiful.

She didn't want anything to do with Old Bill, but she couldn't resist. Ezaara leaned in, staring. Dragons—the swirls of color were dragons. "That's forbidden," she whispered.

"Go on," he murmured, eyes glinting. "Touch it. I know you want to." He held the cloth out.

Someone would see. Ezaara snatched it. Holding it close, she opened her palm and stroked the wing of a golden dragon, then the tail of a bronze. Set against a dark sky dotted with silver pinpoints, the beasts were beautiful. Were dragons really gold, red and bronze? Or was it only the weaver's imagination?

"How much for this fabric with the wheat pattern?" A woman's voice startled Ezaara.

She crumpled the cloth and thrust it into Bill's waiting hand.

Bill tucked the scrap inside his pocket and elbowed his poor daughter, Lovina. She didn't respond, just kept staring at her feet. "Twenty-five coppers a measure, my lady," Bill crooned.

"Twenty-five," the woman exclaimed. "Why, that's preposterous! I'd only pay—"

Ezaara fled past the cobbler's stand, pushing her way through the crowded marketplace, toward Ana's stall. Old Bill was dangerous. If Klaus had caught her staring at dragons …. Swinging her basket to distract herself from her thumping heart, she strode past hawkers, bleating goats and littlings playing tag. The delicious scent of melted cheese wafted over her. If she could sell her last two healing remedies, she'd be done. And it was early, so she'd have the afternoon off. She headed toward Ana's hand-painted scarves. Ana had tried to teach her how to paint scarves, but instead of creating beautiful patterns, Ezaara's had been ugly and splotched.

"Morning, Ana," Ezaara called. "Need any herbs today?" She swallowed. Did Ana know her son had just kissed her?

Ana smiled, eyes crinkling. "What have you got for me today, Ezaara?"

So, Ana hadn't seen, thank the Egg. Ezaara passed a pot of healing salve and a bundle of clean herb across the trestle table. "You're lucky, these are my last."

Ana peered into Ezaara's basket. Her brow furrowed. "No owl-wort?"

"No." Strange question. Ezaara and Ma never usually picked owl-wort unless someone requested it. Most folk didn't need a herb that helped you see in the dark. Ezaara adjusted her basket on her arm. "It's still in season. I can bring some by later if you need it."

"Good, I'll expect you." Ana fumbled with her money pouch.

Was Ana planning on going out at night? Or was the herb for Lofty? He was always sneaking out with Tomaaz, getting into trouble.

Coppers clinked as they passed from Ana's well-worn hands into hers—three coppers. "You've given me too much."

"That last coin is for the owl-wort," Ana replied. "I want to make sure you bring it today."

So, *someone* was going out tonight. "I'll come by later."

Ezaara threaded her way through the villagers, past a weapons stand and Klaus' leather work. Near the cooper's stall, the clacking of sticks came from behind a stack of barrels.

Busy serving customers, the cooper's wife rolled her eyes. "Those naughty boys are fighting again," she grumbled.

"I'll check on them," Ezaara offered. She ducked down the side of the stall.

Behind the barrels, Paolo and Marco were going at it with sticks. Marco, a littling of only six summers, was blocking his older brother's strikes, even though Paolo had the stronger arm and longer reach. Then Paolo gave a mighty swing—too hard, too high.

"Watch out!" Ezaara leaped forward, too late.

Paolo's stick smacked Marco's face. Marco howled and clutched his nose, blood spurting between his fingers. Paolo's face froze in horror.

"Go fetch some water, Paolo," said Ezaara, striding between them. "Quick."

As Paolo dashed off, she sat Marco on a small barrel and checked his face. Luckily, his nose wasn't broken. "Bleeding noses hurt," she soothed him, "but you'll live to fight another day. Here, lean forward."

His blood dripping onto the ground, Marco was still crying.

Ezaara leaned in, whispering, "Even though Paolo's bigger, you almost had him."

"I did?" Marco's tears stopped.

"Definitely." She grinned.

Paolo returned, passing Ezaara a waterskin.

She pulled a cloth from the leather healer's pouch at her waist and sloshed water over it. "Now, be brave, like a warrior." She gently wiped Marco's face.

"Sorry," said Paolo. "We was trying to fight like you and Tomaaz."

Ezaara winced. She'd never thought of littlings copying them. "The first lesson Pa taught me was not to hit too hard," she said. "Remember, you're training with your brother, not slaying a dragon. You need to keep your sword nice and low, and aim at the body, not the head."

Paolo nodded wisely as if she was a great master.

She scooped some healing salve out of a tiny tub in her pouch and dabbed it on Marco's nose. "As good as new."

"You're lucky your folks taught you," Marco piped up, looking a lot better without blood leaking out of his nose. "Ours can't fight, but we're going to battle tharuks when we grow up."

Paolo nudged him. "Hey, I told you there are no tharuks in Lush Valley."

The boy had a good point. If there was no one to fight, why had Ma and Pa trained her and Tomaaz with the bow and sword since they were littlings?

Marco jumped down from the barrel, swinging his sword arm. "Don't care. Want to fight tharuks anyway."

She picked up their sticks. "I'll tell you what, I'll talk to Tomaaz. Maybe we can teach you to fight."

The boys' eyes lit up. "Really?"

She nodded. "We might have a couple of wooden practice swords you can use." The boys grinned. "But not now," she said. "Today, you two need to find something quiet to do."

Paolo put an arm around his brother's shoulder. "What about a game of scatter stones, Marco? You like those."

Ezaara laughed, leaving the boys clacking stones instead of sticks, and wandered back through the market.

"There you are." Tomaaz approached her. "I was looking for you."

"Marco got a bleeding nose from Paolo."

Tomaaz rolled his eyes. "Those two again."

"Now you sound like Klaus." Ezaara grinned. "They don't know the sharp end of a sword from a hilt, and Paolo swings way too hard. We should teach them."

"Good idea," Tomaaz said, tugging Ezaara toward their parents' produce stall. "Now, what was Bill showing you, on the quiet? You looked fascinated."

"Cloth—speckled with dragons of gold and bronze," Ezaara whispered. Her heart started thumping all over again.

"Contraband cloth?" Tomaaz's eyes flitted nervously. "Old Bill's bad news. And his daughter's strange too."

"You'd be strange too, if Old Bill was your pa." Ezaara nodded at a mother with littlings clutching at her skirts, waiting until they'd passed before replying. "Even if dragons are evil, the fabric was beautiful."

Ezaara and Tomaaz skirted a pen of piglets. "Lofty says dragons are honored beyond the Grande Alps," said Tomaaz. "One day, I'm going to look for myself."

She elbowed Tomaaz. "Someone will hear you."

"So what? I'm not going to live here forever, you know."

Turning to face him, Ezaara stopped. "You'd leave us?" Although they sometimes bickered, life without her twin would be like losing a part of herself.

His eyes slid away. "Don't know. Maybe."

Ezaara frowned. "That's why Lofty's ma wanted owl-wort—you and Lofty are planning to go tonight, aren't you?"

Tomaaz burst out laughing. "If only!"

So, he wasn't planning anything. "If you ever leave, take me with you," she insisted. There had to be more to life than Lush Valley.

"All right," Tomaaz said, "but no running off without me, either."

"Course not." They bumped knuckles.

At their family stall, Pa passed a sack of beets to a customer and pocketed the man's money. He faced Ezaara and Tomaaz, hands on his hips. "We didn't teach you fighting skills so you could create a ruckus on market days. What have I told you before?"

Tomaaz sighed. "To save our skills for battle."

"To practice in the meadows, not the market," Ezaara added.

Pa nodded. "Tomaaz, could you take this sack of carrots to the smithy?"

"Sure, Pa." Tomaaz shouldered the sack and left.

Ma glanced at Ezaara's basket. "So, you sold everything. I heard you beat Tomaaz."

"Only just, and through strategy, not skill."

"Strategy is also a skill." Ma put an arm around her shoulder. "Everyone's good at different things. Remember, you were climbing trees way before Tomaaz, because you weren't afraid of heights."

"I guess so." Tomaaz still couldn't climb a ladder without turning green. Who was ever going to be impressed by a head for heights? No one she knew. Ezaara handed Ma the money and basket. "Ana wants owl-wort, *today*."

"Owl-wort?" Her mother's eyes widened. "Collect some supplies for healing salve while you're at it." She gave Ezaara back a copper. "Get something to eat before you head back into the forest."

Pa winked. "Watch out for Lofty."

"I don't know what you're talking about." Heat rose in Ezaara's cheeks. Had Pa heard already? Worse, had he seen Lofty mashing his lips on hers?

"Soon everyone will be gossiping about something else." Ma patted her arm.

Ezaara groaned. This was worse than she'd thought. If only her first kiss had been private, special, not from her brother's best friend. From someone who meant more.

She hurried through the stalls, buying melted cheese on flatbread, then headed down the road to the riverbank, eating it. Water surged around the stepping stones as she crossed the river. Following familiar trails, she tucked peppermint and sage into the leather healer's pouch at her waist. Lifting fern fronds, Ezaara picked some feverweed. The gurgling of the river gradually faded.

Now, she needed arnica and owl-wort. Ezaara strolled deeper into the forest and came to the sacred clearing. Stepping into the sunlight, Ezaara stooped to pick arnica flowers. The ancient piaua, half as thick as a cottage, rose before her at the edge of the clearing, its bark pitted and gnarly. Blue berries peeked from its dark foliage. As a tree speaker, her mother often talked to the piaua whenever she collected its sacred healing juice. Placing her palm against the bark, Ezaara strained to feel a whisper. Nothing—again. She sighed. Not a tree speaker, then. What would her vocation be? Ma was happy as a healer and herbalist, and Ezaara didn't mind helping her, but she wanted something more. Excitement. Adventure. Maybe love.

The owl-wort vines grew among the knobby piaua roots. She parted the undergrowth and plucked a handful of leaves. Rising from a crouch, she opened her pouch.

A strange tingle ran through Ezaara, then a shadow fell over her. Something *swished*, a sudden breeze stirring her hair. She jerked her head up.

A dragon was circling the treetops. Ezaara recoiled in fear. With a snap of fangs or a swipe of talons, it could kill her. The owl-wort fell from her shaking hands. She tensed to flee.

But hesitated.

Sunlight played across the dragon's iridescent scales, making them shimmer. Its graceful wings swished ever closer, rippling with color. This beast was beautiful—beautiful, but deadly. She had to escape. But the tingling grew stronger. The amazing creature circled down toward her. Foliage rustled in the downdraught from the dragon's wingbeats.

A voice hummed in her mind. *"Ezaara,"* it crooned.

This creature could talk to her?

"We're mind-melding, sensing each other's thoughts and emotions."

She held her breath, drawn to the dragon. Rich colors cascaded through her mind. Sunshine poured into her soul. Ezaara wanted to soar. She glimpsed a vision—her riding the dragon, flying above the forest, over the Grande Alps and into the blue.

"This is your destiny, to ride with me."

Warning cries reached her—villagers. If only they knew *this dragon*, they wouldn't be afraid.

The dragon's hum built to a roar inside her. It dived.

Familiar faces shot into her mind. Her family! She couldn't leave them.

Ezaara's love for her family was swept aside as energy rushed through her. She was enveloped in a prism of rainbow-colored light, like reflections in a dewdrop. Music from the purest flute filled her heart. For the first time in her life, she felt whole. The energy coiled inside her and she sprang, lifted by the wind, hair streaming out behind her. In a flash of color, the dragon's scales were beneath her. Ezaara landed on a saddle in a hollow between its wings. She wrapped her arms around the dragon's spinal ridge, hugging it tight.

It felt so right.

The dragon regarded her with yellow eyes. Ezaara could've sworn it was smiling. *"I am Zaarusha. You were born to be my rider,"* it thrummed. The beast turned. Its belly rumbled and flames shot from its maw.

They flew off, leaving her home and loved ones behind.

EILEEN MUELLER

WESTERN PASS

Ezaara clung to the dragon's spinal ridge, wind tugging her hair. They soared above a carpet of bristling green. Her blood sang. Until today, she'd never *lived*.

Beyond the forest canopy, a patchwork of fields and cottages sprawled beneath the snow-tipped Western Grande Alps. Lazy twirls of smoke wound upward. They were nearly at Western Settlement, two days' ride by horse. They'd come so far, so fast.

Just today, she'd vowed she'd never leave Lush Valley without Tomaaz. Now, she was winging further away with each moment—leaving Tomaaz and her parents behind.

She glanced back, the village swallowed by endless forest. Her belly tightened. Could she ever go back?

"You have another destiny—with me. You chose when we imprinted."

She'd felt the connection, and still felt it now. Zaarusha was part of her. Their bond was like one of Ana's scarves—a thing of beauty, of glorious colors, protective and warm.

"Going back means facing the pitchforks of Lush Valley," the dragon mind-melded.

Ezaara swallowed. Everyone in Lush Valley was afraid of dragons—and their riders. She was now their enemy.

"Besides, your family is the reason you're here."

"What? No one in my family's ever seen a dragon."

"They know more than you imagine." A chuckle rumbled through the dragon's belly. *"Your mother and father are dragon riders."*

"No, they—" An image popped into her mind: Ma, much younger, astride a silver dragon; Pa was behind her, arms wrapped around her waist. The way the sun glanced off the dragon's silver scales looked real, but Ezaara wasn't fooled. Then, her mother's hair stirred in the breeze and she laughed. The truth hit her like a punch in the stomach. That was Ma's laugh. Pa's real smile.

"So …," Ezaara said, racking her brain for another answer. There was none. *"This is one of your memories, then."*

"Yes, and dragons can't lie."

"But—"

"I'm Queen of Dragons' Realm. Our families have been intertwined for years."

A dragon family intertwined with hers? And not just any dragon—the queen. *"I don't get it. Why didn't my parents tell me?"*

A wave of sorrow washed over Ezaara. *"Before you were born, your mother, Marlies, accidentally killed one of my royal dragonets."*

How awful. *"I'm sorry."*

"Marlies and Hans fled to Lush Valley to hide the truth, but perhaps that was fortunate, because now, I sense that dragonet's power, latent, in you."

So that's why. Ma was ashamed. Ezaara was here because of a mistake Ma had made, years ago. *"Me? Powerful?"* It was ridiculous.

"Not yet, but you will be." Zaarusha beat her wings, rising up the side of the mountain face.

Ezaara hunched over the queen's back, gripping her spinal ridge with white knuckles. *"But you're a queen and I'm … just me."*

They landed in the snow at the apex of an Alp. Fields lay like lazily-tossed rugs below. Settlements dotted plains that led to a barren range of snow-tipped hills, far to the west. Meandering ribbons of blue fed into lakes nestled among verdant green. A vast forest stretched northward, hemmed in by chains upon chains of mountains that seemed to go on forever.

"This is Dragons' Realm. We protect it. You, me and the dragons and riders that serve the realm."

And to think she'd been cloistered in a valley, afraid of dragons.

Zaarusha chuckled. *"Yes, you've outgrown Lush Valley, Ezaara. You're ready for this."*

It was true. She'd outgrown gathering herbs, and Tomaaz and Lofty's dumb tricks—and the superstitions of Lush Valley. With a surge of elation, Ezaara scanned the vista. It was her new duty to protect this. But how? She was so tiny compared to this vast rugged land of contrasts. The sweeping rivers, the jagged mountains, the homes scattered across the realm. The pristine snow, glinting in the sunlight, full of promise.

"This is what I want," Ezaara whispered. Gods, she already missed her family.

Roars cut the air. Then screams.

Ezaara spun in the saddle. *"That came from the south, Zaarusha."*

Zaarusha sprang. They were airborne, high above the Western Alps in moments.

"There." In a pass, between two steep peaks, was a battle between men and beasts. *"Go, Zaarusha, go."*

"Tharuks, from the scent." Zaarusha's tone was grim. *"Probably a scouting party."*

Ezaara hunkered over Zaarusha's spinal ridges. *"I thought tharuks were monster stories to keep littlings near home."*

"Only in Lush Valley," Zaarusha said, *"but not for long."*

A chill snaked down Ezaara's spine. These beasts were making their way over the Western Grande Alps into Lush Valley. To her people, her family. *"Faster, Zaarusha, faster."*

The queen sped through the sky. Ezaara leaned out, trying to see the fight far below, her eyes watering in the wind. Without warning, Zaarusha dived.

Ezaara lost her balance, sliding down the queen's side. She grasped at the saddle strap.

And missed. Her hands slipped over sleek scales. Then there was nothing—she was in midair. Wind tore at her. The ground charged upward. She was about to die.

A scream froze in her throat.

"Relax and trust me."

The ground was rushing ever closer. What choice did she have? Ezaara let her body go loose.

Strong talons grasped her. Her breath whooshed out of her lungs. Ezaara gripped Zaarusha's legs. They flew to the closest peak and Zaarusha deposited Ezaara on a ledge. She climbed back into the saddle, her legs like Ma's egg pudding.

"Now fasten the harness straps. Tight."

Ezaara gulped. *"I'm sorry."*

"No, it's my fault. It's been a long time since I had a rider." They took off, diving to meet the fight.

On an outpost, high on the ridge, blood from three dead men leached into the snow. A dozen tharuks were attacking two more men, who fought, back to back, trying to keep the beasts at bay. Other tharuks tossed wood down the mountainside.

Tharuks were awful, close up. With sharp tusks, the beasts were covered in thick matted fur and wore heavy boots and leather breastplates. They slashed long claws at the men. Zaarusha snatched up two tharuks, tossing them into the air. Their roars died as they thudded to the rocks, black blood splattering the snow. They stank of rotten meat.

Ezaara groped behind her for her bow. No, it was still at home. And her sword was blunted. She was useless, clinging to Zaarusha as the queen lunged again, flame shooting from her maw.

Tharuks shrieked, flailing on the ground, burning. More beasts ran at the men. Zaarusha flicked flame at them, forcing them back. *"I can't get too close or we'll burn our people,"* Zaarusha mind-melded.

One of the men screamed, clutching at his throat. Red pumped over his hands. He crumpled, dead.

A roar cut through the fighting. A huge beast thrust its fist into the air, bellowing, "Kill him!" More monsters surged over the ridge, joining their leader to surround the last man.

The warrior spun, jabbing with his sword, but he was outnumbered.

Zaarusha blasted a swathe of flame, cutting down a line of tharuks. Their snarls turned to shrieks that trailed off as their smoking bodies dropped, twitching in the snow. She dived, tossing more beasts down the mountainside.

"Zaarusha!" Ezaara's scream died as the last man fell to the earth.

Tharuks closed in, red eyes gleaming.

With a roar, Zaarusha wheeled in midair, her wingtip sweeping a tharuk off its feet. It tumbled down the slope in a flurry of gathering snow, limbs flying.

"Get to Lush Valley Settlement," the tharuk leader bellowed, spinning to face the queen, claws out.

Three beasts fled down the mountain toward Western Settlement and Lush Valley.

Five men dead. Ezaara pulsed with rage. *"Let me kill one."*

"No, that man needs your help."

Ezaara snapped her head around. Her healer's pouch. She *could* help.

Zaarusha threw another tharuk off the slope and swooped in for the leader.

A jolt of pain ripped through Ezaara. But it wasn't her—it was Zaarusha. *"Are you all right?"* Ezaara asked.

"Fine," Zaarusha snarled, ripping the tharuk's body in two. Black blood sprayed over the snow. His body thudded down the slope in the wake of the fleeing tharuk trio.

They landed, and Ezaara undid the straps, scrambling out of the saddle.

Rushing to the man's side, she knelt by him. She took his wrist, feeling his heartbeat, where the blood pulsed weakly over his bone. His chest was a bloody mess, making a wet sucking noise every time he breathed. The poor man. There was nothing she could do for him, except ease his passing. Ezaara raised his head and shoulders, resting them on her knees.

His eyelids fluttered and he groaned.

"Here, chew this." She placed some arnica flowers in his mouth. "They'll taste awful, but will help the pain."

He ground the flowers between gritted teeth. "My wife …" It was barely a moan. "My littlings …"

His jaw fell slack, shreds of arnica petals still on his tongue. His head lolled to the side.

Oh, gods. Ezaara folded the man's hands over his chest and laid his head to rest in the snow. Her eyes burned. She swiped at stray tears. *"Zaarusha, I couldn't save him."*

Throat tight, she went to the other men, checking them. All dead. The snow was a mass of churned black and red, scattered with chunks of wood and bodies of men and beasts. *"We'd better clean up."* Only a few hours' flight from Lush Valley, and they were already burying people.

EILEEN MUELLER

Ezaara gestured at the men. *"They were guarding the pass. This wood must've been for a beacon fire to warn Western Settlement of an attack. Some of those tharuks have slipped through. We have to go back and warn my people."*

"We can't go back," Zaarusha replied. *"I'll tell the blue guards—the riders and dragons who protect this part of the realm."*

"Dragons don't protect Lush Valley."

"Why do you think no tharuks have ever come over the Grande Alps before?"

Klaus was so wrong. Dragons didn't destroy at all. The very dragons he'd despised had kept them safe—unseen, beyond the chain of alps that encircled Lush Valley's wide basin—protecting the three villages cradled within: Southern Settlement, Lush Valley Settlement and Western Settlement.

"Let's light that beacon fire." Ezaara frowned. *"Will people know what it means?"*

Zaarusha replied, *"Your father, Hans, will."*

"First, we'll bury these men."

"We could give them a funeral pyre," Zaarusha suggested.

"No, their families need to be able to find them."

Zaarusha dug a grave and Ezaara buried the men, shoveling icy dirt into the hole with numb hands. She found stones for a cairn, and plucked a pine branch, wedging it between the stones as a marker. If only she could've done more.

Ezaara dragged a log back up to the pass, adding it to what was left of the warriors' wood pile. Zaarusha ripped out dead trees and flew them up. Ezaara could've left the queen to collect the wood, but the burn of her muscles and the ache in her limbs paid tribute to these men who'd tried to protect the pass.

Bit by bit, the pile grew.

"That's enough, Ezaara," Zaarusha said. *"It'll be dark soon. Once I light this wood, the beacon will be seen for miles."*

Ezaara wiped her brow, wrinkling her nose. The stench of tharuks made her gag, and the sight of them turned her stomach. *"What are they? That black blood and rotten stench—they're unnatural."*

"Years ago, a powerful mage opened a world gate and let Commander Zens into Dragons' Realm," Zaarusha said. A vicious face loomed in Ezaara's mind. She tried to block it out, but Zens' enormous yellow eyes followed her. *"Zens created an army of tharuks, without breeding them—the way we take a cutting to grow a plant. They do whatever he commands. They catch and enslave our folk and use plant extracts to make slaves submit to Zens' will."* Zaarusha shared memories of tharuks in mining pits, whipping slaves who were only half alive—thin shells with deadened faces.

Ezaara shuddered. *"Throw the beasts on the fire, too. Erase every trace of them. This is not a funeral pyre to honor them—just their wretched bodies providing fuel to warn our people."*

"My pleasure." A ripple of feral satisfaction radiated from Zaarusha.

When the fire was blazing, Ezaara clambered back into the saddle. Her back and arms ached and her feet were numb.

"Come, it's been a tough first day," Zaarusha melded. *"I know a place where we can rest."*

Gripping the saddle, Ezaara closed her eyes, but couldn't erase the images of the body-strewn snow. *"We have to fight these beasts. Stop them slaughtering our people."*

"I know, Ezaara," Zaarusha said, *"that's why I need you."* Flipping her wings, she flew along the ridge. *"Eighteen years ago, my last rider, Anakisha, my mate Syan, and his rider were lost in battle."*

Zaarusha shared a memory.

Zaarusha was wounded, roaring. Her rider slipped from her saddle and fell, dark hair flying and limbs sprawling, into a horde of tharuks. Claws out, the beasts swarmed over her. A massive black dragon dived into the midst of the monsters, his rider screaming, "Anakisha!" Syan thrashed his talons, sending monsters flying. Tharuks stabbed his belly and fired arrows into his wings, shredding them. His rider was dragged from the saddle and vanished under a pack of furry bodies. Bellowing, the dragon flamed tharuks, but for every beast he burned, three rushed forward. He lifted his tattered wings and flapped, rising, but a seething mass of tharuks grabbed onto his limbs, dragging him back to the ground.

Zaarusha fled, her bellows of rage and anguish ricocheting through Ezaara.

The queen's raw agony swept through Ezaara, making her chest ache and her eyes prick. She'd only left her family behind. Zaarusha had lost everyone she loved.

"Without my clutch of eggs to protect at Dragons' Hold, I would've dived in and died too," Zaarusha said. "I made the right choice. And now, I have you."

Ezaara reeled. "That could've been me, earlier, when I fell."

"Luckily, we were high enough for me to catch you. Riders have broken bones by not trusting their dragons and being too tense."

"I'm glad I didn't know. That would've made it impossible to relax."

"There's only one time when you shouldn't trust me—if tharuks give me swayweed. This herb—"

"—replaces love with hate, changing allegiance between men, or between man and beast," Ezaara recited.

"So, Marlies taught you well." Zaarusha hesitated. "Don't be scared by my past. We have a bright future together. I can sense it. Your name will be honored across Dragons' Realm."

Except in Lush Valley. They'd never honor her there.

Zaarusha dropped down a steep rocky face below the snow line, and landed on a broad scrubby plateau halfway down the mountainside. On the pass above them, the beacon was burning, barely visible in the gold and orange light of the setting sun.

"Don't worry, soon that fire will be blazing against the dark," Zaarusha said. *"Come, I want to show you something before night falls."* Zaarusha paced through scrub, entering a cave in the mountainside. She blew a small flame, lighting a torch in a wall sconce.

A shelf lined the wall, with waterskins and jars of preserves on it. Below, barrels were lined up like warriors. Someone obviously kept this place well stocked.

"A bed." Ezaara slid off Zaarusha and sank down onto the pallet. *"This looks so good right now."*

"Wait, there's something better." Zaarusha went outside and gestured with her snout toward a track winding through the scrub. *"Go on. Take a look."*

Ezaara hesitated.

"You're safe here. Tharuks can't climb down that sheer rock face or scale the cliff below."

Taking a deep breath, Ezaara leaned up and scratched Zaarusha's eye ridge.

The queen nudged her with her snout. *"Enjoy yourself."*

Ezaara followed the goat track through the tussock. The plateau was oddly fertile, given the granite cliff above. Thick grasses and scrub covered the area, with giant ferns towering over her. It was warmer here than up on the snow line, although in winter it would be decked in white. A hidden stream burbled nearby.

The track angled toward the cliff, edged in lush vegetation. The stream was growing louder. Maybe Zaarusha was sending her for a drink of fresh water. The setting sun cast a golden hue over everything. A strange scent hung in the air. The stream was louder now, the gurgle reminding her of Lush Valley and all she'd left behind. Ezaara's eyes burned. Not again. She'd cried enough today.

Stepping through ferns, Ezaara came to the end of the track—and gasped.

Misty tendrils rose off a narrow river flowing along the back of the plateau. But it wasn't mist—it was steam. Ezaara crouched and dipped her hand in the water. She groaned. It was *warm*. Further along the cliff, a waterfall gushed out of a hole in the rock, steam wafting from it as it cascaded into the thermal river. The water smelled like old eggs, but she didn't care. Shucking off her clothes, Ezaara climbed down the bank. She waded a few steps across the river and sat, leaning against the cliff, immersed to her shoulders.

"*Aah, Zaarusha. This is better than food and a bed. It's wonderful.*"

"*I knew you'd like it.*" Zaarusha chuckled. "*You can bathe, but don't submerge your head or drink the water. It's good for aches and pains, but rough on your stomach.*"

Ezaara wanted nothing more than to duck under and scrub the grime from her face, but instead, she leaned against the bank, gazing upward. The water soothed her aching back and shoulders as, one by one, stars winked at her from the dark sky. She craned her neck, trying to spot the beacon. She couldn't see it, but hopefully Pa and Ma would.

"*Actually, Marlies may see the beacon, but she won't be able to help anyone in Lush Valley. She's leaving to help me recover something I lost.*"

"*Zaarusha, stop being so cryptic. What's going on?*"

"*My son is missing. Tharuks captured him. As Queen, I can't leave to look for him, so Marlies is searching for him.*"

So, Ma had a chance to redeem herself with Zaarusha. "*Can you let Ma or Pa know that I'm safe?*"

"Sorry, we're too far away to communicate with either of them." Zaarusha gave a grunt that blew the tired cobwebs from Ezaara's mind.

"Are you all right?"

"Just tired."

Something Zaarusha was saying didn't add up. Ezaara clambered out of the water and tugged on her clothes and boots, not stopping to dry herself. She hurried back along the trail, guided by moonlight. When she came to the cavern, she understood. *"Zaarusha, you're hurt!"* Ezaara rushed forward to examine a gash on Zaarusha's foreleg.

"It's nothing."

"It was that tharuk leader, wasn't it? I felt your pain when you grabbed him." She'd been so overwhelmed, she'd forgotten.

"That maggot-roach sunk its claws into me. But at least those tharuk scouts didn't have any poison-tipped arrows with them. This is simply a cut." Zaarusha flicked her tail, like an impatient cat.

"You should've told me before I bathed," Ezaara scolded out loud. It was strange to speak after mind-melding all day. "This is going to need stitches." She took her needle and squirrel gut twine from her healer's pouch and threaded it. "Hold still." The needle was too small, so in the end Ezaara had to pierce Zaarusha's hide with a knife from the cave and thread the twine through the holes to tug the edges of her wound tight.

Zaarusha was stoic, not uttering a sound, but an image of her ripping apart the tharuk leader's body repeatedly rushed through the queen's mind. *"Helps me manage pain,"* Zaarusha admitted with a dragonly grin.

When Ezaara was done, Zaarusha hooked a barrel toward her with her uninjured front limb. With a swipe of her talons, she pried the lid open. *"Help yourself."*

"Apples. How did they get here?"

"Marlies' dragon, Liesar, leaves supplies for our riders in hide-outs across the realm."

So, Ma's dragon was still alive. How could they bear to be parted? Actually, Ma had had no choice. Ezaara's stomach grumbled. She took an apple and leaned against Zaarusha's side to eat it, tossing apples from the barrel to Zaarusha, who snapped them down.

Spiking an apple on a talon, Zaarusha toasted it with fire from her maw. *"Here."*

Juice ran down Ezaara's chin. *"Oh, so sweet."*

"Are you full?" The queen eyed the barrel. *"Mind if I finish these?"*

Ezaara took one more. *"You can have the rest."*

Zaarusha shoved her snout in the barrel, crunching and slurping until the apples were gone. Ezaara smothered a smile—sharing with a dragon wasn't exactly one for one. Zaarusha curled up on the ledge. Ezaara dragged the pallet and blanket over near Zaarusha and lay down, but her mind was too busy to relax.

"Sleep, Ezaara. We have a long journey ahead of us." The queen folded a wing over her. *"Let me tell you a legend to help you rest."*

Ezaara closed her eyes.

"In the beginning, there was the Egg. Not an ordinary egg, but the First Egg, which held the seed for all dragons. When the First Egg burst into a million shards, Dragons' Realm was born …"

Dragons' Hold

Roberto strode down the tunnel that connected the council chambers to his cavern, the thud of his boots echoing off the stone walls. As he rounded a corner, a familiar figure detached itself from the shadows.

Adelina's smiling face made the torchlight brighter—a welcome face after the council's bickering. "Are you all right?" She hugged him.

There were days, like today, when his sister was the only thing that kept him sane. "I'm fine. Just the usual—more arguing." They walked along the tunnel toward her cavern.

"I'm surprised you didn't enjoy it." She mock-punched his arm, grinning. "I thought you liked arguing. Well, you do with me."

Despite his mood, Roberto managed a weak chuckle.

She arched her eyebrows. "What was it this time?"

"Apparently, Handel has had word from Zaarusha that she's imprinted with the new Queen's Rider."

Her sharp intake of breath betrayed her. "Oh? Has she? I—"

Oh, shards! "Adelina." His voice softened. "We already knew it wasn't you."

She swallowed. "I know. But I still held hope." She gave him a too-bright smile. "It's great news. It's been eighteen years since Zaarusha had a rider. So, why were the council arguing?"

"Because her rider was found in Lush Valley, of all places."

Adelina rolled her eyes. "Really?"

Roberto rubbed the back of his neck, trying to dislodge the tension that had been building all night. "It'll be some ignorant, backward clod, terrified of dragons."

"From a superstitious backwater, dealing with the likes of Lars and Tonio." She shook her head. "And leading the council without knowing the politics here."

Exactly what he'd been thinking. "Tharuks haven't even made it to Lush Valley. How could someone with no fighting or combat experience lead us in war? What was Zaarusha thinking?"

"Maybe she was desperate for a rider after so many years alone." Again, hurt flashed on Adelina's face before she forced another smile. "It's not our problem. Everything will work out."

Typical. She was already looking on the good side again. No wonder she kept him balanced. Stopping outside Adelina's cavern, Roberto faced her. "It *is* my problem. I've been given the honor of training the new Queen's Rider." More of a burden than an honor.

Her eyebrows shot up. "Why?"

"Handel decided, for some unknown reason, and Lars and the council have ratified it, so the decision is binding. Zaarusha will be here tonight."

She grimaced.

The unspoken words hung between them. He'd have to use his talents. "I'll be fine." He had to be. Roberto squeezed her shoulder, then strode down the tunnel toward his quarters.

Huh! An ignorant settler from Lush Valley could be a traitor or a spy—someone Zens had turned without the queen or her rider knowing it. His job was to test this new rider, despite the memories that haunted him each time he had to perform his duty. He'd need to be thorough—for the realm, for Zaarusha. If there was the faintest hint that the Queen's Rider wasn't fit, Zaarusha would be seeking another.

§

Ezaara's chin drooped to her chest. She jerked awake and clutched Zaarusha's spinal ridge. The moon dragged fingertips across the tips of the forest below, not penetrating the dark mass. After three days and nights of flying with only short stops, her backside was sore and her shoulders ached. *"How's your leg doing?"*

"Much better. Thank you for stitching it," Zaarusha thrummed. "We'll be at Dragons' Hold soon. We're expected before dawn."

So, no chance of a decent sleep.

"Yes, I mind-melded and told the blue guards about tharuks entering Lush Valley, and advised them that we're coming."

"I didn't realize you could mind-meld with everyone."

"I can only meld with other riders when they touch me, but I can meld with their dragons if they're not too far away. They're keen to meet the new Queen's Rider."

Whoever 'they' were. *"In the middle of the night?"* Ezaara yawned. *"If they've waited eighteen years, surely they can wait a few more hours."*

Zaarusha snorted. *"Your imprinting bond and loyalty must be tested."*

"How?"

"You'll be fine. Just be yourself."

Fine? That was all right for Zaarusha to say—she wasn't about to face a horde of blue dragons for the first time.

They ascended a snowy mountainside, gliding above a summit. Moonlight caught on jagged peaks that formed a gaping maw around a dark basin.

"These mountains are Dragon's Teeth, the guardians of Dragons' Hold," Zaarusha said. *"Flying is the only way in."*

They swooped down, the basin swallowing them, and flew toward a mountain face, shooting through a tunnel into an enormous cavern.

Inside, the air was filled with dragons, their sinuous necks weaving to stare at her with wild eyes. They swooped and dived past Zaarusha, grim-faced riders upon their backs. Bill's scrap of cloth had been right—they were every color from emerald to blood red. Dragons snarled, flashing fangs. Their wings made torches sputter in their sconces, sending a chill down her spine.

Zaarusha roared, the air reverberating, setting Ezaara's teeth on edge. Her talons clattered on the granite floor. Twelve dragons landed, splayed in an arc on a rock platform that towered above Ezaara and the queen.

Ezaara gripped the saddle tighter. The whole of their farm would fit in this cavern, several times over.

The riders, women and men, dismounted, swords at their sides and dagger hilts peeking from their boots. They looked fierce. Intimidating. Wait, there were thirteen dragons. A bronze rider-less dragon was skulking in the shadows.

A man stalked down from the platform, boots striking the stone steps, moving like a lethal predator. Unlike the men in Lush Valley. Confident. Dangerous. He bowed to Zaarusha, dark hair brushing his shoulders. "Welcome home, Honored Queen." His hard, black eyes flicked over Ezaara. "I see you've brought your new rider for testing."

What a welcome. *"What happens if I fail this test?"* she fired at Zaarusha.

"You'll be banished to the Wastelands."

The Wastelands! *"Banished? But I'm—"*

"I told you, you'll be fine. Climb down, he's waiting."

Ezaara slid out of the saddle, stumbling as her feet hit the ground.

The man's lips twitched into a sneer.

She shrunk back, closer to Zaarusha, as all the stories she'd heard about killer dragons came flooding back to her. *"Zaarusha—"*

Zaarusha snorted. *"Ezaara, you have to do this on your own."* She broke mind-meld and flew to a high outcrop.

"Welcome to Dragons' Hold." His tone was cool, disinterested. Anything but welcoming. "I'm Roberto, Master of Mental Faculties." He was only a couple of years older than her, but his poise and arrogance made him so much older. Intimidating. "It's my responsibility to test you." He waved a hand at the dragons on the stage above them. "I present the Council of the Twelve Dragon Masters. Do you consent to be tested? If not, you'll forfeit your right to ride Zaarusha and be removed from Dragons' Hold immediately."

"Y-yes."

On the platform, the dragon masters bowed. Their dragons towered above her. Ferocious eyes fixed on her. A huge purple dragon roared, its wicked fangs glinting. They all joined in, rearing, clawing the air and shaking the ground.

Her stomach coiled. What had she done to deserve this? *"Zaarusha."* No answer.

Were they going to attack? Better to be impaled on the peaks of Dragon's Teeth than face these beasts. There was no way she'd pass their test. She'd be banished and die in the barren Wastelands across the Naobian Sea. Ezaara froze, rooted to the ground in terror.

Roberto raised his palm. The dragons quieted.

"Good evening, respected dragons and Council of the Twelve Dragon Masters," he said. "In keeping with tradition, Queen Zaarusha has brought her new rider to be tested. She has stood fast in the face of your wrath, passing the first phase of testing."

What? Being too scared to move had saved her from failure? If only her heart would stop bashing against her chest.

"She may have imprinted, with our queen, but how well?" Again, Master Roberto's eyes flicked over her. "We must determine whether she is fit to be trained as the true Queen's Rider."

He looked as if he was battling not to spit on her. Ezaara cringed.

The dragons bared their teeth, nostrils flaring. They roared, a low rumble building until the air vibrated and the stone floor pulsed beneath her.

Roberto flashed a cool smile and gestured at narrow stairs cut into the rock. "Masters, introduce her to your dragons." His voice echoed around the large cavern. "And dragons, be thorough."

Be thorough doing what? Her hands shook. Lofty and Tomaaz would hoot at her fear, call her ridiculous. Ezaara reached out for Zaarusha again. Still nothing.

"Ezaara, proceed to the stage. As you are tested, please remember the moment you imprinted with Queen Zaarusha."

Zaarusha had taken a gamble on her, and here she was, as scared as a littling hearing ghost stories. She couldn't let Zaarusha down. Despite the fear zinging along her veins, Ezaara forced herself to race up the steps toward a formidable purple beast with blue eyes.

The beast lowered its head. A master with a fair beard—and eyes the same shade as the purple dragon's—stepped forward and picked up Ezaara's hand, placing it on the dragon's brow, covering it with his own.

A jolt of energy flew along Ezaara's arm. Her memory exploded in her mind. She was in Lush Valley's sacred clearing, watching Zaarusha approach, her heart on fire as she mindmelded with the Queen of the Dragons for the first time.

The master spoke. "I'm Lars, Leader of the Council of the Twelve Dragon Masters. This is Singlar. Welcome to Dragons' Hold, Ezaara, Rider of Zaarusha, Queen of the Dragons."

Ezaara staggered. How had Lars known her name?

"From your imprinting memories." Singlar winked his purple eyelid. *"Besides, Zaarusha told us earlier."*

Lars motioned to his right. A female master took her hand and laid it upon a green dragon's head, covering it with hers. Ezaara relived her imprinting experience, emotions coursing through her again.

She repeated the experience with each of the dragons in the circle, until only two remained: a blue one and the lone bronze dragon, who regarded her with intense green eyes that reminded her of Pa's.

Roberto led her to the blue dragon. "This is Erob. I'm his rider."

"And the bronze?"

"He's not a member of the council." Roberto placed, not one, but both of Ezaara's hands on Erob's blue brow. "I need to test you more rigorously. Do you consent?"

She had no option. There was no way she was going to give up Zaarusha.

At her nod, Roberto put his hands on her temples.

Surprised, she flinched. Both Erob and Roberto gazed deep into Ezaara's eyes, Roberto's face a mask of concentration. Without a sneer—with his ebony eyes, high cheekbones and olive skin—his face was striking.

§

The girl had imprinted. Roberto was sure of it. Zaarusha had snorted at something, which showed they'd been mind-melding without touching—a sure sign of imprinting. But how solid was their bond? Ezaara had trembled at the sight of dragons, but she'd also stood her ground—so she had courage.

Courage or not, the Queen of Dragons' Realm deserved the best. If Zaarusha had made a mistake, he had to find out. The other masters and their dragons had confirmed the imprinting bond existed. Now he had to test the quality of that bond. And the Queen's Rider. If she wasn't good enough, it was his task to fail this backward girl from Lush Valley, and she'd be dispatched to the Wastelands before dawn.

Roberto took a deep breath, steeling himself. He hated using his talent, paid for with people's blood. He placed both of his hands on the girl's temples. It always came back to using his cursed gift.

He was in her mind.

Zaarusha spiraled down to meet Ezaara. Fear curled in the girl's stomach. Her limbs were paralyzed. She was petrified she'd be raked by talons, or die in the dragon's maw. But even as Roberto wanted to scoff at her naive fear, he was awed at the intensity of her emotions; the sharpness of her memories.

He'd tested many folk. Their experiences had been vivid, but compared to this, they were nothing: an overcast day compared to summer sun.

No, a few halting notes compared to an intricate harmony.

Ezaara's fear of the dragon queen melted into admiration, and her admiration to love. Zaarusha's scales were bright, her voice thrilling. The breeze of the dragon's wingbeats stirred Ezaara's hair. Her emotions soared. This girl's bond was the strongest he'd witnessed. Her jump onto the queen's back was incredible. She'd harnessed Zaarusha's power as if she'd trained for years at Dragons' Hold, not like an ignorant, terrified ….

He'd been wrong. Ezaara's love for the dragon queen was complete. Her imprinting bond was proven. The queen had a new rider.

He should break meld, and announce his conclusion to the council, but doubt nagged at him like a stone in his boot. Lars and Zaarusha were expecting him to be thorough. He didn't like using his gifts—having them was bad enough—but he knew how easily folk could be turned by Zens and his tharuks. So, he delved deeper, searching for treachery.

On their journey to Dragons' Hold, Zaarusha and Ezaara had fought tharuks, and buried warriors. That explained the soot and smears of black and red blood on her cheeks and tunic. He sifted through the experience. Anger pulsed through Ezaara—and grief. Only the queen's wisdom had stopped her from jumping into battle.

She was true to the realm and had bravery in pailfuls. All she needed was training.

Just as he'd been trained. A memory shot into Roberto's mind. *Ten years old, he was crouched behind the kitchen door, clutching Adelina's hand, listening to his parents.*

No! That's where the pain and betrayal had started. Roberto slammed the memory shut and yanked his hands away.

§

With Roberto's hands on her temples and his black eyes gazing at her, Ezaara re-lived her imprinting with Zaarusha: the warmth of Zaarusha's voice slid through her; the scent of the flowers in the clearing; the bright sun glinting off the dragon queen's smooth scales; the bubble of color that had swept her up onto the queen; the rumble of Zaarusha's roar; and the wind tugging at her hair.

Tears of joy slipped down Ezaara's cheeks.

She re-lived her journey to Dragons' Hold: the horror of tharuks killing those warriors; her sadness; the thermal pool and snuggling with Zaarusha; meadows and forests flying past beneath them; and then, the severe peaks of Dragon's Teeth.

A scene entered her head: crouched behind a heavy door, holding the hand of a little dark-haired girl. Voices yelling. Despair. What was this? Where had it come from?

Him. It was from him. A memory.

Roberto flinched, then pulled his hands away, and her mind was her own again. His gaze never left her, although its intensity softened. His voice was soft, too. "It's over." He breathed deeply. "You've been proven."

Proven? How? She didn't feel any different. And what had she seen? The door … the raging hurt was his. Who was the little girl he'd been protecting?

Exhausted and dizzy, she stumbled, her hands falling from Erob's head.

Roberto caught her. He smelled of sandalwood soap. She slumped against him, too tired to care what anyone thought.

His voice rang out, "Hail Ezaara, rider of Zaarusha, Queen of Dragons' Realm!"

The Council of the Twelve Dragon Masters cheered. Their dragons roared. The bronze rider-less dragon leaped into the air, circling the cavern before disappearing through a gap high in the cavern wall, its bellows echoing behind it.

§

Roberto shook his head, banishing the terrible memory that had struck out of nowhere. Burying the pain. Had she seen it? Hopefully not. Surely he'd broken mind-meld fast enough. Now the girl had passed out in his arms. So weak. No stamina at all. And this was the Queen's Rider.

"She's exhausted," Erob melded. "Zaarusha traveled days to get here. You of all people should have compassion."

"True," Roberto replied. He'd arrived here an outcast. "You're right, I should know not to judge newcomers. She does look worn out."

"Carry the Queen's Rider to her cavern," Lars called. "Shari, accompany him and see to her welfare."

That was odd. Why the master of livestock? Lars should have assigned Fleur, the master healer, to help Ezaara. Did Lars intend an insult to Fleur? Not that he'd blame him.

"She looks like a dragonet that's flown itself out," Shari murmured, her dark eyes on the girl's face. "She's pretty."

Pretty? Roberto took another look. Ezaara's eyes were striking green when open, but she was hardly pretty. He huffed. "Come on, Shari. Not even you can tell what she looks like under all that grime."

Shari laughed and slugged him.

They made their way along the tunnels to the cavern of the Queen's Rider. Shari opened the wooden door and Roberto carried Ezaara in. Asleep, she looked peaceful, vulnerable, and way too young to be training as the Queen's Rider. Ezaara had no idea what she was in for.

Roberto laid her on the bed. "Do you need any help?"

"Certainly not." Shari laughed again, making her braids swing. "Why don't you get back to bed? You look like you could use some sleep yourself."

"You know me, I never need much sleep."

"Still having nightmares?" She frowned, serious now. "Are you all right?"

Shari had been his champion when he'd arrived at Dragons' Hold and been treated like an outcast. She'd befriended him, encouraging him to leave his legacy behind and make a better man of himself. It hadn't been easy. There were days when he would've gone mad without her friendship.

"I'm fine." He shrugged, leaving as Shari tugged Ezaara's boots off.

His feet automatically took him along the tunnel. Ezaara was a conundrum. Young and terrified, but brave. Backward and ignorant, with a strong bond to her dragon—a deep bond. Untrained, inexperienced …. He sighed. This was going to be a challenge. War was so close and politics here at the hold could easily implode. He had his work cut out. He'd have to be relentless, tough, to ensure she was up to standard for their queen.

At the passage to his sister's cavern, he took the turn off into the shadows. There was no torchlight shining through the crack below Adelina's door, so she was probably fast asleep. He hesitated. Adelina often helped him order his thoughts. He valued her counsel. He had to tell her they'd underestimated this new Queen's Rider.

Footfalls came along the tunnel accompanied by hushed voices—a man and a woman.

"What are we going to do?" That was Fleur, master healer.

"She's getting old," Bruno, her husband and master of prophecy, whispered. "Hardly fit to rule."

"And now the queen's besotted with that girl," hissed Fleur. "That pathetic scrap of a rider."

Roberto moved deeper into shadow.

"Perhaps Zaarusha is going senile," Bruno said. "We'll have to see Lars."

Fleur's quiet reply was lost around a corner.

Roberto padded along the tunnel in the opposite direction and out of the caverns into the night. He ran along the mountainside on a goat track that led to Lars' cavern and his own. As surefooted as an ibex, he'd often taken bitter refuge on these wild tracks when he'd first arrived at Dragons' Hold.

He slipped past dragons' dens, their occupants opening a sleepy eye to see him pass. As long as Singlar, Lars' dragon, didn't see him, he'd be fine. Before he reached Lars' cavern, he climbed higher, above Singlar's den, and sat near the vent hole to Lars' main chamber.

Urgent voices drifted up. Bruno and Fleur had made good time. Guilt for eavesdropping twanged through Roberto, but, for Zaarusha's sake, he had to know what they were up to.

"She might have made a mistake," Fleur was saying. "It's been eighteen years since she had a rider."

"Are you insinuating that our dragon queen doesn't know what she's doing?" Lars' tone was disapproving.

"No, of course not," Fleur backtracked. "Our poor queen has suffered so much, being without a rider or a mate for so many years. Perhaps loneliness has impaired her judgment."

"We trust our queen," Bruno said, "but, you have to admit, it is odd that she chose a girl from Lush Valley. And one so young."

"Perhaps the girl has manipulated our queen. Or maybe Zaarusha's become a little unbalanced. Reckless." Fleur's voice was smooth, placating. "We don't want Zaarusha hurt."

Roberto clenched his fists. Surely Lars could see through their attempts to discredit the queen.

"You have a point there." Lars sounded weary. "But I won't act on suspicions. Bring me proof. And remember, Roberto has tested her and declared their bond fit."

"Exactly," Fleur purred. "He was a traitor. Maybe he's turned again."

"Enough." Lars' voice was icy. "Out, now! Don't come back unless you have evidence. I need at least an hour's sleep before dawn."

Roberto gazed down at the valley—still shrouded in shadow. It always came back to his past. His actions. Curse his rotten father's watery grave.

§

Ezaara awoke with a pounding head. She was tangled in a snowy quilt embroidered with gold dragons. Sunlight streamed through a hole in a stone ceiling, illuminating a hanging tapestry of more dragons flying across a battlefield beneath distant alps. Across the cavern, near an enormous archway, was a large bathtub with wood under it. The scent of relaxing herbs—bergamot, jasmine and lavender—hung in the air.

"*Good morning,*" Zaarusha hummed. "*Well done on your imprinting test.*"

Ezaara gazed around. Zaarusha was nowhere to be seen. "*I hope there won't be any more tests.*"

"*Not like that one. Only tests of skill.*"

"*Skill? I'm sure to fail, then. I'm not good at much, except herbs.*" Zaarusha should have taken Tomaaz as her rider instead.

"*No, Tomaaz isn't the right rider for me. You are.*"

"*Why me?*"

Zaarusha appeared in the archway. "*When my dragonet gave his life to bless your mother, some of his essence was passed to Marlies, for her progeny. I sense that you—and probably Tomaaz— have special talents, gifts from my baby.*"

"*It's sad you lost your baby.*"

"*Yes, I was devastated, but it was a long time ago.*"

Ezaara sat up. "*So, what talents are you talking about?*"

"These things take time to unfold. Be patient." Snaking her long neck into the room, Zaarusha winked and opened her jaws, shooting a jet of flame along the edges of the metal tub. Soon steam rose from the water. With one last burst of controlled flame, she ignited the timber under the tub. *"Now, relax and enjoy your bath. I'll be next door in my den."*

Ezaara smiled. That was much easier than fetching boiling water from a hearth.

The cavern floor was cool beneath Ezaara's feet. Clad only in her underthings, she shivered. Opening a drawer, she found clean underclothing. In another, dark jerkins and breeches like the masters had worn—dragon riders' garb. A majestic closet held beautiful robes, embroidered tunics and breeches—all made of luxurious fabrics in gorgeous hues. Were these all hers? She stroked a blue satin tunic, then ran her fingers down a soft green dress. She'd never had anything this fine in Lush Valley.

Her family's faces flashed to mind. She missed them: Tomaaz's pranks, Ma's understanding and Pa's teasing. She'd left Lush Valley on an impulse, without a thought for them or a goodbye. She'd broken her vow to Tomaaz. No! Now her eyes were stinging. She squeezed them shut. The Queen's Rider, crying? Surely Zaarusha deserved more.

Shoving her feelings aside, Ezaara strode to the steaming tub. On the wall above the bath were two crossed swords, ancient-looking things with ornately-carved hilts. One hilt was silver, the other, gold. Snarling metal-worked dragons—with tiny engraved scales—curled around the hilts. They were beautiful. She longed to hold one and test its weight, but she didn't dare. They were obviously ceremonial—much too pretty to fight with.

Ezaara dipped her hand in the tub, warm water trailing from her fingers. A bowl of herbs was perched on a ledge. She sprinkled some into the water, a summery scent filling the air.

Stepping out of her underclothing, Ezaara sank into the bath. She had to become a good Queen's Rider. Develop her talents. She could do this. She had to. There was no place among these tough riders at Dragons' Hold for petty worries or loneliness. She had to be strong. But the bath's soothing warmth and herbal scent reminded her of home, washing away her resolve, and soon, her tears blended with the water.

§

Adelina hurried along the tunnel toward the Queen's Rider's cavern. Of all the favors Roberto could've asked! She had a million better things to do than babysitting an ignorant waif from Lush Valley. Why should she look after the girl who'd broken her heart and stolen Zaarusha?

Because Roberto had asked, that's why. She'd do it, but she didn't have to be gracious. Sighing, she knocked on the door.

No answer, but faint sounds came from within.

Adelina pushed the door open, turning on her charm, bowing low. "Good morning, Ezaara, Honored Rider of Queen Zaarusha."

A blonde girl was hunched on the bed, head bowed, half wearing a gorgeous blue satin robe. Seeing the simple ties on the dress, Adelina rolled her eyes. The new Queen's Rider hadn't even greeted her. Couldn't even dress herself. This girl was worse than she'd thought. If she'd been Queen's …. She wasn't. And Roberto had begged her help, insisting the girl was the true Queen's Rider. She had to try. If not for this girl, then for Zaarusha, for Dragons' Realm. The girl sniffed.

Adelina had expected incompetence or ignorance, not some-one melting in self-pity. "Excuse me, are you all right?"

Ezaara's head shot up, cheeks flaming. "Um, yes. I'm fine." She smiled too brightly, her lower lip wobbling.

Familiarity knifed through Adelina—she had a whole arsenal of smiles that masked pain. What was this girl's hurt? At what cost had she come here? She smiled back. "I'm here to help you prepare for your first public flight."

"Thank you, that's kind of you."

She had green eyes, this girl. Brave eyes, despite her sadness. "Here." Reaching into the leather bag slung over her shoulder, Adelina passed Ezaara a bread roll and an orange. "You missed breakfast, but you'll feel better after eating."

"I'm fine, really."

Adelina arched an eyebrow. "Right, of course you are. Especially after a tough imprinting test with a bunch of strangers in the middle of the night, far from home. Absolutely fine."

Wiping her tears, Ezaara laughed.

Adelina had to grin. "I'm Adelina."

"Someone else should be Queen's Rider," Ezaara said. "I don't know how anything works around here. Not even this dress. I mean, I'd never seen a dragon before Zaarusha appeared. What if I fail?"

Obviously humble enough to learn, this girl wasn't so bad after all. "You'll be fine, with my help. Remember, you've already passed your first test."

Ezaara shuddered. "It was hideous."

Roberto had said Ezaara had the strongest bond he'd ever tested, and he'd know. "Master Roberto said you did well."

"I'm surprised he had anything to say about me at all."

"Tough, was he?" He did tough well. "I'll tell you what. He's sometimes tough on me too. Let's pay him back with a prank." She winked.

"But we'll get in trouble. He's a master. I—"

"It's only a bit of harmless fun. I promise."

This time Ezaara's smile was real. "I could use some fun."

Adelina laughed.

Dragon Flight

Roberto paced in the clearing under Zaarusha's den, stones crunching underfoot as he recited the words to the ceremony under his breath. It'd been two hours since Adelina had gone to fetch the girl. What was taking them so long? Over two hundred folk were gathered in the clearing and over a hundred dragons were perched on the mountainside, waiting. This was the biggest event they'd had at Dragons' Hold in years—probably in his lifetime.

Seated on a dais behind him with the other masters, Lars gave the signal. It was time. Ezaara had better show up. Roberto hesitated, remembering the mental ordeal he'd put her through in the middle of the night. Perhaps they should give her longer—last night she'd been so exhausted, she'd collapsed.

Far behind the crowd, Ezaara emerged from the main cavern. What was going on? They'd anticipated her appearance in this clearing, beneath Queen Zaarusha's den. Adelina should've known that.

Roberto raised the horn to his lips, blowing a haunting note that echoed off the granite mountainsides. He gestured toward the new Queen's Rider at the back of the crowd.

And stared.

§

That morning, Adelina had taught Ezaara how to saddle Zaarusha. She'd done her hair, helped her dress, then led her through the back tunnels and into the empty main cavern.

"No one will expect you to come this way." Adelina's brown eyes were warm. "You'll surprise them all."

Hopefully, not in a bad way. "Are you sure? I—"

Adelina hugged Ezaara. "Keep smiling and I'm sure you'll win everyone over. I'll be nearby, if you need me."

It was good to have a friend among these tough riders and fierce dragons.

When Ezaara stepped outside the cavern, a crowd was gathered. Her stomach fluttered. Luckily they were facing away from her, toward the dragon masters.

Roberto blew a horn and flung his arm toward Ezaara. Folk turned to stare.

§

Roberto inhaled. Ezaara was radiant. In place of the fearful travel-weary waif was a young woman worthy of a royal court. Her light-blue robe was threaded with green ribbons that fluttered in the breeze. The crown of her blonde hair was plaited and woven with more green ribbons, leaving long tresses loose over her shoulders and back.

Ezaara talked to those she passed, often touching someone's outstretched hand. Her laugh loosened something in his chest—something that had been tight for years.

Absently, he lowered the horn from his lips. *This* was the same girl he'd tested last night?

She'd passed that test brilliantly, and now she was passing the next hurdle—the folk loved her. They were smiling, shaking her hand. Excitement hummed through the crowd.

It had taken him a year to prove himself at Dragons' Hold. How had she done it in less than a day?

There was more to her than he'd suspected. He cringed at his harsh attitude before he'd known Ezaara was Zaarusha's *true* rider.

She passed through the crowd, murmuring a quiet word here and there, her slim figure coming ever closer to the Council of the Twelve Dragon Masters. Colors flitted through his head. Her, it was her. Ezaara's vibrancy tinged his soul.

Like the crowd of dragon folk, Roberto was awestruck.

But, unlike them, he couldn't afford to show it.

§

The crowd parted. Ezaara swallowed. It was now or never. She could do this. Maybe Zaarusha was right, perhaps she did belong here. Reaching out, she squeezed a little boy's hand. His face lit up and his mother murmured her thanks. Those nearby greeted her. Some smiled, others reached out to touch her. Ezaara made her way through the throng, the warmth of the dragon folk wrapping around her like a fluffy blanket.

Roberto was facing the crowd, his black hair curling where it touched his shoulders. A horn dangled from his fingertips. How had he created such soulful music with a single note?

Nearing the council, Ezaara stopped short of Roberto and inclined her head. She was determined not to give him reason to fault her. "Good day, Master Roberto."

Roberto stepped forward, his voice carrying across the clearing. "Beloved Council of the Twelve Dragon Masters, magnificent dragons, esteemed gentlefolk and riders of Dragons' Hold, I present to you Ezaara, verified Rider of Zaarusha, the Honored Queen of Dragons' Realm." He waved his hand toward her with a flourish.

So formal. What was she supposed to do now? Ezaara nodded in acknowledgment.

Roberto continued, "Before the Council of the Twelve Dragon Masters, she has proven her imprinting bond, her allegiance to the realm and …"

For a moment Roberto looked panicked. He'd obviously forgotten his words.

"This is boring," a little boy piped up.

Ezaara let out a giggle. The stares of the council members turned to ice. She quickly covered her mouth with her hand.

Roberto's cheek twitched, right by a tiny pale scar. He continued, "… her allegiance to the realm and her devotion to our queen. Do you accept her?"

People near them tittered. Others glared.

"Gentlefolk, do you accept her?" Roberto repeated, cheek still twitching.

"We do," the crowd called.

Roberto turned to Ezaara. "And do you, Ezaara, accept your obligation and vow to protect Dragons' Realm—rider, warrior, dragon, wizard, farmer, craftsperson, adult and littling alike—with your very life?"

"My life?" Ezaara squeaked.

Lars, council leader, nodded at her, face grave.

"Ezaara." Roberto's dark eyes bored into her. "Being Queen's Rider carries responsibility. Your decision today is binding and irreversible. You'll be revered and honored by folk in Dragons' Realm and despised by our foes. Your life will be in danger, and you may die fighting our enemies. Do you accept?"

Die? Like Anakisha? Was she ready to die fighting for folk she hardly knew? She remembered the man in the pass, dying in her arms. The weight of responsibility sank through her bones. This was her duty. "My life is Zaarusha's. I will fulfill my destiny as Queen's Rider."

The crowd cheered.

Roberto held his palm up, demanding silence.

"Every new Queen's Rider must undertake an evaluation flight before training begins." Roberto's eyes flicked to her dress.

"Would you care to dress in your rider's garb while we wait, Ezaara, Honored Rider of Queen Zaarusha?" Scorn lurked in his gaze. Challenge. "How *long* will you need?"

Ezaara turned her back to him, facing the crowd, and pulled the ribbons on her gown. The front of her dress flew open, revealing her dragon rider's garb.

The crowd gasped.

Roberto opened his mouth then snapped his jaw shut.

Good, Adelina's trick with the dress had rattled Roberto—sweet revenge for his scorn last night. Twisting her hair into a tight coil on the back of her head, she tied it up with the ribbons. How Adelina had managed to find the exact green of her eyes, she had no idea. She took off the dress and handed it to Adelina, who was waiting at the edge of the crowd. Giving what she hoped was a demure smile, Ezaara said, "You see, Master Roberto, I didn't need *long* at all."

Whatever Roberto replied was lost amid the cheers of dragon folk as Zaarusha swooped down, scales blazing in the noonday sun.

Zaarusha's hum filled Ezaara's mind, *"Jump on. We'll make this flight memorable, so strap in tightly."*

Ezaara climbed up, fastened her harness and pulled the hood of her jerkin tight. Zaarusha sent her a mental picture of the maneuver they were about to perform. *"You're crazy! I'll never survive."* Naked fear sliced through her.

"Ezaara, we have no choice. We have to prove you're fit."

"But I'll slip, fall, I'll—"

"Trust me. I know how brave you are. We can do this." Zaarusha sprang into the sky and circled once, the breeze from her wingbeats stirring the spectators' hair.

"Zaarusha, I don't know if—"

"Trust me."

Her fear would cloud Zaarusha's focus. She had to overcome it. A memory flashed to mind. The first time she'd splinted a broken leg while an injured boy whimpered, she'd been terrified, but despite the boy's anguish, she'd done it with Ma's help. Maybe she could do this too. Ezaara steeled her nerves, patting Zaarusha's neck. *"I'm ready."*

A happy rumble coursed through the queen.

They gathered speed. Below, the upturned faces blurred. Ezaara threw her body forward, sliding her arms through leather loops on Zaarusha's neck, clinging to the hand grips. She locked her knees and dug her feet deep into the stirrups. Wind rushed past her. She was swept up in a whirl of color, and her heart soared with the sweetest music. Her mind was one with Zaarusha, sensing every wing beat, every movement of her dragon's muscles.

Zaarusha's exhilaration rushed through her. Fields whipped by beneath them. The dark forest was a blur. A granite cliff loomed, snow capping its upper reaches. Zaarusha flew straight at the mountainside. Within meters of the rocky face, she roared, folded her wings, and flicked her tail downward, propelling them up the sheer stone wall.

They sped up the mountainside, rock rushing past her dragon's belly. Suddenly, Zaarusha was upside-down. Gravity pulled at Ezaara, trying to claw her body out of the harness. She clung to the leather loops, arms aching. The world tilted and spun. Flashes of treetops. Rock. Snow. Sky. Her stomach dropped. Oh, she was dizzy.

"We're right side up again," Zaarusha announced, flipping over. *"You can relax now."*

Heart pounding, Ezaara released the grips and sat up. *"We did it. That was incredible. Let's do it again!"*

"We'll do many more loops, but not today. Now, take off your hood and unfasten the ribbons from your hair."

They flew toward fields of grain and vegetables.

"*It's time for some fun.*" Zaarusha showed her another maneuver. "*Hold your ribbons high.*"

Ezaara gripped Zaarusha with her knees, tensing her stomach. The dragon queen swooped up and down, leap-frogging across the grain fields, stalks rippling in their wake. Ezaara's blonde hair tugged her scalp as it whipped out behind her. The ribbons fluttered like banners in her hands.

The crowd clapped as they approached, chanting, "E—zaa—ra, Zaa—ru—sha."

The peal of the horn rang out over the basin.

"*Give Roberto one of your ribbons.*"

"*That cold, arrogant fish. Why would I give him anything?*"

"*Trust me. Give him one, but do it discreetly. I'll tell you when,*" Zaarusha commanded.

Ezaara didn't dare question the queen.

§

Erob's chuckle startled Roberto. "*No one's flown a loop since Anakisha. I dare you to challenge Zaarusha's rider now.*"

Zaarusha landed in front of the applauding crowd, facing the council.

Shrugging off his dragon's quip, Roberto approached and helped Ezaara down. Last night, he hadn't noticed the sprinkling of tiny freckles, like precious flecks of gold, across the bridge of her nose. He shoved the thought away, turning to the crowd.

"Honored Queen's Rider." He projected his voice across the stony clearing. "You have been unanimously accepted by the Council of the Twelve Dragon Masters and riders of Dragons' Hold. Tonight, we'll feast to celebrate."

"Thank you." Ezaara's cheeks were flushed. Her windswept hair hung tangled down her back and she was winding a ribbon around her fingers.

Zaarusha roared, drowning out the crowd. She tossed her head high and spread her wings, blocking Ezaara and Roberto from the crowd's view.

Ezaara's small hand reached for his. "This is for you," she said.

Colors spiraled through his mind. There it was again—her.

She darted back to her dragon's side. No one had noticed their exchange.

Roberto opened his hand. Inside was one of Ezaara's green satin ribbons, still warm where she'd held it. He rubbed the satin with his thumb. Did she realize what this meant?

When Roberto looked up, Handel was watching him, bronze tail twitching ominously. Roberto snapped his hand shut and walked away.

FISHING

Roberto lifted the heavy saddlebags and carried them to Erob, who was waiting on the lip of his den. Far below, people were setting up trestle tables for Ezaara's feast. Tonight, fish would be roasted in honor of the new Queen's Rider, and Roberto, being Naobian, was the hold's chief fisherman. He checked Erob's saddle straps were tight, then touched the pocket holding Ezaara's ribbon. The gift confused him. According to tradition, accepting her ribbon made him her protector—unto death. Did Ezaara even know that?

He shrugged. Whether she knew or not, he'd accepted it—and he'd honor that commitment.

Ezaara's dizzying loop had been a spectacular feat. Impressive, along with her trick with her dress. He snorted. Adelina would've been behind that.

At Erob's rumble, Roberto clambered up and rubbed his dragon's neck. *"How did they do it, Erob? Could we fly a loop?"*

Erob huffed his breath out. *"I'd be too tempted to tip you off!"* He leaped off the ledge, soaring high above the folk. They flew north, over fields, toward the dark band of forest and the lake. *"Ezaara trusts her dragon completely—a rare gift."*

"It is," agreed Roberto.

Trust? Could the answer be that simple? And that terrifying. He hadn't trusted anyone for years—except Adelina and Erob. How could he?

After what he'd done, he could hardly trust himself.

The lake glinted silver. Erob spiraled down to the eastern shore and Roberto unpacked the fishing net.

"Work first?" he asked Erob. *"Or are you tired after your arduous flight?"*

Erob gave him a dragonly grin. He grasped each end of the fishing net with his talons and flew over the lake, his forelegs skimming the surface and the net trailing in the water. Erob was taut and focused, yet if there was a threat, he'd be beside Roberto in moments.

"If only humans could share the same bond."

"They can," Erob replied. *"I witnessed it once as an unborn dragonet. Some human mates have such a strong emotional bond, they can mind-meld the way you and I do."*

"What?" He'd never heard of that.

"Apparently Anakisha and Yanir could mind-meld." Erob rose above the lake, the dripping net full of flapping fish, and flew back to the shore. Roberto helped guide the net onto the grass, and opened it. Erob snaffled two large fish for himself, wolfing them down.

Roberto clapped his dragon on the foreleg. *"Good fishing."* He tossed Erob two more. Flipping and twisting, the fish scattered diamonds of water as they arced through the air into his jaws.

"I've finished my work. It's your turn, now." His dragon stretched in the sun. *"I could roast one, if you like."*

"I'm saving my appetite for the feast tonight." Roberto bent to sort the fish, killing the large ones and throwing the small ones back.

"Harrumph." Erob hooked a fish with his talon and roasted it with a moderate dragon flame.

"Erob, just because you're hungry, doesn't mean I am." The aroma of cooked fish making his mouth water, Roberto put their catch into sacks.

Erob shot another tendril of flame at the fish. Its juices sizzled. Shards, it smelled good.

"All right, if you insist." Roberto carried a flat stone to Erob, who placed the cooked fish on it to cool. He flopped on the grass and leaned against his dragon's sun-warmed side.

"A great invention of yours, that net," melded Erob.

He'd always been a good fisherman. It was part of his Naobian heritage. Before the net, he'd hunted for hours from Erob's back with a long-handled net or spear, but now they could catch fish quickly and then take time to relax.

"I bet it's just a rumor that humans can mind-meld." Roberto took a bite of fish.

"When I was an embryo, I met another couple who were mind-melding."

"And?"

"I don't know them, only the timbre of their minds," Erob replied. *"I'd recognize her again, though."*

"Her?"

"Yes, her. She was melding, so I sensed her mind. Through her, I felt his. Their love was like dragon and rider." Erob nudged Roberto with his snout.

Dragons didn't lie. It must be true, then. *"I'm glad we imprinted. Life was grim until you turned up,"* Roberto mumbled. *"Without you, I'd be dead. Or worse."* He bolted the last of his fish.

"Most relationships are not like your parents'." Erob flicked the tip of his tail at Roberto's ear.

Roberto batted his tail away.

"Many humans are happily bonded."

Bitter memories rushed through Roberto. His throat tightened.

"Your father's betrayal was—"

"Not now, Erob," he barked.

"You're not like him," insisted Erob.

His father's face loomed in his head, mocking him. Zens' bulbous eyes leered at him. The bodies of maimed slaves, piled high, stinking. Whips cracked. Screams. Muffled moaning. His forehead broke out in sweat. Roberto threw the sacks of fish into Erob's saddlebags and climbed on his back. It always came back to his father. *"Drop me at Fire Crag."* He broke mind-meld.

Erob landed at their usual spot, an hour's run from the top of Fire Crag.

Roberto dismounted and slapped Erob's flank. He eased his mind open. *"I'm sorry, Erob."* He could never stay mad at Erob for long. His dragon was right—his father had been a traitor.

Erob nudged his shoulder. *"I'll take the fish to the kitchens and be back in a couple of hours."*

Roberto nodded. Letting his dragon's fire blaze through his veins, he set off on the punishing climb to the pinnacle, hoping the burn of his muscles could obliterate his searing memories.

§

Just before dusk, Ezaara and Zaarusha flew down to the feast.

"Finally, you're a passenger fit for a queen," Zaarusha teased. *"Could you spare Adelina for a while so I could have my scales polished and talons clipped?"*

Ezaara swatted Zaarusha's neck. Although her fine clothes and fancy hair made her self-conscious, she knew she looked good.

Zaarusha spiraled upward, sending Ezaara images of a steep dive down to the feast. Heart pounding, Ezaara leaned forward, tightening her grip.

Zaarusha roared.

This was it.

The dragon queen chortled. *"I was only teasing. I wouldn't dive and mess up your hair."*

Ezaara laughed as Zaarusha made a gentle descent.

§

Around Roberto, masters chatted quietly at the head table, which was laid with a creamy linen cloth edged in silver dragons. Murmurs from the crowd drifted on the evening air. Zaarusha roared, and everyone looked up, a hush falling over the crowd. Roberto squinted in the fading light. What were Zaarusha and Ezaara doing up so high? Showing off? Then he understood. Zaarusha was ensuring all eyes were upon Ezaara.

They landed and Ezaara sprang down, rubbing Zaarusha's eye ridge.

Roberto shook his head—the crowd was in awe again.

Ezaara's hair, tied in coils and loops, trailed fine silver and green threads that highlighted her eyes. A silver tunic and matching breeches hugged her curves, and she wore a healer's pouch at her waist. She glanced at him, cheeks flushed from flying.

A dizzying rush hit Roberto, as if he was standing on the edge of Fire Crag. Colors, like a blazing sunset, filled his mind, then they were gone.

Ezaara appeared not to notice. She smiled. "Good evening, Honored Dragon Masters. Thank you for calling this feast."

Roberto passed a glass of apple juice to Ezaara.

Lars raised his arms before the crowd. "We welcome Ezaara, Honored Rider." He turned to her, voice booming, "Enjoy tonight's feast as a token of our respect. On the morrow, you'll commence training for your duties as Queen's Rider. I propose a toast in your honor."

Everyone held their glasses high. "To the Queen's Rider." Their voices echoed off the mountainsides. The crowd drank, then whistled and cheered as Ezaara drained her glass. Roberto gestured for Ezaara to step forward.

"Me?" she replied, wide-eyed.

She obviously wasn't used to feast etiquette. "Of course. You need to reply to Lars' welcome."

She faced the folk. "Good people of Dragons' Hold, I'm honored at your trust. I hope to keep it, and to come to know each of you well. Thank you for preparing this feast in honor of Zaarusha, Queen of Dragons' Realm."

Zaarusha roared at the applause from the crowd.

Ezaara turned back to him. "Was that all right?" she whispered.

Her response? It was a bit short, not very formal, but straight from her heart, and gave honor to Zaarusha. Folk loved it, but that would only get her so far. Roberto nodded. "It was fine, much better than you giggling through your vows today. As Queen's Rider, you'll need more decorum."

"At least I didn't forget my words," she hissed.

It's not as if he had to swear in a new Queen's Rider every week. Anyone would've forgotten a word or two. He couldn't expect a girl from Lush Valley to understand that, but a Queen's Rider should. He guided her to a seat between him and Lars, and refilled her glass with apple juice.

"To a new era," Lars announced, "and Ezaara's successful training."

Everyone raised their glasses again, then helped themselves to food.

Erob's fish had ruined his appetite, so Roberto only put melon and sweet potato on his own plate.

Ezaara was staring at the laden platters, eyes as wide as a newborn dragonet's. Coming from Lush Valley, she'd probably never seen such a feast. She helped herself to some olives, sweet potato and fish and they made small talk.

Lars put a hand on Roberto's shoulder. "You did a good job this afternoon and last night, especially with only a short time to memorize the formal proceedings."

"Thank you, Lars. I'm happy to serve the council and my queen." Well, apart from serving with his mental gifts, but he wasn't about to admit that his strength was his biggest challenge.

"Zens' reach is growing, Roberto. You must train the Queen's Rider thoroughly, but quickly. We don't have the luxury of time."

"I'll do my best, Lars. We'll have to see what else she's capable of."

"I know you'll do a good job."

When Roberto turned back, Ezaara was leaving the dais.

He frowned. The Queen's Rider, abandoning the head table? Unheard of.

QUEEN'S RIDER

Ezaara popped a tiny purplish-black fruit in her mouth. So, Roberto hadn't liked her laughing that afternoon? He was so moody—he could go ride a dragon, for all she cared. She swallowed, but the fruit left a bitter aftertaste, like vinegar. Below the dais, hundreds of people were eating and chatting. She'd much rather sit down with them, than be up here on show.

"Do you like the olives?" Roberto asked, leaning toward her. "We grow them in Naobia."

So, he was being friendly again, was he? "I've never had this fruit before. What did you call it?"

"An olive. Fruit?" He laughed. "They do grow on trees, but we pickle them in vinegar, so they're savory, you see, not sweet."

"Oh." She felt so ignorant and stupid. Had he meant to sound like such a know-it-all?

He smirked. "Don't feel bad. Coming from Lush Valley, you've probably never seen them. You can't help being ignorant, having lived there."

Ezaara snapped her jaw shut. Conversation with him was as bitter as the olives. Everyone down below seemed to be having much more fun. The sooner she could get away, the better.

Ignoring Roberto and his arrogant comments, Ezaara examined the myriad of cutlery beside her plate. This place was dragon-crazy—even the dessert spoons had dragons on them. Luckily, Adelina had told her which cutlery to use for what. Picking up her two-pronged fork with a dragon's tail wound around the silver stem, she nibbled some sweet potato, careful not to drop any on her lovely silver tunic.

Roberto turned away to talk to Lars.

Now was her chance.

Ezaara took her plate and headed across the dais, down the stairs. She glanced back and caught Roberto's disapproving stare, then lost her footing. Her food went flying and she shrieked, landing in a heap, pain shooting through her ankle.

The babble of conversation ground to a stop.

Her cheeks burned. Great. That would impress everyone—the new Queen's Rider, smeared in sweet potato with a busted ankle. People were staring, some concerned, others smothering smiles.

"What do you expect?" a woman murmured. "She's from Lush Valley."

Someone snickered. A few more joined in.

Right, enough was enough. She may be from Lush Valley, but she wasn't deaf. "It's all right, everyone, I'm fine," Ezaara called. "Go back to your dinner and I'll collect mine." She plucked sweet potato and fish off her tunic, putting it back onto her plate.

Scattered laughter broke out. People resumed eating. At least they weren't staring anymore.

Zaarusha melded. *"You're injured. Do you need me to fly you home?"*

"No, my ankle's not that sore. I'll stay until the feast's over."

"Very well, but take it easy."

A blond man, about her age, rushed over. "Honored Queen's Rider, I'm the master healer's son, Simeon. My mother, Fleur, sent me to assist you."

No, not in front of everyone. "I'm fine, thanks. I'll be on my feet in a moment." Ezaara brushed the rest of the food off her tunic. The silver fabric was ruined, stained with dull spots of fish oil. As she clambered to her feet, another spike of pain lanced through her ankle. Oh gods, she couldn't put any weight on it.

Simeon gave her a lopsided smile, offering her his arm. "You need to sit down." Helping her to the nearest table, he asked people to move so she could have a seat. He put her plate of grass-speckled food on the table. "I'll be back in a moment with some salve."

He disappeared before Ezaara could tell him not to bother.

A girl passed a cup of apple juice to her. "Hi, I'm Gret. It's a shame you slipped. Reminds me of the time I fell in a puddle during my sword assessment." She flicked her long brown braids over her shoulders.

Ezaara pushed the food around on her plate with her fork, a plain one without dragons on it—so the special cutlery was only for those at the head table. "Did you fail your sword assessment, Gret?"

"My backside was soggy, but I passed, so it worked out in the end. How are you with a sword?"

Ezaara sighed. "Better than I am with stairs, fortunately, but nowhere near as good as my brother."

Another girl laughed, making her blonde curls bounce. "I'm Sofia. If you need the latest news, come see me."

"Gossip, more like," a blond boy said, taking a bite of bread.

Sofia elbowed him. "Just because I keep up with what's going on, doesn't mean it's gossip, Mathias."

Mathias raised an eyebrow at Sofia, then turned to Ezaara. "Welcome to Dragons' Hold."

Sofia leaned in. "Tell us, what's Lush Valley like?"

Ezaara shrugged. "I've never lived anywhere else."

"Is it true dragons are outlawed there?" Sofia practically held her breath.

How could she admit she'd never been sure if dragons existed?

"Come on, Sofia, you can't believe everything you hear. You also thought Naobia had never had rain. I'm never going to let you live that down." He laughed, dark eyes twinkling against his olive skin, black curls gleaming. From what Roberto had said, he was Naobian too. "I'm Rocco," he said. "You'll get used to Sofia's questions."

"We all had to," said another boy, spearing a piece of fish on his fork. "I'm Henry."

The last of the group moved like a lethal predator around the table toward her. Huge, he extended his well-muscled arm. "I'm Alban." His eyes were gray, flinty. "Welcome," he said, although his stance was anything but welcoming. "You'll be training with us."

Thankfully he'd be on her side in a battle, not fighting against her. Swallowing, Ezaara shook his hand. "Nice to meet you, Alban."

Simeon appeared at her shoulder. "Let's look at your ankle." His amber eyes were soft in the torchlight.

"I'm fine, thank you. Really. It's only a sprain."

"Fine is why you're limping, right?" He unlaced her boot and eased it off.

Ezaara had to grit her teeth to stop herself from groaning out loud. What a fantastic impression she must be making.

"I hope you don't mind me helping you." Flashing his lopsided smile again, Simeon gently propped her foot on an upturned pail. He uncorked a small pot of salve. An arid scent wafted from it.

No way was she having that stinking stuff on her ankle. Ma's salve smelled much better and worked wonders. She'd use that.

Before Ezaara could say anything, Roberto appeared behind Simeon, his voice slicing through the conversation. "I'll take care of the Queen's Rider. Go and enjoy your meal."

"It's no problem, *Master* Roberto." Simeon leveled a challenging gaze at him. "I'm happy to assist."

From the top table, Lars beckoned Roberto.

"Oh dear, duty calls," muttered Simeon.

"Watch your step, Simeon," Roberto threatened. He returned to the top table, boots thunking on the dais.

Irritable was an understatement. That man was downright hostile. "What was that about?" Ezaara asked Simeon.

"I don't know—he's always had a grudge against me." Simeon shrugged. "Don't worry, I'm used to it."

Sofia leaned over the table. "He can be very rude. They say Master Roberto was once—"

"Sofia." Gret gave an exasperated frown. "Ezaara can form her own opinions."

A ripple ran through the crowd as Roberto held his glass high and proposed a toast to Queen Zaarusha. Simeon passed Ezaara her glass, and she nodded as the crowd toasted her dragon's longevity and wisdom.

Glancing down, Gret said, "Wow, your ankle's the size of an apple."

"It looks tender," remarked Sofia.

"It's nothing." Ezaara managed a smile. "I'll be fine."

"Not without piaua juice, you won't," Sofia said, gesturing at Ezaara's healer's pouch. "But then you'd know that."

No decent healer would use *precious piaua* for a twisted ankle. "This is nothing, really."

Opening her healer's pouch, Ezaara extracted a strip of cloth and passed it to Simeon. "Could you please wet this for me?"

"Of course. Use plenty of my salve before you bind it. It will help." Simeon went off to get some water.

Wincing, she rubbed Ma's healing salve into her aching flesh, biting back another groan. She stowed it in her pouch and took the cork off Simeon's stinking salve, letting the harsh aroma mask the smell of Ma's.

Sofia's keen eyes missed nothing, so Ezaara held a finger to her lips and winked.

Grinning, Sofia murmured, "Wouldn't say a word."

Mathias rolled his eyes. "As if."

Simeon returned. "I'm glad you used my salve. That'll help."

Sofia giggled.

Simeon shot Sofia a puzzled glance as he bound the damp bandage around Ezaara's ankle. The coolness of the wet fabric was soothing. Moments later, he was proffering a heavily-laden plate. "You must be hungry, Ezaara. They say you arrived from Lush Valley late last night. That's a long way to travel."

In more ways than one. "That's so thoughtful, Simeon," Ezaara replied. "Thank you."

While she ate, everyone at the table chatted. They were courteous and witty, making her laugh, but although Ezaara thoroughly enjoyed Simeon's company, she felt hollow. No one here really knew her. They were only talking to her because she was Queen's Rider. If she'd failed the tests, it would've been a different story.

Ezaara turned to the top table. All of the other masters were there, but Roberto was gone. She scanned the crowd, but couldn't find him. She shrugged. Why should she care where he went?

Lars stepped down from the dais and perched on a stool before a giant harp. He plucked the strings, his gentle melody weaving its way through the crowd. As the music built, low-pitched notes rumbled through Ezaara like the roar of a dragon. Eyes closed in rapt concentration, Lars caressed the strings, increasing the intensity and pitch until a sweet harmony floated through the dark, making Ezaara yearn for dragon flight, the wild abandon, the sheer color, of winging through the skies.

Her heart soared. She *wanted* to be Zaarusha's rider, not a healer or a painter of scarves. This was her destiny.

The music came to an end, the last note vibrating through the night.

"Thrilling, isn't it?" Simeon whispered. "I've had a very pleasant evening, Honored Queen's Rider. Thank you for allowing me to keep you company."

It *had* been pleasant. "Thank you."

He laughed, touching her hand. "My pleasure, Ezaara." He smiled warmly. "Did you know my parents are masters on the council? As Queen's Rider, you'll soon be on the council too, so I'm sure we'll see much more of each other."

"That would be nice." It was good to be with someone friendly, instead of that arrogant …. Her gaze drifted to Master Roberto's chair. Where had he gone?

The soft note of a horn echoed from the shadows. People started clearing away the tables.

"Please take this and use it regularly." Simeon handed her the pot of his mother's smelly unguent, then helped Ezaara to stand, one arm around her shoulders. "Allow me to assist you home."

Roberto materialized from beyond the torchlight. "That won't be necessary," he snapped. "I'll take her home. Don't let me catch you hanging around the Queen's Rider again."

Ignoring Roberto, Simeon bowed. "Please, let me know if you need anything, my Queen's Rider." He stalked off into the dark.

Who was Roberto to say who could and couldn't walk her home? "Simeon was helping me. He only—"

Roberto stepped closer. "Are you all right?"

"Why wouldn't I be?"

"Simeon's not to be trusted."

She'd been on show since she'd arrived and she could do nothing right in his eyes. "At least *he's* friendly!" Ezaara hobbled away.

Roberto didn't get the hint. He fell into step and put his arm around her back to support her. "You need to be more careful."

"I'm nearly seventeen, and you're treating me like a littling," Ezaara snapped. She didn't dare admit that his support was easing the ache in her ankle.

Within moments, dragons' wings whooshed nearby. Zaarusha and Erob landed on the grass.

"Ezaara," Zaarusha crooned, *"are you all right?"*

"Yes, Zaarusha, I'm fine." Ezaara glared at Roberto. "Did you call them?"

"Erob can bring you home," said Zaarusha. *"You're in no condition to fly solo."*

"I don't want to fly with them."

"Roberto's going to be training you, so you should get to know him." The queen leaped into the sky, her wingbeats whispering through the dark.

Roberto scooped Ezaara up.

"Put me down. I can walk."

"It looks painful." Roberto replied, mint on his breath.

Not as painful as his comments about Lush Valley and her ignorance.

Carrying her over to Erob, he hoisted her onto the dragon's back. When he stepped back, there was sweet potato smeared on his shoulder.

"Oh, I'm sorry." Her cheeks flamed. "There must've been food on my tunic."

"As if that matters!" He laughed, swinging into the saddle.

"Gently," she sensed him think to his dragon, and they ascended skyward.

§

Lars raised his head. There it was again, a knock at the door. At this time of night? Careful not to wake Lydia, he nudged back the covers and pulled the heavy curtain across their sleeping quarters. He padded across the chilly stone in the dining cavern and opened the door.

"Tonio, come in."

The spymaster glanced back down the tunnel and shut the door, his sharp brown eyes flitting to their sleeping chamber. "Are we alone, Lars?"

Lars nodded and threw a log on the dying embers. "Lydia's fast asleep. Take a seat." They sat down. "What is it?"

"It's the Queen's Rider," Tonio said.

In the hearth, the log caught alight, and the fire spat.

So, this was about Ezaara. "Honestly? In the middle of the night?" Lars sighed. "It couldn't wait until morning?"

Tonio leaned forward, firelight flickering across the hard planes of his face. "I've been spymaster for thirty years. Something's off. I couldn't sleep."

Neither could he now. Lars sighed. "Look, I know it's been a long time since Zaarusha's last rider. Ezaara's young, inexperienced and needs training, but she can fly."

Tonio's eyes narrowed as he nodded in reply. "Yes, their stunt today was very impressive. But how do we know she's imprinted properly?"

"Well, Roberto says the bond is strong. That he's never seen one like it before."

"Convenient, isn't it?" There was nothing warm about Tonio's smile.

"What do you mean?"

"Come on, Lars. She's from Lush Valley, far from here. A superstitious place with no connection to dragons. We've never had riders from Lush Valley."

Where was this going? "Yes, we were all surprised."

"What if she's a fake? A traitor?"

Lars shook his head. "Impossible. Roberto has tested her. She's fine."

"Exactly." Tonio stabbed a finger in the air.

"Exactly what?"

"We only have Roberto's word."

"I trust him."

"I know. Others have made that mistake before, Lars."

"He's changed, Tonio, you should know that. As a council member, he's been impeccable." A memory popped to mind. Tonio had voted against Roberto becoming the master of mental faculties and imprinting. Lars gripped the arm of his chair.

Tonio was coiled, like a predator. "What if Roberto's been biding his time, waiting for an opportunity? What if she's a traitor too?" He leaped out of his seat, pacing. "What if Zaarusha's been given swayweed and Ezaara is a spy? It would be simple for Roberto to fake an imprinting test and give us a positive result. He's accomplished, good at what he does. I've never truly believed that he's turned his back on Zens."

"I trust Roberto. And Zaarusha." Lars stood. "With my life." Tonio had gone far enough. "You know if you come with a complaint, I need proof to take to the council, not hunches or gossip. And not at this hour."

The firelight cast shadows on the spymaster's clenched jaw. "Then I shall find you evidence. I'm sorry for interrupting your sleep." Tonio slipped out the door.

The log cracked and fell into the grate in a shower of sparks.

§

Roberto slid his knife under the wooden dragon's snout and smoothed the curve of the beast's neck. A few more shavings and he'd be done. He made small deft nicks in the wood, like scales, then held up his carving to examine it in the torchlight.

There, that was a good night's work. Better than tossing and turning.

He rubbed the loose shavings off his mother's cane, wincing as he remembered her using it in what should have been the prime of her life. Earlier tonight, the head of the cane had been broad and thick, before he'd shaped it into Zaarusha's likeness. He grunted. The dragon wasn't perfect, but it would do. Now it just needed oiling to bring out the hues of the wood.

Should he wait until morning? No, he was too restless to sleep, the colors of his brief mind-meld with Ezaara flashing into his head whenever he lay down. That, and the look on her face at Simeon's attention. He'd have to watch them. Roberto shook his head. Sometimes his talents were more trouble than they were worth. He longed for his littling days, swimming off the Naobian coast, fishing with his Pa, for life before—

No. He couldn't go there.

He laid the cane on his bed. He might as well oil it now. The walk to fetch oil would do him good. If he was quick, he could still catch a couple of hours' sleep.

The torches had burned low, casting more shadow than light, as Roberto walked along the tunnels to the craft halls. On a back shelf, among the woodworking tools, he found an earthen jar of walnut oil, and picked it up before heading back to his cavern.

Quiet footfalls echoed along the tunnel. It was nearly dawn. Who was sneaking around at this time of night? Roberto rounded a corner. A man was in the shadows of the corridor. Simeon? No, not Simeon. Someone with dark hair. Tonio, the spymaster, was emerging from Lars' cavern. Something dire must be going on for Tonio to be skulking around the halls at this time.

Tonio's eyes fell upon the jar Roberto was holding. He frowned as he passed, giving Roberto a curt nod.

"Morning," Roberto replied. Now was as good a time as any to tell Tonio what he suspected about Bruno and Fleur. "Tonio, do you have a moment?"

"Of course not," Tonio snapped. "It's the middle of the night. We should both be in bed." The spymaster strode off.

PROPHECY

"Good morning, Ezaara."

Morning already? Groaning, Ezaara rolled over. Her ankle was throbbing.

"Sorry I woke you." Adelina set a breakfast tray on a table.

Ezaara struggled to sit up.

"Here, let me help you." Adelina raced over to the bed.

"I'm fine. Please. It's bad enough that I hurt myself and ruined my clothes last night. I don't want to be pitied or fussed over."

Adelina backed away. "I'd feel the same. Ready for breakfast? It's cinnamon and honey porridge, topped with fresh cream."

The aroma was incredible. Ezaara's mouth watered. "Soon." She flipped back her quilt and edged her injured leg off the bed. That hurt. She tried to stand, and grabbed the bedpost, wincing.

Understanding flashed across Adelina's face. "I need the latrine too. Shall we go together?"

"Great Queen's Rider I am. Can't even pee on my own."

Adelina smiled. "You've flown the first loop in years. You can't let a twisted ankle beat you."

"I'm just no good at any of this. In fact, I'm not good at much." Ezaara leaned on Adelina. "Back home, my brother was better than me at most things."

Adelina rolled her eyes. "I know the feeling. Mine's like that too."

"You have a brother?"

"Only one, thank a nest full of dragon's eggs! But he's not too bad."

"Mine's all right most of the time too." She'd broken her promise to him. What had Tomaaz made of her disappearing without a word?

Every step was agony, but Ezaara forced a smile and nodded at people in the tunnels. It took forever to get back to her den, and by then, she was starving.

Roberto was slumped in one of her chairs, dozing. Dark lashes swept his olive skin above pronounced cheek bones. Below his left eye was a tiny scar shaped like a crescent moon. Stubble edged his jaw. Last night, without him speaking, she'd heard him telling Erob to be gentle as they'd flown home—strange—she must've heard his thoughts, or Erob's. Asleep, he looked peaceful. Younger.

Adelina helped Ezaara into bed, then slugged Roberto on the shoulder. "Hey, sleepyhead, wake up."

He rubbed his eyes. "I didn't realize I'd dropped off."

What? The master of mental faculties and imprinting hadn't frosted Adelina for punching him? Not like him at all.

Hands on hips, Adelina replied, "You've been up all night again, haven't you?"

Ezaara cringed. She was speaking like that to a master?

"I couldn't sleep." He ran a hand through his hair, then spotted Ezaara and stiffened, a cool mask slipping over his face. "Good morning, Ezaara, Honored Rider of Queen Zaarusha."

"I can't believe you're visiting before she's eaten," Adelina complained. "She's injured, exhausted and needs a break." She picked up the bowl of porridge and walked toward the bed.

"Look out," Roberto called.

Adelina tripped over a long stick leaning against his chair. The tray flew out of her hands. The bowl smashed, and porridge splattered over the floor. She glared at Roberto. "Who put that there? You?"

He jumped to his feet, picking up the largest pottery shards. "Sorry."

Adelina waved at the mess on the floor. "Now look what you've made me do!" Suddenly she laughed. "Between me and Ezaara, we're pretty good at throwing food. I'll grab a cloth and some more breakfast."

Roberto called, "No, I'll get—" but Adelina disappeared before he could finish. He picked up the tray, placing the shards on it, then turned and got the stick. Stepping over splatters of porridge and cream, he handed it to Ezaara. "Sorry about the mess," he said. "I came to bring you this."

It was a cane. The head was wrapped in soft leather. "For me?"

He nodded, onyx eyes scanning her face. "Go on, unwrap it."

Carved into the handle was a likeness of Zaarusha with a girl on her back. "Is this rider me?"

"It is." His voice softened. "Do you like it?"

"Like it? It's amazing. Look, Zaarusha has tiny scales." She didn't dare tell him the rider was much too pretty to be her. "Why did you make it?"

"I thought a cane would help you get around."

After her fiasco last night, she needed some dignity—a cane would help. Ezaara traced Zaarusha's snout and ran her finger down the spinal ridges.

Roberto shrugged. "Besides, I couldn't sleep, so I needed to do something." He took her hand and placed it over the girl's back. His palm was warm. "This is the smoothest place to hold, otherwise the spinal ridges will dig into your palm. If you use the cane on your good side, not the injured side, it'll take the weight off your sore ankle. Here, try it."

Ezaara got out of bed, leaned on the cane and took a couple of halting steps, careful not to go near the porridge. It was slow, but she could get around on her own. She sat back on her bed.

The carving was exquisite, the detail so perfect. He'd made a masterpiece, to save her pride. "Thank you, this must've taken you ages."

He ducked his head, suddenly looking shy. It suited him. "I'm glad you like it."

"Here you go," called Adelina from the doorway. She had a new tray in her hands and a pail and some cloths slung over her arm.

Roberto took a cloth and started cleaning up the spilled food and broken pottery.

Adelina brought Ezaara's breakfast over. "I'm sorry, there wasn't any more porridge left, so I've brought you some fresh bread and fruit. That should—" She stopped, staring at the cane. Spinning, Adelina faced Roberto. "Is that Ma's walking stick?"

Roberto's boot crunched on a shard. His head snapped up.

Adelina stared at him, tension flickering in her gaze.

Ma's walking stick? Adelina's hair was dark, like Roberto's. They had the same dark eyes. His nose was long and straight, while she had a cute snub nose, but they both had that smooth olive skin—Roberto was Adelina's annoying elder brother.

She was the little girl in his memory, crouched, trembling, behind the door with him.

"Yes, it's Ma's old stick," he said. "Our Queen's Rider is in need, Adelina." He finished wiping up the floor, and put the last of the mess in the pail.

"I know *that*, dummy." She took the cane from Ezaara. "Wow, look at that handle." She grinned and slugged Roberto again. "I was right, you didn't sleep last night, did you?"

Ignoring Adelina, Roberto bowed. "Honored Queen's Rider, your training commences today. I'll see you in imprinting class after you've finished your breakfast. We'll be in the orchard. If you need assistance to get there, Zaarusha should let Erob know."

He nodded tersely, picked up the pail of porridge and shards, and left.

Adelina laughed. "He's crazy. Imagine him carving all night."

"You don't mind me having your Ma's cane?"

Unease flashed across Adelina's face. "It's fine. She doesn't need it anymore."

Adelina didn't look fine. "Are you sure? I mean, I can always find another stick." Ezaara touched the handle. Not one as beautiful as this. "How did your Ma hurt her leg?"

Adelina's face shuttered. "It's complicated."

"Does she live here, at Dragons' Hold?"

Her features tightened. "No, Roberto and I came here alone, five years ago. I was ten and he was fourteen." Adelina stared off into the distance, frowning.

Ezaara ate in silence. She'd obviously touched a raw nerve. Adelina looked more like her brother with that dark expression on her face—not that he'd been brooding this morning.

Reaching for her cane, Ezaara made her way across the room.

Adelina passed her some riders' garb. "The jerkin should be fine, but it's going to be tough to get these breeches on over that ankle. What about a skirt?"

Ezaara shook her head. That'd make her stand out even more. "If you don't mind helping me, we could do battle with the breeches."

"Sure." Adelina smiled, looking more like her old self again.

When she was dressed, Ezaara hobbled out to Zaarusha, using her cane. Zaarusha's scales stretched high above her like a multi-faceted jewel glimmering in the sun. How was she ever going to get on her dragon with this rotten ankle?

I'm sure we can manage. Zaarusha crooned, crouching down.

Ezaara tried to climb, but pain shot through her ankle. She grimaced. The last thing she wanted to do was call Erob. She had to prove she could do something.

"Try this." Adelina boosted Ezaara onto the dragon's back. "You'll manage if you always get on this side so your injured leg gets dragged up behind you." Adelina passed up her cane.

"Thanks."

Zaarusha stood, jostling her ankle. *"Sorry."* She leaped off the ledge, and they were airborne.

Relief whooshed out of Ezaara. She was riding on her own again—like a true Queen's Rider.

"What do you mean, 'like a true Queen's Rider'? You are *the true Queen's Rider. Don't you forget it."*

"I keep making so many mistakes."

"Don't be so hard on yourself. You can't learn everything in a day."

They spiraled down toward the orchard. Oh, shards! How was she going to dismount?

§

Roberto's students were clustered in the grass under the plum trees, heads bent as they discussed their parents' imprinting stories, trying to find common aspects. With students of all ages, it was a challenging class, often involving lively discussion.

At the swish of wings, Roberto turned from his students. Zaarusha and Ezaara were arriving. Ezaara's ankle mustn't be that bad if she'd managed to get onto her dragon alone. He was a fool for staying up all night, crafting a cane for that girl. And for risking strife with his sister. He shrugged. It wasn't as if Ma needed her cane anymore.

Zaarusha landed on the grass between the plum trees with a soft whump. Ezaara winced. So, her ankle was hurting. He *had* been a fool—fooled by her bravado.

The dragon queen strolled closer to the class.

The students' whispers were like leaves in the breeze.

"Quiet, please," Roberto said. "Show proper respect to the Queen's Rider." How was Ezaara going to dismount?

Zaarusha lay on the grass. Ezaara swung a leg over the dragon's back, then rolled onto her belly and held onto Zaarusha's spinal ridge with one hand, letting her body slide down the dragon's side until she was fully extended. Her cane was gripped in her other hand.

No, not with a swollen ankle. Roberto wanted to drop his history text, race over and catch her, but that wouldn't do, not with everyone watching. He set his book aside and strolled over. Of course, before he got there, Ezaara let go. She landed heavily on her good leg, letting out an agonized grunt. Facing away from them, Ezaara leaned against Zaarusha's side. She thrust her cane into the ground, her back rising and falling rapidly.

Ouch. He approached cautiously. "My Honored Queen's Rider, are you hurt?" he asked softly.

"I'm fine," she hissed, not turning around. "Continue with your class. I'll be there in a moment."

"As you wish." It was all he could do not to reach out and help her. If only the foolish girl had called for Erob. Smaller than Zaarusha, he was much easier to ride. Roberto strode back to the class. "I want the names of five of the realm's most important dragon riders and their dragons."

"Erob and Roberto," Kierion called.

"Enough flattery, Kierion," Roberto said. "I mean the important riders to the realm, not to you passing this class."

His students laughed.

"Lars and Singlar."

Roberto nodded. "That's more like it."

"Zaarusha and Anakisha, the last Queen's Rider."

"But now it's Ezaara and Zaarusha." The students' heads turned as they watched Ezaara hobble over. Behind her, Zaarusha flew off.

"Please welcome our Honored Queen's Rider," Roberto said.

Roberto observed Ezaara as his students greeted her. She was hurt, all right. Worse than this morning. So headstrong and stubborn. She was Queen's Rider, for the Egg's sake, and tharuks were attacking. War was coming soon. She had to be fit to lead them.

Unable to sit on the grass, Ezaara leaned her back against a tree, taking the weight off her injured leg. She wouldn't last long like that, and it was only early. He should have had Erob bring a stool for her.

"Come on," Roberto asked, distracting the class from staring at the new Queen's Rider, "two more examples of the realm's most important dragon riders and their dragons."

"King Syan and Yanir," Mathias called.

"Master Tonio and Antonika?" Sofia said.

"Yes, our spymaster is very important to the safety of Dragons' Realm," Roberto said. "Could someone explain the naming convention between dragons and riders?" Coming from Lush Valley, Ezaara had probably never heard of it.

Mathias answered. "The dragon's and rider's names share a common syllable. My sister's dragon took on a new name when they bonded."

"Ma renamed my brother after a dragon that was seeking a rider, then one day they imprinted."

Roberto frowned. Had Ezaara's parents deliberately named her so she had a syllable in common with Zaarusha? "It's not only names we share with our dragons, but some of their characteristics," he said. "Can you give me some examples, please?"

Kierion raised his hand. "You asked about characteristics, sir. Over years, the rider's eye color changes to match the eyes of their dragon."

"So, Kierion would lose his pretty eyes if he became a rider?" Sofia called.

Kierion rolled his ocean-gray eyes, flecked with blue, and mock-groaned. "Not much chance of me being a rider."

Always playing pranks and getting into trouble, Kierion hadn't been selected by the council as a trainee rider.

"Enough," said Roberto. "Any other characteristics that you know of?"

Leah raised her hand. Unusual. She was usually too shy to answer. "Sir, they say the spymaster has excellent hearing from his dragon."

"Too true." Roberto winked. "Be careful; he's listening right now. They say even these plum trees work for him."

Laughter rippled through the class.

"Anything else?"

"Prophecy?"

It was more a question than answer. Not surprising, given the lack of accurate prophecy at Dragons' Hold nowadays. Roberto had a theory on that, but he needed evidence. Keeping an eye on Ezaara, he continued. "Our dragons' mental or emotional talents are passed to us. This can happen at imprinting or over time as we bond more deeply. Strengths of the rider can also pass to the dragon."

A student stretched his hand high.

"Yes?"

"What strengths have you passed to Erob?" asked the tousled-haired lad.

There was no way he'd be telling them about his particular strengths. "Fishing."

"Perhaps you could teach us to fish, too, instead of this stuff," Kierion called.

The class laughed.

"Now, tell us what a rider of fire is."

"That's easy," Kierion blurted. "Riders of fire can harness dragon energy to use their talents."

"Exactly. We'll talk more about that next lesson." Roberto glanced at Ezaara. Her face was pale.

Erob, in the grass under some nearby trees, broke through his thoughts, *"Zaarusha is requesting the Queen's Rider."*

"We'll be there right away," Roberto melded back. Good—the perfect excuse to get Ezaara out of class.

§

"Ezaara, wake up."

"Zaarusha, is that you?"

No answer. The torch was low. It must be late. Leaning on her stick, Ezaara made her way out to Zaarusha's den, but the queen wasn't there.

"Ezaara." There it was again—deep, melodious and unfamiliar. *"Come outside."*

She hobbled to the mouth of the den. The valley was peaceful, shrouded in darkness, moonlight catching on the tips of the Alps.

"Look up."

A bronze dragon was circling down toward Zaarusha's den.

"I saw you at my imprinting test," she melded. *"Who are you?"*

"Handel is my name." His talons clattered on the rock, and he crouched, holding out his leg. *"Climb up."*

Ezaara hesitated.

"Your father, Hans, was my rider."

Pa's dragon. Wow. *"Hans, Handel! I should've guessed you were my father's dragon."*

"*I am. Hans is still my rider—or will be when he returns. Climb on, there's someone you need to meet.*"

"*Pa is returning?*"

"*Some day.*" Handel supported Ezaara with his tail as she clambered up his leg and settled herself between his spinal ridges. Tensing his enormous haunches, he leaped into the air. The cool night nipped at Ezaara's bare legs as they climbed up the mountainside to a plateau.

Moonlight shimmered on the snowy mountain face. No, wait, what was that? The shimmer was coming closer. Ezaara sucked in her breath as a silvery shape materialized from the gloom. Moonlight played on silver scales, making them wink like stars.

"*Did you know your father was the master of prophecy?*" Handel asked.

"*No.*"

"*And your mother was master healer.*" The silver dragon's voice tinkled like a bell in a breeze. The beast stretched her neck out and nudged Ezaara's shoulder with her snout. "*I am Liesar.*"

The dragon closed her turquoise eyes—the same shade as her mother's—as Ezaara scratched her eye ridges. *Lies*ar, Mar*lies*. "You're Ma's dragon."

"*No, she's my rider. Dragons are never owned by humans.*"

"*Of course.*" No one could ever own such wondrous creatures. The wind picked up, making Ezaara shiver.

"*Tell her why she's here,*" Handel said.

"*I must share a memory of your mother's.*"

A vision rushed through Ezaara's mind. She was astride Liesar in the middle of the night, Pa's arms around her middle. The vicious peaks of Dragon's Teeth rushed past beneath them, then they were swallowed by the night sky.

"*Years ago, your mother accidentally killed one of Zaarusha's dragonets, so your parents fled from Dragons' Hold.*"

A transparent golden egg loomed before her, with a purple dragonet floating in it, limbs slack and wings drooping—so perfect, she could see its tiny scales and talons. A wave of sorrow washed through Ezaara, leaving her wrung out and hollow. Bitter wind sliced through her clothing. She trembled, tears stinging her cheeks.

"You feel your mother's sorrow at killing the dragonet, and at losing us."

The vision changed. Ma and Pa, years younger, were hugging Liesar's neck, faces pinched with anxiety as they parted. Ezaara's chest grew tight.

"You're feeling your mother's emotions," Liesar said. *"That's the last time I saw them. It took Zaarusha years to understand that the dragonet gave its life willingly to bless your mother with fertility."*

Handel melded. *"Usually a rider can only meld with their dragon, but you can meld with other dragons. This was one of the dying royal dragonet's gifts to you."*

"I never wanted a dragonet to die for me. Will Tomaaz, my twin brother, have this gift too?"

"You have a twin? Zaarusha hasn't mentioned him." Handel's tail twitched.

Liesar answered, *"We'll have to seek him out. Perhaps he also has talents."*

Handel turned his head, his green eyes, the same shade as Pa's, drilling through Ezaara. *"You hold the key to the future of Dragons' Realm."*

The key? She hadn't met a dragon until a week ago.

"Handel and I are leaving tonight to collect your father." Liesar tilted her head. *"We'll collect your brother too."*

"So, I'll see my family? Here?" Ezaara couldn't help grinning.

"Marlies is elsewhere," said Liesar.

"She has to find Zaarusha's son." Handel's voice was grave. *"Once she's proven her loyalty, she may return."*

Ezaara took a deep breath. "Is she in danger?"

"Not yet," Liesar replied. That didn't sound promising. *"Handel, we must leave. I'll meet you near the hunting grounds."* With a flip of her wings, Liesar soared away.

Handel was airborne in moments. Ezaara hugged his spinal ridge as dizzying visions flashed before her.

She saw herself in the main cavern the night she'd arrived, hair unkempt and face streaked with dirt. Roberto, lip curled in disdain, placed his hands at her temples. She collapsed, and he caught her, a rare softness flashing across his features.

A surge of energy flowed through Ezaara as more images from Handel flitted through her head: tharuks killing and maiming people; dragons blasting their enemies with fire; her falling and Zaarusha diving to save her; Tomaaz looking worn and sick; Ma unconscious, battered and bruised; Roberto, face twisted with hate, lunging at her, making her heart thud and breath catch in her throat.

"Handel. Stop!" she screamed.

The images subsided.

"What was that?"

"I'm sorry, I didn't mean to scare you. Usually ancient dragon magic only lets me share prophecies with my rider, or with one whom it concerns. This rush of visions came, unbidden. Perhaps it's because you're the Queen's Rider and the fate of our nation hangs on your actions and Zaarusha's."

Hopefully these prophecies weren't fate. Tomaaz had looked gaunt and thin. Ma was obviously dying. And with the way Roberto had looked, who'd need enemies?

"The future can change, depending on people's decisions. When I know more, I'll let you know. In the meantime, don't tell anyone

that you can meld with any dragon." Handel clattered down on the mouth of Zaarusha's den. *"Be careful, my Queen's Rider."*

Ezaara slid down his side. After seeing his visions, how could she know who to trust?

KNIFE'S EDGE

Ezaara leaned heavily on her cane. "How much further to the mess cavern?"

"Just around this corner." Adelina paused. "Wait, I've got something in my boot." She bent and undid her laces.

Ezaara suppressed a smile. "Adelina, I know there's nothing in your boot. They're laced too tightly for anything to get in. You're making excuses again to spare my ankle. Yesterday, when you said you needed the latrine, you forgot to go."

Adelina's cheeks flushed. "I— um." She grinned. "All right, I'm a lousy actor, but you need a rest. You have to impress the masters and the other riders."

Ezaara grimaced. "Too late for that, isn't it? Everyone saw me fall flat on my backside at the feast."

"They saw you fly a loop, too. Don't forget that."

"Come on, let's get my next blundering entrance over with."

Adelina giggled.

Ezaara smoothed her riding jerkin with her free hand, and they walked around the corner.

The mess cavern was a babbling hubbub of voices, more crowded than Lush Valley's square on market day. Ezaara recognized some of the masters, seated among riders at jam-packed tables. Her stomach grumbled as she helped herself to freshly-baked bread and spicy soup.

A woman rushed over, Simeon at her heels. Wisps of her blonde hair were haloed in light streaming from holes in the cavern walls. Simeon introduced her. "Ezaara, this is my mother, Master Healer, Fleur."

Ma's old role.

Fleur bowed. "My Queen's Rider, how's your ankle?"

"It's all right," Ezaara replied. The last thing she wanted was more fuss.

"I'm sure it's fine." Simeon winked behind his mother's back. At least he understood.

Fleur patted Ezaara's arm. "Simeon can pop by later to check you have everything you need. He often helps me in the infirmary and knows how to treat sprains."

Adelina gave Fleur an overly-effusive smile. "That won't be necessary. The Queen's Rider's ankle will be better in no time." She turned her back on Fleur and Simeon, gesturing to a nearby table. "Why don't you get a seat, Ezaara, and I'll bring your lunch."

"Please, let me help you." Simeon took Ezaara's arm.

It was a lovely gesture. "Thanks, but I can manage. This cane does the trick."

His eyes flicked over the carving. "Surely the help of a friend is better than an old stick?"

Her cane was hardly an old stick—it was a beautiful gift. Before she could respond, murmurs reached her over the clatter of cutlery.

"Twisted her ankle, silly thing …"

"She's too naive, too weak …"

Ezaara lifted her chin, pretending not to hear. So much for Adelina's theory—flying a loop hadn't impressed anyone for long. One fall, and it was forgotten.

As she sat, a tinkling peal cut through the din. Master Lars was shaking a bell. Everyone quieted, and Lars stood. "I'd like to welcome Ezaara, Honored Rider of Queen Zaarusha. She started classes today and will soon be engaged in full training. I trust you'll welcome and befriend her, and I wish everyone a pleasant meal."

Most of the riders applauded. A few snickered. Across the cavern, Roberto was scowling. She'd never impress him.

Simeon was attentive during lunch, but Adelina was as bristly as a boar, eating in silence. Soon Ezaara was laughing at Simeon's anecdotes about living among dragon riders.

"So, you're not a rider yet?" she asked.

"No, but I'll imprint soon enough. My parents are both riders, so it'll happen." He shredded a bread roll, scattering crumbs on the table. "Gives me more time to train before I have to fight tharuks face-to-face."

She shuddered, remembering the battle in the Western Pass. She'd never be good enough to lead an army of dragons and riders against tharuk troops.

Simeon's eyes met hers. "I'd love to fight tharuks beside you."

Ezaara's cheeks grew warm. She broke away from his gaze.

"Enough flirting for today, Ezaara," Zaarusha melded. *"I'm waiting."*

"Unfair!" she melded back. *"I'm not the one flirting. He is."*

"But you are enjoying it."

Adelina snatched up Ezaara's empty bowl. "You won't be fighting until you imprint, Simeon. Your dreams of glory will have to wait. My Honored Queen's Rider, I believe we need to get to knife throwing practice."

§

Ezaara was sitting with Simeon again, laughing at his smarmy jokes. Although she wasn't in immediate danger, Roberto had the irrational desire to wipe the smile off Simeon's face with his fist.

While Adelina was clearing the bowls, Roberto stepped into the space beside Ezaara's seat. "My Honored Queen's Rider." He felt stiff, stilted, as if he had a broomstick strapped to his back. "Please allow me to accompany you to knife throwing."

He led her away without offering her his arm. He wouldn't make her look weak in front of everyone, the way Simeon had. He swept out of the door, a little too fast, just to prove she could manage on her own. "Erob says Zaarusha is—"

"On the ledge," Ezaara interrupted. "She already told me."

"Of course." Shards, that was silly of him.

Soon they were airborne, Ezaara seated in front of him. The scent of her hair reminded him of dandelions; of summer days outdoors, running in the paddocks with his dog, Razo—before his father had changed. He shook his head to jolt his bad memories away as they descended to the knife-throwing range.

Roberto jumped down and helped Ezaara out of the saddle.

"I could've dismounted on my own," she snapped, eyes blazing.

"Of course," he replied, keeping his voice cool. "Good luck for your assessment. I'll wait here and fly you back to your quarters afterward."

"No, thank you." Her pretty green eyes were hostile. "I'll call Zaarusha when I'm done." She stalked away. With her sore ankle it wasn't impressive, but she was determined, he'd give her that.

Trying not to smile, Roberto placed his hand on Zaarusha's head.

"I have to see Singlar and Lars. Stay, please, Roberto," the dragon queen said. *"Watching her knife-throwing will help you assess her."*

"As you wish," he replied. Good. He was curious to see how Ezaara would do.

§

How dare Roberto manhandle her? And keep maneuvering her out of conversations with Simeon. He might be in charge of training her, but he had no right to control her friendships.

Ezaara stalked away—although it was difficult to look indignant while negotiating uneven terrain with a cane. Soon she was near the other trainee riders. Gret, Sofia, Alban, Rocco and Mathias greeted her.

"Are you sure your ankle's up to this?" Derek, Master of Training, asked, shaking her free hand. Behind him, his dragon was shooting flame, blazing a line across the grass.

"I'm fine." Ezaara lied, dropping her cane in the grass. "See, no problem." Ankle throbbing, she tried not to grimace as she hobbled to the line of charred grass.

As the trainees lined up, knives in hand, Simeon rushed out of the trees, up to the line, out of breath. How had he gotten here so fast without a dragon? He winked at her and mouthed, "Good luck."

It was nice of him to support her.

"Have you done much knife throwing before?" Master Derek asked. When Ezaara shook her head, he passed Ezaara a knife and said, "Sofia, please demonstrate."

Sofia held up her blade.

Ezaara copied, but her fingers slipped, buttery with sweat. She wiped her hand on her breeches.

Sofia shot her a sidelong glance. "Hold your knife like you'd grip a hammer."

Adjusting her grip, Ezaara bent her elbow and raised the blade.

"That's better." Sofia flicked her forearm and her knife sailed across the field into a wooden target—a bullseye.

Other knives thunked into targets too, but Ezaara's knife glanced off at an angle, flying onto the grass. It wasn't even embedded in the earth. She stifled a groan. Everyone's eyes were on her.

"Keep your wrist in line with your arm or your knife will veer off. See, like this." Sofia hurled a knife into the target, blonde curls bouncing. Flashing a smile, she passed Ezaara another blade. "Here, try this one. It's my lucky blade."

"All right, wrist in line." Ezaara pulled her arm up and back, poised to throw Sofia's lucky blade.

"Kill the Queen's Rider," a dragon roared. As black as coal, with burning red embers for eyes, it flew straight at her. A wall of flame blasted out of its enormous maw, engulfing her, searing her skin.

Ezaara flung the knife at the dragon. Her ears filled with crackling fire, flames roaring at her. The scent of charred flesh stung her nostrils.

Dry retching, Ezaara lurched and collided with something solid.

The dragon disappeared. So did the heat and pain.

Her skin wasn't burned. She was sprawled on top of Sofia on the ground. The dragon had only been a vision, overpowering, but not real. But she'd smelled burning flesh ….

Sofia was screaming. A knife was sticking out of her thigh. Blood pulsed down her breeches.

She'd stabbed Sofia.

"No!" Ezaara yelled. Easing the blade from Sofia's leg, she ripped Sofia's breeches open and pressed her hands around the gash, applying pressure. "I—I'm sorry, Sofia." She reached for her healer's pouch, so she could stitch the wound. It wasn't there. She'd left it by her bed.

Roberto raced over. "What happened?" Others flocked around them.

"I—I was distracted." Ezaara's hands were covered in Sofia's blood.

Sofia grunted through gritted teeth. "It was an accident. I saw you stagger, like someone pushed you."

"But nobody did." Master Derek frowned. "And you retched. Are you sick?"

"I—uh … don't know." Ezaara ripped a strip from Sofia's breeches. How could she explain where that fiery vision had come from? It had felt like a dragon, but Handel had warned her not to tell anyone she could mind-meld with other dragons. And there hadn't been a dragon in sight.

Above them, Erob was approaching.

Could it have been him? Had Roberto instructed Erob to put her off, to embarrass her in front of everyone? Did he want her to fail? Handel's vision flashed to mind: Roberto—lip curled, face full of hate.

"Sofia needs stitches. Roberto," Master Derek barked, "please fly her to the infirmary at once."

Ezaara bound Sofia's leg, then squeezed her hand, leaving blood on Sofia's fingers.

"Ezaara." Simeon's concerned amber eyes met hers. "You look unwell. Perhaps you should rest."

Master Derek nodded. "Good idea, Simeon. Ezaara, you're excused for the afternoon."

"But I—"

"Take a break," Master Derek snapped. "The rest of you, back to training."

Erob landed on the grass nearby. Roberto carried Sofia over and they flew off to the caverns.

On my way. Zaarusha was flying toward them.

Ezaara hobbled toward the queen, her ankle searing.

Simeon steadied her. "My Queen's Rider. Let me help."

"I'm fine, really." Ezaara leaned on him, tears welling in her eyes. "It was an accident, but it looked like I stabbed her intentionally, didn't it?" She tried to control the quiver in her voice.

"Well … um …" Simeon smiled brightly. "I know you didn't *mean* to hurt her. Come on, a cup of herbal tea will make you feel better."

He'd avoided her question. It was that bad.

Ezaara melded with Zaarusha. *"I've messed up."* She showed Zaarusha her memory of Sofia's wound. *"I've injured a new friend."*

"Stop being so hard on yourself. Riders get injured in training all the time. Sofia will be all right." Zaarusha landed, nudging Ezaara with her snout. *"Erob compared it to a tear in a wing muscle. It'll heal. I'm more worried about the rogue dragon that was imagining burning you. I've ordered all the dragons to search for the culprit."*

"There was a lot of blood."

"If Sofia had scales, she wouldn't have been hurt."

"But she was *hurt. And I did it."*

Simeon helped Ezaara into the saddle, then climbed up behind her and wrapped his arms around her waist. His warmth was comforting.

"My cane—" Where had she left it?

"Don't worry," Simeon said. "I've asked Mathias to bring it back."

"We should go straight to the infirmary to see Sofia."

"No, you've had a shock. You need to rest. There'll be time to see her after my mother has stitched her wound."

"But it's my fault. I should—"

"Ezaara, do you really think Sofia wants to see the woman who just stabbed her?"

"No," she whispered, slumping.

"Sorry if I sounded harsh." Simeon's voice was soft, near her ear. "I'm only trying to protect you."

Zaarusha landed on the ledge outside her den, lying flat so she could dismount. Ezaara's legs were shaking so badly, Simeon had to steady her.

He helped her sit on her bed and pulled off her boots, then took a cup of water out to Zaarusha, who heated it. Pulling a small pouch of herbs from his pocket, he sprinkled some in the cup, then left it to steep. He tugged the covers over Ezaara.

"Thank you." She lay back on her pillows, exhausted. "I keep messing up, Simeon. Now Sofia's hurt. I'm a terrible Queen's Rider."

"I believe in you." He hesitated.

"What is it?"

"Well … no, I shouldn't say disparaging things about Master Roberto." He bit his lip.

"Go on, tell me."

"Roberto has angry outbursts … dark secrets. Watch yourself around him, Ezaara. He's like a rogue dragon, unpredictable and dangerous."

Had Erob given her the burning vision? Did Roberto want her to fail?

"And his sister isn't always as sweet as she seems."

Ezaara frowned. Had Adelina befriended her to work against her?

Simeon smoothed her hair. "Now I've made you worried. Sorry, ignore me, it's probably nothing." He held out the cup. "Here, drink your tea. It'll help you relax."

Ezaara reached for the cup. The tea was bitter and gray; not woozy weed, then. She took a sip and wrinkled her nose. "What is this?"

"Restorative tea." He pulled a comical grimace. "You know, the worse it tastes, the better it works."

"This must be really good for me, then."

He chuckled, watching her drink.

The tea seeped through Ezaara, making her muscles warm and her eyelids droop.

§

Eileen Mueller

Ezaara groaned and dragged her eyelids open. The den was swimming before her. Head pounding and muscles aching, she grabbed a basin and vomited. What on earth had she eaten?

The shrill notes of the dawn chorus pierced her skull. She'd slept from the afternoon, right through the night, until morning. Not a good look for the Queen's Rider. Especially after stabbing someone.

She had to check on Sofia. She should have gone last night. She swung her legs over the side of the bed, but the cavern spun.

After a few moments, everything stilled. Where was her cane? She groaned again. Mathias had forgotten to bring it back. *"Zaarusha."*

"Sorry, Ezaara, I'm in a council meeting. Tharuks are on the move, marching across the Flatlands, destroying settlements and taking slaves."

Great, while the Queen's Rider was in bed, monsters were attacking the realm. Maybe the realm would be better off if she was banished to the Wastelands. Stupid thought. She had to be less of a burden to the queen. Ezaara washed her face, then hobbled along the stone tunnels toward the infirmary.

Her ankle throbbed. She leaned on the rough walls for support, scraping her hands. She passed the mess cavern, but it was early, so few people were about. Torches flickered as she made her way west along the tunnel network. Around the corner, footfalls tromped on stone.

Alban appeared. "Where have you been?" he sneered. "You lowlife, disappearing after stabbing Sofia."

"I've been sick."

"You haven't visited her, haven't asked about her. Haven't even shown your face." His body was taut. His gray eyes, flinty. "You look as guilty as a vulture caught stealing dragonets."

"But I—"

"Stinking ignorant peasant from Lush Valley." He spat on the floor. "Great Queen's Rider you are. All you care about is yourself!" He strode off, his words echoing off the walls.

Heart hammering, she rushed along the corridor, ignoring her aching ankle. She shouldn't have listened to Simeon, although he'd had her best interests at heart. Alban was right. She was selfish for sleeping so long. Selfish for not visiting Sofia immediately. Too selfish to be Queen's Rider.

Ezaara entered the infirmary. Their backs to Ezaara, Fleur and Simeon were bending over Sofia while Fleur swabbed her leg. Sofia was asleep, curls splayed over her pillow. A blood-encrusted bandage lay on the bedside table. The stitches on her thigh were crooked and tight, making the wound pucker over an ugly bump. Ezaara cringed. It was worse than she'd thought. The gash was so awful, it wouldn't stay flat when stitched.

Taking a tub of yellow unguent, Simeon smoothed it onto Sofia's wound. The salve's acrid smell stung Ezaara's nostrils—that same smelly salve Simeon had given her.

When he was finished, Simeon turned, starting. "Oh, Ezaara. I didn't hear you come in." He shoved his medicinal supplies into a drawer in Sofia's bedside table. "How are you feeling?"

Fleur smiled as she bandaged Sofia's wound. "Good morning, Ezaara. Nice of you to visit."

"How's Sofia?"

"We gave her a pain draught so she could sleep, the poor thing," Fleur spoke softly. "Perhaps you should visit another time. You look tired; maybe you should rest."

Alban's accusations bounced around Ezaara's head. The last thing she needed was rest. She had to do something to help. Anything. "Perhaps you two would like an early breakfast while I sit with her? I mean, the accident was my fault."

Fleur cleared the dirty bandage away. "That's not really your role as Queen's Rider, Ezaara. Simeon will tend to Sofia. I must go soon. I've been summoned to a council meeting."

Fleur bustled about while Simeon sat by Sofia. Ezaara hovered, feeling useless.

"We don't use that yellow salve in Lush Valley. What's in it?" Ezaara asked.

"It's my own healing salve containing expensive herbs brought to me by green guards," Fleur replied.

"Green guards?"

"Dragon riders from Naobia, my dear. They ride green dragons. Being from Lush Valley, you wouldn't have heard of them, or their herbs." Fleur smiled. "I suppose you use old-fashioned remedies like arnica and peppermint?"

Ezaara nodded.

"Never mind, they do in a pinch." Fleur bustled out the door.

Ezaara had thought Ma was a great healer, but then, what did she know? Alban was right. She was an ignorant peasant from Lush Valley.

Moaning, Sofia opened her eyes. She scowled at Ezaara. "You! What are you doing here? Come to stab me again?"

Gasping, Ezaara took a step back. "I didn't mean—"

"Get away from me," Sofia shrieked. "Go away!"

Ezaara fled.

She staggered out into the tunnels. Sofia hated her. Blamed her. She'd been so understanding yesterday—a shock reaction? Supporting herself against the tunnel walls, Ezaara stumbled along, her ankle screaming. She welcomed the pain. She deserved it. It was nothing compared to how she'd hurt Sofia.

DEADLINE

Roberto traipsed into the council chambers, Erob's solid footfalls behind him. Council meetings weren't usually at the crack of dawn with the sky tinged honey-gold like the highlights in Ezaara's hair. He forced himself to focus. Zaarusha must have important news for them.

Curling his tail around his body and tucking his snout on his forelegs, Erob took his place behind Roberto's seat, near the back of the cavern, among the other dragons. *I'll catch a few winks while you humans solve the realm's problems,* Erob melded. Although he never actually napped during council meetings, he always threatened to.

Not that Roberto blamed him—their meetings could be boring. *"Don't snore, or Zaarusha might nip you."*

Zaarusha blinked a greeting to Roberto, her scales reflecting a myriad of colors in the torchlight.

He inclined his head, enjoying that familiar surge of pride at being on her council. There was no higher honor than serving their queen. She'd believed in him when he'd first arrived here. He'd never disappoint her.

Lars was already seated, drumming his fingers on the granite horseshoe-shaped table, talking with Tonio and Bruno, the master of prophecy.

Roberto slid into his chair beside Bruno. He nodded at Hendrik, a burly blacksmith and their master of craft. On the opposite side of the horseshoe, Aidan, Jerrick and Jaevin were seated, waiting.

Master of Horticulture and Livestock, Shari, leaned around Hendrik. "Morning, Roberto. Early, isn't it?"

Shari's dragon wasn't here. "How's Ariana doing?"

"Much better," Shari whispered, glancing at Bruno, Fleur's husband, the beads on her tiny braids clicking. "Fleur's tonic didn't work, so I tried the herbs I use on sheep. Ariana's sleeping, but I think they've done the trick."

"Good thinking."

"It's a relief." Shari smiled, white teeth flashing against her cinnamon skin. "A dragon with belly gripe is not a pretty sight—or sound."

Or smell. Roberto chuckled.

On the ledge outside, thumps and the skitter of talons on rock heralded the arrival of more dragons. A blue guard, in riders' grab with a blue armband, opened the chamber doors. Deep in conversation, Alyssa and Derek strode into the room followed by their dragons, who took their spots behind their masters. There were only two seats remaining: Fleur's; and the Queen's Rider's seat, which had been empty for years. Hopefully, Ezaara would soon be qualified to sit in it—although yesterday's abysmal knife incident made prickles of doubt play along Roberto's spine.

Lars cleared his throat. "We need to start. Bruno, can your dragon let us know when your wife will arrive?"

The quiet rumble of conversation made Roberto drowsy. He stifled a yawn. His all-nighter, carving Ezaara's cane, was catching up on him.

"They're almost here," Bruno announced.

Fleur and Ajeuria thudded onto the ledge and entered the council chamber. Ajeuria sat by the other dragons, preening her green scales. Fleur took her seat next to Roberto. Simeon's mother was the closest thing to a healer they had, but a far cry from the

Naobian healers he'd known. Roberto had expected Dragons' Hold to have the best.

"Ajeuria is radiating discontent," Erob melded, *"like she has a tick under her scales."*

"If we de-lice her, Simeon would probably come crawling out," Roberto replied.

Behind him, Erob snorted. Luckily, Erob was excellent at shielding his thoughts from other dragons.

Lars called the meeting to order, and the murmurs died down. "Before we discuss the situation in the Flatlands, I'd like Fleur to report on Sofia's condition."

Fleur stood, her face as tired as unlaundered linen. "I stitched Sofia's gash, but it'll leave a nasty scar. She's stable now, sleeping off the pain draught."

Sofia's wound hadn't looked that bad yesterday. Fleur had probably botched it.

"Thank you, Fleur." Lars nodded. "You may sit."

Fleur remained standing. "It's terrible she was hurt here, at the hold, where she should be safe."

Zaarusha shifted, her talons scratching the stone floor.

Lars frowned. "Thank you, Fleur."

"Will there be steps taken to—"

A low rumble issued from Zaarusha's throat.

Roberto gripped the table so hard his knuckles ached. This was a barely-veiled attack on the Queen's Rider.

"I said, thank you." The tension in Lars' frame carried a threat.

Roberto relaxed his grip.

"Tharuks are harassing our people in the Flatlands," Lars announced. "Our blue guards are currently holding them at bay, but it won't be long until Zens starts all-out war." His voice was gravelly. "We must prepare. Tonio, please report."

The spymaster's gaze flicked over each of the masters. Roberto could've sworn it rested a moment longer on him. Tonio had never trusted him. Sure, they'd grudgingly worked together, but Tonio knew the full extent of his father's treachery, so he'd never given Roberto a chance.

"There's not a lot to say," Tonio barked. "These tharuks seem to be searching for something, but we're not quite sure what, or who, it is. They've burned one village so far. Luckily, only three people lost their lives, but they've taken slaves and until they find what they're looking for, there'll be more deaths. We must prepare our people for war." He sat, muttering under his breath, "How we're going to fight a war with a Queen's Rider who can't carry a dinner plate without spraining her ankle is beyond me."

Zaarusha thrust her head at Tonio, snarling.

Erob piped up, *"Zaarusha's saying Tonio should shut up if he wants to keep his insides on the inside."*

"A shame Tonio doesn't understand dragon snarl." Roberto kept his lips from twitching into a smile.

Tonio leaped to his feet. "With all due respect to the queen, the new Queen's Rider is inexperienced. It was a metaphor, nothing more."

Roberto shifted in his seat. Not a metaphor, and directly aimed at him. Despite flying a loop, Ezaara's track record at the hold wasn't good, and he was responsible for training her. It was his fault she'd left the dais. And he'd been present when she'd had that strange accident and injured Sofia.

Tonio addressed him. "How is the Queen's Rider's evaluation going, Roberto? When will she be fit to lead us into battle?"

Roberto hesitated. They hadn't finished assessing Ezaara. They'd only tested her imprinting bond, flying and knife-throwing. What if her arrows all flew wide and she didn't know how to hold a sword?

"Roberto?" Lars raised an eyebrow.

Derek, master of instruction, cut in, "It's hardly fair, Tonio. We haven't seen her combat skills yet."

"She flies well," Alyssa, master of flight, commented. "Their loop was incredible for such a young imprinting bond. Zaarusha has chosen well."

A few nods rippled around the table. Not enough.

"A battle isn't won by flying a loop," Aidan, master of battle, bellowed.

Unease flickered through Roberto. "Thank you for your solicitous enquiry, Tonio." He deliberately kept his voice cool. "Ezaara's ankle is recovering, and her training is improving. I believe—"

"Improving enough to do what?" Tonio snapped. "Stab her fellow combatants?"

"I'm sure Ezaara—"

"Sure?" Tonio barked. "Be careful what you say, Master of Mental Faculties. I always base my claims on evidence."

"It was an accident. I was there. I saw how upset she was—"

"Upset?" Fleur snarled. "She didn't visit the infirmary last night to check on Sofia. That's how upset she was."

Roberto snapped his jaw shut.

A meaty palm slapped the granite table. Hendrik bellowed, "What sort of Queen's Rider doesn't visit the injured? Especially when it's her fault!"

"Well, she visited earlier this morning," Fleur said hurriedly, "but only briefly, and she fled as soon as Sofia awoke. Not at all what I'd expect of a Queen's Rider."

"I hate to be a harbinger of doom," Bruno muttered.

Everyone turned to him.

"Please go on," Lars asked the master of prophecy.

"Well, I …" Bruno glanced at Zaarusha with a wan smile. "With all due respect to our Honored Queen Zaarusha, I had a vision last night. Things don't bode well."

"Go on, Bruno." Lars' voice was clipped.

"I agree, it appears that tharuks are mounting a war, but my vision showed me that when they find what they're searching for, they'll retreat back over the Terramite ranges, leaving us in peace."

"And how does that bode ill?" Lars asked.

"It doesn't," Bruno answered. "It's good news. Our need to prepare for war isn't as urgent as our spymaster suggests. However, another vision showed me troubling news regarding the Queen's Rider."

Zaarusha shifted her weight, making the torches sputter. Then the room was silent, except for the hiss of the queen exhaling.

"The gift of prophecy is an onerous one." Bruno sighed, melodramatically. "I fear you may not like my news."

He was milking this, as usual.

"Spit it out, man." Hendrik slapped his enormous hand on the stone table again. On either side of him, Shari and Fleur flinched.

Bruno met Lars' gaze. "The Queen's Rider will betray us."

Zaarusha stood. Her roar juddered through Roberto's bones.

"My dear Queen," Bruno placated, "I cannot help what my gift shows me. To protect you and the realm, it's my duty to report what I see."

Roberto bristled. That whole family was rotten to the core. How dare Bruno accuse the Queen's Rider of treachery? It insulted Zaarusha's fitness to rule. It also insulted him—he'd tested her. Ezaara didn't have a disloyal scale on her hide.

"No chance of sleeping through this," Erob muttered. *"Almost makes me yearn for boring meetings again."*

"Our queen is a great dragon," Fleur added, "but she was lonely and desperate for a new rider. Maybe her judgment was flawed."

Bruno shook his head. "The queen is getting older …"

Zaarusha snarled. Yelling broke out. For the queen. Against her rider. Dragons raised their hackles. Masters leaped to their feet. Roberto ducked as Ajeuria's tail whipped through the air. Erob rose, beside Zaarusha, yellow eyes glowering at Ajeuria.

"Silence," Lars bellowed, cutting through the cacophony.

Lars placed his hand on Zaarusha's head. "Our queen commands no more slights on Ezaara. She has chosen her rider. Now, sit down. Everyone. I'm pleased Bruno advises us that war will not come, but however pleasing his prophecy is, we must prepare the Queen's Rider for battle. Roberto, please answer Tonio's original question. How long until she's ready?"

Roberto had to save face, for himself, for Ezaara, but mostly for Queen Zaarusha. They needed a trained Queen's Rider—and he'd give them one, if it meant slogging day and night. "She'll be ready by next moon," he announced.

Annoyance flashed across Tonio's face. "A moon? Ready to fight against tharuks? How? She's only been here a few days, and she's had one disaster after another. She's injured one of our most promising trainees, and you want to turn her loose in battle?"

"Maybe she'll injure some tharuks too," Roberto snapped.

Lars rapped the table with his gavel. "Roberto, are you sure you can do this?"

Of course not, but he had to try. "Yes, sir."

"Good. If you're that confident, I'll give you two weeks, at which time we shall reconvene and evaluate her worthiness as Queen's Rider."

"Yes sir." Roberto nodded. Dragon's fangs! How was she ever going to be ready in time?

§

"Ezaara! What are you doing here?" Gret crouched, her voice sharp.

Slumped against the wall halfway between the infirmary and the mess cavern, Ezaara shrugged. "Uh, resting …"

Gret's face softened. "It's your ankle, isn't it? Where's your cane?"

"Simeon said Mathias would bring it back from the field."

"Good," Gret said. "Mathias bunks in the boy's cavern, along here. I'll hunt him down."

"Thanks." Ezaara struggled to her feet. She couldn't put weight on her foot.

Soon Gret returned, out of breath. "Mathias didn't have your cane. Says Simeon never asked him to bring it back."

"But Simeon—"

"Forget Simeon," said Gret. "He has a reputation, you know."

Everyone was tough on Simeon. Were they all judging him, the way they were judging her? "Simeon's been nothing but friendly."

"Of course he has." There was an edge to Gret's voice. "Your ankle looks worse. What were you doing? Running on it?"

"I'll be fine. Just give me a hand, please."

Gret supported her along the tunnel, their footsteps echoing off the stone walls. "How are you going to train if you can't walk?"

Exactly what she'd been wondering. "Things will work out."

"They're saying you stabbed Sofia on purpose."

"It was an accident."

"I know that!" Throwing her hands in the air, Gret took a step back, leaving Ezaara unsteady. "I'm loyal to the realm and to you, but not everybody is. We have to combat these vicious rumors or you'll be put on trial and Zaarusha will lose her rider."

"Combat rumors? I'm struggling to walk. I can't even get back to my den."

Gret laughed.

"What?"

"Only dragons have *dens*. Riders have *caverns*."

"I have so much to learn, haven't I?"

Voices echoed beyond a bend in the tunnel. "Someone's coming," said Gret. "By the Egg, Ezaara, put a smile on your face, or everyone will think you're guilty."

Alban strolled around the corner, deep in discussion with another boy. "I was there." Alban stabbed a finger in the air. "The blood was horrendous. Poor Sofia."

"Ssh, she's coming," the boy replied. "She'll knife you next, if you don't watch it."

"Like to see her try." Alban's gaze was steely as he stalked past Ezaara.

Although she felt like screaming, Ezaara forced a smile as more footsteps sounded around the corner.

Roberto and Adelina approached.

"Ezaara!" Adelina hugged her.

"You're coming from the infirmary, I take it? Good." Roberto's eyes narrowed. "Where's your cane?"

"Simeon said Mathias would bring it from the knife-throwing range, but it's missing."

"Simeon?" Roberto's face tightened. "Leave it to me, I'll find it." He strode down the corridor, his boots striking the rock.

Shards, she'd lost the beautiful cane Roberto had carved for her—his mother's cane. Ezaara bit her lip, glancing at Adelina guiltily.

§

Roberto was astounded. He'd seen it again. When Ezaara had answered him, brilliant color had flashed through him. It was her. The brightness of her intellect, her mental resilience, whatever it was, they had a connection without touching.

He rushed down the corridor. The tunnels were too stifling, too narrow and confined for emotions this big. He needed to fly. He melded with Erob, *"Meet me on the ledge outside the mess cavern."*

"On my way."

Roberto broke into a run. The sooner he had space to think, the better. He took a bolt hole out onto the trails and ran along the goat track on the mountainside. Anakisha and Yanir had been able to mind-meld, so it was possible. But why Ezaara? Did she have a propensity for mind-melding like him?

He shuddered. He'd paid a terrible price for his skills.

Above the mess cavern, Roberto vaulted onto Erob's back. Two steps later, Erob was airborne. Roberto let out a gusty sigh. *"Sometimes I think the politics in this place are going to do my head in."*

"You're used to the Naobian Sea, the wide open coasts and endless blue. Living in this basin is hard on you."

"Not as hard as life in Naobia."

Erob coasted over fields of crops. *"Those memories will fade soon enough. You have your whole life in front of you. Where to?"*

"The knife-throwing range. That shrotty louse Simeon has hidden Ezaara's cane."

Erob roared, a tremor running through his body.

Roberto grinned. He felt exactly the same.

They descended toward the field. In the distance, a green dragon was returning to the caverns.

"It's Ajeuria," said Erob. *"The master healer must've been foraging for herbs."*

Roberto dismounted by the targets, scanning the grass. He'd felt Ezaara's anguish in the corridor; he knew Sofia's stabbing was an accident, but those keen to discredit the Queen's Rider were using this to their advantage. His boots tapped something in the grass—Sofia's lucky blade, crusted with blood. He stuck it in his belt and checked behind the targets. The cane wasn't there. Where had Simeon put it?

Erob melded, *"They flew off from over there, so perhaps it's nearby?"*

Roberto searched the bushes, the long grass at the edge of the field, and then scoured the surrounding trees. *"What a waste of a morning, and all before breakfast."*

Erob shot him a mental image of himself: face dirt-smeared, a twig in his hair and grass seed stuck to his jerkin. *"All in service to your Queen's Rider."*

"All in service to that slimy cockroach who's furthering his political interests and worming his way into the Queen's Rider's trust. Huh!"

But when Erob shot him the image again, Roberto had to chuckle. He looked a sight.

"Jealous?"

"What? Of that creep? Of course not."

§

Roberto found Kierion sharpening his blade against a grindstone. "Kierion."

The boy looked up. "Yes, Master Roberto?"

"I have a challenge for you."

Kierion's face shone as he sheathed his sword. "I'm your man."

"The Queen's Rider's cane has gone missing." How could he phrase this delicately? "I believe one of the trainees has played a prank on her."

"It wasn't me, sir." Kierion's voice was earnest. "I'd own up if I'd done it. Promise."

Roberto chuckled. A true prankster, Kierion was the most inventive of his students. "I'm not here to blame you, but to ask for your help."

"So, you want me to find it?"

"It was last seen at the knife-throwing grounds."

Kierion hissed through his teeth. "They're saying Ezaara knifed Sofia on purpose. I don't believe it, but I bet that's why someone hid her stick."

Roberto corrected him. "Her cane is ornately carved, much more than a stick, but speculation leads to gossip, Kierion. It's probably just a joke." *If only.* "Let's go. Erob's waiting."

"Erob!" Kierion grinned. "Wow, I'm definitely in. I've never been on a royal dragon before."

Roberto had to smile. Kierion's enthusiasm was catchy.

As they jumped off the ledge, Kierion let out a whoop. Roberto sighed—so much for searching without anyone noticing. They descended to the grass at the edge of the trees.

Kierion slid down from Erob, all business. "Where have you already searched?"

"Throughout the grass, among these trees and in those bushes. It could be anywhere. It might not even be here anymore."

Kierion bit his lip. "That's possible, but there are a few great hiding places around here. Follow me."

Traipsing through the trees, they came to a rotting log in the grass. Kierion knelt at one end and peered inside. "Empty. We'll try the next spot." They headed toward a cluster of bushes and tangled vines. Kierion and Roberto lifted up the edges of the vines and poked their swords into the bushes. Still nothing.

"There's one more spot, before we search the whole area," Kierion said. "Have you looked high in branches in case someone tied it in the top of a tree?"

"I had a cursory look, but nothing that thorough. Erob will scout from above."

"If your search wasn't that thorough, why did you end up with leaves in your hair?" Erob asked.

"Cheeky dragon," Roberto melded. *"If I admit it, Kierion will show me up."*

Erob chuckled and, within moments, was airborne, surveying the treetops.

Kierion took Roberto back toward the field. "We should've checked this spot first, but I thought it was too obvious." He stopped in front of a lightning-struck strongwood tree. "Give me a leg up?"

Roberto hoisted him up and Kierion's head and shoulders disappeared into a hole in the trunk.

"Found something." His voice was muffled. He pulled his head out. Burnt bits of bark were stuck in his hair and his face was soot-smudged. He yanked Ezaara's cane from the hollow, grinning. "We did it."

Roberto's breath caught in his throat—the cane was jagged, the shaft broken in half.

"Shards! Let me have another look." Kierion reached back into the hollow and fished out the other piece of the cane. He whistled. "That'll take some fixing."

Roberto's gut was hollow. A whole night's work, viciously broken. He took the pieces from Kierion, swallowing. "Thanks for finding it."

"Wow, look at that handle. Is that Ezaara on Zaarusha?"

Roberto nodded.

"Who made it?"

"I did, when she first hurt herself." Roberto coughed. "To show respect for the Queen's Rider." Warmth crept up his neck. Kierion was bright, but hopefully he wouldn't notice.

"Shards! What a way to frost Ezaara. Someone wants to delay her recovery, I'm guessing."

Too bright—he'd hit the nail on the head—but at least Kierion was gazing at the cane, not his face.

"That's only speculation," Roberto replied. "It was probably a prank." He attempted a laugh. "You know all about those."

Kierion turned beet red.

§

Roberto cornered Simeon near the infirmary. "It was you, wasn't it?"

Simeon grinned that same slow self-satisfied smile he'd grinned when Trixia had fled Dragons' Hold. No one had been able to pin anything on him then, either, but watching him now, Roberto was sure it was Simeon who'd fathered Trixia's littling. And, if the rumors were true and he'd taken the young woman by force, he was dangerous.

"What are you talking about?" Simeon's eyes widened in innocence, acting again.

"This." Roberto brandished the pieces of Ezaara's cane.

"What a *terrible* loss." Simeon's sarcasm made Roberto's skin writhe. "I'll have to escort Ezaara places, now, won't I?"

Roberto's hands clenched around the walking stick. "Don't you go near her."

"I'll do what I want," Simeon snapped. "You can't be everywhere."

"You lay so much as a talon on her and I'll make you pay."

"Is that a threat?" Simeon asked. "I wonder what Lars would say about a master threatening a subordinate? Did you inherit that talent from your father?"

Roberto forced himself to ignore Simeon's jibe. "Lars would have something to say about your antics."

"Oh no, he won't." Simeon smiled. "I've heard Lars likes proof, and plenty of it. And apart from some dumb broken stick, you're empty-handed."

Roberto wanted to smack the insidious smile off Simeon's face. "You can't hide behind your parents forever, Simeon."

"At least I have parents." Simeon smirked. "I bet your father used to beat your mother with that stick before he—"

"You've. Gone. Too. Far." Sword drawn, Roberto was icy with fury.

Although Simeon fled, Roberto stood seething, knowing he hadn't won at all.

A Testing Time

Adelina bustled into the Queen's Rider's cavern. Ezaara was already up and gone. Dragon's eggs, something stank. There, by the bed—a basin of vomit. Ew. She didn't mind helping the Queen's Rider, but she'd never thought her duties would involve *that*.

Putting down the breakfast tray, she picked up the basin and trotted off to the latrines. There was something odd about the smell. A strange, but familiar, tang. It was only when she arrived back in Ezaara's cavern that she realized what it was. Skarkrak, a herb used by the Robandi assassins from the Wastelands. How had it got to Dragons' Hold?

Snatching up a cup by Ezaara's bedside, Adelina sniffed it. It was skarkrak all right. Who'd given it to Ezaara, and had they realized that, while a mild dose helped with sleep, too much could cause vomiting or death?

Simeon worked in the infirmary. A shiver snaked down Adelina's spine.

She couldn't really tell Lars without proof, but she'd definitely mention her suspicions to Roberto.

§

"There's something I need to show you." Erob flipped his wings and glided across the lake.

"What is it?" Roberto shaded his eyes against the glint of the water.

"Brace yourself."

A vision shot into Roberto's mind. A wall of dragon flame seared his skin, stinking of singed hair and burned flesh. Blinding pain fried his nerve endings.

"That's a powerful illusion." He shook his head, focusing on the water lapping at the lake's shore. "Why are you showing me this?"

"Sorry, I should have told you earlier." A wave of Erob's guilt hit Roberto. Then Erob sent another image: Ezaara, screaming, her knife flying into Sophia's leg. Doubled over, she retched.

So that's why she'd been sick—from the stench of her own burning flesh.

"Someone forced that vision on Ezaara?" Someone with special mental talents. Who? Wait a moment. *"Why have you withheld this? Did someone suspect me?"*

Erob's guilty silence spoke for itself.

"Erob, answer me. You can trust me."

An indignant rumble came from Erob's throat. *"Of course I trust you. I just showed you the vision, didn't I?"*

"Come on. For the Egg's sake, Erob."

"It would be better if you asked me questions."

"You want me to guess, so you can say you didn't tell me?" Roberto slapped Erob's scaly hide. *"Who's told you not to mention this?"*

Erob spiraled down to the grassy lakeside. *"Ezaara was so distressed, she tried to push the vision out of her head, inadvertently relaying it to all the dragons on the council. We all agreed not to mention it to our masters until we knew who'd tortured her with it."*

Roberto dismounted, approaching Erob's head. *"She can send a vision to multiple dragons? That's crazy. No one's done that since Anakisha."*

"She has talents ..."

"Did she send it via Zaarusha?"

"No."

"Ezaara can meld with dragons other than Zaarusha?"

The silence hung heavy between them. Erob sprung, his wings flashing above the water. Within moments, he'd gulped a maw full of fish and thudded down beside Roberto again.

"Maybe a dragon sent her the vision, then. Or it could've come from a rider with hidden mental talents." Roberto let out a gust of breath. His past was still shadowing him. *"Did* you *think it was me?"*

"No. I've told Zaarusha it wasn't."

Roberto scratched Erob's eye ridges. *"But not every dragon believes you, right?"*

"I'm sorry." Erob butted his snout against the flat of Roberto's stomach. *"You were so against having a Queen's Rider from Lush Valley. You keep everything so close to your heart. Can you blame them for not realizing you've changed? That you're loyal to the Queen's Rider?"*

"Ezaara's in danger." Roberto's hand gave an involuntary twitch above his sword. *"We must protect her."*

§

Ezaara gripped her knife and raised her arm. Again.

"Not like that." Simeon stepped closer, his warmth playing along her back as he adjusted her grip. "There, that's better. Remember how to hold your thumb?" His breath tickled her earlobe.

Heat flooded her cheeks. "Thank you, Simeon." It was bad enough being back here after what she'd done to Sofia, without blushing like a strawberry whenever he touched her. This was instruction, not a romantic interlude. She had to stop behaving like a besotted turkey.

"I know this is hard after yesterday, but take it easy. Throw when you're ready." His voice was gentle.

She'd known all the boys in Lush Valley since she was small. Here, the men her age seemed older, more confident. More experienced. She had to focus, throw the knife, not think about him. Ezaara flicked her arm forward, and the blade sailed through the air, hitting the bottom of the target.

"You're improving," Simeon said over-enthusiastically. "Well done. If you throw with more force, and aim a little higher, we'll have you hitting the bullseye in no time." He dashed toward the target to retrieve her knife.

It sounded so easy, but sweat coated her hands whenever she lifted the knife. She'd hurt Sofia. Another tremor ran through her. Remembering her skin bubbling and blistering made her feel like vomiting all over again.

"Have another try." Simeon was back, urging her on. "You can only get better." His cinnamon eyes were warm and encouraging. At least she had one true friend here.

She could do this, for him. Ignoring the flash of fire in her head, the twisting of her gut, her damp fingers, she threw the knife.

"That's better. I'll retrieve it for you."

If only she had her cane. Her ankle was aching, but she didn't want to admit it to Simeon when he was trying so hard to help.

Simeon grinned as he handed her the knife again. "Go on, one more."

As Ezaara raised her arm, a shadow fell over her.

"Here comes trouble," Simeon muttered.

He was right. Erob was here—and Roberto's expression was as dark as a storm cloud.

Ezaara sighed.

"Hard to please, isn't he?" Simeon murmured, squeezing her hand. He got it. He understood her so well, and he obviously knew Roberto. "Come on, Ezaara," Simeon urged. "Let's show him what you've learned."

She raised her arm. Simeon reached around her body, adjusting her grip again. "A little higher," he whispered. He stepped back as her knife sailed straight into the target.

Erob thudded to the ground, and Roberto swung out of the saddle, face thunderous. Striding toward them, he nodded at the target. "Much better," he said. His gaze flicked over Simeon. "What are *you* doing here?"

Simeon's lip curled. "Training the Queen's Rider."

"Training Ezaara is my job," Roberto snapped. "Not yours."

"Well, it's a shame you were too busy, isn't it? Anyone would think you want her to fail."

Roberto flinched. "Get back to the infirmary and your assigned duties."

"Yes, *Master* Roberto," Simeon spat. "Farewell, Ezaara. It was a pleasure being with you this morning." He flashed a sparkling smile and strode off.

"Let's get back to training," Roberto said.

"Until you two start treating each other civilly, I have no inclination to train with either of you." Ezaara stalked toward the target, masking her aching ankle.

Roberto caught up with her. "Ezaara." His deep voice shimmied through her. "I need to talk to you."

She was about to ignore him, when Erob mind-melded, "*Ezaara, listen to him. He has your best interests at heart.*"

"*His rudeness is a strange way of showing it,*" she melded back.

Erob chuckled as Ezaara pulled her knife out of the target and sheathed it in her belt.

Roberto put his fingers in his mouth and whistled. With a flap of wings, Erob leaped over to them. Roberto reached up and untied her cane from his saddle, holding it out toward her. His expression softened.

His mother's beautiful cane. "Where did you find it?" Her irritation evaporated.

He waved an arm at the nearby trees. "Hidden near here." His fingers traced a hairline break in the wood. "It was snapped in two. I used a dowel and some tree sap to fix it. It's not as good as it was, but it should do the trick."

"Broken in two?" That was hard to swallow. "That's pretty low."

Roberto's eyes flitted toward Simeon's departing back.

Of course, he suspected Simeon—her friend. Ridiculous. It was more likely to have been Alban.

"Thank you for mending it." Ezaara put her weight on the cane. "It's as good as new."

Roberto leaned against Erob's side, crossing his long legs. "Today, Ezaara, you and I are going to get to know each other a little better. And then we'll start training in earnest. You need to be ready for battle."

What if she didn't want to get to know him? And how could she train in earnest when her ankle was throbbing?

"Come on." He extended his hand and helped her onto Erob. He climbed up in front of her and slid her cane into a saddlebag. "Hold on tight."

Ezaara put her arms around his waist, inhaling his sandalwood scent. They took off, heading toward a lake that glinted silver among a dark carpet of trees.

"Is this where you go fishing?" Ezaara asked. It was a tranquil refuge from the gossip in the mess hall and tunnels.

Erob settled on the grassy shore.

He smiled. "Yes, and I swim here in summer."

Erob shot Ezaara an image of Roberto, muscular and sun-bronzed, cutting through the water.

Her cheeks grew warm. *"Honestly, Erob!"*

"What is it?" asked Roberto, sliding down, then helping her off Erob. "Don't you like swimming?"

"I love it." He'd noticed her blush, which made her blush even more—a vicious circle. "Um, what did you want to talk about?"

Roberto sat by the lake and patted the grass. "Please, sit down." He took a package wrapped in waxed cloth out of his pocket, then took his jerkin off and rolled it up. "Rest your ankle on this, it might help."

Simeon hadn't paid any attention to how her ankle was today. Maybe there was more to Roberto than she'd thought. "You seem to have practice in looking after invalids," she joked.

His face grew grave. "My mother was badly injured. I nursed her for three moons." He unwrapped the waxed cloth, revealing bread, a jar of relish and a wedge of cheese.

"What happened to her?"

His fingers were motionless for a moment. "She died."

The hollow ache in his voice made Ezaara's eyes prick. "I'm sorry."

"It was a while ago." He cut some bread off the loaf with his knife.

"How was she hurt?"

Roberto's face darkened. "Another time, all right?" He passed her the slab of bread, and sat with his blade poised. "Cheese?"

When they'd finished their makeshift sandwiches, Roberto asked, "Why didn't you tell me about the vision you saw when Sofia was hurt?"

"I, uh ..." Handel had told her not to tell anyone she could meld with other dragons. Handel's prophecy of Roberto's face twisted with hate flashed before her. He didn't look hateful now. Concerned, maybe curious, but not hateful. "I haven't told anyone."

"Erob showed me. Is that what caused your accident with Sofia?" He looked at her as if he was really seeing her.

Something loosened in Ezaara's chest. Words tumbled out of her in a torrent. "My skin was searing, blistering. It was agony. My whole body was on fire. Made my stomach turn. When my mind cleared, Sofia was ..." She shuddered. "Sofia was ..." Tears stung her eyes.

She. Would. Not. Cry.

"Her blood was everywhere .... Everyone thought I'd done it on purpose."

"I didn't think that." Roberto's gaze was gentle. "I've tested you. I know you." Again, his gaze, *seeing* her. "And last night?"

"I meant to visit Sofia, but Simeon gave me a cup of tea and I fell asleep. The shock made me sick. Or maybe I ate something bad."

"Maybe."

Alban's words popped into her head. Incompetent, that's what he'd called her. Ezaara's shoulders slumped. "Zaarusha should send me home."

Roberto put an arm around her. Again, mint and sandalwood.

Her master was hugging her? She pulled away. "I, um ..."

He dropped his arm, scratching his neck awkwardly. "Ah, how's your ankle now?"

"Still throbbing. It'll be a few more days until it's healed. I should stay off it."

"Ezaara, we don't have time. The council want you battle-ready. They're not prepared to wait." His eyes slid to the healer's pouch at her waist. "Is there something you could take?"

Piaua, but no, it was too precious. "It only needs rest."

He leaped to his feet, pacing. "Tell that to the council when they demand that you go to battle unprepared. I told them you need time. They wouldn't listen. We have two weeks to give you a lifetime's training."

"Two weeks!"

"Only if tharuks don't attack before then." Roberto's face was tight. "We have to heal you, Ezaara. Is there anything that could help?"

She couldn't fail Zaarusha or the realm. "Piaua," she whispered, gazing down at the grass. "But we can't …"

"Why not?" He crouched before her.

"I took a healer's oath. We only use piaua for grievous injuries."

"Ezaara," he breathed, raven eyes pleading. "It's urgent. You're the Queen's Rider. You have to be ready for anything."

As Queen's Rider, she needed to be fit—but she wouldn't waste such a scarce resource on a stupid ankle. Ezaara thrust his jerkin to one side and scrambled up. "Look, I'm fine."

In a flash, Roberto drew his sword and lunged.

She leaped back, pulling her sword from its scabbard and parried his blow. Her ankle twinged as she sidestepped his next move. Whirling, she ignored the throbbing, thrusting and counter-thrusting. Metal scraped on metal. Sweat stung her eyes. He swept his sword along the ground, making her jump and land on her ankle awkwardly.

"Aagh!" In a fit of anger, she lunged for his chest and struck home.

Flinging his sword aside, Roberto raised his arms. "You win."

"No," Ezaara moaned, "you do! Now I've ruined my ankle, so I have to use piaua." She sheathed her sword and slumped onto the ground.

§

Roberto crouched beside Ezaara, untying her boot. He sucked in his breath. He'd thought she'd give up and concede. But no, she was a fighter.

She glared at him. "You're a—"

He didn't wait to find out what she thought. "Shards! I'm sorry, Ezaara, I never expected you to fight back."

A glint of triumph shone in her eyes. She was breathing hard. "I should have stabbed you there and then."

Wincing, she let him roll up the leg of her breeches to check her ankle. It was swollen and red, almost as angry as her. "Sorry, I—"

"Curse it. Stop apologizing. You win. I have to use piaua juice so I can get on with training." Ezaara glared at him again with those startling green eyes. Wisps of blonde hair blew across her face. She jammed them behind her ears.

"I really didn't think you'd fight me with a sore ankle."

"So you said." She reached into her healer's pouch and passed him a slim vial of transparent green liquid. "Piaua juice is precious. The trees are rare, and draining their juice can kill them, so we only use it in dire circumstances." She frowned, lips pursed. "Not for a swollen ankle."

He'd forced her into this. "It's for the best."

Her eyes met his. "I know. Knifing Sofia and falling off the dais hasn't helped. I have to be ready for tharuks, and I have to prove to these tough old riders that I'm Zaarusha's rightful rider."

She understood. Roberto's breath whooshed out as he pulled the tiny cork stopper out of the vial.

"Wait. Don't spill any. Only use a drop or two." Her face showed her apprehension.

"Is it really as effective as they say?" he asked.

"Better. We play down its effects so people aren't tempted to drain the trees."

"I'd heard only tree speakers could collect the juice."

"True, and I'm not one, so this is doubly precious."

He held the vial over her ankle, tipped two droplets onto her swollen flesh, then passed it back to her. Ezaara capped the vial, and rubbed the oily residue over her bruised skin.

"Are you all right?"

"It burns a little. It's nothing." She bit her lip, and her brow furrowed as she worked the oil into her skin.

The swelling was receding before his eyes. The blotchy purple bruise was fading, growing lighter. Within moments, her ankle was normal. Incredible.

"This stuff's amazing." She had pretty ankles and feet, not that he'd ever noticed a woman's ankles before. Roberto coughed, glancing away.

Ezaara flexed her ankle and leaped up, dancing across the grass. She snatched up his sword and tossed it to him.

Dragon's eggs! She was beautiful, full of life.

There was no way he could ever act on how he felt—as if he'd be that stupid. Masters weren't allowed relationships with trainees. He'd never risk banishment after all he'd done to earn his position as master at Dragons' Hold.

"Now we can duel," she called.

"You'd better get your boots on," Roberto growled. "I'm going to put you through your paces."

TRICKERY & STUNTS

Erob flapped his wings. Exhausted, Ezaara clung tighter to Roberto. Except for that first time, no matter how hard she'd tried, Roberto had beaten her every time they'd dueled today. He'd been remorseless, goading her with jibes as they'd clashed swords. Her beating him earlier had been a fluke, like when she'd beaten Tomaaz in the marketplace.

Erob descended to the edge of the forest and Roberto jumped off, making no move to help her. He strode toward a strongwood tree and hung a leaf on the rough bark of its trunk.

Ezaara slid off Erob. Although she was tired from dueling, it was great to walk and run properly again. She shrugged off her guilt about using piaua. It was too late now.

"Let's test your archery skills," called Roberto. "The leaf is your target."

Stifling a smile, Ezaara called, "It looks awfully small." This would be a cinch. She and Tomaaz had grown up shooting as soon as they were old enough to fetch arrows.

Roberto took two bows out of Erob's saddlebag. "Which one do you want to use?" He held a longbow in one hand, and a recurve in the other.

The elegant longbow needed more strength, but was taller and more cumbersome. The recurve was her favorite, the type her family used. The ends of the bow curved forward, creating more tension on the string so arrows could travel faster and further.

"This one, thanks." She took the recurve. It was similar in feel and size to her one in Lush Valley. Ezaara rubbed her fingers along the string, then sniffed them. Good, it had recently been treated with beeswax.

Roberto observed her, narrowing his eyes. "Do you need any tips?"

He was assuming she couldn't do anything—why not humor him? Ezaara sighed dramatically. "I'm fine, really." This could get interesting.

He passed her a quiver of arrows and she slung them across her back. Ezaara wiped her palms on her breeches, nocked her arrow, and raised it to sight the center of the leaf. It took a seasoned archer to evaluate a new bow with only one test shot. As she loosed the arrow, she twitched her bow to the side. The arrow whistled through the air and went wide, hitting a bush.

"Hmm," Roberto pursed his lips. "Although you sighted well, the bow jerked as you fired. Try again." He crossed an arm and rested his elbow on it, rubbing his chin.

This time, she let the bow jump to the opposite side.

"Same problem. Let me show you." He strode toward her.

"No, thanks, I'm fine. I'm just warming up." Ezaara bit her cheeks to stop herself from grinning. Her next shot was wide, and the one after, too high. All of her arrows had missed the trunk.

"Ezaara, allow me to help you." Roberto's jaw was tense.

She'd probably pushed him far enough. "One more shot, please?"

A terse nod.

She loosed an arrow, hitting the center of the leaf. Bullseye. Then she loosed another and another, until the leaf was shredded, prickling with arrows.

If Roberto's eyebrows rose any higher, they'd meet his hairline.

"What did you think of that?" She ran to the trunk and pulled out the arrows, tucking them back into her quiver.

"We have two weeks to train you, and you think we have time to play games?" He shook his head, then snapped, "Double your distance."

So, he'd lost his sense of humor? Fine. Two could play that game. Ezaara paced back from the tree to where she'd been standing, then paced that far again. Roberto replaced the leaf with a fresh one. Raising her bow, she loosed an arrow. Another bullseye.

"That far again," he called.

Pacing off, she turned and fired another shot. Her arrow hit the edge of the leaf.

"Center, this time," he barked.

"I'd like to see you try," Ezaara muttered under her breath as she nocked an arrow and let it fly. The arrow hit the leaf, knocking her earlier arrow off the bullseye.

Roberto gave a short nod. "A spinning shot, this time."

Ezaara faced away from the trunk, nocked her arrow and spun, slamming her front foot down, aiming and loosing the arrow in one fluid motion. It hit the leaf.

Roberto nodded and called her over.

He should be pleased, but no, he was frowning again.

He took her bow and quiver. "Since you're so proficient at archery, draw your sword."

Groaning, Ezaara obliged, and they clashed blades again.

§

At the crack of dawn, Ezaara and Zaarusha flew down to the archery range.

I could've easily slept longer. Ezaara yawned, muscles aching from yesterday's sword bouts with Roberto. She had bruises too.

He's a good trainer, Zaarusha melded. *And not bad company, once you get to know him.*

"I'd rather befriend a wolf."

Zaarusha just chuckled.

Roberto was already there, oiling a dry patch on Erob's neck. He swung back into the saddle as Zaarusha landed. "Good morning, Ezaara. Don't get down. Today we're going to be shooting arrows from dragonback." He nodded at her bow and quiver.

He seemed pleased she'd brought them with her—as if she was a littling that would forget her weapons. Well, his weapons. He'd promised to take her to Master Archer Jerrick to get her own bow today. A shame she'd left hers in Lush Valley.

"I didn't exactly give you time to pack," Zaarusha rumbled.

Or say goodbye. Her eyes pricked. Tired, she was just tired.

Roberto's charcoal gaze focused on her, then flicked across her face. He always seemed to know when she was melding with Zaarusha. Could he hear them?

"No, he can't," Zaarusha answered. *"He can only access your mind when he touches your temples. That's his gift. I haven't seen another like him. Well, there is one, but …"* A dark shiver flitted across Zaarusha's mind.

Ezaara suddenly felt cold. *"Who?"*

"Later. He's been patient enough."

Roberto, patient? Yesterday he'd goaded, commanded and prodded her until she'd nearly dropped from exhaustion. She raised her eyebrows at him.

"Have you ever shot arrows from horseback?" he asked.

"A few times." More than a few. Pa had drilled them until they could hit a target galloping. It had been a while, though.

"Good. It's different from dragonback, but you'll soon get the hang of it."

That was it? No hints or tips? "How is it different?"

His smile was wry. "You'll see. Hit the red targets. Erob and I will fly behind Zaarusha, so I can evaluate you."

So helpful.

Erob took to the skies, and Zaarusha followed, skimming along the tree tops at the edge of the meadows. Her bow and arrow at the ready, Ezaara scanned the trees. There, a red scrap of cloth was tied to a high branch. Ezaara sighted, aimed, fired. And missed. This was harder than it looked. She nocked another arrow, and aimed at the next target, fluttering in the breeze among the foliage.

Another miss.

Ezaara snatched another arrow out of her quiver. Zaarusha was flying a steady slow course and these targets were all at a similar level. If she was in battle, she'd be dead from a tharuk arrow by now. She aimed at another scrap of red, missing. And another, missing again. And again.

And again.

Erob popped up beside Zaarusha. "Want a few hints?" Roberto called.

Now he asked? "Not yet," Ezaara replied, then melded with Zaarusha. *"Could you slow down a bit and fly closer to the targets?"* There, that should be easier. Her arrow speared a branch. Closer, but not a hit. Pitiful. Absolutely pitiful. *"Why is it so hard?"* she asked Zaarusha.

"It's the air currents from my wingbeats."

"Well, that's great. If you stop flying in battle, I'll be too dead to shoot anything." Ezaara sighed. *"Unless you glide each time we pass a target."*

"That often works."

"So, if you knew, why didn't you tell me?" Ezaara sighted, aimed. Slightly closer.

"Sometimes, experience is the best teacher."

She snorted, still feeling the bruises on her ribs from Roberto's sword, and nocked yet another arrow. *"Gentle,"* she commanded Zaarusha.

A memory popped into her head: Pa teaching her to shoot from horseback. "It's all about the balance and the rhythm," he'd said, demonstrating how to rise up in the stirrups as he fired, to counteract the movement of the horse's gait.

As the queen steadied her wings, gliding past a strongwood, Ezaara rose in the stirrups and aimed. Her arrow snagged the edge of the red cloth. A hit, her first hit. Only a ragged corner, but better than a miss. She reached into her quiver, but it was empty.

Behind her, Roberto laughed. "Retrieving them is part of your stamina training." Zaarusha and Erob landed in the nearest clearing and Roberto dismounted. "Get down," he said. "We haven't got all day."

Ezaara dropped to the ground.

"Now, run." He gestured behind Zaarusha. "Back the way we came. Go and get your arrows."

She'd fired her first arrow ages back, but there was no way she was going to groan in front of Master Roberto. Ezaara set off at a run. She'd loved running through the forest back in Lush Valley and had done far too little of it at Dragons' Hold, thanks to her ankle and having Zaarusha to take her everywhere.

"I heard that," quipped the queen.

Roberto drew level, running beside Ezaara. His feet fell into time with hers. The steady cadence of their breathing contrasted with the rustling foliage and twitter of birds in the trees above. Ezaara was scanning the trees, trying to figure out which one she'd fired at, when he motioned toward a tree with a rope hanging from one of its branches.

"This one." He held the rope out toward her. "Start climbing, it's good for fitness."

Great—tree climbing, running and dragonback archery all in one.

It took Ezaara the rest of the morning to retrieve most of her arrows. When she was done, there were still four missing. Roberto motioned her to sit on a rock at the edge of the clearing. Moments later, Erob and Zaarusha dropped to the grass.

Striding to Erob's saddlebags, Roberto took out a small cloth bundle. "How are you feeling?"

Hungry and tired, but she wasn't about to tell him that. "As perky as a dragonet." If dragonets were even perky—she had no idea.

Opening the bundle, he passed her some bread, cheese, an apple, and a waterskin. He motioned at the skin. "Drink that first, it'll revive you."

It was sweet, delicious and vaguely familiar. "This is great. What is it?" Ezaara took another swig.

He grinned. "Watermelon juice, a Naobian treat."

So that was it. "I tasted watermelon once, when I was young. A trader brought some over the Grande Alps. He sold them straight from the river, where he'd submerged them in a huge sack, cooling. It was delicious. Such a strange, foreign delicacy." A pang of loss for Lush Valley shot through Ezaara. He was far from home too. "Do you miss Naobia?"

A wince shot across Roberto's face, so fast she almost missed it. "It's a beautiful place, but no, I don't miss it." His face shuttered. "What strategies could you use to find your lost arrows? They're a valuable resource. You won't find them, unless you're smart about it. Think, Ezaara. Think."

She'd hunted around the ground underneath the targets and searched the foliage to see if they were hidden there. She chewed her breakfast in silence.

"A Queen's Rider has to use strategy," Roberto said.

"Well, you're master of mental faculties. You should be an expert at that."

His face darkened. "This is an essential part of your training."

"I could ask the littlings from Dragons' Hold to find them."

"Now you're thinking. Delegation. What else could you do?"

"Get Zaarusha to shake the trees, and see if any of them fall out."

"How would you know which trees to shake?"

"All the ones with the ropes hanging from them."

"All of them? But you only lost four arrows."

Ezaara sighed. "I guess I should've marked the trees where we lost the arrows."

"Yes," Roberto answered, "you should have. But don't worry, today I did."

Biting into her apple, Ezaara said, "So now I have to search around four trees. Those arrows could be anywhere."

"Strategy, Ezaara, strategy."

The best strategy would be to walk away from his insufferable questions, but he was her master, so she didn't dare. "All right, I give in. What's your brilliant idea?"

Roberto gestured at the vast forest around them. "There was no way I could explain to you the effects of wingbeats on arrow flight, before you'd tried. Just as there's no way I can explain to you how to develop good strategies that will save you time in battle. Some things have to be done through trial and error. Sometimes experience—"

"—is the best teacher. I know. Long ago, someone wise once told me that."

"Not that long ago." Zaarusha chortled. *"And very wise."*

"I know, perhaps Zaarusha could help."

His eyebrows shot up. "How?"

"Maybe she saw where the arrows went."

"Of course I did. I always look." Zaarusha gave a small trium-phant roar. *"I told him you were good, and now you've proven it."*

He just raised another stupid eyebrow. "Did you cheat and ask our Honored Queen?"

Ezaara threw her apple core at a tree trunk with more force than necessary. It splattered against the rough bark. "No. I. Did. Not." She got up and climbed on Zaarusha. "Now, let's find those arrows."

§

Ezaara was a fast learner, he'd give her that. And resourceful. No one else he'd trained had ever thought of using the dragons to shake trees, let alone asking them to mark where their arrows had fallen. Although dragons, with their superior intellect and excellent sight, often noticed details that riders missed, most novices were unaware of it. Formidable in battle, dragons were deadly enemies. Roberto was glad he wasn't fighting against them.

Within a short while, they'd found three arrows and were thrashing around in the bush, searching for the fourth. "Come on," Roberto said. "It's not worth spending any longer on this."

"I thought they were precious?" Ezaara snapped, her face streaked with dirt, and her hair fraying from her braid.

"When you're done questioning your master's ability to teach you," he said, "we'll do more shooting from dragonback."

"Sorry," she mumbled, her eyes the same shade as the foliage.

He grunted. "When you're back in the saddle, focus on Zaarusha's every movement: the flip of each wing and how she rises and falls on the breeze. Rising in the stirrups to make your shots was a good technique, but you have to perfect it. In battle, your targets won't be static. So far today, you've been shooting within close range, alongside a target. I'll know you're truly proficient when you can shoot at targets ahead, alongside, and behind you. Are you ready?"

She raised her chin, determination flashing in her eyes.

§

Ezaara ached all over. The last few days' training from dawn until dusk had been grueling, but at least she could now hit most targets from her saddle. Sitting on the edge of her bed, her stomach muscles groaned in protest as she bent to unlace her boots. Dragon's sit-ups, Roberto called them, but they were more like torture. He'd made Zaarusha run along the edge of the orchard, and every time a low branch hurtled toward Ezaara, she'd had to lie back to avoid being hit, then pull herself up using her core muscles. She snorted. And that was the least of it. Her days had been filled with sword fighting, tree climbing, running, balancing on ropes above a churning river, scaling rock faces, and eternal target practice. He'd even had her kneeling on the saddle to shoot. Of course she'd missed, how could she not miss when she wasn't balanced properly?

And through it all, he'd goaded her to be better, try harder, think more like a Queen's Rider and less like a girl from Lush Valley. She missed her family. Where were they? What was happening to them? Did Tomaaz miss her too?

Sometimes, she glimpsed another side of Roberto, the gentle side that gave her watermelon juice, or a special green apple from the tree his parents had planted. He never talked about them, nor his littling days. No matter how often she asked, he'd always change the subject.

Ezaara threw her boots near the bed so she could easily find them when Roberto came back for her tonight. So tired—and now he wanted her to do flight training. Why in the night, when she was exhausted? Ezaara collapsed on her bed, in her riders' garb, and drifted to sleep.

She awoke to a thud in Zaarusha's den.

"Erob's here," Zaarusha warned.

Moments later, Roberto appeared. "You skipped dinner."

"I was tired." She'd been asleep before her stomach had rumbled, but now she was ravenous.

"As Queen's Rider you need to take care of yourself."

"That's why I was sleeping." Ezaara rolled her eyes. "I'm exhausted. Is that any surprise after the last few days?"

"Not really," Roberto admitted, a flash of sympathy in his eyes. "Here." He reached into his pocket and passed her a small cloth bundle.

"Mm, smells divine." Like lemon and something. She unwrapped it. A lemon poppy seed cake. Ezaara moaned in pleasure as she bit into the warm gooey center and crunched the delicate seeds. "Thanks." It was just right. Not too sweet, not too sour.

He smiled, watching her eat. "I'm glad you like it." His voice was soft.

When she was finished, he strode out to the queen's den. Ezaara threw a heavy cloak around her shoulders and joined him.

"Sometimes riders lose their seat in battle, or half slip out of the saddle," Roberto said. "Tonight, we're going to practice stunt riding, so you have the skills to right yourself again if you get into trouble. You have to trust your dragon. Zaarusha knows what's best, so follow her commands, even if you can't see why she asks you to do something. Obedience is key."

"The cheek of him, after you and I flew a loop." Zaarusha's voice was more playful than indignant. *"Let's have some fun, shall we?"*

"Anything you say, My Queen. Obedience is key." Ezaara smothered a smile as she climbed into the saddle.

§

Ezaara's hair shone in the moonlight as she tied it back with her slender fingers. She was suppressing a smile. Her emotions were always so bright, so colorful, so close to the surface, like a bubble welling up in a spring.

He was falling for her, a little more each day he worked with her. He'd pushed her hard, demanding only her best, driving her to her limits. She hadn't cracked, rising to each challenge, her competitive spirit taking the bit and thundering for the finish line. Even her knife throwing had improved. Today she'd hit every target. But he didn't dare let her know how much he admired her. He had to maintain a hard exterior. She was his student. A slight whiff of indiscretion and he'd be banished, and everything he'd worked toward since his father's betrayal would crumble. His whole world would be lost if he revealed he loved her.

Lars and the council would soon test her to gauge whether her skills were up to scratch. He had to make sure she was ready.

They rose above the basin, the forest a shadowy cloak around the lake—glinting silver in the moonlight.

"Ezaara," he called across the air between them. "Take your feet out of the stirrups for a start."

Grinning, Ezaara did as he asked.

"Now you need to—" He gaped as she knelt on the saddle, then crouched and straightened to stand. "Ezaara!" He couldn't help the strident warning that crept into his voice. "Be careful."

"Why? You said we were going to do stunts." Ezaara grinned, full of life and mischief. She stepped—onto nothing. Arms wheeling, shock flew across her face. She plummeted into the darkness.

Zaarusha flipped her tail, plunging after her.

"Dive, Erob! Dive." Fangs! They were going to lose her.

Like a hawk after prey, Zaarusha sped down.

"Faster, Erob, faster." Roberto leaned forward on Erob's neck, willing him more speed. If she died …

Roberto glimpsed a bright thread of color, stretched taut between him and Ezaara. A thread that brought him joy and hope. That had given him hope since the day he'd tested her. A strong thread that could help him be a better person, if he could cling onto it. If she survived.

Still she fell.

No, not Ezaara, so vibrant and full of life. She couldn't die, not now. Not when he'd just realized how he felt about her. She was special, the first Queen's Rider in years. He'd always admired her: her bravery in facing the council after imprinting; her courage to try anything; her horror at injuring Sofia; her healing skills; and her joy of life. She hadn't had her littling life ripped away by someone she loved. She hadn't had her innocence destroyed, or been used as a pawn. She was wholesome, a backwater girl from Lush Valley, who loved life and trusted her dragon implicitly.

With a slap, like a whale's tail on the ocean, Zaarusha snatched Ezaara in her talons.

The Queen's Rider laughed.

Erob chuckled too.

And that's when Roberto realized it was a stunt.

§

The plunge through the night sky was exhilarating, making every fiber of Ezaara's being jump to life. To trust so completely, love so completely, to place her life in Zaarusha's hands—well, talons—*that* was living. This is what she'd yearned for in Lush Valley. She'd risk her life for the queen, give her life for her realm. She was Ezaara, Queen's Rider.

"I told you back in Lush Valley, you were born to be my rider."

"If only I'd believed it."

"Get ready."

With a whump, Zaarusha caught her, cradling her in her talons. *"I think we've frightened the scales off Roberto."*

Ezaara laughed. *"I didn't know he had scales; he must keep them well hidden. Maybe we've scared him into being nicer. Maybe he won't be so tough on me now. Not that I'd intended to scare him."*

"Really?"

"Well, maybe a little."

"He's not being tough. He's challenging you, so you can better serve the realm."

"Not tough? I'd hate to see him when he's trying to be."

"Roberto has faced things that would break most men." Zaarusha flipped her wings, spiraling down toward a field. *"Stretch your legs, and tell me when to let you go. It'd be a shame to squash you when I land."* The queen chuckled.

Ezaara's feet brushed the tall grass. *"Now, let go."*

She rolled as she hit the meadow. Luckily it was soft, not stony. Zaarusha thudded to the grass nearby, and moments later Erob landed.

Roberto dismounted and strode over, sword hilt glinting in the moonlight. He took her by the shoulders, onyx eyes stormy. "Ezaara." His breath was ragged.

She was about to mumble her apologies when he pulled her against his chest, murmuring into her hair. "Dragon's bleeding fangs! I thought I'd lost you." The scent of mint and sandalwood enveloped her.

For once, Ezaara had nothing to say.

THARUK ATTACK

L ast night he'd failed. He'd slipped up, taken her in his arms
out of sheer relief that she was all right. And once she'd
been there, it had been hard to let her go. The smell of her hair
reminded him of the days before his father had turned. Happy
days playing in the sun, fishing and tending the animals. Running
through meadows, swimming in lakes and laughing.

His last few years with his family had seldom given him reason
to laugh. And many reasons to cry. Until he'd hardened himself,
locked away his tears and moved on. Only Adelina remained. His
father had destroyed everything else in his life. Roberto kicked at
an old shoe lying on his cavern floor.

Ezaara reminded him of everything good in the world. Of
innocence. Of loving family bonds. Of fun, dare he think it. Of
warmth and friendship. Everything he'd denied himself for years.
He sighed and tugged his jerkin shut. And he would deny himself
her, for her own sake, and his.

"I'm ready. Will you stop mooching around?"

Roberto snorted. *"Mooching?"*

"Now you're snorting almost as well as me." Erob gave a
dragonly snort that echoed off his den walls outside.

Roberto chuckled. Where would his life be without Erob?

A shiver ran down his spine as he remembered his life among
tharuks.

§

Whatever Roberto had demonstrated last night was gone. The
tenderness she'd felt as he'd held her. The vibration of his deep

voice through his chest. The warmth and firmness of his torso. The peace she'd felt, the sense of one-ness at being in his arms—it was gone.

All gone.

He struck her shoulder with the flat of his sword. "Faster." A tap on the hip. "Block, Ezaara."

She lunged, sweat trickling into her eye, and missed him. Their swords clashed again.

"A sleeping tharuk could do better. Try."

Whirling, she advanced, gaining ground. He beat her back.

They'd been training for hours. She was dying of thirst. "Water," she gasped.

He nodded. "Only a sip. There's no time to stop in battle."

No sooner had she taken a swig, he bellowed, "Run. Race you to the knife-throwing range."

Groaning, she ran after him. So unfair, he had a head start. She couldn't let him win. Sprinting, she chewed up the ground between them. Where in the Egg's name did he get his energy from?

Panting, Ezaara reached the range on his heels, spurted past him and threw her knife without stopping.

He whistled. "Good shot, but it may be a fluke. Another.

"And another.

"And another."

Roberto drew his sword and they were fighting again. His blade smacked her knuckles. This would never end. Dragonback archery was bound to be next. Ezaara's life was one endless, merciless round of sweat and pain.

§

Roberto woke to a battle horn.

"Wake up," Erob melded. *"River's Edge is under attack."*

Throwing on his clothes and boots, Roberto grabbed his weapons and jumped on Erob. *"To the council chambers,"* he melded. *"Tell Zaarusha that Ezaara should prepare for battle."*

"Already done."

Roberto and Erob reached the council chambers at the same time as Shari and Jerrick. Behind them Tonio, Bruno and Fleur were arriving. They dismounted and strode inside. Aidan and Lars were deep in discussion over a weathered map. Within moments, the council was gathered.

"River's Edge, a village near Montanara, is under attack by tharuks." Lars announced. "The village only has a small fighting force. Unless we engage, they'll be slaughtered. We're sending dragons and fighters. Our battle master will instruct us."

Aidan pushed the map along the table. He pointed his stubby finger at a village a few river bends south of Montanara. "The villagers are outnumbered. The fighting is so thick, dragons can't use flame for fear of hurting our people. Jerrick, we need a squad of forty archers on dragonback to circle the area and prevent tharuk reinforcements from reaching the village. Jaevin, ready your sword fighters. Alyssa's squad will drop them close by, for hand-to-hand combat. Alyssa, only three people per dragon, we don't want to tire them. The archers will form two squads to pick off beasts from the air—one led by Tonio, one by me. Bruno, any foresight about this fight?"

Roberto repressed a snort. They were asking *Bruno's* opinion.

Bruno's voice was assured. "This is nothing but a minor skirmish. My prophecy tells me you'll be successful."

"Tonio, any other intelligence?" Aidan demanded.

"Nothing," said Tonio. "We don't have any dragon corps spies near River's Edge, but blue guards from Montanara are on their way."

Aidan nodded. "Good. We'll leave as soon as everyone has formed up. Lars, the time is now yours."

Lars stood. "Fleur, prepare the infirmary for wounded, and take supplies and healers there." Lars stabbed the map, indicating the next village over. "We may have to ferry patients to you. Roberto."

Roberto's head whipped up.

"I want you to—"

The doors burst open. Ezaara rushed in.

Lars' surprise was painted across his face. "My Honored Queen's Rider, you haven't finished your training. This isn't a drill. We need capable archers, not novices."

Ezaara's chin lifted and her eyes flashed. "Master Roberto." She turned to face him.

Great, she was going to drag him into this.

"Am I a capable archer?"

A ripple of tension ran around the room. Roberto nodded. "Yes, of course. More than capable." Apart from Shari, all the masters looked incredulous. "Ezaara is one of the best archers at Dragons' Hold."

Jerrick's head snapped up. "Best archer? I don't believe it!"

"What's not to believe? I'm the Queen's Rider," Ezaara retorted, "not an ornament to be left on a shelf."

Erob melded with him. *Zaarusha has warned me that Ezaara won't be fobbed off.*

Time to stick his neck out. Roberto stood. All heads swiveled to face him. "Our Honored Queen's Rider has a point," he said quietly. Was that relief that flashed across Ezaara's face? "We've waited long for a Queen's Rider. Now that we have one, she should fight."

The room erupted.

Zaarusha swooped through the doors, her roar bouncing off the chamber walls. The queen of the dragons stalked to Lars.

Lips pursed, Lars placed his hand above Zaarusha's eye ridges, so they could mind-meld. Turning to the council, Lars announced, "Zaarusha wishes to take Ezaara to battle. She says they've fought tharuks together before. I concur: she may go."

Excitement radiated from Ezaara. Colors cascaded through Roberto, then they were gone.

Lars stabbed a finger in the air toward Ezaara. "Honored Queen's Rider, you must stay on dragonback. You may engage as an archer, but only from the air. You are not, under any circumstances, allowed to fight on foot at close range with tharuks."

"Certainly," Ezaara replied, lashes lowered.

Her manner reminded Roberto of their first archery session and her flight stunt, putting him on edge. Was her concurrence a ruse? Would she put herself in danger? He touched the pocket holding her ribbon. He'd vouched for her, and whatever she did, he was sworn as her protector.

§

Zaarusha landed in the clearing below her den, Erob next to her. Ezaara could hardly sit still in the saddle, she was so jittery. The clearing was filled with dragons, gravel crunching underfoot as they landed. Roberto dismounted, pulled a bundle out of his saddlebags and came over, motioning her to get down. She slid down Zaarusha's side.

He passed her some rolled-up fabric. "Here's an archer's cloak to keep out the cold."

"Thank you." Ezaara wrapped the thick cloak around her shoulders and fastened it down the front, slipping her arms out the arm holes. Roberto adjusted her quiver so her arrows poked through the tailor-made hole.

Roberto took a deep breath. "Please, heed Lars' warning. Fight from dragonback only. You're too valuable for us to lose." Without waiting for an answer, he strode to Erob and jumped astride him.

Valuable—what was that about? Another way of pressuring her to keep Lars' rules?

A figure hurtled out of the main cavern, running through the dragons to Erob. Adelina reached up to squeeze Roberto's hands and murmured something to him. He smiled, a gentleness coming over his face that Ezaara seldom saw.

Adelina came over to Ezaara and squeezed her hands too. "Good luck, My Queen's Rider, may you fly swiftly and come home unharmed." A moment later she was gone.

Ezaara climbed into her saddle and cinched herself in.

Clatter filled the air like stones bouncing down a mountainside. Ezaara spun. It wasn't an avalanche, but the rustle of a hundred wings as more dragons swooped down from the mountainside.

All these dragons for a fight in a village? What would all-out war be like? Weapons clanked and leather creaked around her as riders adjusted the girths on their dragons' saddles.

A few dragons over, Gret was perched behind two others, sword at her side. She waved to Ezaara, grinning. So Gret would be fighting on the ground. Ezaara waved back. Hopefully, she'd be safe, facing those monsters up close.

Master Jerrick thrust an extra quiver of arrows into Zaarusha's saddlebag. "Make these count," he said. "If you're as good as Master Roberto says, every arrow should find a tharuk."

Ezaara nodded. "Yes, Master Jerrick."

Roberto raised his eyebrows. "Ready?"

Ezaara swallowed. "Of course." Around them, riders were watching. She forced herself to smile and sit straighter in the saddle.

Zaarusha melded, *"Whatever happens, hold on tight. I don't want to lose you in midair."* In the moonlight, her scales were glorious.

Aidan stood before the assembled warriors. "We've sworn to protect the realm, to preserve the peace, and not to let Zens' tharuks enslave our people. Get in fast, strike hard and save the settlers of River's Edge." He pumped his fist in the air.

Amid dragon roars, riders cheered. Zaarusha and Erob took to the sky. Tugging Roberto's cloak around her against the chill, Ezaara marveled as the undulating mass of dragons broke into four squadrons, North, South, East and West, each with a master at the front.

She and Roberto were at the center of the compass, protected on all sides.

"And from below," Zaarusha rumbled in Ezaara's mind. *"I'll blast anyone who attacks you, and Erob will protect you from above."*

"Above?"

"If necessary."

Ezaara gazed up at the dark sky, the stars like a littling's shiny scatter stones on a dark blanket. Could her family see the same stars tonight? Hopefully Ma was safe. And Tomaaz and Pa. Her chest tightened. If anything happened to her tonight, she'd never see them again.

Soon, the long fingers of dawn were stretching across the horizon, smearing yellow paint above the flatlands, glancing off the mountains to their left. The golden light cast Roberto's face a beautiful shade of bronze.

"Focus," Zaarusha rumbled. *"We're nearly there. Ready your bow."*

Alongside, Erob snorted and Roberto fastened his waist harness and nocked an arrow in his bow.

Ezaara leaned low, her bow nocked, as Zaarusha descended toward a plume of smoke. River's Edge was nestled in the sweeping bend of a broad river. Houses were on fire. Tharuks swarmed through the streets, attacking men, women and littlings. Screams and roars rent the air. More tharuks were flooding into the village from the forest. Isolated pockets of beasts were chasing villagers across fields.

Fleur broke formation first, flying further along the river with a few riders to set up her healing outpost. Aidan and Tonio's squads swooped over the town, shooting tharuks. Alyssa's squad flew to the far side of the village, depositing sword fighters where the battle was thickest. Dragons from Jerrick's squad defended the perimeter, blasting flame at monsters as they swarmed from the forest. Dragon riders' arrows were thick in the air.

A tharuk broke from the forest, zigzagging past arrows and sword fighters. Standing in her stirrups, Ezaara shot at its head and missed. She loosed another arrow, hitting the beast in the chest.

"Nice kill," Zaarusha purred. *"Let's get some more."*

A tharuk had a man cornered against a barn. Roberto released his arrow, shooting the monster through the back of the neck. Whipping another arrow from his quiver, he spun and shot another brute through the gut.

A desperate scream rang out. There, beneath her, a young girl was running away, a toddler on her hip. The girl tripped, regained her footing, and kept running. A tharuk pursued her across a meadow, grass trampled in its wake. Two more appeared from the trees.

Zaarusha swooped and blasted the rear tharuk with fire, incinerating him. *"The next is yours."*

Heart pounding, Ezaara pulled back her bowstring and fired. Black blood sprayed from the beast's chest. It collapsed to the ground. She whipped out another arrow and nocked it. More monsters were coming.

With a roar, Zaarusha sped toward a gangly tharuk. It glanced skyward, giving Ezaara the perfect shot. The arrow flew true, piercing the brute's forehead.

The girl kept her head down, running. The littling on her hip screamed as the girl stumbled, then kept going. The monster chasing her mowed through the tall grass, intent on his prey.

Ezaara tried to line up a shot. It was impossible. She'd hit the girl. *"Zaarusha, let's try from the side. I can't get a clear shot."*

The dragon queen swerved, changing her angle, but the tharuk changed his position too.

"It's no use, Zaarusha," Ezaara cried. *"I'll hit the girl or the babe."*

The monster leaped, tackling the girl and slamming her to the ground. Her scream rang out above the sound of the distant battle.

"Zaarusha, let me down. Now." Ezaara unfastened her waist harness and pulled her feet out of the stirrups. *"I'm not having the lives of littlings on my conscience."*

Zaarusha swooped low. Ezaara swung her legs over one side of the saddle and eased herself down. A meter or two above the ground, she let go and dropped to the earth. Rolling to stand, she unsheathed her sword and ran at the monster.

The beast was holding the girl up by the neck, crushing her throat. Her fingers scrabbled at his furry hands. She was gasping for breath. The toddler ran at the beast, beating at its leg. The tharuk kicked it, and the littling went flying into a tree trunk, then dropped to the ground, motionless.

Ezaara's pulse sped. Racing up behind the monster, she plunged her sword through its back. The tharuk dropped the girl, swinging its arms wildly. Her arms aching from the impact, Ezaara ducked to avoid its savage claws. She held tight, pushing the sword with her full body weight. The beast groaned, dropping to its knees, black blood pumping onto the grass.

A roar split the air in the meadow. Ezaara yanked her sword out of the beast and turned.

Brilliant blue, Erob blew a gust of flame over three tharuks until they were smoking heaps of debris.

"Send the girl to me," Zaarusha melded. There she was, near a grove of trees.

The girl was kneeling by the littling, weeping and stroking its hair. More tharuks were pounding toward them.

Ezaara ran to the girl, shaking her arm. The littling was a boy. A wee boy, unconscious but breathing. "Quick, take the boy and go." She pointed to Zaarusha. "Flee."

The girl scooped the littling to her chest and ran.

"Ezaara, behind you."

Ezaara spun. A tharuk as wide as three men swiped at her with its claws. She ducked. Sliding forward on one knee, she drove her sword up into its belly. The beast's agonized roar nearly split her head in two, before it crumpled, knocking her flat. Sharp pain ran up her sword arm. She was trapped under its shoulder, its matted fur mashed into her face. The tharuk jerked. Her body twitched in response. She gagged on its stench.

"Ezaara," Roberto bellowed. "Incoming tharuks."

Pushing up, she tried to force the dead beast off her. Its enormous torso pinned her legs, preventing her from rolling. She was wet with its blood. The pommel of the sword, still lodged in its gut, was digging into her side and her hand was throbbing.

The ground thudded with footfalls. Something was getting closer. Ezaara frantically shoved and grunted, but she was trapped.

There were roars, grunts and cries, the wet thump of bodies hitting the ground.

"Ezaara!" It was Roberto. On his knees, he lifted up the tharuk's hip. "Dragon's eggs, this thing is heavy."

It gave her enough space to force one knee and her arms up. Together, they pushed. As the tharuk's weight slid off her, fresh air rushed back into her chest, making her gasp.

"Are you all right?" His face was tight with concern.

"Look out," she gasped. A tharuk was charging him. She scrambled to her feet.

He spun to fight the beast. Easily two heads taller than Roberto, its claws shredded his cloak as he danced out of reach.

"I've got the girl and littling," Zaarusha melded, now airborne above them. *"I'm taking them back to the healing post."*

Erob swept above the far side of the meadow, blasting any tharuks who dared approach.

Gripping the pommel of her sword with two hands, Ezaara placed her foot on the dead beast's gut and yanked. With a squelching suck, the sword slid free and she stumbled backward. Regaining her footing, she faced the monster attacking Roberto. After this one, there were two more to deal with.

Standing just beyond their swords' reach, the three monsters formed a wall, cutting off their retreat to Erob. A scar-faced tharuk crouched, ready to pounce. The largest brute waved his sword menacingly, advancing on Roberto. The third rushed at Ezaara.

She feinted to the left, then thrust her sword to the right, gashing the tharuk's arm. Snarling, the beast swiped at her and she spun out of reach, standing at Roberto's back. This tharuk was smaller. With her sword, she had the longer reach. She leaped, attacking the beast.

Behind her, grunts and groans ripped the air before a high-pitched scream rang out.

"Scar-face is down," Roberto yelled amid snarls.

Ezaara's tharuk tried to knock the weapon from her grip. She chopped at its clawed furry hands. Her sword found its mark, piercing the monster's palm. It howled, then wrapped its other hand round the sword blade. Not caring about slicing its fingers further, the beast pulled, yanking Ezaara closer.

For an instant she resisted, then let her bodyweight fly, slamming the beast to the ground. Pulling a dagger from her boot, she thrust the blade through its throat, then stood, chest heaving, to retrieve her weapons.

The tharuks were dead. The meadow was silent, save for the crackle of Erob's flames as he kept further tharuks at bay.

Ezaara spun. Roberto was hunched over near the large brute, his body curled in pain.

She ran. Crouching next to Roberto, she examined him. Three gashes across his jerkin were stained red with his blood. Ezaara reached for her healing pouch at her waist, but cursed. In her haste to get ready, she'd left it behind. "Come," she said, "let's get you to Fleur's healing post."

His breathing was shallow, eyes wide with pain. "No, not Fleur. You can heal me back at Dragons' Hold."

He could bleed out before they got there. "No, Roberto. Fleur's closer."

"Never." He winced.

"Roberto, this is no time for prejudice. I know you don't like Simeon's family, but this is your life we're talking about."

"That's why I don't want Fleur," he spat through gritted teeth. Roberto gripped her hand, hurting it. "Promise you'll take me straight home."

Erob was still busy battling tharuks, but beyond the trees, she saw the glint of Zaarusha's wings. She nodded. *"Zaarusha! Hurry! Roberto's hurt."*

Healing

Zaarusha thudded onto the ledge. Slumped over Zaarusha's saddle, Roberto twitched. Ezaara shook him. He groaned. A trail of his blood ran down Zaarusha's side.

"Roberto," she urged. "We're home. I can't lift you down."

"Get help," Zaarusha commanded. *"I'll let you know if his breathing changes."*

Leaving Roberto tied to Zaarusha's saddle, Ezaara dashed through her cavern into the main tunnels. Adelina wasn't in the mess. Nor the training cavern. She stopped a girl. "Do you know where Adelina is?"

"Try the infirmary. Lars asked her to relieve Simeon for his meal break."

Good, she'd need a few supplies to treat Roberto. Ezaara raced along the tunnel. The infirmary was empty except for Adelina.

"Hi, Ezaara, why are you back so early? Is the fight finished?"

Ezaara deliberately kept her voice low. "It's Roberto, he's injured."

Dismay shot over Adelina's face.

"A tharuk gashed his chest," Ezaara said. "I need your help to lift him off Zaarusha. At my den, um, cavern." She yanked open a drawer. "First, clean herb and bear's bane." She opened another drawer. Where was the vigor weed, clear-mind or heat herb? Not to mention basic supplies such as arnica or slippery elm powder.

"There's nothing in those drawers," Adelina said. "The only things I've found are endless tubs of smelly yellow salve, some green paste and grayish leaves."

Ezaara yanked open a cupboard, but only found more of the ghastly yellow stuff. "Fleur says it's made of special ingredients brought by the green guards."

"Green guards come from Naobia, like me, and I've never seen that stuff there." Adelina leaned closer. "Roberto doesn't trust Fleur's remedies, and I don't either."

Of course, Adelina shared her brother's ridiculous prejudice. Ezaara picked up a small pot of yellow salve. "I'd better try this, in case Fleur's right."

"Not on my brother, you don't."

"What's behind that old curtain?" Ezaara asked. While Adelina was distracted, Ezaara tucked the tiny pot in her jerkin pocket.

"I don't know," said Adelina. "Let's check."

Ezaara flung the curtain back to reveal an alcove of shelves crammed full of pots and jars all filled with the yellow salve or a sticky green paste. A few pouches contained gray leaves.

As she was turning away, Ezaara spied some earthenware jars at the back of the bottom shelf. "What's in those?"

Dropping to their knees, she and Adelina pulled pots of yellow salve off the shelf to get at the earthenware jars. They uncorked a few.

An oniony scent filled the air. "That's bear's bane," Ezaara said, pointing at Adelina's jar of clear salve. "This one's freshweed." She put the cork back and opened another jar of dried pale-green leaves with a familiar tang. "Clean herb! I've got what I need. Let's go."

"This stuff has obviously been hidden," Adelina said. "I knew they were up to no good."

"Hurry, Ezaara," melded Zaarusha. *"Roberto's breathing is getting more labored."*

"Quick," Ezaara said. "Roberto's getting worse."

While Ezaara hurriedly replaced the pots at the back of the shelf, Adelina took off her jerkin and bundled the clean herb and bear's bane pots inside it.

"So no one sees," Adelina whispered, her face tight.

They'd just stepped out of the alcove and pulled the curtain shut when footsteps echoed outside the infirmary. Ezaara jerked her head toward the doorway and she and Adelina rushed across the room, slowing as Simeon entered.

Ezaara smiled, stepping in front of Adelina so Simeon wouldn't see her bundle.

"My Honored Queen's Rider." He smiled warmly. "Are you hurt?" He took her in, head to foot.

She was splattered in black tharuk blood and red smears from Roberto. She had to think fast so Simeon didn't suspect anything. Not that she'd ever hold anything back from him, but Roberto's business was his own. "Zaarusha sent me to check on any injured riders, but none have arrived yet."

"You look a little nervous. Would you like a restorative tea to help calm you?"

"Hurry," Zaarusha melded.

"No, thanks. I'd better get back to the queen," Ezaara called. She and Adelina walked swiftly to the door.

"Adelina, aren't you staying to help?" Simeon asked.

Adelina smiled sweetly. "I've been asked to help in the kitchens, but I'll send someone right along."

Moments later, they were running along the corridor.

"He's losing more blood."

"Come on, Adelina." Ezaara rushed through her cavern to Zaarusha's den. Adelina dumped the remedies on a table and ran after her. Climbing onto Zaarusha, Ezaara fumbled with the ropes around Roberto's waist, untying him from the saddle. He groaned as she and Adelina lifted him down.

He was as heavy as a horse, but they managed to carry him to her bed. Blood soaked into the white quilt. Grabbing half a palm of clean herb, Ezaara threw it into a cup and thrust it at Adelina. "Fill it halfway with water and ask Zaarusha to warm it."

Roberto's eyes slid open. His gaze was unfocused, bleary. He gripped her arm. "Thank you … no Fleur." He slumped back on the bed, eyelids fluttering.

Slashing his tunic open, Ezaara examined the wounds. Three claw marks, not deep enough to puncture any internal organs, but deep enough to make him bleed like a stuck goat. "You're going to be all right, Roberto," she murmured as Adelina returned with the infusion and some cloths.

After cleaning Roberto's wounds, Ezaara smeared bear's bane over the edges, the pungent onion scent making her eyes water. Surely it was the onion—not his pale pain-laced face—that made her want to cry. This was her tough master, impossible to please, cool and detached.

"That stuff stinks like leek soup," said Adelina. "What's it for?"

Blinking back her tears, Ezaara answered steadily, "Numbs the wound, so it won't hurt when I stitch it." Hands trembling, she drew her needle out of her healer's pouch and started stitching his gashes.

Adelina clenched and unclenched her hands, then started pacing back and forth, her footsteps gnawing a hole in Ezaara's patience.

"Would you like something to do to keep your mind off things?"

"Please." Adelina's voice shook almost as much as Ezaara's hands.

"Fetch him some clean clothes."

"Good. I'll be back soon." Adelina rushed out the door.

Hands coated red, Ezaara pushed the needle through Roberto's skin, pulling the edges together. She hated stitching. Although she

EILEEN MUELLER

knew it helped, it always felt strange to put holes in people's bodies to make them better.

"Colors, so many colors," Roberto murmured, the trace of a smile on his face.

Great. Here she was, fretting over him, while he was having a pleasant dream. She shook her head. This was worse than she'd thought—he was delusional.

§

She was near—so close, but so far. Deep sea-greens and marine blues danced through Roberto's mind as Ezaara smeared onion salve over him, numbing his skin, making the stabbing in his chest ease to a blunt ache. He could feel her tugging at his wounds, but the sensations were disembodied, like they belonged to someone else.

And through it all was the bright thread that joined them together.

"Roberto." Ezaara sounded like she was calling through water.

He forced his eyelids open, but they kept sliding shut as his body dragged him back under.

"Roberto," she called, sharper this time.

Bolts of pink shot across his vision, behind his eyelids. She could do that? Just with her voice? He was riding a sea of sensation, like a raft on the ocean, drifting away from her again.

The tugging stopped.

Her hands rubbed across his chest, leaving trails of blazing fire in their wake. His wounds seared, the burn biting deep inside him, aching through his chest. His eyes flicked open to glimpse a slim vial in her hand, then thudded shut again. Piaua. This was piaua— the reason she'd winced as he'd applied it to her ankle. It burned its way through his flesh, knitting his chest together, the deep healing fire purging his damaged tissue.

By the Egg, it hurt.

"At least it won't leave scars." Warmth washed through him. It was her, speaking in his mind.

Roberto forced his eyes open. The fog lifted, his vision clearing. There she was: green eyes wide, leaning over him, rubbing his chest, her golden hair shining in a shaft of sunlight.

She smiled. "How are you feeling?"

Dragon's claws, she was beautiful. "Uh, all right. I didn't know piaua burned." He glanced down. His wounds were gone. Thin pink lines ran from below his collar bone, down across the right side of his chest. "That's incredible. I thought I felt you stitching me …"

"I used bear's bane so you wouldn't feel much. By stitching you before I used piaua, we avoided ugly scars. I could have just used piaua, but it seemed a shame …"

She hadn't wanted to mar his chest.

His gaze dropped to her fingers absently tracing the lines of his new scars.

Her cheeks tinged pink under his scrutiny and she snatched her hand away. He wanted to tease her and make her laugh. Nothing would please him more than flying through the skies on Erob with her in his arms. But he was her master.

Attachments led to betrayal. He'd learned that the hard way.

"Thank you for healing me, Ezaara." He sat up, flexing his arms and chest. "I feel as good as new." His shirt and jerkin were shredded. He pulled them off and cast around for something else to wear.

Ezaara corked the piaua vial and tucked it in her healer's pouch.

There was a knock at the door, and Adelina came inside, carrying a bundle of clothes. "Roberto." She raced over, throwing the clothes on the bed and hugging him. "You look amazing. I can't believe it!" She pointed at his new scars. "This is incredible."

He stood up, flexing and bending. "As good as new."

"You mustn't tell anyone," Ezaara warned. "I'm only supposed to use piaua in dire circumstances."

"Those gashes were dire enough." Adelina flung her arms around Ezaara. "Thank you. I won't breathe a word." She headed for the door. "I'll catch up with you two later. Benji wants me in the kitchens to help prepare food for our hungry warriors. Come and grab something to eat when you're done." She shut the door behind her.

Ezaara passed Roberto an open tub of pungent ointment. "I used some of this healing ointment on the cut on your arm." She gestured at a bandage on his left forearm.

This yellow stuff didn't look like any healing salve he'd ever seen.

"Use it sparingly," Ezaara corked the tub. "Fleur said the ingredients are expensive, only brought in by the green guards."

Green guards? They patrolled Naobia, yet Roberto had never seen such a strange salve in use in his homelands. "This is from Fleur? I told you I didn't want to be healed by her."

"She told me it was better than anything I had. I thought—"

"Well, next time don't. That family's worse than a scorpion's nest. They—" A knock at the door silenced him.

Shooting him a scathing glance, Ezaara strode to the door. "Why, Simeon," she said. "Come in."

That shrotty leech was here.

Simeon stepped over the threshold, his gaze sweeping over Roberto's naked torso and the bloodstained clothes on the floor. His eyebrows rose. "Oh? Am I interrupting something?"

"Not at all," said Ezaara, folding her arms. "Roberto was just leaving."

"No, no, don't leave on my account," that sycophantic leech said. "I was only wondering where Adelina is. Wounded riders have arrived, and I need her help in the infirmary."

"She's in the kitchens, on duty," Roberto snapped, tugging his clean shirt and jerkin on. "You'll have to find someone else."

"No problem." Throwing a greasy smile at Ezaara, Simeon left.

Ezaara shot Roberto daggers. "You didn't have to be so rude to my guest."

Perhaps he should tell her. "I've warned you about Simeon."

She folded her arms, fuming.

"Look, Ezaara, the council let you fight today because you promised not to get off Zaarusha."

Her jaw tensed. "So, you expected me to let that girl and her littling brother die?"

This was not a battle he was going to win. "No, you did the right thing. We had to help them, and you fought well, but if the council hears about this, we'll be flamed. Get changed so no one sees the blood all over you. Although it might be too late, because Simeon already has."

The look she shot him could have curdled blood. Even covered in tharuk gore and angry at him, she was stunning. She must never, ever get an inkling of how he felt. Roberto tamped his feelings down tight. "It's your job to heed the rules, Ezaara, not break them." He strode out the door.

§

Roberto was so sharding stubborn, so pigheaded. Ezaara scrubbed her face and arms and changed into clean clothes. They'd fought so well together. She'd saved a girl and her brother, but all he could do was lecture her. No kind word of praise. Not even a smile.

She flexed her torso, aching all over where the monster had pinned her. No doubt there were others more badly wounded. She'd forgotten to go to the infirmary when Sofia was injured, but she wouldn't make the same mistake twice. A Queen's Rider needed to serve her people. Making her way as quickly as possible down the tunnels, Ezaara came to the infirmary.

Fleur was back. She, Simeon, and two assistants were tending wounded riders and sword fighters whose moans echoed off the stone walls.

Ezaara went straight to Fleur. "Who should I first attend?"

"Oh, um … him." She pointed. "He's loudest."

She frowned. Her mother had always triaged patients, knowing the loudest often wasn't in the worst condition. Ezaara hesitated. She really should obey Fleur—it was her infirmary. She went to the man Fleur had indicated, and sure enough, his injuries didn't appear as bad as the lad next to his, who was lying silently on a spreading stain of red.

"How were you hurt?" she asked the boy.

"Arrow in my back," he answered through gritted teeth, staring at her with pain-filled eyes.

The man's moaning in the next bed was driving her to distraction, so Ezaara gave the man a stick to bite on and rolled the boy from his back onto his front. The arrow had gone deep, but from what she could see, the wound had been enlarged by whoever had removed it so clumsily, ripping the flesh further. Her blood boiled. This poor boy couldn't be more than thirteen. "Who removed this arrow?" she muttered.

Suddenly standing at her shoulder, Simeon smiled. "I did," he said.

Simeon was the son of a healer. He should know better. She bit back a scathing comment, only saying, "Please, fetch me warm water."

When Simeon returned, she was about to ask for clean herb, but remembered it was hidden in the alcove, so she muttered, "Thank you," and waited until he was gone to slip clean herb out of her healer's pouch and crumble it into the water. She cleansed the boy's wound, threaded her needle with rabbit gut twine from Lush Valley and stitched the ragged edges of his flesh together. The boy's body was tight with tension. Even when she gave him a stick to bite on, he whimpered.

"Simeon, do you have anything to numb the wound?" she called.

Tending a man nearby, Simeon shook his head. "Supplies were dreadfully low when my mother took over here. Sorry."

Hang on, there was bear's bane in the alcove. What were Fleur and Simeon playing at? Perhaps Simeon didn't know. Maybe his mother had kept supplies in reserve for an emergency. Surely this boy constituted such an emergency?

"Great job, Ezaara," Simeon called as he passed to fetch more bandages. He dropped some off at the boy's bedside. "Those are nice even stitches."

Ezaara's chest swelled with pride. It was true, her stitches had always been neat and tidy. Despite her not wanting to be a healer, her mother had taught her well. Thinking of Ma made her throat constrict. She blinked, hard. She had to focus on this boy and other patients. There'd be time enough later to dwell on family.

Hours later, when they'd finished treating the wounded, Simeon thanked her profusely and kissed her hand. Grateful at least someone had appreciated her today, Ezaara stumbled from the infirmary to the empty mess cavern.

Adelina greeted her. "You look exhausted. Here, take a seat. I saved you dinner."

"Infirmary," Ezaara grunted, ripping a bread roll, too tired to talk. She bit into the crust, groaning in pleasure.

Adelina bustled off, returning with a bowl of dark meaty stew, and sat beside her. "It's been a long day."

Nodding, Ezaara spooned stew into her mouth, occasionally pausing to dip bread into her bowl. When she was finished, she sat back and sighed. "Now, that was good, the best part of today."

"Thank you for healing Roberto." Adelina kept her voice low. "He said you fought valiantly, saving a girl and a littling."

Roberto? Ezaara bit back a bitter retort. During training, he was so tough, never giving a scrap of praise. "You know the strangest thing?"

Adelina shook her head.

"Simeon said they didn't have anything to numb wounds, but there's bear's bane in the alcove. Maybe Simeon doesn't know about the supplies in the alcove, but Fleur must do. I should have asked her. I …" Ezaara hung her head.

"What is it?"

"I did my patients a great disservice by not challenging Fleur."

"I don't trust Fleur," Adelina replied. "Neither does Roberto."

Despite her cynicism about her master, a prickle of mistrust ran down her spine. She'd have to watch Fleur.

§

Sitting on the edge of his bed, Roberto circled his arms again. He could still use his injured arm, but the gash was puffy and red. He rolled his eyes. That was probably due to Fleur's rotten salve. What had Ezaara been thinking? Well, at least his chest was as good as new, thanks to her.

He'd heard two healers in Naobia whispering about piaua when he'd taken his mother to them for her back … no, he mustn't think about that.

Now he'd seen piaua in action—and Ezaara using her healing arts. Queen's Rider, compassionate healer, competent archer, with a fierce loyalty and a wild beauty that nearly made his heart stop each time he glimpsed it. As her master, he had to know everything about her—talents, strengths, weaknesses, so he could truly prepare her to lead their army against Zens.

It was no good, he couldn't sleep. *"How about a flight?"*

Erob's snores were his only answer. Fair enough. His dragon had only returned a few hours ago, after ensuring every tharuk was either dead or gone from River's Edge. A walk would have to do instead.

Roberto pulled up the hood of his jerkin and strolled along the tunnels. Lost in thought, he realized he was near the Queen's Rider's cavern when Simeon appeared, sneaking along the tunnel. Roberto froze in the shadows. Simeon, furtively glancing back, stole down the short tunnel to Ezaara's cavern.

Roberto slipped after him.

Hand on the Queen's Rider's door handle, Simeon paused, listening.

"What are you doing here?" Roberto hissed. Grabbing Simeon's free arm, he twisted it behind his back. Simeon went limp, but Roberto knew that trick, keeping his grip tight as he marched him down the tunnels.

Simeon blathered. "I couldn't sleep for worrying about Ezaara. I just had to check she was safe."

"I'm not listening to your sniveling dragon dung," Roberto snapped. He'd tried his best to keep Ezaara busy, away from Simeon, Alban and Sofia, but he couldn't be everywhere.

When they reached the infirmary, and Simeon's family's living quarters, Roberto released him. "Stay there. All night. Every night. Or you'll see the sharp end of my sword." He gave a cutthroat grin.

Glowering, Simeon slipped into the infirmary.

Roberto exhaled. That had been lucky. He could've been asleep. If he hadn't been there, who knew what could've happened to their new Queen's Rider—to Ezaara. Dragons' Hold would be a lot colder without her smile.

RIDER OF FIRE

A few days later, as her bruises from their fight at River's Edge were fading, Ezaara opened her door at Roberto's knock.

In usual terse form, he nodded. "Good morning, Ezaara. I have news. Lars has scheduled the Grand Race for today. All trainees must participate, including you." He passed her a pair of light shoes with flexible leather soles. "I thought you'd like these. They'll be easier to run in than your boots."

The shoes were made of supple leather, and hand-painted with a likeness of Zaarusha soaring over a lake, her shining scales reflecting all the colors of the rainbow in the water. These shoes were as beautiful as Ana's scarves. More so, because someone had made them for her. She scarcely dared breathe. "Did you make these?"

His smile warmed his eyes. "No, but I did ask our master craftsman, Hendrik, if he could make you some pliable shoes, suitable for running."

"When did you get time to do that?" Over the past week, they'd been together every waking moment, training.

"Right after the imprinting test." He shrugged. "I saw that you'd arrived in only what you were wearing, with a sword at your side. Once I knew you were Zaarusha's true rider, it was logical you'd need something to run in."

He was a man of such contrasts—a harsh taskmaster, but thoughtful. His mother's cane, these shoes, the treats and tiny things he was constantly doing for her. The way they'd fought together at River's Edge. There was hidden gentleness inside him.

"Thank you."

"Please, try them on. If they don't fit, you'll be running in your boots." He laughed, his face open and free.

She put them on and pulled the leather laces. "They fit perfectly." Ezaara took a few steps. They were light enough to dance in.

§

Hundreds of dragons settled on the ridges above the clearing, their rustling wings and restless feet sending stones skittering down the mountainside. Although riders were scattered among them, perched on outcrops or ledges, most of the crowd were gathered at the edge of the clearing and along a track leading through the meadows to the forest.

The race was due to start at any moment. Stretching her calves, Ezaara evaluated her competitors, all in cut-off breeches, stones crunching as they limbered up. Sofia was flexing her thighs, her vivid pink scar puckered over the awful bump on her leg, as if she was deliberately reminding everyone of Ezaara's blunder. Although Ezaara had several remedies that would help that scar tissue, she doubted Fleur or Sofia would want to know.

Sofia ignored her, but Alban scowled enough for both of them, shooting her dirty looks. Due to Roberto's rigorous training schedule, she hadn't seen much of Sofia or Alban—almost as if Roberto had intentionally kept her away. But whenever she had seen them, they'd snapped or muttered insults. So much for the Queen's Rider being respected. Alban was deliberately frosting her.

If she did well in the race today .... No, she'd scarred Sofia's leg. Nothing would help. She swallowed, missing the easy banter she'd enjoyed when she'd first met Sofia.

Rocco gave her a wave. He jogged on the spot, the breeze ruffling his dark curls. They looked fit, all of them. Henry had a much smaller stride than hers, so she should be able to beat him, but the others …. She'd messed up so many times, she had to prove herself today.

Bright laughter echoed around the clearing—Kierion was here. Lucky he wasn't running, or everyone would've found lizards in their shoes, or their boots nailed to the floor. Ezaara rotated her ankles. Shards, her new shoes were light.

Gret was the only one who approached her. Shaking her hand, she said, "Good morning, My Honored Queen's Rider. It's a privilege to be running beside you." Her voice carried across the clearing. Standing tall, Gret met the gaze of every competitor, including Alban and Sofia.

Ezaara clasped Gret's hand. "Thank you, Gret. Run well."

"Good luck. Here, at Dragons' Hold, it's tradition that a master also runs in the Grand Race." Gret flashed a grin. "They draw straws."

Beyond Gret, lanky Mathias gestured. "Here they come now."

Lars was talking with the masters as they approached. When they were alongside the competitors, Roberto sounded the horn. The crowd quieted.

"Good morning, riders, trainees, and gentle people of Dragons' Hold," Lars boomed. "Our trainee riders are participating in the Grand Race as part of their evaluation. There is only one rule: if there's any foul play, the perpetrator will be disqualified and banished." Ezaara could have sworn his gaze lingered on Alban. "Now," Lars said, pausing theatrically, and waving a bunch of straws in his fist as he scanned the competitors. "One lucky master will be racing with you. Masters, choose—the shortest straw runs."

Ezaara's stomach knotted. Who would it be? Tonio, always skulking on the edge of every crowd observing everyone? Or Lars himself? Hopefully, not Roberto—he beat her every time they ran. In Lush Valley she'd won a few races, but here, everyone was tougher, fitter, older. She wasn't racing the village littlings or Tomaaz and Lofty.

A hush enveloped the crowd. The masters drew straws. One by one, they held them up. Not Lars. Nor Tonio. Not Hendrik, who'd made these wonderful shoes. Ezaara flexed her feet. Alyssa held up a long straw, then Fleur and Bruno. Roberto had the short one.

Racing against him? She'd never win. So much for proving herself.

She'd have to get out in front early, or she'd be chewed up and spat out. Using the old techniques Pa had taught her, ignoring the tightening in her throat at the thought of her family, she visualized herself speeding ahead of everyone. *Good thoughts speed us*, he'd always said. A shame he wasn't here. *"Zaarusha, Handel and Liesar left ages ago to get Pa and Tomaaz. When will they be back?"*

"I don't know, Ezaara. Now, focus."

Lars stepped up to the mark, motioning the racers forward. Roberto gave her his usual nod of acknowledgment and joined them. Ezaara placed her hands on the ground and bent her front leg, ready.

"We'll start at Queen Zaarusha's roar," Lars announced. "May your feet be like wings of air."

Zaarusha melded, *"Good luck, Ezaara. Win by a decent margin!"*

Win?

Zaarusha was already roaring. The other runners were off, gravel hissing as they sped across the clearing toward the fields.

She'd missed the cue. Startled, Ezaara stumbled. Gaining her footing, she leaped forward.

Adelina cheered her on. "Go, Ezaara. Catch up!"

Ezaara pounded after her competitors.

Henry was clutching his side. "Cramps." His face was a tight grimace. Ezaara shot him a sympathetic look as she passed. As a healer, it didn't seem right to leave him, but she had to catch up to Roberto and the others. They were already through the first wheat field, and she was only halfway across.

Ahead, Roberto broke away from the main group. Someone followed—Alban. Sofia's mass of wild curls, the same hue as the golden wheat, bounced as she loped with the group, favoring her leg. Thankfully, she could still run. Ezaara swallowed the thought. She had to focus.

She caught the main group of runners as they ran between vegetable fields, dust flying under the warm sun. The scent of kohlrabi hung in the air. Her vest was already sticky.

Rocco spurted ahead, trying to catch Alban and Roberto. Shoulders tight, he was straining too hard. He'd never last the distance.

Ezaara forced herself to relax, her legs flowing across the ground. She moved along the outside of the group.

Sofia veered and stumbled, jabbing Ezaara in the ribs with her elbow.

"Ow!"

"Sorry." Sofia smirked, dripping sarcasm.

"Hey," Gret yelled at Sofia, "that's not on."

"A *mistake*, just like when that cow hurt me."

A flash of anger spurred Ezaara on. Pumping her arms and legs, she dashed forward, leaving the group behind.

She deserved every hit and blow and slur. If someone had hurt Tomaaz like that, she would've been livid. She couldn't blame Sofia for being angry, especially when Alban kept poisoning her with his nasty barbs. If she was ever to be a just Queen's Rider, she couldn't let peer politics get her down. But doubt and fear ate away at her as she ran on.

Rocco was closer, now. With steady paces, Ezaara chewed up the ground between them and overtook him as she crossed the last meadow. Glancing back with a sneer, Alban entered the forest. Roberto was long gone, somewhere among the trees.

Gradually, Ezaara increased her pace. She hit the tree line, welcoming the cool shade of the forest canopy. She blinked, helping her eyes adjust. This part of the forest was dense, branches woven together in a lattice of foliage. Vines with broad shiny leaves hung from boughs, occasionally twining their way across the path. As a tree-speaker, Ma would love this place. A pang of loss hit Ezaara. Alone. She was so alone here. Her family couldn't celebrate any of her successes. Or support her through her failures.

§

Roberto pressed ahead, Erob's power singing through his veins. Last time he'd glanced back, Ezaara had pulled away from the group and Alban was entering the forest. The muted thud of Alban's feet was back along the trail.

Leaping over a mass of vines, Roberto headed around a corner. A master running against trainees seemed unfair, but it spurred the trainees to push their limits. Masters, with the advantage of accessing their dragons' power, would always win. He, Lars and Tonio were the fastest at Dragons' Hold, although rumor had it that Lars had once been beaten by a master who was no longer here.

Roberto grinned. He'd beaten Lars the last few times they'd raced. His success was as much due to the strong bond between him and Erob and his mental aptitude, as it was to his fitness. Although he enjoyed training hard, exorcising the demons of his past.

Behind him, Alban's footfalls stopped. Roberto cocked his head as he ran. The winding path must be masking Alban's tread. He slowed, pacing himself for the descent into the stream and the grueling climb once he left the trees.

§

Ezaara skirted a patch of sludge and raced over some gnarly roots. This part of the track was tricky. Up ahead a mass of vines lay across the path, with no way around them. A leap should do it. She sped up and took a huge stride, launching herself into the air. The vines whipped up, smashing into her legs. She crashed to the forest floor, smacking her ribs on a root and whacking her shoulder. Rolling, Ezaara came to her feet. A wall of muscle was before her. Alban.

She ducked. Too late. His fist connected with her stomach. She dropped and rolled, staggering up as he pounced after her. With her back to a tree trunk, she feinted to the left, then jumped, aiming a flying kick at him. He sidestepped, but not fast enough. The full weight of her body hit his groin. They crashed to the ground and she rolled away.

Alban sprawled on the ground, grasping his groin. Ezaara whipped a knife from her waistband and held it near Alban's neck, breathing hard.

"So, you're going to slash me too," he spat, "the way you butchered Sofia? Do it. I'll report you, and you'll be banished."

The panting and footfalls of other runners were audible further along the track. A few more corners, and they'd be here.

Despite the anger sparking through her, Ezaara spoke softly, "You'll be banished too, Alban, for attacking the Queen's Rider."

"No one will know," he said staunchly. "No one will believe you." But his eyes were panicked. She had him.

"Nor you," she said. "Vow to keep your mouth shut and not breathe a word to anyone, even Sofia, and I'll do the same."

Nodding, he tried to sit up.

"Don't move yet." She pressed her knife more firmly against his throat. "Swear it, upon your life."

Alban made the vow, then, in the same breath, swore at her.

"What a shame you've fallen over these vines. I guess you'll be too sore to move until someone can help you up." Aiming a foot at his chest, Ezaara pushed Alban back to the ground and took off along the trail, tucking her knife into the back of her waistband.

She'd deliberately worn a vest that hung to her backside, disguising her weapon. Her hands shook as she ran. She'd never expected to use it.

She was the outsider. No one would believe her if she testified against Alban. Her gut ached, and her ribs and shoulder were sore. Heart pounding, she raced down the track, toward burbling coming through the trees. Good, a stream. Her mouth was dry. She could grab a drink.

§

Stooped in the calf-deep water, Roberto was taking a drink when he glimpsed Ezaara racing through the trees. So, she was faster than Alban—impressive. Mind you, she'd given him a run for his money when they were training, although he'd never let on, constantly pushing her to be better. He waited. He had nothing to lose. He'd pull away again as soon as they sped up the mountainside.

Face flushed and frowning, she looked worried.

Her expression cleared when she saw him and her green eyes widened. She splashed through the stream, then bent, scooping water into her hands. As she raised them to her lips to drink, sun slanted through the trees, and their eyes met.

She was beautiful. Something ached deep inside him. So beautiful.

Parting her lips, she drank, water droplets catching like crystals in the sunlight as they fell from her hands.

Vibrant colors flitted through his mind, swirling and eddying, stronger than ever before. A whoosh rushed through his chest, as if it was too small to hold his emotions.

Shards, she was gorgeous.

§

So beautiful. The words flashed through her in a deep male timbre.

It was him, Roberto, thinking about her. They were mind-melding. She saw an image of her, drinking from the stream. The way he saw her took her breath away.

Roberto grinned, the sun striking his dark eyes, turning them to burnished gold.

Water dribbled through her fingers as she stared at him, seeing him as she never had before. Every part of his face was painted with tenderness and wonder.

Something fluttered in her chest.

He was beautiful too. More than beautiful.

She reached up and stroked his cheek. A surge of strange energy hit Ezaara, rushing through her. Anything felt possible.

His eyes sparked as he spoke in her mind, *"Harness it. Run, run like the wind."* He tugged her hand. Sliding on the stones, they scrambled onto the bank and ran through a meadow of wild flowers toward the mountain.

Roberto laughed and his eyes met hers.

Ezaara's stomach jolted. *He liked her.* Her tough arrogant master, *more than liked* her. Every fiber of her being sang. He cared about her deeply.

Letting go of her hand, he smiled. *"Go, Ezaara, go! You're a rider of fire."*

Energy flooded her, pushing her on. She raced across the meadow, heading for the mountainside, Roberto keeping pace.

"Follow the flags." He pointed at a narrow trail dotted with red flags, leading up the granite mountain face and back down to the basin floor.

"I know."

They took off toward the thin trail. Ezaara's blood was on fire, the familiar heat of imprinting burning in her veins as she raced to the top of the track. Somehow, she was harnessing Zaarusha's energy to run.

Roberto melded. *"That's what we're called when we harness our dragons' energy—riders of fire."*

"I can see why." Her soul was ablaze, feet speeding along the mountainside. *"Can every rider do this?"*

"Most masters can harness their dragons' energy, but only a few are able to use it for running. You, Tonio, Lars and I can. Tonio also has dragon sight—he can see much further when he uses Antonika's energy."

"We're melding. How is that possible?"

"I don't know. I have certain mental abilities, and Erob told me that you can meld with other dragons, so you probably do too."

"Did Erob really say that?" she blurted out loud.

Roberto laughed.

They raced down the stony incline, Ezaara barely feeling her feet touch the ground.

She'd always loved running, but this was something else—so effortless and powerful. The sprint they'd maintained up the mountain and back down the path to the valley floor was phenomenal. Her body seared with dragon fire, driving her into a rapid dash, faster than Roberto, across the fields to the finish line.

§

Dragons were wheeling in the sky near the caverns. Heart pounding, Roberto crossed the finish line behind Ezaara. He'd expected her to run well, but this was incredible. Zaarusha's bellow shook the ground underfoot, signaling Ezaara's win. Ezaara leaped upon Zaarusha and rode her in a circle over the crowd's upturned faces. They erupted into a roar. Everyone was going wild, hollering, whistling and clapping.

Zaarusha landed, and Ezaara slipped off her back. Roberto was about to greet her, but Simeon dashed forward and snatched Ezaara in his arms. Spinning her around, he planted a kiss on her mouth. Ezaara turned tomato-red. Her surge of anger flared in Roberto's mind.

Simeon was taking liberties. Roberto's blood boiled. His hand automatically went for his sword, but it wasn't there.

"Easy," Erob melded. *"You still have fire in your veins. Don't do anything rash."*

Shards! What was he thinking? He was a master, not some lovesick youngling.

Simeon grinned and blew Ezaara another kiss. Someone in the crowd whistled. Others cheered. People surrounded Ezaara, pounding her back and congratulating her. Simeon hovered nearby—as if he'd trained her. As if he meant something to her.

Roberto was so enraged, he could barely think straight. He slipped his impassive mask into place, the one he'd learned to wear in Death Valley, and strode through the crowd.

"Roberto." Adelina reached out to him.

He shoved his way past her, ignoring the hurt that flashed across her face.

Ezaara had seen how he felt about her. If she revealed his feelings to anyone, he'd lose everything he'd worked for. He'd be banished, no better than his father. He couldn't afford to love her.

§

It was tradition for Lars to wait for all of the racers. He shaded his eyes. The last two runners would be here soon. The crowd had gone inside to feast Ezaara's victory. Knowing Lydia, she'd save him a bowl of stew and a good spot in the mess cavern. Behind Lars there was the thump of a dragon landing. Probably Tonio's.

Someone tapped his shoulder. Not Tonio. "Ezaara, what are you doing here? I thought you'd be enjoying your glory inside."

She shrugged. "It's too noisy. I'm not used to so many people."

"That was a fine performance. I've only seen a few run like that," said Lars. "Lately, Roberto's been first home, but years ago, your father beat me with an unprecedented burst of energy."

"Pa can run like that too? He's a rider of fire?"

"Hans was one of the best. It's a great feeling, isn't it?"

Ezaara rubbed Zaarusha's neck. "It took me by surprise."

Lars chuckled. "It always does, the first time. Different masters have different talents, not always running. It's all part of being a rider of fire."

"Master Roberto mentioned that."

"We've decided your sword evaluation will be tomorrow."

Her eyes widened. "Tomorrow?"

"Get a good night's sleep and stay warm." He pointed to the distant sky, voice grim. "There'll be snow in the far ranges tonight."

"I will." Ezaara got on Zaarusha, and they flew back up to the mess cavern.

The last two runners were nearly here. Sofia's leg seemed to have healed nicely. She was running with Alban, at a steady careful pace. Good, he didn't want her injured leg playing up. The scar was ugly. Fleur's half-botched attempts at healing didn't come near Marlies' skill, all those years ago, but she'd fled after that terrible incident with Zaarusha's dragonet. He shook his head. What a waste of a dragonet and a healer.

His dragon, Singlar, had told him Ezaara was Marlies' daughter. Poles apart, Ezaara had looked unpromising when she'd arrived. Knifing Sofia hadn't made things any better, but hopefully that was all behind them.

"Well done," he called from the finish line. "Your leg's holding up well, Sofia."

Flushed, Sofia gave a tired smile. "Thanks, Master Lars."

"And thank you for supporting her, Alban."

Alban stopped and bent, putting hands on his knees and taking a few deep breaths.

"Are you all right?" Lars asked.

"Fine," he said.

Sofia grinned. "He tripped over some vines. I slowed down to keep pace with him."

Alban glowered. "I said I'm fine."

"Come on, it's all in good fun." Lars clapped him on the back.

"Just like knife training," Alban shot as he stalked off.

Face clouding, Sofia rushed after him.

So, it wasn't behind them. Grudges were brewing—and grudges were not healthy for morale.

Lars lingered to watch a pair of dragons shoot across the basin. Now, there was competition at its finest—no grudges, no malice, just pure fun. The dragons reached the western mountain faces, then spun back toward him. He frowned. Over the ranges, in the far west, ominous storm clouds were brewing.

TEST OF THE SWORD

Ezaara was cold. There was fresh snow dusting Dragon's Teeth and a chill in the air. She pulled her cloak tight around her, blocking the draft from Zaarusha's wingbeats.

"*There's an unseasonal blizzard raging in the west and to the south,*" Zaarusha said. "*We got off lightly, but it'll be cold there for a few more days. Don't worry, your sword evaluation will soon warm you up.*" The dragon queen flew along the eastern side of the valley. "*There's the sword fighting arena.*"

Below them, two stone outcrops jutted out of the mountainside, forming a natural arena between them, walled on three sides by granite. Dragons were perched on the higher outcrop and people were sitting on the other, on heavy blankets, legs dangling over the rocks. More onlookers were gathered on the ground around the arena, Roberto, Adelina and Simeon among them. Blue guards, in their striking uniforms, were stationed around the edge of the crowd.

"*You told me I had a sword evaluation,*" Ezaara shot at Zaarusha. "*Not a ceremony with hundreds watching.*"

"*It's traditional to have a crowd,*" the dragon queen replied.

"*Of course, I should have realized. In Lush Valley we're well-versed in the traditions of Dragons' Hold.*"

Her sarcasm wasn't lost on Zaarusha—the queen was still chuckling as she landed.

The arena was strewn with rocks and tussock, a challenging surface for dueling. Luckily, the sun had melted the frost. Ezaara dismounted. "*Thanks, Zaarusha.*"

The queen flipped her wings and shot up to the outcrops, perching between a blood-red dragon and Erob. *"Good luck. Show Jaevin what you're made of."* Head high, she surveyed the arena with a regal air.

Zaarusha was right. She had to prove herself. Winning the race had been a good start yesterday, but running would never win a war. She had to show these riders she was worthy of Zaarusha. She had to honor her queen.

Swordmaster Jaevin inclined his head. "Good morning, Ezaara, Honored Rider of Queen Zaarusha." He gestured toward the red dragon. "May I re-introduce you to Vino, my loyal companion. You met him at your imprinting test."

Thanks to her new feelings for Roberto, she could finally think of her imprinting test without cringing. *"The pleasure is mine,"* Ezaara melded, nodding at Vino.

He dipped his head in response.

Master Jaevin continued, "Today, I'll put you through your paces, testing your skills to determine what further training you require."

As if Roberto hadn't been putting her through her paces already. She ached from their training sessions. "Thank you, I look forward to it."

"Every time you strike me, you gain an advantage," he said. "Your time is up once you strike me twice, or I strike you five times. Vino will keep count, roaring for each strike."

On a wooden rack near the rock face were two ornate swords with engraved hilts—one gold and one silver. Both were sheathed in decorative scabbards. Familiar swords. They'd been on her wall above the bathtub until yesterday.

The swordmaster followed her gaze. "I see you recognize these. They're the ceremonial swords for the Queen's Rider's evaluation, passed down through generations. You may have heard of them?"

Of course, she hadn't, but she smiled and nodded anyway.

Master Jaevin turned to the assembled crowd, his voice booming. "The official swordsmanship evaluation for Ezaara, Rider of our Honored Queen Zaarusha, is about to commence." He flourished a hand at the swords. "Through the ages, every Queen's Rider has been evaluated with these ceremonial swords, blunted to ensure no one suffers grievous injury. Please present the Queen's Rider with her gold-hilted sword."

Roberto took the golden-hilted sword from the stand and pulled it from its scabbard. He strode over to Ezaara. Bending on one knee, he offered it to her. The blade had a strange sheen. The hilt was engraved with dragons—talons out and fangs bared.

"Nervous?" Roberto waited, gazing up at her.

A soft gasp escaped her. It was there again, that unnerving but thrilling power surging through her. *"So many people, just to see me."* Wiping her palms on her jerkin, she accepted the sword. "Thank you, Master Roberto."

"Relax. If you impressed me, you can impress Jaevin."

Impressed? From his attitude, she'd never have guessed. *"You never let on. I thought I was hopeless."* Her breathing eased. Despite the crowd—despite making a fool of herself so many times since she'd arrived—she could do this. After all, she'd beaten Tomaaz in the market. And she'd scored quite a few hits on Roberto over the last week. She only had to get two strikes. If she got in fast, she might catch Jaevin off guard.

"You're right. I never let on how good you were ... or how beautiful you are ..." Roberto's words shimmied through her mind, lighting every corner within her, taking her breath away. He was still on bended knee before her, in front of the crowd.

"Please stand, Master Roberto," she said, voice strong enough to carry.

Roberto's onyx eyes scanned her face as he rose.

"I thank you for training me so well." Her success would be his.

He bowed his head again. "Good luck, My Honored Queen's Rider." Her face was reflected in his midnight eyes—as if her likeness was seared into his soul. Roberto walked back to the crowd.

Master Tonio presented Master Jaevin with the silver-hilted ceremonial sword, then stepped back.

Jaevin towered above her. Broad and well-muscled, he twirled the sword absent-mindedly. He was good. To strike him, she'd have to use every strategy and trick she knew.

Upon the outcrop, a purple dragon flexed its wings—Singlar. Astride him, Lars lifted a horn to his lips and blew it.

The crowd cheered.

Master Jaevin lunged. Ezaara parried a flurry of thrusts. As quick as an asp, he struck her arm. Vino roared. Strike one.

If this were a real fight, she had no doubt Jaevin could kill her in an instant. Thank the Egg, it was only an evaluation. She parried a downward strike, the force reverberating through her arm. Jaevin feinted and she deflected it, blocking his next blow.

"Good," Jaevin called. "Nice block."

"Graceful move," Roberto melded, and an image flashed through her mind—her braid swinging and arm muscles flexing.

She looked like that? *"What? Oh, thanks."* Ezaara missed blocking Jaevin's next blow and had to duck sideways to avoid being hit.

"Timing is everything," Master Jaevin called.

"Yes sir," Ezaara replied.

"Your braid looks like spun gold in the sunlight." Warmth flowed through her at Roberto's words.

"At a time like this, you're admiring my hair?" Ezaara side-stepped as Jaevin swung again.

"Everything."

Her arm shuddered, blocking another strike.

"You're a powerful melody thrumming through me, setting my bones on fire."

Bones on fire. She got that. Hers melted every time they melded.

Faster and faster, Jaevin whipped his sword at her, keeping her on the defensive. His style was similar to Tomaaz, driving her backward, giving her no chance to attack.

"Lift your guard a little," Master Jaevin called.

Ezaara did and their swords clanged.

"Nice move." This time Roberto sent her legs, bronzed from the sun, thighs flexing to parry Jaevin's last blow.

Jaevin's sword shot past her guard, the tip tapping her shoulder. Vino roared.

"Your left side was open," Jaevin called. Strike two.

"Noted." She parried his next thrust. *"You cost me a strike, Roberto. How can I concentrate when you keep leaking emotions?"*

A rush of sweetness engulfed her.

"It's wonderful, but not now." Ezaara danced out of Jaevin's reach.

"Sorry." Just like that, Roberto was gone and her head was her own again.

§

A dam had broken. For years, Roberto had kept his feelings on a leash. He'd escaped a crucible of pain and never wanted to revisit it, so he'd barricaded his emotions behind a thick wall.

Ezaara had destroyed all that. From the first glimpse of her imprinting, she'd created a chink in his defense. He'd plugged the hole with cold indifference, austere instruction and dogged determination.

But her loyalty to the queen had created another rift in his wall. Her courage, another. By stealth, the chinks had widened. And during the race yesterday, at the river, the fire of dragon power had swept away his last flimsy pretense of indifference.

It had sneaked up on him like a wildcat and sunk its claws deep into him, and no matter how he tried to shake it loose, it clung to him, worming its way deep inside him.

He loved her.

And she knew it.

And if he acted on it, he'd be banished.

§

Jaevin's sword thudded against Ezaara's leather breastplate. Vino roared. No! Strike three, and she hadn't landed a blow yet.

She had to bide her time. She was used to holding out against larger opponents. Tomaaz was a head and shoulders taller than her. Lofty, even bigger. Dragging their bulk around, they often tired before her. But Jaevin wasn't showing any sign of tiring. It was a joke—she hadn't come near to landing a blow. At this rate, she'd only be proving her incompetence.

Ezaara dodged another strike and swung around so Jaevin couldn't back her up against the rock face. Sweat pricked her eyes. She darted back, out of range. Jaevin lunged again, intense thrusts driving her across the arena. Get in fast and attack him? How naive she'd been.

The clash of steel on steel rang among the rock faces as Jaevin launched another flurry of attacks. Her arms were tiring. Her breath rasped in her throat. Everyone's eyes were on her. She couldn't back down. She had to prove herself. Had to strike him, if only once.

She stumbled over a rock, and Jaevin tapped her leg. Vino roared, his scales shining blood red in the sun. Four strikes. None to her. One more from him and they'd be done.

"A short break," Master Jaevin called. "Water, please."

Ezaara slumped onto a rock.

"Well done, Ezaara," Adelina called out. "He's already beaten all of us, so you're in excellent company." A ripple of laughter floated across the arena.

Even though they weren't laughing at her, Ezaara wanted more. They had to take her seriously. Everyone had to see that she could fight, lead them, think strategically. If she were to lead them, they needed to feel confident in her abilities. She had to land a blow on Jaevin—and soon.

Roberto brought Ezaara a waterskin. She drank deeply, wiping her mouth while he held her sword. "Thank you," she gasped. "I needed that."

"Think strategically," Roberto mind-melded.

She nodded, too tired to reply.

"Come on, Ezaara. What's his biggest weakness?"

"Jaevin's fast, but he sometimes keeps his left side open. I'll try to use that move you used on me the other day." Roberto had repeatedly slipped his blade past her guard, tapping her forearm. She took another swig of water.

"It'll impress him if you can carry it off." Roberto's eyes rested on her face a moment longer than necessary before he passed her sword to her, took the waterskin, and went back to the sidelines.

Impressing Jaevin was no small order. She was up against the most practiced swordsman in the realm.

"Go, Ezaara!" Adelina and Gret pumped their fists in the air. Cheers broke out. Lofty was the only one who'd ever cheered for her at home. These riders wanted her to do well. She had to try. Mustering her determination, Ezaara stood to face Jaevin.

A deep note rang out from Lars' horn.

Ezaara leaped forward, but Jaevin was already there, aiming a blow at her chest. She parried, sword ringing, and lunged. He deflected her blade. She ducked low, feinting to Jaevin's left and leaped to his right. His side was open. She thrust up, hard. He twisted, sword flashing, but he was too late. Her blade hit his forearm.

Caught by the sun, red droplets sprayed through the air as he drove his sword across her blade, flicking the sword out of Ezaara's hand. Her blade clattered to the stone.

Dragon's fangs! She'd swung so hard, the blunted blade had cut him.

Vino roared, counting her first strike. But the crowd was silent—she'd injured a master.

Belly hollow, Ezaara gasped. "Sorry, Master Jaevin."

He grimaced. "Good hit. A little too much force for training, but it's only a scratch. I'll survive."

It was more than a scratch—although not a deep gash—but was bleeding impressively. Perhaps he was a bleeder, whose blood didn't clot properly.

"When unevenly matched, use more leverage," Master Jaevin said. "Strike with the strong part of your sword against my tip. Now, pick up your sword, Ezaara, and keep fighting. A tharuk wouldn't show you any mercy."

She snatched up her blade.

Blood running down his arm, Jaevin fought with a ferocity that made her knees tremble. Again and again, he struck and she blocked.

Blood ran down his hilt, drops flying—so much blood for such a small cut.

Her arms ached. Her legs were tired. If she faltered now, he'd strike her again—the last strike.

"*Steady,*" Roberto murmured.

She rallied, blocking the master's blows.

Gradually, Jaevin slowed. A sheen of sweat coated his face. His strikes weren't as strong as before. Face pale, Jaevin leaped onto a rock, deftly flinging his sword from his right hand to his left, then jumped back down to engage her.

Even using his left hand, he was good, but definitely weaker than before and tiring too fast. Ezaara parried him easily. She drove him back. He stumbled.

Lips tinged blue, Jaevin's breathing rasped as he lifted his blade to strike her—and dropped it, clutching at his chest.

"Master Jaevin, are you all right?" Ezaara sheathed her sword and leaped forward to support him.

Pale. Blue-tinged lips. Rasping breath. The edges of his gash were puckered and he was bleeding way too much. Dread filled her. Dragon's bane—it had to be.

But who had poisoned him? Amid murmurs from the crowd, Ezaara lowered Jaevin to the ground, positioning him against a rock.

She picked up her ceremonial blade, examining the tip. Despite the bloody end, the blade glistened with a clear substance. She sniffed it. Yes, it *was* Dragon's bane. Deadly if not treated. She had the remedy in her healer's pouch, back in her cavern.

"Unhand him!" A shrill voice yelled. Fleur.

"It's dragon's bane. He needs—"

Sofia yelled, "Another victim. She wants us all dead!"

"She's Zens' spy!" Alban joined in.

"Get away from him." Rushing over, Fleur knelt beside Jaevin. "Poison!" She pointed at Ezaara. "Seize her. She's poisoned the master of the sword."

If they didn't listen to her, Jaevin would die. "No, you don't underst—"

The blue guards grabbed Ezaara's arms.

In a flash, Roberto's sword tip was at a guard's throat. "Unhand the Queen's Rider," he demanded.

Within a heartbeat, Tonio leveled his dagger at Roberto. "You're threatening the blue guards?" he asked in a deadly-soft voice.

"They're threatening the Queen's Rider," Roberto snapped.

"Who has poisoned the swordmaster," Fleur barked, bent over Jaevin.

This was crazy. They were all at each other's throats. "Stop," Ezaara called. "There's been a misunderstanding. Jaevin needs—"

Zaarusha roared and swept down from the outcrop, thudding to the arena. *Don't worry, Ezaara, this is preposterous. I'll sort it out.*

Lars blew the horn as Singlar landed. "Order," Lars yelled. "Order, now!"

Everyone froze.

Shards, these riders had discipline.

"Stand down, Tonio and Roberto," Lars barked. They sheathed their weapons, glowering at each other. "Fleur, take Jaevin to the infirmary at once and purge this poison from him."

"Yes, Master Lars. I won't rest until I identify it."

"Master Lars," Ezaara said, "it's dragon's bane." The antidote was in her healer's pouch, tucked under her mattress for safe-keeping, but it was common enough. Fleur probably had it by the jarful—or maybe not. "I have the remedy."

Fleur's gaze was glacial. "It's probably a ruse to feed him further poison and finish him off." She and Bruno bundled Jaevin onto Ajeuria, between them.

Ezaara watched, helpless. No one trusted her.

"Don't let anyone get their hands on the remedy," Roberto melded. *"Except you. Keep its whereabouts secret."*

"Why?" No answer.

Lars addressed the crowd. "No one will be apprehended without proof. However, there are suspicious circumstances, so we'll need the standard precautions. Everyone except the council members and blue guards are to go straight back to their assigned duties, now. If you know anything about Master Jaevin's poisoning, report to the council this afternoon."

The air was a flurry of murmurs and flapping wings as riders left for the caverns.

Lars addressed the masters and guards. "We'll meet as a council to discuss who may have poisoned Master Jaevin. Tonio, you will be disciplined for raising a weapon against another master."

Tonio's face flashed annoyance, but he nodded.

"Ezaara, as prime suspect, and I mean suspect only, you and Zaarusha will be kept under guard until we've sorted this out." Lars nodded at a hefty blue guard nearby. "Jacinda, your troop are assigned to guard the Queen's Rider and the queen in their quarters until the trial."

"We'll go quietly," Zaarusha said.

"Of course." Ezaara kept her head high.

Jacinda and her blue guards surrounded Ezaara and the queen at swordpoint, removing Ezaara's weapons.

"Roberto, for raising your sword against a blue guard, and as Ezaara's training master, you and Erob will also be confined to your quarters. Seppi, your troop will look after Erob and the master of mental faculties and imprinting." At Lars' words, guards manhandled Roberto onto a blue dragon.

Ezaara mind-melded one last time. *"Roberto, it wasn't me."*

There was nothing from Roberto, not even a backward glance or a mind-melded thought. It was as if she wasn't there.

Lars' gaze was fierce. "Jacinda, Seppi, you're tasked with everyone's safety as much as their containment. Check their food and water aren't poisoned. Make sure no one reaches their quarters to harm them. I intend to get to the bottom of this with everyone intact."

Suspicions

Guards hustled Roberto through the onlookers, the air a soup of murmured rumors and fetid body odor. He swiped a trickle of sweat from his forehead. It wasn't the first trial he'd attended—although at every one, memories of his father's banishment loomed. That old bitterness flooded his mouth. He swallowed it down.

The council chamber was packed with people, crammed into a makeshift gallery of chairs. More were standing, six-deep, around the walls. The other masters were seated, the granite horseshoe a giant shield around them. Ezaara should be sitting behind that table, not facing it on trial. The realm's ruling dragons were lined up along the rear wall like warriors ready for battle. Zaarusha's eyes were golden slits, focusing on a point in front of the crowd—Ezaara.

There she was. White-faced, on a chair facing the council, stiff-backed guards on either side of her. Even under duress, she was beautiful. Her smattering of freckles stood out like scattered stardust. Her head was high, gaze directly on the council. Facing them head on—like she'd faced every other challenge since arriving here.

Beyond her, Fleur, Bruno and Simeon were seated in the accusers' chairs. Fleur should be healing Jaevin, not here on a witch hunt. Roberto shrugged off the guards and strode forward, stopping before the council table.

"Nice of you to finally show up," Erob said from his spot among the other dragons.

Roberto sent him a mental snort.

Lars rapped a gavel on the table. The crowd hushed.

"We're here to establish who poisoned Master Jaevin." Lars scanned the room. "As spymaster, Master Tonio has been appointed as spokesperson for the accusers. Master Roberto, as Ezaara's official trainer, you are responsible for defending her."

Keeping his face a mask of disinterest, Roberto replied. "You're right, Master Lars, it is my duty—unless someone else volunteers."

He melded with Ezaara, *"Do you trust me?"*

"I do."

"Then, please, no matter what I say, don't protest." Tonio was Fleur's spokesperson. Tonio, who mistrusted Roberto and hated his father. Tonio, who was brilliant at slanting evidence to suit his case.

"I promise … but—"

"Ezaara, they'll banish you if they believe you're guilty. Do you want to lose Zaarusha? Life here at the hold?"

"Are you going to lie?"

"I may have to. We can't afford to have you banished."

"You mean innocents can be banished?"

Roberto shifted his weight. *"I've seen it happen."*

The air was sticky with anticipation.

Lars shuffled some parchment and dipped a quill in his inkwell. "Master Tonio, I turn the time to you. Please outline the accusation and question the accused."

It was dehumanizing, hearing Ezaara referred to as *the accused*, but Roberto held his tongue, and steeled himself for Tonio's questions.

Tonio stalked around the table to stand near Fleur. Eyes fixed on Ezaara, Tonio addressed him. "Master Roberto, permission to question the accused directly."

A demand, not a request. And one he didn't want to submit to, but he couldn't refuse without making Ezaara look guilty, and Tonio knew it. "If you must." Roberto stepped back.

"The accused—*Honored* Queen's Rider." Tonio's tone was derisive. "Do you recognize these ceremonial swords?" He gestured at the swords Ezaara and Jaevin had dueled with that morning, now lying on the council table.

"Yes."

"Where have you seen them?"

"They've been hanging on the wall in my cavern since I came to Dragons' Hold," she replied.

Already things looked bad. She'd had access to the blades every day.

Tonio addressed the council. "When Zaarusha melded to let us know she was bringing a new Queen's Rider, Swordmaster Jaevin checked the ceremonial blades were blunted in preparation for her sword evaluation. He then hung them back in the Queen's Rider's cavern." His face darkened. "No one thought to check them again until after Jaevin was injured." He turned to Ezaara, his voice hard-edged. "*Your* blade was not only coated in poison, it had also been sharpened."

Ezaara met Tonio's dark gaze. "I didn't know what those blades were for. I thought they were decorative. It would make no sense for me to poison a decorative sword, or any sword. Besides, I've been training day and night, so anyone could've tampered with them."

"Good point."

"No, Ezaara. Not anyone." Tonio's smile was feral. What did he have up his sleeve? "I call Fleur, Master of Healing, as my first witness."

Fleur rose, her chair grating against the stone, setting Roberto's teeth on edge.

"Master Healer, Fleur, what was the poison on the defendant's blade?" Tonio was charming—now he wasn't questioning Ezaara.

"I've never seen it before," Fleur said. "Neither have any of my assistants. It's something foreign to Dragons' Hold."

"It's dragon's bane," Ezaara announced, before Roberto could stop her, "as common as clover in Lush Valley. Any healer worth her salt knows that."

No! He'd been too slow. Now Tonio had rope to hang her with.

Tonio pounced. "What did you call it? Dragon's bane? Sounds dangerous." He flashed his teeth. "So, you brought the poison here, then?"

"I object," Roberto called. "He's planting a connection in everyone's minds, where there is none."

"Agreed." Lars rapped his gavel. "Continue questioning along a different line, please, Tonio."

"Did you bring this poison, this dragon's bane, to Dragons' Hold? Answer, please," Tonio snapped.

"No, I didn't. I'd never poison anyone. I've learned the healing arts, so I recognize some poisons."

"A healer must know many poisons."

"Well, that's true, my mother taught me to—"

"Your mother? Now, who was that?" Tonio purred dangerously.

Why was Tonio aiming at Ezaara's family? Was there dirt in their past?

"This isn't relevant," Roberto interjected. "We're investigating Jaevin's poisoning, not Ezaara's upbringing."

"Upbringing can have an effect on behavior, Master Lars," Tonio countered.

Lars scratched his beard. "You may proceed, Master Tonio, but please keep your questions relevant."

"Who was your mother?"

"Marlies."

Gasps rippled around the room. Those a generation older than Roberto looked shocked. Who was Marlies?

Tonio could barely conceal his triumph. "You mean the infamous healer who killed a royal dragonet, then fled before she could be convicted?" His face hardened. "Perhaps her blood flows too strongly in your veins. Perhaps you, too, had the desire to kill."

Lars rapped his gavel. "Order, Tonio. Keep your questions relevant."

But it was too late. The atmosphere was poisoned, as if Tonio had leaked dragon's bane into the air. Council masters' faces were tight, their posture rigid. Onlookers were pointing and whispering, hostile gazes on Ezaara.

"Don't answer any more of Tonio's questions," Roberto melded.

Ezaara's face was paler than before. *"I've messed up, haven't I?"* She was biting her lip, the picture of guilt. *"If only I hadn't struck Master Jaevin."*

"It was a duel. You were supposed to strike him. Someone has set you up. I know you're innocent. We need to convince the council. Try to relax." Shards! If she didn't change her expression, she'd be convicted on that alone.

Zaarusha roared.

Lars approached her and laid his hand on her snout. "The queen would like to give evidence." He nodded at Tonio. Both men placed their hands on Zaarusha's forehead. It was customary for two people to listen to a dragon's evidence, so no one could falsify it.

Lars spoke. "Zaarusha says to judge her rider upon her merits, not the mistakes of her mother. It's been years since she's had a rider, and she doesn't want to lose Ezaara."

Good, the queen was vouching for Ezaara.

As Lars and Tonio sat down, murmurs broke out. Lars rapped his gavel, then had to rap it again to get the crowd to settle.

"Tonio," Roberto said quietly. All heads swiveled to him. "This has all been coincidental. Do you actually have *any real* evidence?"

With a scathing glance, Tonio snapped his fingers.

A blue guard approached, passing Tonio a package.

"We searched her quarters." Tonio unwrapped the package and uncorked a terracotta pot. "My spy found this in the top drawer of Ezaara's nightstand. Fleur, would you please identify it?"

Fleur dipped a fingertip in the pot and sniffed it. "The same poison that's been used on Jaevin." She pointed at Ezaara. "Dragon's bane, she called it."

Dragon's bane in Ezaara's room. Roberto hadn't expected that.

"It's not mine," Ezaara blurted, panic etched on her face. "I've never seen it." *"Roberto, it isn't mine, honest."*

"Sit tight. Don't say another thing."

"But I have the antidote in my healer's pouch, hidden under my mattress. I could help Jaevin."

"Don't mention it."

"But—"

"Not a word. It's vital." Someone was plotting something far larger than ousting Ezaara. Her antidote could be their only chance of saving Jaevin. If Fleur got her talons on it, she'd destroy it and Jaevin wouldn't stand a chance.

Tonio slammed the pot of poison on the table, his voice as hard as granite. "What other lies are you going to tell us, Ezaara?"

Now—when Tonio had the whole crowd against her—he used her name. Intimately, as if he knew her. But if he knew her, he'd never accuse Ezaara of treason. She didn't have a treasonous bone in her body.

A guard burst into the council chamber and pushed through the crowd, rushing up to Lars.

The weary lines in Lars' face deepened. "Master Fleur," he said, "Jaevin is rapidly declining."

"I don't think I can save him." Fleur shot Ezaara venomous daggers, snapping, "I hope you're happy."

"Roberto, the antidote. I have to tell them."

"No!"

Fleur drew herself up. "Before I leave this chamber to attend to Jaevin, I would like to say one more thing."

Lars nodded. "Permission granted."

"The Queen's Rider is talented, that's undisputed," Fleur said. "My own son is quite enamored of her, and I'd considered her an asset to the realm."

Simeon's eyes roamed over Ezaara as if he'd devour her.

Clenching his fists, Roberto stuffed them in his pockets.

"After Jaevin was wounded, other incidents came to mind," Fleur continued. "When Ezaara was in the infirmary helping me, she questioned my judgment, often suggesting alternative remedies. Was she trying to poison my patients? And why did Ezaara knife Sofia? That incident has never been explained."

Roberto stood. "Master Lars, this is nothing but personal opinion and has no bearing on this morning's case."

Alban jumped to his feet. "If I may, Master Lars?" At Lars' nod, he continued, "Ezaara did not only knife Sofia. She also attacked me during the race, threatening me if I spoke up. You saw me yourself, sir, limping over the finish line."

"He attacked me and I defended myself!" Ezaara melded.

Alban had had it in for Ezaara since the knife accident. This had to stop. "Do you have any witnesses, not just people bearing grudges?" Roberto snapped.

Alban glowered, not answering.

Roberto nodded. "I thought so. No proof. This is another attempt to malign the Queen's Rider. I—"

"Sit down, Master Roberto."

Roberto sat, fuming. This was nothing but slander. Ezaara would never betray Zaarusha.

Or could she? Perhaps he was letting his heart get the better of him. He'd been betrayed before by someone he loved.

Fleur tucked a strand of hair behind her ear. "I must attend Master Jaevin and make his last hours more comfortable. Thank you for the opportunity to express my concerns." She exited the chamber, escorted by the guard who'd brought the news.

Tonio swept his hand toward Ezaara. "I present to the Council of the Twelve Dragon Masters, Ezaara of Lush Valley—daughter of Marlies, the dragonet slayer—who wheedled her way into our dragon queen's trust, only to smuggle poison into the hold and strike down Master Jaevin in an attempt to weaken our council. She planned to make this look like an accident, using a public event to disguise her murder attempt. No one suspected she'd poisoned the blade, except our intuitive healer, Fleur. I warn you, we have a traitor in our midst and would do well to be rid of her."

"They don't believe it was an accident!" Ezaara's anguish sliced through Roberto's mind, making him wince.

These coincidences were stacked against her. He had to find a sliver of proof that showed Ezaara's innocence.

"Master Roberto, please present your defense."

"Master Lars, council members, and esteemed folk of Dragons' Hold, with all due respect, we have no concrete proof and no witnesses against our Queen's Rider. It's all supposition. No one saw Ezaara poison the sword, because she didn't. The dragon's bane found in her cavern could have been put there by someone else. That she recognizes a poison from her home is unremarkable, especially when she's been trained to ease afflictions and promote health. She's an ignorant Lush Valley girl, who has imprinted with Zaarusha—not an assassin." He paused, letting the weight of his words settle. "I tested her imprinting bond. It's strong. I admit, she's been clumsy—dropping her dinner, twisting her ankle and then harming Sofia in an accident—but she's been training hard to be the best Queen's Rider she can be. And she adores our queen. Why would she throw all that away? It makes no sense. Master Lars, with your permission, may I perform a mental test on Ezaara to see whether she poisoned the ceremonial blade?"

Lars nodded. "It's within your role as Master of Imprinting and Mental Faculties. I trust you to be impartial."

It was ironic. Life had taught Roberto to be careful, to mistrust, to always question—and that was why Lars trusted him. "Ezaara, may I?"

"Of course, I have nothing to hide."

Roberto locked down his own thoughts, so Ezaara couldn't read them, and placed his hands upon her temples. There it was again, a bouquet of vibrant color swirling through him, as if he'd stepped into a summer garden. He flitted through her memories, accidentally stumbling upon their first mind-meld at the river. He tried to control the warmth spreading up his face. How did she do that? Make him feel so much, when he hadn't for years? He dug further. Despite how he felt about her, he had to prove the Queen's Rider hadn't fooled him.

Wait, what was that? Ezaara and Adelina, smuggling pots out of the infirmary. His gut hollowed. Was she guilty? Had she tricked Adelina into helping her? He chased the memory to its end. No, those were the medicinal herbs smuggled out to heal him after his chest was gashed. A breath of relief slipped out of him. He tracked further through her memories—her loyalty blazed like a beacon fire in the dark.

What a fool for doubting her.

Roberto released his hands and stepped away from Ezaara. "I'm satisfied, Lars. Ezaara did not poison the Master of the Sword. Someone is trying to blame her. They hid the dragon's bane in her room. We have a traitor among us."

Gasps rippled around the chamber.

"Excuse me, Master Lars," Simeon interrupted. "If I may ... I mean, I don't want to interrupt, but I fear there may be more to Roberto and Ezaara's relationship than trainee and master."

What was Simeon inferring? *"He's bluffing,"* Roberto warned. *"Look surprised."*

The crowd tensed.

"I once stumbled upon Master Roberto half naked on Ezaara's bed. She was with him."

"What? When?" Then he remembered. "I was injured, and Ezaara was healing me." The words burst out of him before he could think.

Simeon screwed up his face. "I work in the infirmary. I don't recall you being injured."

"I took a tharuk gash to the chest when we fought at River's Edge. Ezaara treated it."

"That must've left a nasty scar."

"Of course it did," he barked.

"No, it didn't, Roberto," Ezaara melded. *"It's faded—I used piaua."*

Simeon had them backed into a corner.

"I don't suppose you'd be happy to show this scar to us, would you?" Simeon asked, all reasonableness. That leech.

"I'm not disrobing in front of half the hold, just to please you," Roberto snapped. "Master Lars, please call this man to order."

"To the contrary," Lars said. "A romantic relationship with Ezaara would prevent you from being impartial, invalidating your mental testing as well as being cause for banishment. Please show us the scar as proof of your injury. Or otherwise explain what you were doing half-naked in the Queen's Rider's quarters."

Roberto was silent. There was nothing he could do. *Sorry, Ezaara.*

Guards stepped up to hold Roberto's arms and Tonio pulled his jerkin and shirt open.

There was an audible hiss as Tonio sucked in his breath. "No new scar," Tonio announced. "Only old ones."

At the front of the crowd, Adelina's face was stark, eyes wide with shock.

Tonio's voice sliced through the silence. "Son of a traitor! The apple doesn't fall far from the tree. You're the lowest of the low, consorting with your trainee, who's the daughter of a dragonet slayer and plotting to poison the council—of which you're an honored member." Tonio spat at Roberto's boots. "Honored no more."

"Steady, Tonio," Lars cautioned. "The council haven't cast their votes yet." He motioned to the guards, who circled Roberto, Ezaara and Tonio.

Ballot papers were handed to the council masters. The scratch of their quills made Roberto's scalp crawl. Masters passed their papers to Lars.

He opened and read the votes, his brow furrowing. His mouth grew tighter as he separated them into two piles. Only two papers were on Lars' right. The rest were piled up on his left.

"Ezaara, please stand," Lars called.

Chairs creaked as people craned past others to look at her. Roberto wished he could send them all away. Her legs were trembling. Hands shaking. But her shocked green eyes were the worst.

He'd failed her.

"Honored Rider of Queen Zaarusha," Lars said. "We find you guilty of attempted murder and treason. If Master Jaevin dies as the result of this incident, you will be guilty of murder."

Zaarusha bellowed, talons raking stone, shards of rock skittering across the floor.

They were convicting Ezaara. They'd throw her in the dungeons. Then banish her. There was no way she'd survive the Wastelands—the harsh red desert full of scorpions, rust vipers and Robandi, the tent-dwelling assassins who scoured the hot sands. If she didn't get caught in one of their cut-throat feuds, then the heat or a sandstorm would finish her.

Banishment was a death sentence.

He had to save Ezaara. He'd do anything to help her. Anything to secure the queen's rightful rider. Thoughts spiraled through Roberto's head with dizzying speed. Flee. Make a stand. Fight. Burn their way out and escape on Erob.

But all of those options led to Zaarusha losing her rider.

"Steady, Roberto. You're only one man. You can't change the world." For once, Erob wasn't teasing.

His mind cleared, settling on one irrevocable course of action. Straightening his shoulders, he faced Lars. Roberto's thoughts slid over Dragons' Hold: the snow-capped peaks of Dragon's Teeth soaring high against the blue sky, fertile fields and forest sprawling at their feet. All he'd ever wanted was here. Especially now that he'd met Ezaara.

Roberto held his hand up. "Stop. I have more evidence, upon my word as a dragon master." Guards gripping his arms, he moved to the council table and met each master's gaze. "I poisoned Jaevin. I planted the poison in Ezaara's cavern. I'm part of Zens' plot to overthrow Dragons' Realm."

Lars gaped at him.

"No!" Shari gasped. "That can't be true. I know you, Roberto. You'd never do that."

Erob roared.

Tonio nodded, eyes narrowed. "I saw you with that pot after the feast. Is that when you did it?"

Adelina paled, mouthing, "No."

Shari's hand flew to her mouth.

What? Ezaara's shock seared him, burning through his bones. He'd saved her, but he'd lost her. She'd never trust him again. He tightened his resolve, slamming his mind shut. He pulled his mask down and turned to face her, sneering. "You were fools for trusting me," he said. "All of you."

Ezaara's face paled further, her freckles standing out like blood stains on snow.

BETRAYAL

Ezaara gasped. What about them mind-melding? What about their feelings for one another? *"So, it all meant nothing to you?"* Ezaara reached out to mind-meld with Roberto, but she came up against a wall of granite. She tried again. And again.

And again.

Nothing. Not a sniff of Roberto's thoughts. He'd blocked her out. Withdrawn.

Tonio's eyes were sharp, tone cutting. "Did you administer the poison? Or did your accomplice, Ezaara?"

"Ezaara!" Roberto snorted. "Hardly. That silly fool had no idea I'd poisoned the weapon. You heard her, she didn't even know what the blades were for."

Ezaara's stomach jolted, her breath knocked from her. She'd been a fool, all right. He'd deceived her and gained her trust—and she'd believed he loved her.

"When did you poison the blade?" Tonio asked.

"Yesterday, during the after-race celebrations."

The race had only been yesterday. A lifetime ago, when the world had been full of possibility. And love.

"Where did you source the poison?" Tonio asked. "If dragon's bane only grows in Lush Valley, did Ezaara give it to you?"

He rolled his eyes. "It's common in many places, including Naobia. Any *proper healer* would know that."

Master Bruno yelled, "I'll not have you speak about my wife like that!"

Roberto laughed, a hard, arrogant bark that made Ezaara's skin break out in cold prickles.

How could she have believed him? Their love had felt so real. So beautiful. Just what she'd dreamed of. His icy arrogance fit him like a natural skin. This was reality. The man she loved was a traitor, a liar, plotting against her queen.

Lars sighed. "Roberto." His voice was tender, as if he was speaking to a son, but grim lines furrowed his brow. "You saw the damage your father did. You vowed never to be like him. Your talents are valued here. Why would you do this?"

What had Roberto's father done?

Roberto stared at Lars, eyes cold, refusing to speak.

Lars tried again. "And your relationship with the Queen's Rider?"

Roberto's upper lip curled. "Relationship? What relationship?" He regarded her the way a buyer at a market would gaze upon rotten fish entrails.

Her cheeks burned with shame. She met his eyes. There was nothing warm there now. *"Roberto, this can't be true. Tell me it isn't. Please."* It was a desperate plea sent into a cold hard void.

"She's not the real Queen's Rider, is she?" Tonio's words struck Ezaara like a whip. "You only *pretended* to test her."

"Yes, I am," Ezaara cried.

Zaarusha roared.

"She is the Queen's Rider," Roberto said. "Their bond is strong. But banish me, and you won't have anyone to test your imprinting bonds again."

"Or feed that information to Zens," Tonio snapped.

Lars looked sick, his face tinged gray, sweat on his forehead. "Master of Mental Faculties and Imprinting, Roberto, son of Amato, is now stripped of his title and is no longer a part of this council," he announced. "He'll be banished to the Wastelands within the hour. Take him to the dungeons. His sister may farewell him before he goes. Ezaara, our Honored Queen's Rider, has been cleared of all charges. This trial is adjourned." The crack of Lars' gavel nearly split Ezaara's heart in two.

At the rear of the chamber, Erob bellowed, lashing out with his talons. Blue Guards restrained him with javelins and ropes as more guards marched Roberto out of the chamber through a side tunnel.

"Adelina," Ezaara called out, but Adelina ignored her, striding after Roberto, chin high and eyes shiny with unshed tears.

"Clear the room," Lars commanded. "The masters and dragons have urgent matters to attend to."

"Zaarusha!"

"It's all right, Ezaara. It was a mistake to trust him. It was lucky he confessed before you were cast out."

Gods, it *was* lucky. Because of his confession, her name had been cleared. *"What if he's lying?"*

"Erob said the same. But I doubt it. Roberto has obviously inherited his father's disposition, like Tonio always feared."

Ezaara was swept out the main doors amid the crowd. Although she was surrounded by people, everyone avoided eye contact and no one came near. Fleur's and Tonio's accusations had created a granite wall between Ezaara and her people.

§

Adelina stumbled along the tunnel. Roberto. No, not Roberto. Ma, dead. Roberto, banished.

She had no one left. No one.

Not that her father had been a loss. They'd all been glad to see the back of him. Life had been peaceful after his death. After he'd paralyzed Ma. She choked back tears, cursing his watery grave. She hadn't swum in Crystal Lake again since he'd died there.

It hadn't been easy, growing up with an older brother who was fighting inner demons, but Roberto had always been gentle with her. More gentle than with anyone else. As if he'd understood her need to be protected, after what they'd been through. He'd become her mother and father. And fought tooth and talon to keep her, refused to foster her out, although that's what most thirteen-year-olds would've done if their parents were dead.

And now he was imprisoned, headed for the Wastelands.

He had no chance. Although Roberto had survived other forms of hell—everyone had said he'd never come back from Death Valley—he wouldn't be coming back this time. If cats had nine lives, Roberto had used all of his twice over.

There was something about the whole trial that was off. Roberto loved being a dragon master, loved the realm. There was no way he would've hurt anyone or risked being half naked in—

That must have been the day Ezaara had healed him and Simeon had walked in.

Why hadn't Roberto told Lars about piaua? Why hadn't he asked Ezaara to testify? Questions swirling in her mind, Adelina traipsed down the dingy tunnel to the dungeons, following her brother, the only other surviving member of her family.

§

"Adelina." Roberto's face was haggard. They clasped hands through the cold bars of the dungeon. "They'll banish me, they have to." He slipped something between them, into her pocket. His eyes were fiery with some insistent message that she couldn't grasp.

"Over my dead body!" Adelina snapped. By the Egg, they'd been through so much. It couldn't end like this.

"No," he insisted. "They have to, can't you see?"

He *wanted* to be banished. "After all you've worked for." Her throat tightened.

"And undone." His eyes flicked to the guards behind her. Those eyes were pleading with her to understand something important—but what?

"Time's up," a guard called.

"Yes," said Adelina. "Of course."

Eyes burning, she made her way back up the tunnels, determined not to cry. She'd had years of practice at hiding her emotions.

Slipping her hand into her pocket, Adelina drew out the Queen's Rider's green ribbon, warm where Roberto had held it. Oh, shards! He'd taken the blame to protect Ezaara. She blinked back tears, but it was useless. Warm rivulets coursed down her cheeks.

This was harder than Pa's treachery. His abuse. His death.

Harder than Ma's death. Because Roberto had been there.

And now, she had no one.

§

Ezaara raced to her cavern. She lifted her mattress, and snatched up her healer's pouch.

Roberto had been lying. He'd melded and shown her his true self, only it wasn't his true self. The man she'd glimpsed and loved had been a traitor. The admiration in his eyes, the way he'd lit every corner of her being with light, shone a torch on her darkest fears and given her strength to race with fire in her veins—it had all been a ruse. Some sort of mental trick to get her onside. The first step in destroying her.

A sham, nothing but a sham. Lofty's clumsy kiss had been more genuine than her mind-meld with Roberto.

But Gods, how she loved him. How she wanted him back.

Master of mental faculties, well, he'd proven that. He'd mastered melding and fooling her, easily. By the Egg, she was so ignorant. So trusting, so easy to dupe into love.

Only it wasn't love. It was *a lie*.

His lie. The master of lies, deceit and murder.

She ran, her feet pounding a tattoo into the stone floors to Jaevin's door. Hopefully, the dragon's bane hadn't finished Roberto's work. Hopefully, they had a chance …

Ezaara knocked.

A woman opened the door, wisps of sweat-drenched hair clinging to her worry-creased brow. She started. "What do *you* want?" she snapped. "Have you come to gloat?"

"Who is it?" a feeble male voice called.

"The one who poisoned you," the woman spat, pushing the door to shut it.

Ezaara jammed her foot in the gap, so the woman couldn't shut her door. "They've banished someone else. It wasn't me," she shot, her chest squeezing as she pictured Roberto's face. Shards, no! It was him. "I have the antidote. I can save Master Jaevin."

"I'm not letting you near my husband. You'll probably give him more dragon's bane." Jaevin's wife shoved on the door, but Ezaara held it fast.

"Threcia, let her in," Jaevin called. "I'm dying. If she finishes me off, at least I'll be out of my misery. But you never know, she might just save me. Any remedy is worth trying."

"Master Jaevin," Ezaara called. "I've been trained as a healer. I don't kill people—I save them, if I can."

"Go on, Threcia, please." Jaevin sounded exhausted.

His wife looked dubious. "Come in, then." Threcia barely held the door open wide enough for Ezaara to squeeze through.

Jaevin lay in a makeshift bed, in their living area, near a stoked fire. His face was pale and his breathing raspy. Ezaara felt his forehead—cool, but beaded in sweat.

"He's cold, always cold," said Threcia, tugging his blanket up. "And his breathing's shallow."

"What did Fleur give you?"

"This tea." Threcia thrust a cup at her.

Ezaara sniffed it. Woozy weed—a sleeping draft. No use against dragon's bane. "Did she give you any other remedies?"

"This, against the pain in his chest." Threcia passed her a tonic. Again, to ease a symptom, not the cause.

Dragon's bane made the airways, throat and lungs tighten and slowly close down. If the dose was strong enough, the victim would die within a day. Without an antidote, there was no chance of survival.

Roberto had done this.

It didn't make sense. His kind gifts, his tenderness, love and wonder when they'd melded …

But he'd looked every bit a hardened killer as he'd confessed, spurning her and the realm. He'd taken advantage of her ignorance. A slow burning anger spread through her, each thud of her heart a count of the ways he'd fooled her.

"Jaevin, can you swallow?"

He nodded, face pale, lips tinged blue. Threcia's eyes were locked on his face, shiny with tears. This was true love, tested over years, not the flashy show of emotion Ezaara had felt for her master.

"Threcia, get Vino to warm a third of a cup of water."

Threcia rushed off and was back within moments. Ezaara mixed eight pinches of antidote—a pale green powder made of finely crushed rubaka leaves—stirring until it had dissolved, then propped Jaevin up and helped him drink.

Once he'd swallowed the last drop, she sat, holding his wrist where the veins ran across the bone, feeling his heartbeat. Now that she'd administered the antidote, Ezaara fought her urge to rush out the door. She had to make sure this worked. Jaevin's life was more important than what was happening to Roberto.

Deep in the bowels of the caverns, a drum boomed. Then another. The stone under Ezaara's chair pulsed like a dragon's heartbeat, the floor resonating with a deep cadence that throbbed through her boot soles. Waves of sound kept rolling around them. The mournful keening of a dragon was a sad counterpoint to the drums' rhythm.

"The banishment drums." Threcia's gaze softened. "I'm glad it wasn't you."

"Who poisoned me?" Jaevin wheezed.

"Master Roberto." Ezaara's voice cracked.

"No," Jaevin whispered, face lined with shock. "No, not Roberto, I trusted him."

Exactly. Ezaara hardened her heart. She couldn't allow space for traitors. She mixed another draft and put it on the table. "Drink this in two hours."

Jaevin drifted to sleep, his breathing not completely right, but improved. Threcia walked her to the door and clasped Ezaara's hands. "Thank you."

"Please don't mention I've been here. If anyone else comes by, tell them he's sleeping."

Threcia narrowed her eyes. "Why? Master Roberto will be gone."

Gone. He flashed to mind, standing calf-deep in the water, eyes golden in the sunlight. Laughing and carefree as they'd raced together as riders of fire, his love washing over her. She'd never see him again. A pang shot through Ezaara, as strong as Alban's stomach punch. No! She fought it. He was a traitor. It was good riddance. "Keep Master Jaevin safe until he's fully recovered. He'll be weak for a few days, and it may be a while before he's himself again. Until then, it's best he doesn't have visitors." Especially Fleur, who was as good as useless. "I'll be back in a couple of hours to check on him, after you've given him the draft."

Threcia kissed Ezaara, her tears spilling onto Ezaara's cheek. "Thank you for saving his life."

It was a healer's duty to save lives, not take them. "I'm glad I could help."

"The Egg bless your mother for teaching you. I don't care what Tonio says, my family will serve you and yours." She bowed. "My Honored Queen's Rider."

Ezaara's eyes pricked. "Remember, not a word to anyone."

"Of course," Threcia said. "Master Roberto may have accomplices."

Adelina? She hadn't thought of her. Ezaara left, and ran, drums pulsing beneath her feet, Erob's howls filling the tunnels. She had to find Adelina. And, despite him being a killer, she yearned to see Roberto, one last time.

§

Heart thudding, Ezaara tried one passage after another. Strange—most of the corridors were empty. Finally, she found a tunnel with stairs winding down into the bowels of the mountain. It was cold down here, so cold. She pulled her jerkin tighter.

Feet pounding stone, she came to another tunnel with a locked door. Guards blocked it, swords drawn. "No admittance to the dungeons. Only the traitor's sister may see him."

Ezaara mustered her haughtiest tone. "Please move aside for the Queen's Rider."

"Sorry. Master Lars said you weren't to see him. It's for your own protection."

Nothing would sway them.

Ezaara tried to meld with Roberto. Nothing.

She'd have to wait for Adelina. She retreated along the tunnel, ducking into a deserted chamber, ricocheting drumbeats throbbing through her head, and her boots gnawing a hole in the stone.

Time seemed to last forever.

The drums stopped. Erob's keening died. The sudden silence stifled Ezaara like an overly-thick cloak.

Finally, along the tunnel, the door thudded. A small cloaked figure bolted past the chamber.

"Adelina," Ezaara called out.

Adelina sped up. She mustn't have heard.

"Adelina," Ezaara yelled.

Adelina raced up the winding stairs. She was deliberately ignoring her. No one could've missed that.

Ezaara quickened her pace, following Adelina along the deserted tunnels. When they'd walked so long that Ezaara was in a passage she'd never seen before, Adelina stopped outside a door.

She whirled to face Ezaara, eyes red-rimmed. Her usually cheerful face was closed. Hard. "I know you're following me, but don't."

"I need to talk to you."

"No, you don't. You're the last person I want to talk to."

It was a knife to her gut. "I want to check you're all right." And Roberto … she wanted to see him.

Adelina rolled her bloodshot eyes.

"What have I done?"

"What. Have. You. Done?" With each word, Adelina stabbed a finger in Ezaara's face. Eyes fiery, she snapped, "You've sentenced my brother to death."

"No!" What? Ezaara reeled, gut-punched. "No, Adelina, he poisoned Jaevin." The pot of dragon's bane, his confession, had sealed his fate, not her. "Tonio saw him with the pot …" The scathing hatred on Adelina's face stopped her.

"You're as dumb as Fleur." Adelina thrust open the door, strode through it and slammed it in Ezaara's face. "Go away!" she yelled through the wood.

That hurt. But not as much as Adelina was hurting. Hang on, this wasn't Adelina's cavern. Whose was it?

Ezaara pushed the door open. It was Roberto's. Erob's ornate saddlebags were leaning against a wall. Adelina was slumped on Roberto's bed, one of his jerkins in her hands. The cavern smelt like him—mint and sandalwood and male. A memory of flying with him came flooding back. Of him holding her, safely cocooned, after her stunt. She tried to swallow it down, but couldn't.

"You don't get it, do you?" Adelina wrung his garment in her hands. "I asked Roberto to tell the truth, but he refused."

"But he did tell the truth. At the trial, he said—"

"How could you be Queen's Rider and be so dumb?" Adelina's face was frankly incredulous. "My brother sacrificed his life to save yours. He's innocent."

"Oh!" Ezaara's stomach was a hollow yawning chasm. She was spinning, dropping into an endless void. "I—I—" She'd been too angry, too blind, too stupid to see …

"Why didn't you vouch for him?" Adelina demanded.

"He made me promise not to argue with him …. What about that pot Tonio saw?"

Adelina bit her lip. "The night you arrived. Oil for *your* cane."

Adelina's mother's cane. Roberto had freshly carved and oiled it, after only just meeting her. He'd cared for her, right from the start. And how had she repaid him?

"My brother would never poison Jaevin. How could you believe that?"

"When I told him I had the antidote, he said to keep it secret. Not to heal Jaevin … it seemed off. Why would he keep the remedy secret?"

"Well, think about it." Adelina tapped her foot against the bed like a mad woodpecker. "Do you trust Fleur?" Adelina's glance stabbed Ezaara. "Oh, figure it out yourself!"

Oh shards. He'd been preventing Fleur from destroying the remedy. She'd been a double fool. Now they'd lose him. But it wasn't too late. Surely she could do something. "I have to talk to him. Have to vouch for him, tell Lars."

"It's too late. He's gone." Her voice hollow, Adelina slumped on the bed. "Didn't you hear the banishment drums?"

"Yes, but—"

"When the drums sounded, everyone went to the main cavern to jeer at the *traitor* before the blue guards loaded him into saddlebags. I couldn't bear to go." She wrung his jerkin, twisting it into a tight coil. "He'll never survive the Wastelands. Never."

Oh shards, her *brother*. Her only living family member. This was so much worse for Adelina. Ezaara reached out to hug her, but Adelina shoved her away.

"My brother's life is worth more than a cheap apology. Just go."

It stung like tharuk claws raking flesh. This was her fault. She should have realized. Believed in him. Spoken up. Now it was too late.

Secret Plans

Ezaara ran to Zaarusha's den and threw herself against her dragon's side. Zaarusha's scales were warm, but nothing could ease the dark icy hollow inside.

"It's been a grueling day. How are you faring?" Zaarusha snuffled her hair, her breath tickling Ezaara's neck.

"Terrible. Adelina blames Roberto's banishment on me. Says he did it to save me. That it's my fault he's gone." It was. There was no other explanation. He loved her, she'd known that, but she'd taken his lies to save her too literally. She'd been too shocked to see the sacrifice behind his actions.

"I was surprised he'd betrayed us. I trusted him too." Zaarusha nudged her shoulder with her snout. *"He even fooled Erob—and it's difficult to maintain a facade around a dragon. Erob bellowed at the council, trumpeting on about going to save Roberto until I pulled rank on him. Not pleasant at all."*

"If you trusted Roberto, what changed your mind?"

"One traitor at Dragons' Hold puts the whole realm in danger," Zaarusha replied. *"Roberto is clever. His mental abilities make him a dangerous foe."*

His mind. Shards, his mind was beautiful. But dangerous? *"But Adelina knows him better than anyone else, and she says he's innocent. What if we're banishing him wrongly?"*

"Roberto's past holds dark secrets. Secrets that would make your stomach turn and send you running. I know you've developed a fondness for him, but it must stop. He's not what he seems."

Fondness? That's what Zaarusha thought these powerful feelings were?

Their love was an avalanche, hurtling headlong down a mountainside. Unstoppable. And she'd let this man go to his death.

"I disagree. We should save him, go tonight. We could try melding with the blue guard's dragon on the way. Perhaps we'll catch them before they abandon him in the Wastelands."

"Abandon him? Ezaara, he's been tried and banished. He poisoned Jaevin. You're probably his next victim."

Zaarusha might never understand. *"Adelina says the pot Tonio saw was oil for my cane, not poison."*

"Her sisterly affection is blinding her. He's been banished. And if you try to rescue him, you'll forfeit your right to be Queen's Rider and be banished, too."

Lose Zaarusha? *"But Zaarusha, I—"*

"You're as bad as Erob. We've had to put him under guard until he quiets down. My own son, imagine!" Zaarusha's voice was steely. *"I'll do the same to you, if I have to. I won't lose you, Ezaara. I won't have you assassinated."*

Ezaara clamped her thoughts down tight, so Zaarusha couldn't sense them.

Zaarusha was making her choose: Zaarusha, whom she'd imprinted with in a burning flash of color; or Roberto, whose love seared a fiery pathway through her soul.

A current of bitterness ran through her. She didn't want to choose. She loved them both.

"Thank you, Zaarusha. It's been a long day, and you're giving me good advice," Ezaara replied.

"You've been under a lot of stress. It must've been a big shock, being charged with murder, then released, only to have your master banished."

"Yes, it has been. I'm exhausted."

"Why don't you have a meal before bed? That might restore your energy."

Did dragons think food fixed everything? Ezaara didn't feel like eating, but she was hungry for action. *"Good idea. I'll be back soon."*

She ducked into the mess cavern and grabbed a bowl of stew. By keeping her ears open, she soon learned where Erob was being kept.

§

Ezaara hefted the lump of meat. Convincing Benji, the head of the kitchens, to give it to her so she could console poor grieving Erob had been easy. The hard part was going to be persuading the guards to let her feed him.

Low snarls rippled down the tunnel. Erob had stopped roaring a while ago, but he hadn't given up protesting.

"Erob," she melded.

"You!" he snarled back.

Ezaara swallowed. One word—so much venom.

"Erob, we have to rescue Roberto." She rounded a corner, the flickering torchlight making her shadow skitter along the wall.

"As if Zaarusha would condone that," Erob spat. *"I've been shackled by my own mother—for loyalty to my rider."*

"Zaarusha threatened to strip me of my role, but I'm going anyway."

"So, you saw through his subterfuge to save you?" Erob sounded surprised.

Ezaara swallowed, keeping her thoughts masked. Thank the Egg for Adelina.

"How could everyone believe him? How could they not see his innocence?" Erob's questions stabbed her.

Shards, she'd been so dumb. Guilt wormed its way through Ezaara. She had to phrase this right. *"We could go together."* Her heart thumped twice before she dared continue. *"But we'll have to convince them we're being obedient or we won't stand a chance."*

Ezaara rushed along the tunnel, bloody meat dripping on stone. There, on the right, was a barred cavern, in the shadows. Behind the bars, Erob sat on his haunches, yellow eyes slitted, still snarling.

"Halt. No one has permission to be down here." A blue guard stepped out, blocking her way. He was massive with a thick scar running down his neck. Two more were behind him.

"I've brought food for the dragon," she said. "It might soothe him."

The scarred guard grunted. "Orders are orders."

A smaller guard spoke up, "He's quite upset. Perhaps food would calm him."

"What if she doesn't touch him?" the third guard muttered.

The scarred guard grunted. "All right." They stepped aside.

"They think we can only meld when you touch me," Erob whispered in her mind, the perfect picture of a brooding dragon. *"If only they knew."*

Ezaara held up the meat, advancing slowly, letting her arms shake as if she were nervous. *"We have to be quick,"* she melded.

Erob's snarls ceased as he sniffed the meat. *"What's your plan?"*

"You need to calm down. We have to convince them that you don't need guards."

"Got it. As soon as they let me free, I'll meld and let you know." She passed the meat through the bars. His lips curled back and he took it in his fangs, retreating to the back of the cave. *"We can't leave until after dark."* Erob chomped on his meat, tail curled around himself protectively, as if he wanted to hide in a corner and lick his wounds.

"I can't believe the change in him," said the scarred guard.

Ezaara nodded. "In times of crisis, dragons need a source of comfort." She wasn't lying—their plan to rescue Roberto would comfort Erob more than any chunk of meat.

"Maybe that's why she's Queen's Rider," the third guard whispered, nudging the small one.

"Mm," murmured the small guard. "That and the way she can fly. Remember that?"

Ezaara retreated down the tunnels. Great, they'd believed her. Now for phase two of her plan.

§

After checking on Jaevin again, Ezaara returned to the mess cavern and pocketed some food. When she reached Roberto's cavern, Adelina was nowhere to be seen. She glanced about for somewhere to hide her supplies.

"*Ezaara,*" Zaarusha's voice nearly made Ezaara drop the food. Dashing to Roberto's wardrobe, she stashed apples, smoked meat and bread among his clothes and slammed the door. The scent of his clothes conjured up his face, raven eyes tinged with sunlight, regarding her at the river. *Loving* her.

"*Ezaara!*" Zaarusha again.

Ezaara jolted the image away. "*Yes, Zaarusha?*"

"*You've been gone a while. I wanted to check you're all right.*"

"*I've been stretching my legs.*" Well, that was true, she had traipsed back and forth between the mess, Jaevin's, Erob's holding pen and Roberto's quarters.

"*Come back soon. I'd like to see you settled before I go hunting.*"

"*On my way.*"

When Ezaara returned to their quarters, Zaarusha was pacing in the den, hungry.

"*You seem more energized,*" the queen said.

"*Eating helped.*" It *had* helped Erob.

"Stay right here," Zaarusha warned. *"I know you were keen on going after Roberto earlier."*

Had the queen seen through her?

"But I'm glad you've seen sense," Zaarusha continued. *"Colluding with a traitor would strip you of your privileges. The last thing I want is to lose another Queen's Rider."* A potent wave of sorrow enveloped Ezaara with that same memory of Anakisha falling into a seething mass of tharuks.

"What an awful way to die." Ezaara squeezed her hands tight, her nails biting her palms. She didn't want to lose Zaarusha.

"Not as bad as at the hands of a traitor." Zaarusha glided off the ledge toward the hunting grounds.

Whichever path she chose, Ezaara would hurt someone she loved—the queen she'd pledged her life to, or the man she'd given her heart to. She sighed, walking with heavy feet through the archway to her cavern.

"Ezaara, the guards have let me go." It was Erob. *"I'll meet you at midnight in my den."*

It was happening. In a few short hours, she was walking out on her life as Zaarusha's rider. Walking out on everything she could ever dream of—except Roberto. She couldn't stay here and let him die in the Wastelands. Life without Roberto would be like living in a dead and empty shell, walking on knife-sharp shards every day.

"I'll be there." Ezaara checked the supplies in her healer's pouch and added more of the clean herb and bear's bane she'd retrieved from the infirmary when she'd healed Roberto.

From what she'd gleaned in the mess caverns, the Wastelands were vast fierce deserts, inhabited by feuding tribes and rust vipers, four days' flight from Dragons' Hold. Roberto would be dropped off with a few mouthfuls of water, but no weapons or food. If she and Erob could leave tonight, they'd only be a few hours behind him—although it might take days to find him.

"Ezaara, I need your help!" a dragon's voice called faintly, as if it was far away.

"Who are you?" Ezaara mind-melded.

"Septimor, a dragon with the blue guards. I have a young girl, attacked by tharuks, who needs healing."

She had to leave. She had no time. *"Master Fleur is in the infirmary."* Guilt rippled through her. Sending patients to Fleur went against her grain. Fleur's healing was clumsy at best, her salves seemed useless, and Adelina was worried that Fleur would destroy the antidote to dragon's bane. She couldn't trust her with a master or a rider, but surely Fleur would heal a girl with a few cuts or scrapes.

"I can't send her to Fleur," Septimor answered. *"I want her to survive."*

Ezaara didn't miss the cynical edge to the dragon's reply. Or the urgency. *"What's wrong with her?"*

"Her arm's been mutilated and infected with limplock, a tharuk poison. She's dying."

Dragon's fangs and bones! *"Bring her to me. When will you be here?"*

"Soon. Master Roberto knows the remedy."

Septimor obviously didn't know Master Roberto had been banished.

Ezaara ran down the tunnels toward Adelina's quarters. Being Roberto's sister, maybe she knew the antidote too. *"Erob, something urgent has come up. Someone's dying and needs my help."*

"Yes," his answer came, *"Roberto in the Wastelands."*

"Come on, Erob. It's four days' flight, he won't even be there yet."

"True, but most die within two days of arriving. We can't delay forever."

"I have to help this girl. I can't let her die."

Erob melded again. "If you can't come soon, I'll have to leave without you."

"Erob, please, I'm a healer. This is my duty."

"And what of your duty to my rider?" Erob snorted. "I'll give you one day. If you're not done by midnight tomorrow, I'm going without you."

§

Gret sheathed her sword and left the practice cavern. Adelina was leaning against the tunnel wall, her eyes red. "Hi, Adelina."

"Erob wants to talk to you," Adelina said, pushing off the wall.

"I've never melded with any dragons in the royal bloodline," Gret replied. "Why would Erob want to talk to me?"

Adelina shrugged. "There's only one way to find out. He's on the ledge outside the mess cavern."

Gret put an arm around Adelina's shoulders. "Anything I can do for you?"

"I'm all right." Adelina's voice was brittle. "It's not the worst thing that's happened to me." She strode off.

That was true, but having your brother banished and sentenced to die must be tough.

The mess cavern was deserted, and Erob was the only dragon on the ledge. His large yellow eyes gleamed at Gret as she touched his head.

"Gret, thank you for coming." His voice rumbled through her mind. "With Roberto gone, someone must protect the Queen's Rider. Are you up for this task?"

"Of course, but why me?"

"I can trust you. Ezaara trusts you. You're fast with a sword and nimble on your feet, and you're young—you can keep vigil overnight without dozing off." He showed her a vision of a secret alcove near Ezaara's cavern. *"Hide here. Be vigilant. There are some at Dragons' Hold who would do Ezaara harm."*

"I'll be vigilant. I owe it to my queen and Ezaara." Gret's heart swelled with pride. A royal dragon, no less, respected her swordsmanship.

"Thank you." Erob flapped his wings, sending the stray hair on Gret's forehead wafting in the breeze, then he was airborne.

Gret flicked her braid over her shoulder. Should she trust Erob? If Roberto was really a traitor, couldn't his dragon be traitorous too? She shook her head. No, Erob would never betray his mother, Zaarusha, and the realm. And despite what everyone was saying, neither would Roberto. Something strange was going on.

After careful inspection, she found the hidden alcove in the corridor opposite the door to Ezaara's cavern. Deep in shadow, a lip of rock obscured the entrance. She hid inside, starting her vigil.

Hours later, after midnight but still a while before dawn—the worst part of night watch—Gret stretched wearily, easing a kink in her neck. It was cramped in here. She didn't dare stamp, and there wasn't room to walk. She blinked and shifted her weight from foot to foot. So much for Erob's vigilance of the young.

A faint scrape on rock jerked Gret awake. There it was again. Moving her weight forward, she placed her eye against a spy hole. Someone was around the corner. Gret eased her knife from its sheath. Heart pounding, she waited.

A shadow flickered. Simeon crept down the tunnel, glancing furtively over his shoulder.

She should have known. That shrotty weasel had forced himself upon her best friend, Trixia, but no one had believed her—not with Simeon's parents, the highly-esteemed council masters, accounting for his whereabouts. Everybody had assumed Trixia's betrothed, Donal, had fathered the littling. Fleur and Bruno had insisted that Trixia be banished for tainting their son's name, but Lars had sent Trixia and Donal both back to Montanara. Trixia had lost her lifelong dream of becoming a dragon rider.

That rat—no, that tick on the backside of a rat—was nearly at Ezaara's door.

Simeon peered through Ezaara's keyhole.

Now was her chance. Gret slipped out of the alcove. Approaching Simeon from behind, she grabbed his hair in her fist, and held her knife to his neck. "This stops right here, rat."

Simeon froze.

"Stand up. Slowly." She gripped his hair, keeping her knife at his throat, and marched him toward Lars' chamber.

§

Lydia had been asleep for hours, but Lars hadn't touched his pillow. Pacing in front of the fire, he rubbed his shoulder, trying to ease a stubborn knot. It was crazy, he'd trusted Roberto, but now he'd admitted he was a traitor. It felt wrong. Everything was off. But he was already gone to the Wastelands.

And Tonio was like a dog, yapping at his heels, determined to believe Roberto was evil. What if Tonio was wrong? There wasn't anyone else with Roberto's skills. Who would now test their imprinting bonds? Who would now ensure dragon riders were trained to withstand tharuk mind-benders?

There was scuffling outside his door. Lars strode over and flung it open.

Gret was outside, her knife at Simeon's throat. Eyes shining in the torchlight, she announced, "I've brought you a traitor."

Another one?

A trickle of blood rolled down Simeon's neck.

"Gret, stop! What are you doing?"

"I caught Simeon sneaking up to the Queen's Rider's cavern." Gret kept her knife at Simeon's throat.

"Come in, both of you." Lars waved his hand. "Down with the knife, Gret." He turned to Simeon. "It's the middle of the night. What were you doing near the Queen's Rider's cavern?"

Simeon's voice was smooth. "Master Lars, I was concerned for the Queen's Rider's health. There's talk that a rogue dragon wanted to burn her. I had a nightmare that she'd died, so I wanted to reassure myself that she was all right."

Gret snorted.

Lars had heard too many rumors to believe everything Simeon said. He turned to Gret. "Your opinion?"

"Like I said, he was sneaking around. It's not the first time he's wanted to harm—"

"I was only looking through the keyhole," Simeon interrupted, "to make sure she wasn't harmed."

"Liar. You were figuring out how to sneak in," Gret snapped, eyes fiery.

Simeon rubbed the scratch on his neck.

"Gret," asked Lars, "what did you actually see?"

"Ah, I—" She scuffed her boot on the stone floor. "He was acting sneaky, skulking along the corridors and peering through the keyhole—"

"And you?" barked Simeon. "Hiding in the shadows of the Queen's Rider's corridor, late at night? What were you doing?"

"Waiting for you," Gret snapped. "You're more trouble than a rat's nest."

Lars' instincts aligned with Gret's, but he had to have proof. "Simeon," Lars said, thinking fast, "turn out your pockets." Hopefully they could pin something on him this time.

Only healing salve. Not a weapon on him. That made sense, he was a healer's son. But something about this was wrong. If his parents weren't dragon masters, he wouldn't have believed him—about Trixia, or tonight.

Lars ran a hand through his hair. "Simeon, this is a warning. If you're caught near the Queen's Rider's cavern alone again at night, you will face trial and possible banishment. This is not your first warning."

That business with Trixia had never been resolved to Lars' satisfaction, but with two council members vouching for Simeon, there hadn't been much he could do. "Simeon, go straight to your quarters. Gret, please stay a moment."

Lars waited until Simeon left, and shut the door. He turned to Gret, whose fists were balled tightly against her sides. "Gret, I know your intentions are good, but you can't hold people at knife point. You can be aware and alert. You can keep an eye out. But you cannot draw weapons because someone is looking through a keyhole. No matter how much you dislike him. No matter how angry you are at him. Understood?" He sighed. "Tomorrow, report to the kitchens for duty. I can't have you injuring Simeon and going unpunished—no matter how slight his injury was."

Gret's shoulders slumped. The skin under her eyes was dark with weariness. "Yes, Master Lars."

"Now," he said, placing a hand on her shoulder, "go back to bed. You look like you need some sleep."

HEALING CALLS

It was late and Septimor still hadn't arrived. Ezaara paced between her cavern and the queen's den—waiting, doing nothing, while the blue guards were taking Roberto closer to the Wastelands. She couldn't even prepare for the trip with Adelina sitting on her bed. "Are you sure that's the right remedy?" Ezaara asked.

"Absolutely sure. I'm glad you remembered seeing these in Fleur's alcove." Adelina placed a vial of yellow granules back into the fleece-lined box. "Will you relax?" she said. "All that pacing is wearing me out."

Ezaara slumped in a chair, jiggling her leg.

"Quit that wiggling too." Adelina sighed. "All right, I'm sorry for snapping at you. It was Roberto's decision to banish himself, not yours. Did you realize what you were doing when you gave him this?" She fished a green satin ribbon out of her pocket.

Ezaara gasped. "That's mine. I gave it to Roberto the day Zaarusha flew a loop."

"I know. I put them in your hair, although I wouldn't have, if I'd known this would happen."

"What?"

"You still don't get it!" Fists on her knees, Adelina leaned forward in her seat. "By accepting your ribbon, Roberto vowed to become your protector until he dies."

"What?"

"You already said that." She rolled her eyes. "Ribbon gifting is tradition. Look, I don't want to be angry with you. I've been thinking about it. Roberto would've done the same for me. In fact, he probably would've done the same for you without this." She tossed the length of green satin at Ezaara.

The ribbon unfurled in the air, falling in a tangle in Ezaara's lap. "I didn't ask anything of Roberto. Zaarusha told me to give it to him."

"You should never underestimate a dragon, especially our queen."

Zaarusha had engineered Roberto to be her protector and had then allowed him to be shipped off? He'd been too convincing for his own good. Ezaara wound the ribbon around her finger, the smooth satin soothing her skin. She wound it onto the fingers of her other hand, and then jumped out of her chair and paced to the den and back. "*When* are they going to get here?"

"Why are you so uptight?" Adelina frowned, then her eyes flew wide. "Oh. This is about my brother, isn't it?"

Ezaara opened her mouth, but before she could protest, there was a whump in Zaarusha's den.

"Septimor's finally here!" Ezaara ran to the den, Adelina on her heels.

Septimor's wings were limp by his sides. *"I think she's unconscious from limplock and blood loss."* He craned his neck toward the girl slumped in one of his saddlebags.

"You look exhausted," Ezaara said.

"I'll hunt soon." Septimor glanced around. *"Where's Master Roberto?"*

"Banished." Ezaara was careful to mind-meld, so Adelina wouldn't get upset.

Septimor's eye ridges flew up. *"Whatever for? He's one of our best."* He lowered himself so they could lift the girl out of the saddlebag.

She was about thirteen and as pale as goat's cheese, with a deep bloody gash on her forearm and one of her little fingers hanging off by a scrap of flesh. Her hands were cold, fingers stiff and curled, but her forehead was burning.

"Her name is Leah. Take care of her, Ezaara. I have to get back to Seppi—he's still fighting tharuks." The blue dragon flapped his wings and left.

They carried Leah to Ezaara's bed.

"What's wrong with her hands?" Ezaara asked, trying to pry her fingers open. "I've never seen anything like it. And her breathing's shallow too."

"That's limplock. It sticks to your nerves, slowly paralyzing you." Adelina unlaced the girl's boots. "Roberto taught me about tharuk poisons when I was small. Look." She pointed to the girl's toes. Leah's feet were curled in and her legs were spasming. "I hope we're not too late."

"She needs a full vial of the remedy, sprinkled on her tongue, a little at a time." Adelina grimaced. "It'll be tricky because she's unconscious."

"No problem." Ezaara pushed Leah's lip against her tooth, making Leah automatically drop her jaw. "You give her that, while I staunch the bleeding."

"Good trick." Adelina sprinkled a few grains onto Leah's tongue.

Ezaara made a tourniquet on Leah's upper arm, out of a shirt and her knife, to slow the blood supply to her forearm. The bleeding eased. She examined the gash. Deep, but it could be stitched, and with the help of piaua … She dribbled the pale green juice into the ripped flesh, to heal the deepest layers. The girl twitched and groaned. The flesh slowly knitted together, but it could use some help. Ezaara threaded her needle with squirrel gut, then stitched the wound while Adelina held the edges together. Then she rubbed more piaua along the scar.

"Now we've got to deal with her finger." Ezaara exhaled forcefully. Although this wasn't a job she relished, she had no choice. The finger was already pale and bloodless. She had no way of stitching bones and nerves back together.

Ezaara went out to the den and called, *"Zaarusha?"*

"Coming. Septimor told me you have a limplocked girl here." The queen flew down to the ledge. *"How's she doing?"*

"Not good. I have to amputate her finger. Could you please heat my knife?"

"Hold it out." Zaarusha's grim tone reflected how Ezaara felt. The queen heated the blade until it glowed.

Ezaara dashed back into her cavern. She swallowed. "Adelina, c-could you help me with this?"

Adelina's eyes were grave as she held Leah's hand still upon a clean cloth on the bedside table. "We're ready."

It wasn't *physically* hard to cut off the flimsy flap of skin holding the girl's finger in place—yet it was the hardest job Ezaara had ever done. It felt like slicing off hope. Damning someone to a bleak future.

It felt like losing Roberto all over again.

As she held the hot knife against the stump of Leah's finger to cauterize it, Leah, still unconscious, whimpered. Ezaara tried not to breathe in the stench of heated flesh. Hot tears ran down her face. Adelina was crying too.

Ezaara dribbled piaua juice onto the cauterized stump, and then bandaged Leah's finger. With Adelina's help, she slowly released the tourniquet.

"She'll need feverweed tea," Adelina whispered, sloshing water into a mug and crumbling feverweed into it. She passed the mug to Ezaara and sprinkled more anti-limplock granules on Leah's tongue. "We're not over the pass yet."

Exhaling violently, Ezaara paced to the den, holding out the cup to Zaarusha. *"Not too hot."*

Zaarusha leaned in and shot a tiny flame at the cup. *"There, that should be warm now. You're doing a good job, Ezaara."*

Then why did she feel so hollow?

When Ezaara came back into her cavern, Adelina was sponging Leah's forehead. "She's burning up."

"This should help."

They propped Leah's head up and took turns dribbling tea into her mouth. She swallowed reflexively. After half an hour, her fever had cooled a little. Ezaara gave her more antidote, while Adelina and Zaarusha made more tea.

"Tell me more about limplock and numlock," Ezaara asked while they waited.

Adelina settled in a chair. "Numlock stops your emotions and reasoning and makes people seem slow and dull."

"How does it feel? Do you know anyone who has had it?"

"Like you're dead inside." Adelina's eyes slid away. "Anyway, limplock is different. It gradually paralyzes you, starting with your hands and feet and working its way through your body until you stop breathing." She dribbled tea into Leah's mouth. "If the dose had been stronger, she would've been dead already. We're lucky Fleur had the antidote in her alcove."

§

Ezaara awoke to whimpering. Leah was having another nightmare. Only it wasn't yet night—the sun was setting outside. They'd been up tending her all of last night and only dropped off this afternoon, when her fever had broken.

Adelina raised her head from the pallet next to Ezaara's.

"I'll go," Ezaara croaked. "Get some more sleep." She scrambled from her makeshift bed into a chair at the bedside.

Leah was shivering again. Ezaara pulled the quilt up and grabbed some sleeping furs from a chest, piling them on top of her. Adelina had said that the antidote could make Leah tremble and vomit. So far, they'd only had trembling, but Ezaara had a supply of pails near the bed, just in case. She held Leah's hand and stroked her forehead. Touch seemed to soothe her.

Erob melded. *"How's the girl?"*

"Not conscious yet. I can't leave her with Adelina until she wakes."

"I'm going hunting. It may be days before I can eat again." Erob hesitated. *"Ezaara, whether you can come or not, I'm leaving in a few hours."*

Ezaara twisted a button on her jerkin. *"Erob, please ..."*

"I can't keep delaying. Neither of us want to find Roberto dead."

"But if he's injured, I can help heal him."

"Not if you're here, you can't."

All the people she loved were slipping, like salt, through her fingers: Roberto was gone; she had no idea where Ma, Tomaaz or Pa were; and when Leah was well enough, she'd be running out on Zaarusha. How had it come to this? A tear slipped down Ezaara's cheek. Why was life full of choices that hurt?

"I know he cares about you."

Ezaara froze.

Adelina was awake, watching her.

"I—"

"I know you care about him too," Adelina said, "but I don't think I can look after Leah properly if she's unconscious. I mean, what do I do if she never wakes up?"

"No one's asking you to."

"I know. I also know Erob well. I'm guessing he'll be leaving soon. You've been stretched as tight as a bowstring since yesterday. You want to go with him, don't you?"

Ezaara nodded. Leah was peaceful now, sleeping with a trace of a smile.

Adelina gestured toward her. "Let's hope she rouses. In the meantime, I'll visit the mess room and get some food. Where have you been keeping your supplies?"

Ezaara's cheeks burned. "In Roberto's cavern, so I can load them into Erob's saddlebags."

"Logical. I'll strap his saddlebags on him and start loading." Adelina hugged her. "I'm so glad you're going. I've been crazy with worry about him."

"How do you hide your anxiety so well?"

"You mean like this?" Adelina flashed her a sparkling smile. "I've had years of practice." Face grim, she strode out the door.

§

A scream woke Ezaara. Leah, again. Her neck hurt—she'd dozed off in her chair.

Sitting up in bed, Leah was wide-eyed. "Who are you? Where am I?"

"It's all right." Adelina put an arm around her. "You're with friends, safe at Dragons' Hold."

Ezaara patted Leah's hand. "You've been sick, but we're helping you." The torches had burned low. How late was it? Had she already missed Erob?

"Ezaara, I'll take care of Leah. Zens and his tharuks ruined my family, and I swore I'd always help any victim." Adelina gestured to the door, her eyes full of meaning. "Go. Give him my love."

A jolt ran through Ezaara.

She hugged Adelina. "Thank you." She fastened her sword at her hip. Snatching up her healer's pouch and the archer's cloak Roberto had given her, Ezaara ran out the door.

"Erob, I'm ready!" she cried.

"Good, I'll be back at my den shortly."

A surge of energy ran through her. They were finally leaving.

The tunnels were dim, torches low, as Ezaara raced toward Roberto's cavern, glad to be burning off some energy after caring for Leah for a night and a day. Jaevin's poisoning, her being accused and Roberto's banishment made no sense, but they were all connected. If only she could fit the pieces together, she'd be able—

A figure stepped out of the shadows. Simeon's teeth flashed in a grin. "You seem to be in a hurry, My *Honored* Queen's Rider. Going somewhere?" His eyes slid over her body, stopping on her face.

"Not really, I've just been busy and need exercise."

"So late? With such a warm cloak?" He approached her.

The blizzard in the south-west was still raging. She'd need the cloak as she traveled. Ezaara stepped back. "It's cold out."

He moved closer. Ezaara backed away. Her foot hit the wall behind her. Simeon crowded her, his body only a hand's breadth from hers. "I can keep you warm." He ripped her cloak off, tossing it aside.

Ezaara snatched her sword. Before she could raise it, Simeon grabbed her wrist, squeezing. Gods, his grip was an iron vice. Her bones crunched and she let go, sword clattering onto the rock floor.

Simeon slammed her hands above her and thrust his knee against her groin, his body pinning her against the wall.

Ezaara bucked and twisted. It was no use.

His eyes slid to her breasts. Trapping both her hands with one of his, he ripped a button off her jerkin, yanking the fabric open.

His breath was hot, harsh in her ears. "You're mine," he growled. "No running off to rescue him. He won't want you once I've had you."

Ezaara opened her mouth to scream, but Simeon slammed his hand against it, knocking her head on the rock wall. She bit down, hard. Grabbing his flesh between her teeth, she ripped.

His hand slid out of her teeth, smacking into her head as he lurched backwards. Ezaara shoved him, and Simeon sprawled on the rock. Snatching up her sword, she held the tip at his chest.

Gret ran around the corner. In a flash, Gret had Simeon on his feet, her blade at his throat and his arm twisted up behind his back. "Caught in the act, you filthy rat!"

Simeon hung his head. "I'm sorry, Ezaara. I truly am. I shouldn't have—"

"Shut up!" Gret snapped, then addressed Ezaara. "Let's get him to Lars. With two witnesses …" Her eyes took in Ezaara, picking up her cloak, sheathing her sword. "You're going, aren't you?"

"Ezaara! Where are you?" Erob. It was time.

Ezaara nodded.

"But Lars won't believe me without you to back me up. He's always asking for proof. Please," Gret pleaded.

Questions would turn into a trial, and a trial wouldn't happen now, in the middle of the night. She didn't have time. Roberto could be dying, right now.

"Ezaara."

"Thank you, Gret, but I'm sorry."

As Ezaara raced to Erob, Simeon's gloating echoed down the deserted tunnel. "Once again, little Gret, it's your *pathetic biased* word against mine."

THE WASTELANDS

Tangerine sand, as bright as the orange on Ana's scarves, undulated in endless rippled hillocks. Ezaara's nostrils burned, just from breathing. Stinging sand grains whipped into her eyes, and sweat slicked her back. She'd always imagined the Wastelands as bleak, but this cruel land was also breathtaking. The rolling hills were etched with mysterious patterns from the wind's fingertips, and stretched so far they made her eyes ache.

"They're called dunes," said Erob, *"those hills."*

"It's hopeless, Erob. How will we ever find him?"

"Keep mind sweeping. Roberto's got to be somewhere."

"It's been two days. I haven't sensed a thing, except you. Apart from those tents near that oasis and a few Robandi tribes, the only thing we've seen is sand."

"Don't give up. We have to find him."

Hopefully alive. Although the longer they searched, the less likely that was. Ezaara gripped Erob's spinal ridge with tired fingers. Her throat ached and eyes stung—and it wasn't from the sand.

§

The heat pressed against Roberto, like a scratchy blanket. Despite the undershirt wrapped around his head and mouth, his throat rasped. He shook his waterskin. Not a drop left—he'd drained the last trickle hours ago. It was a miracle the paltry contents had lasted that long.

He dragged his heavy legs through the endless shifting sand, longing for the cool kiss of night—although dark brought its own challenges. Last night had been so cold, he'd been wracked with shivers by the time the sun had glared over the dunes, but right now, that would be better than being scorched alive. Ezaara's awful vision flashed through his mind: being burned alive by dragon flame. This furnace was burning his lungs—he was roasting alive, inside and out.

Shards! He had to pee.

Hope spurted inside him. Something to drink. By the Egg, had it really come to this?

He peed into the waterskin. Only a dribble, but it burned and his pee was so dark it was the color of this cursed sand. Shrugging, Roberto took a sniff, wrinkling his nose. Foul and stinking, but it was liquid. It could keep him alive. He raised the waterskin.

No, he couldn't drink it. Dropping the skin, he staggered toward the next dune. If only he could fly on Erob's back, traversing the desert by air. He blinked. Erob wasn't here, but something was clinking over the next dune.

His brain was so foggy, he nearly rushed straight up the sand. No! Caution. He dropped to his belly and crawled until he crested the hill. Robandi. Two feuding tribes. If he read the battle right, red headdresses were pitted against white.

A man ran a saber through the stomach of another, blood turning the amber sand to deep red. The man whirled, scarlet drops flying from his blade and slashed an arm, a chest, a face. Men, only men. Fierce, desperate, sabers flashing in the sun, until they were stained so red, they were too dull to flash. No cries, no yells or moans marked this battle. Feet muffled by sand, they fought with precision and uncanny silence, as if they were afraid of being heard. Only grunts and clashing blades scarred the stifling air, the strange silence as oppressive as the heat.

A man fell, throat slashed, his blood gurgling as his eyes turned lifeless.

Still on his belly, Roberto retreated down the dune, leaving a deep furrow. Curse this sand. He'd be easy to track. Scrambling to his feet, he turned to flee—and came face to face with two men with red headdresses whose white clothes were splattered with blood.

A grin flashed white in a dark weathered face. An instant later, a bloody saber was at Roberto's neck, its tip sharp against his skin.

He was their enemy. No sudden moves. Roberto edged his hand down his leg toward the blade hidden in his boot.

The pressure of the saber on his neck increased.

The other man flicked his sword across Roberto's fingers. Blood welled up across his stinging knuckles.

In a hiss of sand behind him, a shower of particles tumbled down the slope. Orange-clad camel riders were racing down the dune.

Shock registered on his captors' faces. One lunged at Roberto, sword slashing.

The pain was instant, blooming across his gut like a jellyfish unfurling thousands of stingers. Clutching his torso, he looked down. His clothes were sliced straight through, his guts spilling out of his broken flesh. He sunk to the sand, grasping at the edges of the wound, trying to hold the contents of his stomach together.

His gut rippled with fire. Lights ricocheted through his head. It was no use. In this blasted sun, his insides would dry out and disintegrate, as fragile as the crust of paper round the rim of a rice pot.

"Ezaara!" He'd never see her again.

ZAARUSHA

Zaarusha was wroth. That fanged Ezaara had risked the kingdom for infatuation. That silly volatile new rider. She roared, sending a sprinkling of shale tumbling down the mountainside. Undignified and irresponsible behavior for a queen, but she didn't care. Her rider was gone.

Gone. After eighteen years of waiting.

After loss and despair and deceit. Right when Zens was marshaling his armies.

Liesar alighted on the lip of Zaarusha's den and bowed her silver neck, her snout nearly scraping the ground.

"The Queen's Rider is gone." Zaarusha knew the wave of despair she'd sent to Liesar would have left a lesser dragon cowering. But that's why she'd summoned Liesar. Not Ajeuria the Sly or Antonika the Stealthy, but Liesar the Strong. Liesar who'd arrived home last night with a sick girl from Lush Valley.

"I know," was Liesar's reply. *"Erob melded with me as I was flying here and he was going south."*

"Erob told you, but deceived his own mother!" Zaarusha snarled, blasting Liesar with a gust of fire.

Liesar stood solid, immovable, silver scales reflecting the flames. *"Yes, me. When you were enraged and would've killed Marlies, all those years ago, I ferried her away to Lush Valley to protect her lineage. I guessed correctly that your dragonet had passed his life force to her."*

"Don't remind me of your traitorous actions."

"Traitor or savior?" Liesar's turquoise eyes regarded Zaarusha. *"There are many facets to our actions, My Queen. My actions provided you with a Queen's Rider of exceptional capability, a rider as good as Anakisha herself."*

"A rider who has fled after her lover—a traitor!" Zaarusha snarled, bunching her legs to pounce.

Liesar bowed her head, now submissive. That was better, the way a subject should treat a queen.

"Shall we hunt them down and kill them?" Liesar asked. *"Roberto, Ezaara—and Erob too? Would that avenge your wroth? Would that appease My Queen?"*

Zaarusha froze.

"Or would you rather listen to reason?"

Motionless, Zaarusha watched Liesar, feeling the timbre of her mind as she relayed Erob's message.

"Tell My Queen and mother that I honor her and love her." A wave of love flooded Zaarusha's chest. That was Erob, loyal and true. *"Tell her Roberto is innocent, that he lied to save the Honored Queen's Rider, Ezaara, and that she fled to find him. There's a traitor at Dragons' Hold, but it's not Roberto or Ezaara. Someone is plotting to undo the realm. Someone who doesn't want Anakisha's prophecy to come true."*

As much as she hated to admit she was wrong, Erob's words rang true. *"Why should I listen to his message?"* Zaarusha scoffed, but the heat had gone out of her words. It was all bluster.

Liesar, now grinning, knew it too.

The queen changed her stance, airing her wings. *"Let's hunt down this traitor before they do any more damage."*

There was a rap at Ezaara's door and the pounding of hurrying feet in Ezaara's cavern.

Adelina burst into Zaarusha's den. "My Honored Queen, Master Jaevin is dead!"

SILENT ASSASSINS

Ezaara winced. *"No, Erob, we can't return without Roberto."*

"It's been days. We need more food," Erob insisted, flapping his wings, his shadow rippling over the wind-streaked orange below. *"Unless we find a food source here, we'll have to return to Naobia for supplies. We're no use to Roberto dead."*

"It'll take two days to fly to Naobia and back here. Anything could happen to Roberto in that time." Shards, they couldn't leave yet, not without him. Panic gnawed at Ezaara's gut. He'd die.

"Ezaara, don't despair. We have to eat. We're useless to him dead."

"And he's useless to us dead too!" she snapped.

Erob was silent, his slowing wingbeats speaking for him. Days of trawling the desert were wearing them down. They'd seen signs of skirmishes—ominous dark stains in the sand—and caravans of Robandi, but there'd been no sign of Roberto. What if he was hidden in a tent or a sandy grave?

"Sorry, I shouldn't be morose." She had to keep hoping. Roberto's face flashed to mind. His sardonic smile. His ebony eyes flashing as he laughed with Adelina. The way his arms flexed as he wielded his sword. The warmth of his torso as he adjusted her grip on her knife. His love—his mind-searing, heart-bursting, fire-in-her-veins love. He couldn't be gone. Mustn't be gone.

She sighed. *"All right, let's go back."*

Erob ascended to fly back to Naobia, the desert dropping far below them.

Ezaara stared out over the endless gut-wrenching orange, one last time.

There, what was that? Hidden over some distant dunes was a smudge. *"Look, Erob. Is that an oasis?"*

"I can't fly much longer without decent food." Despite his protests, Erob flew toward the blur of color nestled between orange dunes.

Their flight seemed to take forever.

"Yes!" A turquoise jewel was nestled in the sand, fringed by palms. *"Look, a lake, shade."* It was strange—all the other oases had been inhabited by Robandi tribes with their brightly-colored tents. *"You'd think an oasis this big would have people here."*

Erob didn't answer. His wingbeats were flagging and he was flying low. He banked and aimed for the lake edge.

"Unless we find food, we'll have to fill our waterskins and fly back over the desert and the Naobian Sea."

That vast ocean with its slate, lapis, cobalt and turquoise tones. She'd never expected the sea to be everchanging, writhing and seething far beneath them, whipping up white tips far out from the shore, sheltering enormous creatures that created dark blots, like ink stains, under the water. This life Zaarusha had given her was bursting with possibility. Except she didn't have Zaarusha anymore. She'd forsaken her dragon, her role and title.

And she didn't have Roberto. If she returned empty-handed, she'd have nothing.

"Let's rest and drink," melded Erob. *"It helps stave off dark thoughts."*

Ezaara stretched her mind out, reaching for Roberto. *"Roberto!"* Hundreds of times she'd tried mind sweeping, and hundreds of times there'd been nothing except the bite of windswept sand on her cheeks. Infusing every last scrap of her love into her message, she thrust out her mind again, *"Roberto."*

"E-zaa-ra …" Faint and foggy, but it was him.

"Roberto!"

Nothing.

"Roberto!"

Again, nothing.

Had she imagined it? Was she sun-struck? Going crazy?

"No, I heard it too." Erob thudded to the ground, and staggered, his snout hitting the sand and wings askew.

Ezaara slid to the sand. *"Are you all right?"*

"Need to drink." Dragging his tail, Erob crawled to the water.

"Wait!" Ezaara called out loud. *"It might be tainted. Maybe that's why no one's here."*

Erob sniffed it. *"Seems fine."* He submerged his snout.

Ezaara followed, scooping crystal water into her mouth. It was pure, like fresh rain on spring grass. It beat the stagnant water from their skins. *"Erob, Roberto must be near. We can't leave."*

"We can eat and drink here. Look." Erob waved his snout at heavy clusters of dates hanging from the palms.

Ezaara roamed over to the palms, accidentally disturbing a herd of goats dozing in the shade. *"Strange. Goats, but no people."*

"Maybe they're wild." As quick as a wink, Erob killed one and settled to feast.

They collected dates, Erob shaking the trees until the fruit fell down, and Ezaara gathering them into his saddlebags. She found an orange grove, the juicy fruit stinging her chapped lips as she wolfed it down. Why was this place deserted?

"Look, footprints." Ezaara pointed at the churned-up sand near one of the groves. *"Lots of them."*

"I noticed camel prints from the air. Someone else must've been hungry."

"Maybe Roberto was with them. Maybe they've just left with him …"

"Let's check."

They searched the perimeter of the lake, filling their water-skins. The whole time, Ezaara and Erob stretched their minds out to Roberto. There was no reply.

"We heard him," Erob melded. *"He must be here somewhere. Be patient."* He settled on the sand and she slid off.

Ezaara sank down, leaning against him. *"What if he's dead and that was his last cry? We've got to do something. To come this far …"* Her chest grew tight and she broke down, sobbing, burying her face in Erob's side.

§

A cool caress brushed Roberto's brow. A trickle of water slid down his throat. He swallowed, his gullet thick and clogged. A dull ache throbbed across his middle, laced with a filigree of dancing fire. Exquisite pain. Zens had taught him pain was exquisite and that there was an art to enduring it—Roberto had learned that the hard way.

His mind was slipping again. Faces flitted before him. Eyes, watching: Erob's golden ones, shining as they'd imprinted; Ezaara's sad green eyes when he'd been banished; Zens' giant yellow orbs, enticing him to cruelty, mocking him when he succeeded.

He *was* a mockery. He'd thought he could make a difference to Dragons' Realm, right his father's wrongs and help send Zens back through the world gate. But instead, here he was, banished and dying.

A gentle burble floated through his mind, like the babble of a stream, an accompaniment to the waves of fire rippling across his belly. If he lay perfectly still, would the water put the fire out? Only there was no water here in the desert, in the dark.

§

"Ezaara."

Erob's sharpness woke Ezaara. Eyes gritty with sand, she rubbed them.

Then rubbed them again. This wasn't a nightmare. They were surrounded. Warriors were thrusting a nest of sabers at her throat and Erob's belly.

A tall warrior paced around the dragon, her kohl-rimmed eyes sizing him up. Ezaara followed her with her gaze, helpless. No wonder this oasis had been deserted. These warriors infested it.

"What are you doing here?" The woman's voice was soft, sibilant, like the hissing of wind on sand.

"Ah, Ezaara," melded Erob, *"I know these people. You'd better be polite."*

That sounded dire. Were they Robandi? Their faces and hands were sun-darkened like Robandi, but they were dressed differently—clad in gauzy headdresses, breeches and shirts the same orange as the sand. "We were refreshing ourselves at these beautiful waters." Ezaara inclined her head a fraction, as far as she could without being stabbed. "We also partook of your delicious fruit. Um, and a goat. Thank you for your hospitality." Shards, what was she supposed to say?

The woman hissed, "Seize the scorpion with the flattering tongue and confine her lizard." Swords flicked from her to Erob. Strong arms grasped Ezaara, removing her weapons in a heartbeat. "Now we'll find out what you really want," she whispered.

"We're seeking a friend," Ezaara said. "He may be injured. Dark hair, dark skin, black eyes."

Snorting, the woman whispered again. "Convenient, but not believable. That could be any Robandi. Take them below."

Below?

The warriors moved with lithe elegance and strength. They were women—all forty of them. They marched Ezaara and Erob at sword point to a grove of trees at the far end of the lake. Among the palms was a giant amber boulder with trees growing over it. A latticework of roots hung over the rock's overhang, enveloping it like a spider's web. Two figures stepped out from the overhang, their orange-and-brown-splotched clothing camouflaging them until they moved. They pulled aside some roots and the guards marched Ezaara down a tunnel leading underground.

"What about Erob?" she asked.

"He will be well-tended," a guard answered in a hushed tone.

So, the tall warrior didn't have a speech defect. All of these women whispered.

"Of course they do," melded Erob. *"They're the Sathiri, the Wastelands' infamous silent assassins. Whatever you do, don't mention men, especially not Roberto."*

§

Kohl-rimmed deep-brown eyes studied Roberto. The woman's skin was darker than his, the shade of rich pecans. Hawk-nosed, her face was a mask of tranquility. She was Robandi—and he was alive. High above her was a vaulted ceiling of amber rock. Still in the Wastelands, then. Fangs, his gut ached, a deep sharp throb that sent sparks of pain skittering across his skin whenever he thought of moving.

The woman lifted a cool compress to his brow, murmuring in Naobian, "Lie still. Rest."

As if he could go anywhere. Gods, he probably couldn't even sit up. More fire, pain. "Who—" His voice came out in a broken croak.

"Ssh. Let me tell you."

Roberto had heard similar accents from the Robandi traders in the Naobian markets. She held a cup of sweet cool water to his lips and he swallowed. Bliss. A faint smile traced her lips and she stood, moving with strength and calculated economy. Clothed in orange breeches, headdress and a loose shirt, a saber hung at her hip. A warrior, then.

Who was she and where were they? That babbling was still here. Slowly, Roberto turned his head, not wanting to risk stabbing gut pain. A spring was trickling out of the rock into a pool, feeding an underground stream. He hadn't dreamed the water. It was real.

"Robandi Duo slit your gut and left you to desiccate in the desert. The fools didn't recognize you were Naobian or a *dracha ryter*. How do you call this in your tongue?"

So, she knew what rider's garb looked like. "Dragon rider." Still croaky, but his words were now recognizable.

"Ah, yes, those magnificent beasts, so fierce in combat." A feral flash of teeth.

And she had an interest in dragons.

"Your road to healing will not be fast, but at least your fever has broken. Luckily, we found you and brought you here to the Retreat of the Silent Assassins." Fire stirred in the depths of her dark eyes.

The band of women, renowned for their fighting prowess, who sat in judgment over feuding Robandi tribes. Their skills were many. Ruthless, most trained from the age of seven, learning the spiritual and fighting arts. "And you are the Prophetess of the Robandi Desert?"

A nod.

An assassin prophetess. He coughed, his throat dry, gritting his teeth against the ache in his stomach. If he survived this, he'd never take coughing or laughing for granted again.

"Rest. It is your first time waking in hours. Do not strain yourself." She clicked her fingers, and a young girl of about thirteen approached his bedside.

There were other sounds, hidden by the spring: faint rustling, the chink of someone working. He lifted his head, stifling a groan of agony. Girls and women were working nearby, lit by shafts of sunlight angling through the ceiling. By the Egg, his guts. He'd never move again.

The prophetess frowned, voice stern. "Lie still. You must not rip the stitches."

The young girl lifted the cup to his lips, her fingers twisted and scarred.

"Little and often," the woman said to the girl. Then to Roberto, "Underestimate us at your peril. Every girl here is trained to kill." She slipped the knife out of his discarded boots, and stalked away.

There must've been something in the liquid he'd sipped, because soon Roberto was dreaming again. He hung in a dark void dotted with stars, body endlessly spinning. No matter how hard he tried, he couldn't move. Everything was numb—mind, body and emotions. Then he heard her.

"*Roberto,*" she called across time and space, her bright colors flashing through him. "*Roberto!*" Ezaara—the woman he loved. She'd brought vibrancy and meaning to his life, making him strive to be better.

He tried to answer, but his lips wouldn't move and his limbs were rubbery. He struggled against the darkness dragging his body down, down, spinning … He thrust her name outwards, "*E-zaa-ra,*" then he was gone, suspended in the void again.

§

Ashewar turned her head from the sleeping Naobian as footfalls approached. "Izoldia, have you secured that *dracha*?"

"The *dracha* escaped, my highly-esteemed Beloved One." Izoldia's bow was so low her nose nearly scraped the floor. "But it'll be back for food."

Her darling sycophant had hoped she wouldn't ask. "Trap the *dracha*. Or I'll be tossing your hide to the rust vipers."

"Yes, my Revered Prophetess."

Ashewar turned back to the Naobian. *Sathir* was strong in him. She sensed a ruthless discipline in his spirit, or perhaps it was a disciplined ruthlessness, a darkness. He would serve her purpose well. With this core of steel, his seed would provide good lineage. She surveyed the geography of his face: hollows under defined cheekbones, high brow, strong chin, dark lashes. It was a shame she wouldn't get to lie with him herself, but she had no need of more twisted progeny. Her loins had produced only bitterness: boys to be culled at birth and one daughter of inferior quality.

She needed good fruit. Strong female fruit, to be raised to carry on the legacy of the *Sathiri*. She'd selected ten protégés for the honor—women experienced in cajoling the seed from unwilling men. And when they were done with him, he would die. Just as he'd been about to die when they'd found him.

Izoldia appraised the male. "Good choice, Revered Prophetess. You show such excellent wisdom and foresight. He will give us many strong daughters."

"He will indeed. It's rare to find such a specimen, a man in his prime, on our doorstep. This is a good omen." She hesitated. Izoldia was tough, cruel at times, but that would serve them well: if the others begot boys, Izoldia would have no hesitation in feeding their bodies to the carrion birds. "Would you like to oversee the process?"

Izoldia's grin was fierce. "Thank you, Revered Prophetess. I'll make sure he complies and kill him swiftly afterward."

§

Roberto awoke with a start. "How long have I slept?"

"A day," murmured the girl, bunching her twisted fingers in fists and hiding them in her sleeves.

"Was that a sleeping draught? That sweetness?"

"It promotes sleep and healing."

His head was groggy, limbs still dead, but he was awake and his mind was his own. He'd dreamed of Ezaara, remembering the trial in horrible detail: Ezaara had believed him. Believed he'd poisoned Jaevin. By the Egg, that hurt—he'd only lied to save her. But even worse was the bleak expression on Adelina's face: eyes hollow, face drained of hope. He knew that look. He'd been beside Adelina when Ma had died from injuries inflicted by Pa.

In saving Ezaara, he'd abandoned his sister.

"You must get strong and heal quickly." The girl spoke quietly, her eyes slipping away.

Something in her glance sparked a memory: while he'd been dreaming, he'd heard Ashewar discussing him and harvesting some sort of fruit. What had it been?

Gods, his seed—they wanted to force him to give up his seed. Horror engulfed him.

When the girl offered him the sleeping draught again, he drank readily, falling back into the dark void.

Imprisoned

Guards marched Ezaara before the same imposing woman with kohl-lined eyes, now sitting on an ornately-carved throne. A prickle of dread ran down Ezaara's back. Every carving on her throne was of a woman killing a man.

"Your name?" the woman whispered, torchlight glinting off three diamond studs in her beaked nose.

"Ezaara of Dragons' Hold." She didn't belong there anymore, nor in Lush Valley—she was an outcast from the only homes she'd ever known.

"So, you are the new Queen's Rider, but where is your queen?" Even whispering, this woman was haughty.

The woman had heard of her, but Ezaara had never heard of these silent assassins. Not in Lush Valley. Nor at Dragons' Hold. "I have no queen," Ezaara mumbled, staring at the floor.

"Without a *dracha*, you are not much use. Unless you can fight?" The woman clicked her fingers and her assistants lunged, swords aiming for Ezaara.

She ducked, instinctively thrusting her arms up to block— but their blows never came.

"With training, you might amount to something," the woman hissed. "Izoldia, take her to the dungeon near the training room."

With a sneer at Ezaara, a towering barrel-chested assassin squeezed her arm.

"But I have to—"

"Silence," the burly Izoldia hissed. "You must not address Ashewar, Chief Prophetess of the Silent Assassins, until spoken to." She raked a dagger along Ezaara's arm. A line of red beads appeared. Ezaara sucked in her breath. That stung. Izoldia yanked her toward a narrow tunnel, more female guards in orange clothing trailing behind.

"Wait." The prophetess' eyes narrowed. "What is that pouch you wear?"

No, they couldn't take her healer's pouch. "My mother was a healer. I've learned some of her skills."

Ashewar snapped her fingers and a guard brought the pouch over for her to examine. "Hmm. Let her keep her pouch. She can heal cuts from training skirmishes. Now, take her away."

Roberto! Since they'd caught her, she'd forgotten to mind sweep. *"Roberto."* Nothing. But she wouldn't give up. He'd been alive a few hours ago. Why had Erob warned her off asking about him? *"Roberto."*

They went through a catacomb of tunnels and crossed a large cavern, where women were moving in an elaborate dance, swords and bodies flowing in time to some unseen rhythm. The guards paused at an adjoining cell, unlocking a door of iron bars.

Izoldia's fetid breath washed over her face. "If you're useless, Ashewar will give me the pleasure of killing you, but if you train hard, you'll become one of us." The guard shoved her, sending Ezaara sprawling onto a lumpy mattress against the rocky wall. The bars clanged shut.

Marching to the center of the cavern, the guards joined the dance.

So, this was their training area.

And hers. She had to survive until she could escape. Shrouded in shadows, her cell was barely longer than the mattress. Torches in the main cavern illuminated a spring near the front of her cell, flowing from the rock wall into a pool. Picking up a long-handled dipper, Ezaara drank. At least the water was good.

The women in the cavern moved in unison with supple fluidity, their robes swishing, feet slapping on rock and their sabers flashing. Their dance was beautiful, but their moves were deadly. Kill or be killed.

Ezaara stayed in the shadows, copying them. With no sword, she used the dipper, thrusting the handle at imaginary opponents. The assassins ignored her.

"Roberto."

"Don't give up," Erob melded. *"I think he's here. I've escaped, but I'll be back. Find him."*

"I'm imprisoned. I'll try." Ezaara kept at the killers' dance. Here, her right hand needed to be higher, her left leg more controlled. She danced. *"Roberto!"*

And danced.

An assassin's sword clattered onto the rock. A chain of echoes bounced around the chamber. Everyone froze. In a swish of orange gauze, Ashewar swept into the cavern, striking the offending assassin's face with her saber. The smack of metal against flesh echoed in through the cavern, ricocheting against the walls like a macabre drum beat. A bloody gash split the woman's cheek, but she retrieved her sword, slipping back into stance. Ashewar stalked out as the women continued, not missing a move.

Izoldia unlocked Ezaara. "You. Heal her." She stood over Ezaara while she rubbed healing salve onto the woman's wound, then marched her back to her cell. "If you don't shape up, you'll need more than healing salve when I'm through with you," she sneered.

Heart pounding, Ezaara slumped on the mattress, sweat beading her limbs and torso. It was hopeless. She lacked these assassins' control and finesse. She was weak from hunger. She'd never be good enough.

"Roberto." Would he ever answer?

Across the training hall was a girl in the shadows, as still as a marmot scenting a predator. She was watching Ezaara, clumsily holding a silver dish. Her hands were covered by the ends of her sleeves. Maybe the dish was hot. The girl approached and passed the dish through the bars.

Dates, oranges and a grainy cereal containing smoked meat—not hot food. Then why had the girl covered her hands? "Thank you," Ezaara said.

The girl held a finger to her lips—a finger that was scarred and bent out of shape.

Silent assassins.

Ezaara took the dish, catching the girl's hand in hers. The girl shrunk back with terrified eyes, but Ezaara didn't let go. She set the dish down and examined the girl's fingers. Her fingers had deep scarring, as if by fire, all ten digits bent and twisted. The scarring looked like burns, but burns wouldn't melt bones and twist them. Had she been born that way?

Ezaara examined the girl's fingers, one by one, then pressed the tips with her nail to see if she flinched. She had some nerve damage. It'd be difficult to work with such fingers. Ezaara reached into her healer's pouch—thank the Egg, the assassins hadn't taken it—and pulled out a vial of piaua. Quickly unscrewing the lid, Ezaara tipped a drop onto the girl's smallest finger and rubbed it over the scar tissue.

A soft hiss escaped the girl. Her scars slowly faded into healthy tissue and her finger straightened. Wonder lit her features. Ezaara picked up her piaua vial to work on the girl's next finger, but she shook her head. Her eyes flicked to the dancing assassins and she motioned to the dish.

Ezaara scooped the contents into her mouth, then handed the dish back.

"I am Ithsar," the girl whispered.

"Ezaara," she whispered back.

"To complete the training, you must sense *sathir*, the energy of all living things, interwoven in the rhythm of the dance." With that, Ithsar melted back across the room and out the exit.

What did that mean? *"Roberto,"* Ezaara melded. No reply. She picked up her dipper and started the dance moves again. What was *sathir*?

The next morning, when Ithsar brought food, Ezaara healed another finger. In return, Ithsar mentioned the first step in sensing *sathir:* feeling your heartbeat in every movement, while reaching out to sense what was around you.

It took Ezaara hundreds of attempts before she could move in time with her heartbeat.

"Roberto." Would he ever answer? Was he alive?

When Ithsar came again, Ezaara was prepared. A drop of piaua, rubbed along her next finger, with a whispered question. "There is a man I seek: dark hair, with olive-black eyes and a tiny crescent-shaped scar on his cheek. Do—"

Ithsar's eyes flashed recognition. She stiffened and turned away, curling her healed fingers into her palms. Izoldia was approaching.

Picking up the dish, Ezaara used Ithsar as a shield to bolt some of her food, then made a show of chewing and eating while the small assassin waited.

With a hand signal, Izoldia dismissed Ithsar.

Ezaara practiced the intricate dance of killing again. For every ten beats of her heart, she sent out Roberto's name. It was easier now, the rhythm of the exercises counted in heartbeats gave a fluidity to her movements, but she doubted she'd sensed whatever *sathir* was.

That night, Ezaara jolted awake. A lamp flickered in the shadows across the cavern. Someone was sneaking around the perimeter, toward her dungeon. She grabbed the water ladle and slipped into the back of the dungeon, waiting in the deepest shadow.

As the figure came closer, she let out a breath of relief. It was Ithsar. Ezaara dropped the ladle and rushed to the bars. "What is it?" she whispered, mindful of the cavern's echo chamber.

"Thika is unwell." Ithsar set down the lamp. She drew a wan-beige lizard with dark stripes from the folds of her robe, cradling him on the underside of her forearm. Its head was nestled in her palm and tail curled around her elbow.

"Tell me about Thika."

"My father gave me Thika when he was a tiny lizard, only this long." She waggled her little finger.

"What's wrong with him?"

"I don't know."

Ezaara touched his dry cool hide. "Is he usually warmer than this?"

"Only when he basks in the sun or snuggles me. His skin can be fiery-orange, like Robandi sand, but today he's pale. Usually, he scampers around, catching midges, or crawling all over me. I found him limp in a corner and he hasn't moved since." Ithsar's bottom lip wobbled. "Please, use the juice. Help him."

She couldn't tell her only friend in this forsaken place that it would be a shame to waste piaua on a lizard, not when Ithsar cared so deeply for him. Ezaara reached into her healer's pouch. "Piaua doesn't heal everything."

Ithsar forced Thika's mouth open and Ezaara shook two drops of piaua into his maw. "There, he should be better in a few moments."

Ithsar stroked his skin. Moments stretched and there was no change.

"Ithsar, this juice cures most illnesses and heals many wounds, however it has limits. It can't treat infection or poison."

"Thika has been poisoned?" Ithsar's hand flew to her mouth. "It must've been Izoldia." She thrust Thika through the bars at Ezaara. "I know where the poisons and remedies are kept. I'll be back." Ithsar left the lamp and dashed away.

Ezaara sat on her mattress, stroking Thika. The lizard blinked and slumped on her lap. His hide reminded her of Zaarusha's—soft and supple. She released a long sigh, missing the queen.

Ithsar returned with a sack of earthenware pots. "I haven't done my poison training yet, so I'm not sure what is what," she whispered, her gaze hopeful.

"Let's see." Ezaara put Thika on the mattress and eased the sack quietly through the bars. Opening the pots, she held them near the lamp, examining the contents and sniffing each one. "I've never seen any of these before," she whispered.

"Thika was my father's. He's the only thing I have left of him." Ithsar's eyes pooled with tears.

"Is your father …"

"Dead? Yes. Ashewar killed him once they'd finished using him to breed. I guess I was lucky. He lived longer than most. I was nearly four when he died."

Ezaara took a sharp breath. "That's why there are no men here?"

"Ashewar hates men. She murders them once they provide enough offspring. Any man who comes here—" Ithsar's eyes flew wide. "I'm sorry. I—"

Oh, gods. They were going to use Roberto for *breeding*, then *kill* him. Ezaara's body ran cold. A gulf opened inside her, wide enough to swallow her.

Ithsar froze, her dark eyes huge.

"T-tell me." Ezaara tried to force a smile, but couldn't.

"You love this man with the olive eyes?"

She nodded.

"It is the new way of the silent assassins—since Ashewar destroyed the former leader and purged the ranks of men. I'm sorry …"

Breeding and murder. She had to get out of here with Roberto. She'd need Ithsar's help. "Where is he?"

"Under sedation while he heals."

"What's wrong with him? Is he poisoned too?"

"No, Robandi slit his gut in the desert."

Shards! The rock walls spun, then closed in on her.

"He is healing well, but it will be slow. Gut wounds are." Ithsar's eyes dropped to Thika and a tear tracked down her cheek. "I have no one else." Her whisper was barely audible.

Ezaara counted her heartbeats. She couldn't panic. One step at a time. First heal the lizard. Then Ithsar's fingers. Then plan an escape and rescue Roberto. And find Erob. Closing her eyes, she breathed deeply.

When she opened them again, there was a faint red glow around Ithsar. Must be the lamp light. She picked up a pot, sniffing the acrid black paste inside. When she held the pot near Thika, a sickly green shimmer enveloped the lizard and the paste. It disappeared when she moved the pot away.

"I think that one is rust-viper venom," Ithsar murmured.

Setting it down, Ezaara took another pot which also had a faint sheen of greenish light around it. "Is this special clay? Is that why the pots glow?"

Ithsar's face lit up. Her whisper was full of suppressed excitement. "*Sathir*. You can see *sathir*."

"This light? *That's sathir*?"

Ithsar nodded. "If you can see it around the pots, that is a miracle. I can sense most people's *sathir* and Thika's. Some can sense animals and plants. Perhaps you have that gift." She held a pot near Thika. "Sathir shows the effect of things on one another. Here, what do you see?"

"Sickly green."

Another pot.

"A tiny thread of red."

"Red is Thika's *sathir* color. This substance strengthens his life energy, so it may heal him."

Rapidly, they tried the others, but only that one pot glowed red. Ezaara administered the liquid from the pot, a few drops at a time. Gradually, Thika perked up, his skin growing more orange with each dose. A wide ribbon of shining red connected him to Ithsar.

"His *sathir*, it's connected to you."

Ithsar grinned. "We are all connected to one another." The lamp sputtered. "I have to go." Ithsar shot to her feet and hid Thika in her clothing. Reaching through the bars, she gathered the pots up and shoved them in the sack. "Thank you."

"Wait." Ezaara grasped her hand and healed another two of her fingers.

"I must go. At dawn, the morning's training will commence." Ithsar rushed away, keeping to the perimeter of the cavern so her footfalls weren't amplified in the natural echo chamber.

Ezaara lay down, but before she could sleep, assassins filed into the cavern to perform their training rituals. She lay, watching through half-lidded eyes, seeing flashes of *sathir*. Maybe one day she'd be good enough to see more. But first, she had to escape and find Roberto.

Ithsar appeared, carrying a small dish of food, her hands hidden in the folds of her sleeves. "Give me the juice. I'll heal your friend and help you escape." Her murmur was barely detectable.

Shielding Ezaara from view with her body, she held out her hand for the vial.

Five fingers healed in total and five to go. Ezaara could give Ithsar the piaua to heal Roberto, but the girl might use all of the juice on herself or her friends, saving none for Roberto.

She breathed, staring into Ithsar's eyes. One heartbeat.

Two. Three.

A connection, like a thread of color, wove between them, shimmering. The thread grew stronger, thicker, flowing between them. It felt right to trust this girl, as if their paths could influence each other's destiny.

"*Sathir* is strong between us," whispered Ithsar—she felt it too.

Ezaara handed Ithsar the piaua juice. "A few drops on the wound and two on the tongue. It's precious."

Ithsar retreated through the shadows.

Ezaara sank onto her mattress. She'd given her most precious healing remedy, the scarcest of her resources, to one of her captors. What had she done?

A LINK REFORGED

Roberto woke to the girl with the twisted fingers. By the Egg, he was sick of sleeping. The dark haze made his world turn upside-down and inside out. She lifted a cup to his lips. He shook his head. "Not the sweet water," he croaked.

"It will soothe you," she said, widening her eyes and shooting him a meaningful glance. She held the cup up, urging him to drink.

Strange. She meant something with that glance. Could he trust her? He took a sip. It was water, cool and pure, not tainted with the sickly-sweet draught that knocked him out. He gulped it down.

"Sleep now, while I change your bandages." That widening of the eyes again, with a casual glance at the other workers behind her. She subtly wriggled her fingers. Some of them were *no longer scarred and twisted.*

Roberto shut his eyes, feigning sleep. She peeled back his bandage, a twinge rippling across the dull ache of his wound. Something dribbled on his injury, burning. He nearly cried out, until he remembered the burn of Ezaara's piaua. Was it possible this girl had piaua too? Where from?

And then he heard Ezaara. Felt her.

"Roberto!" Vibrant colors flashed through him—with a potent wave of love.

"Ezaara!" He fought to keep an insane smile from his face. Ezaara was here. Ezaara believed him. Ezaara *loved* him. Every

corner of his body was filled with light. He was a feather floating on the breeze, a bubble rising to the top of the sea.

The juice burned along his stomach. He opened his eyes. The girl re-bandaged his wound and shielded him from view as she leaned over, pretending to give him the cup, but slipping a drop of piaua onto his tongue. "For your insides," she barely whispered. "Ezaara is here."

"I know," whispered Roberto, smiling. He closed his eyelids, pretending to sleep.

§

It was him—Roberto! Her whole body was singing with joy. A rush went through her, like she was imprinting all over again. He was here. Alive. Ezaara counted her heartbeats, concentrating on *sathir*, but it was hard to focus, especially when Ithsar made her way across the training room holding a dish of sliced oranges. She was clever, curling her fingers so they looked unhealed.

"Quick, my mother is coming," Ithsar whispered.

Ezaara took the dish—and the vial of piaua hidden beneath the orange wedges. She pocketed the vial immediately, then sat down to eat her oranges while Ithsar watched, her face inscrutable.

Within moments, Ashewar, the chief prophetess of the silent assassins, appeared. So Ashewar was Ithsar's mother. Ugh.

The assassins turned to face their leader, right hands on sword hilts, left fists over their hearts. Ashewar strode through the room on noiseless feet. As one, they followed her, their bodies like the hands of a giant clock, always facing their master.

The chief prophetess stopped in front of Ezaara's cell. "Stand," she hissed.

Ezaara passed the dish of empty orange peels back to Ithsar and stood.

"You were asking about a man when you arrived," Ashewar said. "We have interrogated a Naobian man, found in the desert with his gut slit. He says you injured him in an attempt on his life." She shook her head. "To forfeit a life in the desert, without our sanction, is a grave crime, so you will be executed tomorrow at dawn."

"But I didn't—"

"Silence." Izoldia stabbed through the bars with her sword.

Ezaara leaped back.

Ashewar waved a hand at the assassins in the training area. "Choose who will kill you."

Ezaara's mind spun. She scanned the rows of stony-faced warriors. She pointed at Ithsar. "I choose her."

Ithsar's expression froze, her eyes piercing Ezaara.

Rage flashed across Ashewar's face. Her voice turned to ice. "Very well, Ezaara *formerly* of Dragons' Hold, soon queen of a shallow grave in the Robandi desert. May the buzzards pick your bones dry before they're bleached by our sun."

Ashewar gestured to Ithsar, and she joined the ranks of the trainees, keeping her fists in her sleeves to hide her healed fingers. She had no weapon.

Suddenly, Ezaara understood. She'd chosen the one assassin who couldn't properly wield a sword, disgracing both mother and daughter.

Izoldia bowed to the prophetess.

"Speak, Izoldia," commanded Ashewar.

Izoldia gave a nasty grin. "My Most Revered Prophetess, Ithsar may finally have her first kill." She barked out a harsh laugh.

The prophetess gave a curt wave, cutting her off mid-laugh. "This is Ithsar's last chance. If she is not successful in killing Ezaara, you will execute both of them."

§

In the deepest night, the faint slap of feet woke Ezaara. Someone was coming. She felt for her sword but, of course, had none. She got up and crept to the side of her prison, gripping the dipper.

A light flared. Ithsar was there, a tiny lamp in her hands. She unlocked the dungeon door and gave Ezaara a bundle of orange clothing. Hurriedly, Ezaara pulled the garments on over her own. Ithsar fastened an orange headdress over Ezaara's head, and darkened her face with earth. She passed Ezaara her sword and daggers. Then, tugging her hand, she led her into the training cavern.

"Where to?" Ezaara's whisper sounded unnaturally loud, reverberating in the chamber. No! She'd forgotten the echo effect in the middle of the cavern.

Ithsar's eyes flew wide. She doused the lamp, but it was too late. People were running along the tunnels toward them.

Grabbing Ezaara's hand, Ithsar dashed with her into the darkness. Heartbeats. Ezaara tried to focus on her heartbeat to stay calm and stop her breath rasping. But her traitorous heart boomed like banishment drums.

Assassins pounded the stone behind them.

Racing along the network of tunnels, Ezaara was soon disoriented.

Ithsar pulled her to the floor, whispering, "Lie down. Squeeze under this bridge. Don't move until I return."

Ezaara obeyed. She wriggled under some planks—a hand's breadth from her nose. Below, was the burble of distant water. Ithsar pushed her in further, then raced off to draw their pursuers away.

Moments later, footsteps thundered over the wood, so close their breeze brushed her face. Ezaara froze, counting her heartbeats until they passed.

Hundreds of beats after their steps had faded, Roberto melded with her. *"Ezaara, what's happening?"*

"I'm trying to escape."

"Me too, but—"

Ezaara tried to meld with him again, but couldn't. Time crawled as she lay, squeezed in that confined space. Her fingertips grazed slatted wood above her. To her side, her other fingers met air. One wrong move and she'd tumble into the water far below. Swallowing, Ezaara kept counting.

Ithsar was used to hiding in the tunnels. Used to avoiding the unwanted gaze of her fellow assassins. Used to crawling into tiny spaces to escape their taunting. But she wasn't used to the new strength in her fingers, the strange energy that had surged along her half-dead nerves as Ezaara, she of the golden hair and green eyes, had *healed* her. Ithsar had never experienced such kindness from anyone. And although the *dracha ryter* from a far-off land had given her a vial of healing juice, Ithsar honored Ezaara, so she hadn't dared use any on herself.

So, Ithsar ran for her life and for Ezaara's. Having hands that didn't work well had helped her hone the rest of her body. Whenever she was off-duty, she practiced the *sathir* dance for hours on end, her limbs nearly brushing the walls of her tiny cavern. Her legs were strong, feet agile and her endurance was akin to the legendary *Sathiri,* who had established the ancient dance. Not that any of her fellow warriors realized. She'd hidden her prowess, deliberately acting clumsier than she was. Deliberately fooling everyone—especially her mother, Ashewar.

On through the dark, Ithsar ran, through winding tunnels to a hidey-hole they'd never suspect. When pursuers passed her, she doubled back until she reached an alcove near where the Naobian lay healing. *Healed*. She'd healed him. He of the dark eyes shining like ripe olives under the sun. No wonder Ezaara loved this man—it was evident in her *sathir* when she'd asked after him. And he had cried, calling Ezaara's name in his fever with such love, babbling about her color. The color, Ithsar had understood. Ezaara's presence radiated all the colors in her mother's prism seer. Another talent Ashewar was unaware of—Ithsar could *see* without a prism. And she'd seen a vision of these two *dracha ryter*.

The Naobian had also ranted about banishment, murder and poison. It appeared he'd saved Ezaara, the healer. For that, Ithsar owed him.

Ashewar planned to kill him.

But no, Ashewar would not kill this man, loved by her healer. Ithsar would see to that. He would go free to love Ezaara. Perhaps one day, she, Ithsar, would have a man like this, who called her name with a voice that ached with tenderness.

Her breathing now quiet, Ithsar stepped out of the alcove. The Naobian had only one person guarding him at night—but tonight it was Izoldia. Ithsar's birth defects meant she was smaller than other girls her age. Izoldia, the largest, had led the bullying, and was always the last to finish beating her—the most savage, the cruelest. Bruises, black eyes, and, later, cuts and burns had been Izoldia's mark—until one day, Ithsar had wrestled the brand off her and burned Izoldia, keeping her brutality at bay.

Ashewar, noticing Ithsar's hurts, had said nothing. Disciplined no one. If Ithsar had been the daughter of another assassin, Ashewar would've been ruthless in punishing Izoldia. But she wasn't. She was Ithsar, Ashewar's only daughter—the chief prophetess' malformed disappointment.

Perhaps Ithsar owed Izoldia, for driving her to artistry in *sathir*, for making her stronger than she otherwise would have been, but Izoldia had also twisted what the Naobian had said, conjuring up stories so Ezaara—*she of golden beauty* the girls called her in hushed whispers over their evening meal—would die.

Not while Ithsar breathed.

Opening the healing room door, Ithsar kept the anger from her face, instead, offering congeniality and supplication.

"What do *you* want?" Izoldia snapped.

"Did you hear the disturbance?" Ithsar asked, eyes downcast.

"You think I'd miss that lot, thundering around like a herd of Robandi camels?"

"I came to fetch you because you're much stronger. You'd be better at fighting an intruder than me."

Izoldia sneered at Ithsar, her chest swelling with pride, but then her eyes narrowed in suspicion.

Although she hated groveling, Ithsar had to be quick. She held out her twisted fingers, hiding the healed ones in her palms. "My hands … I'm useless, afraid …" She let her lip wobble.

"You miserable wretch, Ithsar. I should make you go and face the danger." Izoldia's bark was harsh, loud. She'd never been good at silence—gloating didn't sound right in a whisper. Izoldia got up, hand on her saber. "Watch that man."

The moment Izoldia shut the door, the Naobian's eyes flicked open.

"I am Ithsar," she murmured. "Ezaara's friend. I'll take you to her so you can escape."

"My hands and legs are fastened." His whisper was papyrus-thin. He was obviously used to stealth—good, that would serve them well tonight.

The ropes on his hands and feet were quick work for her saber. Ithsar thrust the cut ropes into her pocket and pulled some clothing and a headdress from a drawer. He threw them on. On close inspection, he wouldn't pass for a woman, but it was better than the *dracha ryter* clothes he wore underneath. She passed him his sword and dagger. They slipped out the door, sliding through the shadows along the walls and nipping into side tunnels or alcoves whenever someone neared.

Finally, they made it back to Ezaara, hiding under the bridge.

When she'd crawled out and they'd retreated to a nearby side tunnel, Ezaara whispered, "Ithsar, quick, give me your unhealed fingers."

In the darkness, something dripped onto Ithsar's fingers, then Ezaara rubbed the oil into her skin. The slow healing burn built until her bones were on fire and *moved and straightened.* An ache pierced her chest and her eyes stung.

She was *whole.*

Ithsar clutched Ezaara's hand for a moment longer, placing it on her wet cheek. "My life is yours."

The Naobian's hand rested atop theirs, enclosing them both. "Thank you, Ithsar," he whispered. "Thank you for risking your life to save ours."

They stood in the darkness, her and these two strangers, their breath flowing and ebbing together in the inky black. And then the vision descended upon Ithsar again—these strangers on mighty *dracha,* with *her* beside them on another. *Sathir* built around them, tangible, like a warm caress full of color and life, a force connecting the three of them. She belonged to these people. This was her destiny.

From Ezaara's soft gasp and the grunt the Naobian gave, they'd sensed it too.

Footsteps slid over rock nearby. They froze, waiting until they retreated, then Ithsar led them into a tunnel far away from the main thoroughfares. Winding under the heart of the lake, deeper and deeper into the earth, she took them toward a hidden exit on the far side of the oasis.

§

Roberto rubbed Ezaara's hand with the back of his thumb. Her palm was warm and soft in his as they followed the tiny silent assassin through the winding tunnel, guided by the light of her lantern. They stooped to avoid sharp rocks protruding from the ceiling and slithered over piles of rubble nearly as high as the tunnel itself. Thank the Egg, he could move again. Brilliant colors swirled at the edge of his mind—Ezaara was trying to communicate with him. How was he going to tell her? The assassins' sleeping draught had set all his old nightmares writhing and churning inside him. Perhaps it was better to get it over with. Letting his barriers melt away, he melded, *"Ezaara."*

"What's wrong, Roberto? Why won't you talk with me?"

She'd picked up on his emotions in spite of his effort to shield them. How could he ever protect her from himself, from the monster inside? He squeezed her hand. She was as bright as a thousand stars, her multi-colored light streaming through him. He reached for his resolve. *"Ezaara, I won't be coming back to Dragons' Hold with you."*

Her steps faltered. *"Why not?"*

Because his past had caught up with him. Because he'd lived a life before he'd become a dragon master. Because he feared Tonio was right: sooner or later, he could turn traitor. It was not only in his blood, it was in his past. Before Erob.

He tugged Ezaara forward, keeping pace with the assassin.

"I thought you loved me."

Pain speared through him. *Exquisite pain.* Shards, Zens' words were still shaping him. Would he ever purge the evil from his soul?

ESCAPE

There was a ripple in the fabric of the *sathir*, a rip in the cloak that surrounded them. "What is it? What ails you?" Ithsar turned to the *dracha ryter*, holding up her lantern.

They were no longer holding hands. The Naobian's face was stoic.

Ezaara's … Ezaara's look haunted Ithsar. Hollow-eyed, bereft of hope.

"With such disunity, Ashewar will feel the disharmony and find us immediately. If you are to be reunited with your *dracha*, you must put this pain aside."

§

Dragons' Hold without Roberto? Every fiber inside Ezaara screamed. And she wasn't Queen's Rider anymore. Her life was meaningless. Worse than before she'd left Lush Valley. Then, she'd been ignorant of mind-melding, of the depth of love, the wonder of dragon flight, the *potential* of life.

She reached deep inside herself, stretching her mind out to Roberto, and showed him how to find *sathir*. He joined her and they found that place of peace, sensing the cord that bound them to nature, and to each other. And Ezaara found hope.

§

Ithsar's lamp shone on a series of hand and foot holds in the rock, leading up a chimney into darkness. Ithsar went first, Roberto next and Ezaara took the rear. Melding with Erob, Roberto was surprised Ezaara was also talking to him.

"*Erob, we're climbing out a tunnel on the other side of the lake, apparently near a cluster of date trees,*" she informed him.

"*Date palms? With hundreds of palms around, that should be an easy landmark to spot in the middle of the night.*"

Erob's wry response made Roberto's heart lurch. Could he take Erob away from Dragons' Hold? Would Erob leave his mother and kin? Or would he lose Erob, too? What about Adelina?

"*Stop disturbing the* sathir *with such morose thoughts,*" Ezaara melded. "*We'll sort out what we're doing once we're out of here.*"

She was right. He'd tell her everything when they got to Naobia. If they got to Naobia—there were still dozens of silent assassins to get past. His hands bit into dusty rock handholds. The footholds were gritty with stone particles, often making his boots slip.

Ezaara spat. "*Tastes great, thanks.*"

He'd flicked dirt on her. "*Sorry.*"

"*I'd rather be underfoot than without you.*" Her response was glib, making him smile, despite his heaviness.

"*Erob, we're nearing the top. Where are the assassins?*" Roberto asked.

"*Amusing themselves by thinking they're guarding me.*" Erob sent Roberto an image of him toasting an assassin on a talon. "*Only joking. They have me surrounded with their sabers.*"

"*Careful. I don't want you wounded. We have a long flight ahead of us.*"

"*Yes,*" Ezaara chimed in. "*It's four or five days to Dragons' Hold from here.*"

Roberto said nothing. Let her think she'd won. It would keep her happy for now.

Above him, Ithsar whispered, "We're here." She put out the lantern hanging on her belt.

There was a faint rustle. Foliage above them parted and the cool kiss of night air rushed in to meet them. Roberto climbed out to a sky scattered with stars, and date palms whispering in the breeze like hundreds of silent assassins. Moonlight cast a shaft of brightness across a lake. Beyond, a hillock was silhouetted among a fringe of trees. The sky was dark, but it wasn't long until dawn. They had to get out of here.

"Are you that lump in the trees?"

"A lump?" Erob snorted. The hillock on the other side of the lake moved. *"See that?"*

"Yes. We're straight across from you." Roberto grasped Ezaara's hand and pulled her out into the open. She stumbled on the edge of the chimney and he grabbed her to stop her falling backward. She landed with her cheek against his chest, and their eyes met. Dragon fire raced in his veins. His heart thrummed.

She was in his mind, against his body, her floral scent and her presence filling his senses. *"You can't deny what we feel."*

And he couldn't. He brushed his lips against her hair.

§

"No," Ithsar whispered, but it was too late. The Naobian's lips touched Ezaara's hair, lighting up the *sathir* connection between them like a million stars. Any assassin tuned into *sathir* would know where they were. So much for stealth.

On the other side of the lake, a sand-shifting roar split the air. A belch of *dracha* flame lit up the palm grove, and the mighty blue-scaled beast took to the sky.

He was coming. Both *dracha ryter* would be saved.

"Traitor." Izoldia stepped from behind a date palm, saber out.

Ithsar snatched her own saber and pointed it at the Naobian. "Now, you're coming with us!" she cried.

The Naobian spun, flinging Ezaara aside. He was fast. When had he unsheathed his sword?

"You," he spat at Ithsar, lunging at her. "You've outlived your usefulness."

He was absolving her of blame. Ithsar parried with her saber, letting it fly out of her hand as he struck, as if her fingers couldn't hold it. Izoldia wouldn't know any different.

The Naobian held his sword to Ithsar's throat. "Drop your weapon," he said to Izoldia. "Or the girl dies."

Izoldia threw her head back and laughed. "She's worthless. Kill her. It'll save me the trouble."

The slow burning anger that Ithsar had harbored all these years blossomed like a bruise, staining the *sathir* purple-black. The stain spread across Ithsar's vision, blotting out the stars, blotting out the date trees, blotting out Izoldia.

Ithsar had never deserved such scorn. Despite her deformed fingers, she had tried her best. Izoldia had seen to it that everyone despised her, including her own mother.

A breeze stirred at her feet, whirling the sand into a flurry. It rose, faster and higher around her, whipping her clothes in the wind. It shook the date palms, rustling their fronds and swaying their trunks. Thrusting out her anger, Ithsar's whirlwind made the date palm over Izoldia tremble.

A huge bunch of dates fell, hitting Izoldia's head, knocking her to the ground.

Instantly, the purple stain was gone.

The Naobian released Ithsar and spun, checking for more assassins. Ithsar could sense them across the lake, running toward them.

Ezaara rushed over to Izoldia. "She's unconscious." She hesitated for a moment.

"I'm sorry," whispered Ithsar. "I've never done that before."

"A good job you did," the Naobian said, putting a comforting hand on her shoulder.

Ezaara opened her pouch and took out a tiny sack of powder. "Ithsar, quick," she hissed, "fetch a little water."

Ithsar snatched the empty waterskin at her belt and collected water from the lake.

Ezaara threw a pinch of powder into the skin, and they held up Izoldia's head, letting the water trickle down her throat. Izoldia swallowed reflexively.

"This is woozy weed," Ezaara said. "It will make her sleep and leave her confused about what happened over the last few hours. She probably won't remember any of this."

Ithsar had been prepared to die to free these strangers. She let relief wash through her, not trying to control it. If anyone had seen the dark bruise in *sathir*, they'd believe the *dracha ryter* had caused it. She fished the ropes she'd cut off the Naobian's limbs from her pockets and thrust them deep into Izoldia's tunic. "Hopefully, they'll think she's a traitor who led you here."

The *dracha* bellowed.

"Fast," said the Naobian, "go back to your quarters through the tunnel."

Ithsar flung herself down the chimney, and he pulled foliage back over the entrance. Only when she reached the bottom and turned on her lamp did she realize she'd forgotten to farewell the *dracha ryter* and tell them about her vision.

§

With a flurry of wings, Erob landed. Roberto was liquid motion, snatching the dates that had hit Izoldia and flinging them into a saddlebag, then throwing Ezaara on Erob's back. He jumped up behind her, wrapping his arms around her waist, his touch kindling flames in her heart. Roaring, Erob took to the sky as the first rays of the sun turned the sand to honeyed amber.

Below, in the oasis, silent assassins waved their sabers, and a cry went up as Izoldia was discovered.

Ezaara squeezed Roberto's hand. She had to know. *"You said you weren't returning to Dragons' Hold, but it's not true, is it?"*

Roberto's arms tightened around her as if he was afraid to lose her. A wave of sadness hit her, and her throat tightened with grief.

The rumble of his voice carried through her back. "Let's enjoy the journey and talk about it in Naobia."

They didn't really speak much in their long flight across the dry and arid desert. Maybe she'd feel better when she saw the ocean again.

But when they reached the Naobian Sea, it was overcast. Instead of a sparkling jewel box of lapis, sapphire and jade, the sea was flat slate, its dark secrets roiling below the surface.

The day turned to dusk and darkness settled. Ezaara drifted to sleep, head against Roberto's shoulder, his warm arms around her.

She woke to that same slate sea rushing in to the Naobian shore. Today, Roberto would tell her why he wasn't returning. Ezaara felt emptier than ever before.

NAOBIA

The salty tang of the Naobian Sea woke old memories inside Roberto as Erob's wingbeats made currents, stirring wisps of Ezaara's hair against his cheek. She was breathing softly in her sleep, peaceful. He steeled himself against a wave of tenderness. Love led to heartbreak. He'd seen enough lives cut short by traitors like Amato. And he'd destroyed enough himself. It would be better to lose Ezaara now, before he destroyed her too.

There, it was time to face it. Amato, his father, had scarred him. Flying back to his homeland was like facing his past—the nightmares: his father, and himself.

It had started that night when he was ten.

Thirsty, he got up for a drink of water. His parents were yelling. They'd argued more since Pa had been lucky enough to escape from Zens. Adults didn't make sense—surely they'd be happier now Pa was home. Roberto crouched behind the bedroom door, listening. Adelina, only six years old, joined him, tucking her small hand in his.

"They're incompetent," Pa shouted. "The whole bunch of them. With wizards gone, they can't even protect our lands anymore. We'll all be destroyed unless we join Zens."

"Don't be ridiculous," Ma said. "Dragons have protected the realm for thousands of years."

"You ignorant fool, it's obvious." Wood splintered.

And splintered again.

Roberto's heart pounded. He put his arms around Adelina. She clung to him, trembling.

"Amato." Ma's voice was shaky. "What's happening to you? This is treason."

"Lucia, Zens makes sense. He has new blood and muscle at his command. He will win."

"How can you say that?"

"Lucia, my darling," Pa reasoned, sounding tender, "I'm only worried about the family, the littlings. I love you all so …"

His father wanted to follow Zens, the enemy of Dragons' Realm. Roberto pulled Adelina away from the door, taking her back to her bed. He was no longer thirsty.

Everything had gone downhill from there. Family life became tense and discordant, and his father, violent.

One day, after Roberto had fed the hens, Razo limped up to him, whimpering, trailing bloody footprints. Roberto knelt, patting his fur. "Hey, boy, what's wrong?" His dog's hind leg was gashed from haunch to paw, his tan fur laid open in a viscous slice of red.

Razo whined and sank to the ground, licking Roberto's hand. His leg was a mess. "Hang on, boy, I'll get Ma." Roberto spun.

"No, you won't." Pa's voice was dangerously soft. "Lazy dog, lazy boy. Both, good for nothing." Amato flicked a whip.

In a surge of anger, Roberto knew who'd hurt Razo. His fists balled. "What did he do?"

"Absolutely nothing. Should've been working, keeping the stock. Instead he was lying in the sun."

"That's not fair! You made him run those goats too far last night. He came home worn out." He gritted his teeth. "You're nothing but a coward, Pa. No one whips a good work dog."

"And no one whips a hard-working son," thundered Amato. He flicked his whip. The tip lashed out, striking Roberto just below the eye.

Razo leaped up, barking, to defend him. "No, Razo, no!"

Pa drew his knife and sunk it into Razo's throat.

Blood sprayed.

Over Razo's chest. Over Roberto's face and clothes and hands.

He knelt in the sun, blood dripping from his fingers, his chin. His dead friend. Roberto was numb with shock.

"Clean up this mess and bury him deep. Then you've got the hens to tend." Amato kicked the twitching dog with his boot and stalked off to the river to cleanse himself.

Roberto's tears mingled with the blood on his face, dribbling into his mouth. Chest heaving, he pulled Razo against him, crying until he couldn't cry anymore.

His mother arrived. Her warm arms folded around him, and she held him wordlessly until Razo's body was cold.

Ma's face was also streaked with red and tears. Adelina was clutching Ma's tunic, eyes red.

"Let's give him a proper funeral," Ma had said. "I'm sorry, Roberto, so sorry."

He and Ma were covered in blood and dirt by the time they'd buried Razo.

Along with his dog, he buried the playful innocence of his littling days and his love for his father.

It hadn't always been like that.

Pa had been loving and fun until his green guard troop had been captured by tharuks. All six riders were taken and enslaved, although their dragons escaped.

His ma, Lucia, had never given up hope that Amato would return, even though he was missing for nearly a year. Matotoi, Pa's dragon, had never stopped hunting for him, and one day, he brought Pa back, chasing the sorrow from Ma's face.

Roberto and Adelina were overjoyed. No one except Amato had survived. Naobia celebrated his return and mourned the loss of the other riders.

A few weeks later, Amato's angry outbursts began. Naobian leaders thought his rage would subside. It didn't.

Tharuks kidnapped settlers—one by one—from their fields, the woods or down by the coast. Over a year and a half, fifty or more disappeared, taken to rot and die as tharuk slaves.

No one suspected Amato. The best rider in the whole southern region, he'd been reinstated as the leader of the green guards, stationed in Naobia. Although his family life was tempestuous, Naobian leaders didn't want to interfere when Amato had been through so much and was valiantly trying to serve.

But Amato was addicted to swayweed and working with Zens and his tharuks.

"Roberto, would you like a ride on Matotoi?" Pa's eyes gleamed with excitement.

Ma was out with Adelina. Pa was in a great mood this morning.

"Can I? Really?" Pa's fiery green dragon, Matotoi, was the envy of all Roberto's friends.

Pa gave a belly laugh. "Why not?"

They made their way to the sacred clearing, where Matotoi was waiting.

A band of tharuks were waiting too. Pa held Roberto, while the beasts tied his hands and feet. He screamed and struggled, but Pa only laughed. "Come on, boy, do you want that ride or not?"

The tharuks gagged him and stuffed him into Matotoi's saddle-bag, and Pa flew him straight to Zens, who trained Roberto as his protégé.

Sorrow ached deep inside Roberto. The things he'd done. The person he'd been. Hardly a suitable companion for a Queen's Rider who'd lived a sheltered life in Lush Valley. What had he been thinking when he'd admitted how he'd felt?

He hadn't—he hadn't been thinking at all. They'd simply melded, stripping away every pretense, revealing their love.

The cold gleam of the distant stars did nothing to light their way across the ocean. It would be a few hours until the sun rose, but Roberto didn't expect any warmth. Ezaara's hair stirred against his cheek again. He brushed his lips against the top of her head, one last time. Her love could never be his.

DARK SECRETS

fter visiting Naobia's early morning market, Ezaara sat with Roberto on a cliff, the churning tide smashing into jagged rocks below. Leaning against Erob, Roberto broke some bread and sliced a round of goat's cheese with his knife, passing some to her. After days of desert fare, the scent of crusty fresh bread made her mouth water. Although the cheese was creamy and mild, it was hard to eat with the unspoken question hanging between them.

After a few bites, Roberto said, "I have to show you something, and it's not very pleasant."

"What is it?"

"Me."

"Don't be silly. I'll always—"

"I can't come back with you, Ezaara." His face was etched with sorrow. "You won't understand my decision until you understand who I was. May I?" His hands hovered near her temples, his upper lip beaded with perspiration. He was nervous.

"Of course." Ezaara smiled, trying to make it easier for him. "It's all right. I'll always love you, no matter what."

"Maybe." His expression grim, he placed her hands on his temples.

Ezaara wanted to slide her fingers down his face and stroke his cheeks, reassuring him he was fine. Instead, she closed her eyes and focused.

Instantly, her stomach blossomed with pain.

"Pain is exquisite," *a male voice said in her mind.*

Sharp stabs pierced her legs. She screamed, but made no sound. A slow burn licked along her arms, and a vice tightened on her head, an excruciating ache throbbing through her skull. Her head was going to burst. Ezaara blacked out.

She came to in a dingy cavern, a man with bulbous yellow eyes looming over her. Zens. A huge tharuk thrust water at her and she drank, but the water coated her mouth with an odd tang.

Roberto's voice was gentle in her mind. "*Swayweed. Amato, my father, gave me to Zens, who tortured me, fed me swayweed and corrupted me.*"

It felt real, as if it was happening to her, but she was reliving Roberto's memories.

Slammed against a wall, Roberto slid into a pile of filth, battered and bleeding. A nasty stench filled his nostrils, turning Ezaara's gut. A kick thumped his ribs. His head smacked a rock wall, and he blacked out again.

When he woke, Roberto struggled to his feet. "I won't. I won't do it." His breath rasped, chest aching. "I won't hurt people just because you want me to."

Zens gestured at a man in riders' garb, chained to the wall. "Are you sure, Roberto? I'd hate to force you. Just lay your hands on this dragon rider's head and use your new skills. A little pain will make him talk."

"No!"

"Very well." Zens' silken voice caressed his mind. Roberto shuddered as Zens' eyes took on a feral gleam. "You leave me no choice." Zens turned to a massive tharuk with a broken tusk. "Tharuk 000, bring in the others."

"Yes, beloved master." 000's red eyes gleamed and dark saliva dribbled off his tusks, splattering on the floor.

Moments later, he was back with four littlings. Pitifully thin and hollow-eyed, they were about four to six years old. Littlings—

slaving for Zens. The eldest had a festering lash mark on her cheek. Faces slack and expressionless, they were victims of numlock, wasted and broken.

What were they doing here? Did Zens want him to test them too? Well, he wouldn't.

"Place your hands upon that man's temples, Roberto. Extract the information."

"No."

"If you don't, I'll kill this girl." Zens gestured to the blank-faced littling with the lash mark.

It was an empty threat to bully him into submission. Roberto lunged for Zens' knife. "I'd rather kill myself than help you."

Tharuk 000 leaped between them and grabbed Roberto, tossing him against the stone wall, smacking his shoulder. That hurt.

"First, the girl. We'll see if he cooperates afterward." Although Zens was mind-melding with 000, his voice slithered into Roberto's skull, battering him from the inside. "Remember, Roberto, this was your choice. Now, she'll die, and it's your fault."

That's why the littlings were here. As hostages, to get him to cooperate. "No! Don't! I'll do anything you—"

000 raked his claws across the girl's throat. For a moment, her eyes flew wide. Blood welled along the gash, then spurted down her neck. Her mouth went slack and her head lolled to the side, eyes dead.

"No!" Roberto screamed. Through his memories, Ezaara felt the scream rip through him, again and again.

000 held his dripping claws to another littling's throat.

"Ready?" Zens asked.

Numb with horror, Roberto stumbled to the rider. He placed his hands on the man's temples and followed Zens' instructions.

Moons of Roberto's life passed in servitude. Amato visited, flashing gleeful smiles at his son's progress. Slaves died at Zens' hand,

Roberto herding them, broken and bleeding, into Zens' cavern for mental torture—littlings, women and men.

Ezaara's gut churned with nausea. So young, only twelve. Roberto's hope died. His resistance was gone, and he did everything Zens commanded. He was a shell, obeying his masters' orders— almost eager for Zens' approval.

His subversion was sickening. Panicking, Ezaara dropped her hands from his temples and opened her eyes. Was this his horrible secret? Was Tonio right? Had he been a spy for Zens all along, only acting a role as master of mental faculties? Was Zaarusha right too? Had he been plotting to destroy her?

Roberto looked at her with strange intensity. "Are you all right?"

She shrugged.

"Let's continue. It's not over yet." His tone was flat, devoid of emotion.

He was as strong as the waves pounding the shore, as beautiful as the sparkling ocean she'd first traversed, and as dangerous as the gargantuan dark creatures that lurked in its depths.

He could destroy her.

Her stomach churned. "So how …?" She couldn't talk. Couldn't unsee those awful memories. The desolation, the torture and pain.

"How did I escape? Zens trusted me. It was his downfall," Roberto murmured. "Well, he trusted his ability to keep me under control. I had freedom to roam Death Valley because he knew the swayweed in my rations and numlock in my water would keep me subservient. After a year of slavery to him, things changed."

He placed her hands on his temples and his memories cascaded through her mind.

Roberto strolled through a horde of slaves, gloating at his ability to control them.

Ezaara recoiled. This wasn't the man she loved.

"Zens stole people and turned them into drudges, enslaving them physically and mentally, breaking their minds," Roberto melded with her. "I had less numlock than the slaves, so I was capable of some independent thought and emotion, but not much."

His memories continued.

Roberto headed over the hill, coming out of the fog. His forehead prickled with sweat. He should go back. Zens could call upon him at any time, but he had the strange urge to explore. He trudged down the hill to a nearby valley, then over another hill. Something tugged him forward, further than he'd ever been since arriving at Death Valley.

Soon he came to a grassy valley of wildflowers with a stream running through it. Salt beading his upper lip, Roberto stooped to drink. His taste buds zinged with life. Fresh and pure, this water stirred distant memories in his fog-shrouded brain. Water was supposed to taste like this, not like the foul stuff he drank every day.

Scooping up handfuls, he swallowed greedily, drips running down his chin. He splashed his face, dribbled it over his hair, then drank again until his belly was tight.

Sudden cramps wracked his gut. Stumbling away, Roberto vomited behind a bush and kept on vomiting until he was dry retching. He spat and wiped his face on some leaves.

His gaze had cleared. Everything was more focused. The Terramites, the chain of mountains standing between him and the rest of the world, were pristine, snow-tipped and formidable, but his memory of life beyond those mountains was hazy.

Shards, he wouldn't drink Zens' fetid stuff anymore—it made his head foggy. From now on, he'd have fresh water. Zens didn't need to know. Taking the waterskin from his side, he tipped the tangy water out and rinsed it, then filled the skin from the stream. Ah, this felt good. He could slip out regularly and replenish his supplies. If he had to, he could alter the minds of those who noticed him leaving. As long as Zens or 000 didn't spot him.

Something blue flashed near the Terramites. A thrill ran through Roberto.

It flashed again, closer.

A dragon. Bright blue.

Roberto stole a glance back toward Death Valley. He was safe. No one could see them here. A surge of energy ran through Roberto as he and the dragon imprinted, breaking the hold of the swayweed and numlock. He had to leap upon this dragon, leave Death Valley and never return.

But Zens and Amato had threatened to kill Adelina if he left.

A rumble coursed through Roberto's mind, "Ah, Roberto, I'm Erob, named in your honor. You're my new rider."

Roberto stared into Erob's yellow eyes.

A yawning pit opened inside him as he remembered his actions among the slaves. "What have I done? Who have I become?"

"You've been a pawn in Zens' hands, twisted by him and your father, but you can be better. Become more, ride with me."

A strange energy thrummed inside his chest. He could feel his heart again. And hope.

But he'd been crossed by his own father. Maybe the dragon was tricking him too. "You think I'd believe you? Zens has helped me to become strong and powerful."

"Zens has shackled your true power, the power to lift mankind to a better place. Roberto, fly with me."

What if this was a devious beast trying to enslave him? Body trembling, Roberto fought Erob and the imprinting bond. "What about my sister? Amato threatened to kill her if I leave."

"I'll take your sister to a safe place, then meet you here at dusk in ten days. Drink only the stream water. Don't eat Zens' food." *The dragon's instructions blazed through Roberto's mind.* "Don't let

Zens test you mentally, or he'll discover you're no longer under his influence. Being a dragon rider is your true destiny, Roberto of Naobia."

"And if I don't like this new life with you?"

"I'll return you to Death Valley."

"What if Zens suspects?"

Erob rubbed his eye ridge on Roberto's hand, and Roberto couldn't help scratching it. "You could come now."

Amato's angry face flashed before Roberto and he shook his head. "No, we must protect my sister."

"Here, take one of my scales. Eat a little each day. It'll give your eyes, skin, and fingernails a gray sheen, like you're numlocked, but you'll need to act sluggish."

Roberto stopped his memories. Ezaara reeled. So much information. So much hurt.

"Zens nearly caught me, but I pretended I had a belly gripe, blocking his probing mind with memories of nausea so he'd think I was too sick to eat," Roberto said. "On the tenth day, when I went to meet Erob, tharuk troops were combing the hills, so I had to sneak to the foot of the Terramites. Erob sensed me before I saw him. Under the cover of night, we escaped. He returned me to my home so I could uncover my father's treachery and bring him to justice."

"What happened to your father?"

"He was banished at his trial, but escaped on his dragon, Matotoi, who he'd turned with swayweed after he returned. My mother wouldn't tell him where Adelina was, so my father threw her off Matotoi's back onto some rocks. She never walked again." He stopped speaking, his throat bobbing as he swallowed. "She died a few moons later."

Ezaara gasped. "That's awful. Horrible."

"For a moment, my father was wracked with anguish that he'd hurt her. Matotoi felt his self-hatred, so he dived to the bottom of Crystal Lake, killing himself and Amato." Roberto gestured inland, his voice hollow, lifeless. "It's a short flight away, over those hills. Adelina and I used to swim there, but we haven't been back. The villagers searched for their bodies, but they were never found."

Her life in Lush Valley had been paradise compared to his. No wonder he'd been so distrusting when she'd first met him. His father had murdered his mother. Sure, it had taken moons for her to die, but he'd killed her. And tortured Roberto and sold him out.

If Amato wasn't dead, she'd finish him off herself.

"Ezaara." Roberto's voice pierced her thoughts. "I can't return to Dragons' Hold. I've been a traitor already, controlled by Zens, and I could fall again."

"You've turned your back on Zens once, proving you're true. If he ever catches you, you can do it again. You can resist him." Ezaara wanted to grab him and shake some sense into him. She hadn't come all this way, risking her life and giving up Zaarusha, only to have him give up.

Handel's vision flashed across Ezaara's mind: Roberto's face twisted into a cruel mask, lunging at her. She pushed the image aside. She wouldn't let that prophecy come true.

"Tonio's right." Roberto ran a hand through his hair. "Just say, they let me back as a dragon master again—if Zens gets hold of me and the information in my head, he'll learn enough to destroy the realm and its leaders."

"But you love the realm. You'll weaken the leadership if you're not part of it. No one has your mental talents. No one knows Zens' weaknesses better than you." She took his hand.

He pulled it away. "I can't go back. They think I was romantically involved with you. As a master, I'd be banished anyway."

"We didn't do anything! I was treating your wounds."

"But you weren't supposed to get off Zaarusha."

"I don't care if they know. I saved someone's life. Two lives."

"And endangered your own."

"So what?" Ezaara ripped a crust off the loaf and tossed it to some gulls that were wheeling and shrieking in the wind. They landed, squabbling over crumbs.

"Anyway, they think I poisoned Jaevin." Roberto uncrossed his long legs, scattering the birds.

"We know you didn't. There's a traitor at large at Dragons' Hold. If we don't find them, they may strike again. They may have already."

"No, they're better off without me, and so are you."

Ezaara threw her hands up. "Roberto, can't you see? I love you. I want you by my side."

"I'm not fit for you. You could do so much better. Besides my past with Zens, I'm a broken man. Even Erob tells me I don't trust enough."

"True," Erob interjected.

Roberto raised an eyebrow and gave a sardonic smile. "See?"

Ezaara took his hand again, rubbing the back of it with her thumb. "In time, you'll come to trust me, despite what's happened in your past. We can do this. Together."

He sighed. "I'm really not a fit companion for a Queen's Rider."

"Well, then, that's fine, because I'm no longer Queen's Rider. I gave up Zaarusha to come and find you."

His eyebrows flew up. His jaw dropped. "You gave up the queen for me?"

Ezaara nodded.

A tear ran from Roberto's eye. His voice dropped to a hoarse whisper. "You did that? For me?"

She stroked her finger along the track of his tear. "Yes, for you, Roberto of Naobia. You're worth it. But don't make me return alone."

§

Roberto was filled with a thousand swirling colors. Ezaara had chased away his darkness. She'd glimpsed the horror of his past and loved him anyway. *We can do this together,* she'd said. And he believed her.

"How can you want me, when you've seen what I've done?" His scarred cheek twitched where Pa had whipped him.

Her smile was like sunrise after a long night.

"With me no longer a master, and you no longer Zaarusha's rider, I don't know how we're going to get anyone to listen to us." Roberto sighed. It was worth a try. "If we're going back, it's time to hone your mental talents. I've designed training to help our riders beat tharuk mind-benders, but the council haven't let me test the training on my students yet."

"Why?"

"There are one or two masters who are resistant."

"Let me guess. Tonio?"

"No, he's for it." The spymaster was reasonable, except for his prejudice against him. Mind you, with his history, Tonio had reason. And someone had poisoned Jaevin …

"Roberto?" Ezaara jolted him back to the present. "What's a mind-bender?"

"Some tharuks can shape your thoughts, emotions or actions. They're called mind-benders. You can block them by keeping a fixed picture in your mind. The more detailed the image, the better. Picture something now, and I'll try to bend your thoughts."

Ezaara closed her eyes. There were dark circles under them. She was exhausted. The days in Robandi Desert hadn't been easy on her either. In fact, not much had been easy for her since she'd come to Dragons' Hold. Roberto placed his hands on her temples and accessed her thoughts.

She was imagining a bay fawn, sitting in sun-dappled light in the forest. He pushed the image away.

"More detail, Ezaara. Sounds, scents and sensations will all help."

Startled, the deer flicked its ears and raised its nose to scent the breeze rustling the nearby leaves. Roberto tried to push the deer aside. Not bad, a solid enough block against an average mind-bender, but not solid enough for him. He punched a hole in her image.

Flames danced in his head and heat rushed through him. He'd opened a floodgate. She was thinking about *him*—about how she felt. Shards! His arms ached to squeeze her against him, to lose himself in the touch of her lips, but he'd never be able to face Tonio with a clear conscience if he kissed her now.

§

"Ezaara, try again. Bring a little more life to it." Roberto's words floated through her. He'd pushed her image aside like a leaf in the wind. Oh, it had held for a few moments, before he'd shattered it.

Fire danced in her veins. With him, she felt so alive. So full of possibility and wonder. Strong.

He was only a hand span away, his breath caressing her cheek. Roberto closed his eyes, lashes dark against his olive skin as he slowly drew a deep breath.

He was struggling for control too.

His eyes opened and fell to her lips, lingering.

Every fiber of her being screamed out to kiss him. It was now or never. On tiptoes, Ezaara stretched up and brushed her lips against his. A jolt ran through her being. This was so right, so—

"No!" Voice hoarse, Roberto pushed her away. His face was tormented. "No, Ezaara."

Shame knifed through her. Oh, shards! Her face burned. "Sorry."

"Don't be. I just can't." Onyx eyes sad, he grimaced. "If we're returning to the hold, I can't kiss you."

"But you're not my master anymore." Ezaara thrust her desperate emotions deep, managing to stay calm. "We're free."

"Not if we're returning, we're not."

Ezaara wanted to throw herself on her knees and beg him for a kiss, but she could see conflict in every line of his body and hear chaos roaring in his head. Swallowing, she nodded.

"Go on, Ezaara, try again." Roberto urged her. "Use something you know well. Something deeply personal."

So, she did.

§

Shards, she was sly. Him, it was him. Seeing his own face, painted with the beauty of a skilled artist, made Roberto's breath catch. She saw him like this? Where was his hardness toward his father? His anger at Zens for shattering his core? Where was the broken man?

She showed him a face touched with compassion and admiration. A face that loved and cared and held human life precious. A face without the harshness he saw in his polished bronze mirror.

She brought out the best in him.

More reason not to kiss her now. To wait, and earn her love the hard way.

Face radiant, she stared up at him. Gods, he was tempted. *"Another picture. Choose something else."*

A cottage on a farm, nestled on the forest's edge, alps stretching to the sky. He shoved and pushed at the image, but it was anchored. It must be her home in Lush Valley. *Well done; try something different.*

A tree, bark rough against her cheek as she hid from two boys below, hunting for her. Birds flitted through the branches, among rustling leaves. The scent of summer hung in the air. He tugged, pried, punched, but the trees and boys held fast.

"Excellent. We can practice more on the return flight."

She stood. "We should get back and warn people there's a murderer at Dragons' Hold."

"Ezaara …" Roberto hesitated. Her biggest stumbling block could be her loyalty to her friends. "I suspect Simeon and his family may be involved."

He hadn't anticipated the icy rage that flitted across her face. Her voice was deadly calm. "Whether the council accepts us or not, we can do better than warn them: let's hunt that traitor down."

DEADLY INTENT

Roberto had his arms around Ezaara as she slept, the warmth of her back seeping through his jerkin. His eyes were gritty and drooping, but he was too tense to sleep, despite the peaceful rhythm of Erob's wingbeats. The Egg knew what would be facing them when they arrived at Dragons' Hold. His whole life, he'd wanted to be a dragon master, but he'd gladly thrown it away to save Ezaara from banishment. He'd never expected her to sacrifice being Queen's Rider—it was nearly impossible to deny the bond between rider and dragon. But she'd done it—for him.

It had been a long hard flight and his backside was aching. Roberto shifted in his saddle. Erob was slowing.

The first rays of sunset hit the crags of Dragon's Teeth, making the snow-clad reaches catch fire. His breath caught. This is what he lived for. Flying. Nature in all its glory. And now, Ezaara in his arms, her breath rising and falling, and her hair smelling of the Naobian Sea.

She stirred and woke.

"Look," Roberto whispered. "Isn't it stunning?"

She exhaled, eyes wide at the sight. "Roberto, we can't let tharuks destroy this."

"They will, if we give them a chance."

"All this bickering and in-fighting … we've got to turn our gaze outwards and work to save the realm."

"If we regain our standing with the council …" He sighed. "One step at a time. First, we have to get there."

As they neared the ranges, blue guards took to the sky.

Erob melded. *"So, they're awake and alert. What do you want me to tell them?"*

"That they're a bunch of idiots for believing I was guilty."

"Well, you were pretty convincing," Erob replied.

"You didn't believe me. You knew I was innocent."

"Of course I did. You have a dragon of superior intellect."

"With a mild sense of exaggeration." Despite his trepidation, a chuckle broke from Roberto.

"And a wicked sense of humor. Don't forget the humor." A rumble rippled through Erob's belly. *"I'll manage them, shall I?"*

Ezaara broke in. Whenever she melded with him and Erob, it was like an extra string on Lars' harp, producing a new exciting thread in an existing melody. *"Remind the blue guards that they've pledged to serve our queen, and it's in her best interests to reunite her with the Queen's Rider. At least, I hope she wants to be reunited."*

"Did she banish you outright?" Roberto asked her.

Ezaara winced. *"Only because I went after you. But I'm glad I did."*

"Of course you are." Erob snorted. *"Neither of you are guilty. Which means someone else is."*

Erob melded with the blue guards' dragons. They were closer now, their talons visible. Were they coming to drive them off? Or to escort them into the hold?

Septimor, Seppi's dragon, roared, and Erob replied, a tremor running through him. *"We're to follow them to the council chambers."*

So, no longer outcasts, but not yet welcomed either. Well, that was better than being chased off outright.

"What's happening?" Ezaara straightened. *"I can't meld with Zaarusha."*

"That's strange." Roberto took his hands off her waist. *"Maybe she's hunting or asleep."*

Blue dragons flanked them on either side. Roberto gave Seppi a nod, and they flew on. When the peaks of Dragon's Teeth were below them, drumbeats started pounding.

"So much for a quiet entrance," Erob said.

"What's that drum signal?" Ezaara asked.

"Something's afoot," Roberto said. A repeated seven-beat rhythm. *"A death toll. Someone's died."* Shards! His breath got stuck in his throat. Adelina? Lars? Who? Another poisoning or an innocent death?

Ezaara sat bolt upright. *"Our traitor may have struck again."*

Seppi's grim expression conveyed similar thoughts. Erob swooped down, flanked by blue guards, and landed outside the council chambers. Roberto thumped to the ground with Ezaara and the blue guards close on his heels. They rushed into the chamber, drums reverberating through the stone.

No one was there. Two chairs were up-ended, the others pushed back haphazardly. Papers were scattered across the table and half-eaten food sat on plates. Cloaks were hanging on hooks, but there were no weapons in the weapons stand. The masters had left in a hurry, armed.

"Come on, we've got to find Lars," Roberto yelled to Seppi as he spun for the door.

Seppi grabbed his arm. "Not so fast, Roberto. Septimor's melding with Singlar to see if Lars wants you free or in chains."

That stung. And Roberto hadn't missed the fact that Seppi hadn't addressed him as 'master'.

Seppi's face blanched, right as Erob melded with Roberto, *"It's Master Shari. She's dead,"* said Erob. *"I'm sorry."*

Knees faltering, Roberto grasped the back of a nearby chair, the wood biting into his clenched hand. No, not Shari.

Her smile flashed to mind. When no one else had accepted him at Dragons' Hold, she'd welcomed him, trusting he'd changed when he'd imprinted with Erob. She'd stood up for him at his trial, seeing through his lies to save Ezaara. She was the closest thing to family he and Adelina had.

By saving Ezaara, he hadn't been here to help someone else he loved. Eyes stinging, he forced himself to speak. "Seppi, please ask Lars if I may see Shari."

Seppi waited a few moments, obviously asking Septimor to meld with Singlar, then replied. "Lars would like you and Ezaara in Shari's cavern, right away."

§

Ezaara glanced at Roberto's pale face as he gripped a chair. Shari had obviously been close to him. She kept trying to meld with Zaarusha as she and Roberto followed the blue guards down the tunnel, that strange drum rhythm echoing around them. *"Zaarusha."* Still no answer. Was the queen too angry to mind-meld?

They rounded a corner and met a troop of guards stationed outside Shari's door, swords drawn. "Halt!" A guard addressed Seppi. "Why are you bringing these traitors into the heart of the hold?"

Seppi nodded curtly. "Lars wants to see them immediately."

Moving aside, the guards opened the door, and they entered.

Face haggard, Lars was on his knees next to Shari's bed with his hand on her shoulder. He waved them in. Masters Tonio, Bruno, Aidan, Hendrik, and Fleur were in discussion, clustered at the foot of the bed.

Shari lay curled, with her hands around her stomach. Even in death, she was beautiful. Her braids were scattered around her face and across her pillow, their copper and silver fastenings glinting in the torchlight. Her dark eyes were blank, staring into nothing.

"We're not sure what caused her death," said Lars, voice husky. "But we'll find out."

Maybe the poisoner had struck again, not satisfied because Ezaara had thwarted their attempt on Jaevin's life.

"How's Master Jaevin doing?" Ezaara asked.

Lars' gaze was flat. "He's dead."

Ezaara's stomach jolted. "But I healed him. He should have been fine. What happened?"

"We don't know." Lars shook his head. "We've been trying to find out, but Master Fleur hasn't been able to get to the bottom of it."

Fleur chimed in, pointing at her and Roberto. "These traitors were banished for colluding to kill Master Jaevin. I told you Ezaara left a substance with Threcia, saying it was medicine, but it killed him. It was probably more dragon's bane."

Rising to his feet, Lars gave Master Fleur a withering look. "All masters, report to the main cavern to address the assembled folk. Tonio, you're in charge. Have your people circulate among the crowd and see if they can pick up anything. Fleur, once Shari's death has been announced, bring the other female master, Alyssa, back to prepare Shari for her death rites. Seppi, Roberto and Ezaara, you stay here. We have to get to the bottom of this before anyone else is killed."

Bruno strode across the room. "I'm not leaving you with two banished outcasts and only one blue guard for protection."

"Very well." Lars' gaze was icy. "Seppi, choose another blue guard to stay. Now, the rest of you, get to the main cavern." He glowered until Bruno left.

Roberto melded with Ezaara. *Bruno and Fleur seem very keen to have us out of the way.*

"And to tarnish our reputations," she replied. *"I'm going to check something."*

But before she could move, Lars spoke, "Two Masters dead since you've been banished, so it obviously wasn't your fault. Roberto, I'm guessing you said you'd poisoned Jaevin to deflect the blame off Ezaara. You'd rather we lost a master of imprinting and mental faculties than the Queen's Rider, huh?" He shot Roberto a shrewd gaze. "We need to get to the bottom of this matter, then I'll have you both reinstated. But first, I need to know if you've been romantically involved."

"No, sir."

"Lucky we never kissed," Ezaara shot.

"Agreed." Roberto's answer was heartfelt.

"But you do care about her, don't you?"

A brief nod was the only sign Roberto gave.

"I'm glad you showed me how you feel or I wouldn't believe it," Ezaara said.

For a heartbeat, Roberto's cheeks took on a red tinge as he addressed Lars. "Tell us what happened."

The booming of the drums stopped, the air suddenly hollow.

Lars cracked his neck. "Jaevin's dragon, Vino, melded with Zaarusha and showed her Jaevin's dying thoughts. He insisted that you'd helped him to recover, then someone else had slipped poison into his evening meal. He had no idea who it was." Grief lined Lars' face. "I'm sorry. I owe you both my deepest apologies. Now we have to hunt down the killer before they strike again."

This was awkward. Ezaara had expected hostility or accusation, not contrition. "Thank you, Lars," she said. "There's something else that concerns me. I haven't been able to meld with Zaarusha since we arrived."

"When Zaarusha realized you two hadn't poisoned Jaevin, she barricaded her mind and hasn't let any dragons meld with her since," Lars replied. "Fleur's dragon, Ajeuria, insists that Zaarusha needs peace and quiet and that solitude will help her heal."

Odd. Ezaara would've expected Zaarusha to be angry, filled with fire and flame, not retreating in self-pity. Then again, Ezaara had never seen her heartbroken. Could Ajeuria be right? *"What do you think?"*

Roberto shrugged. *"I don't trust Fleur, Bruno or Simeon, but Ajeuria should be loyal to the queen."*

Ezaara's eyes were drawn to a bowl of half-eaten soup on Shari's bedside table. "Why was she eating here, not in the mess cavern?"

"She'd been feeling off-color, so she chose to miss tonight's council meeting and eat here." Lars pulled Shari's blanket up to her shoulders.

Except for her staring eyes, she could've been sleeping.

There was a knock at the door, and the guards let Fleur and Alyssa enter. While Lars and Roberto were greeting them, Ezaara used the opportunity to examine Shari's meal. She bent over, as if to tighten her boot, and sniffed the bowl. Odd. The soup had a strange but familiar scent. She quickly moved away before anyone noticed. Where had she recently smelt that?

"Alyssa and I will dress Shari in her ceremonial robes now." Fleur held the door open—a blatant invitation for Lars, Roberto and Ezaara to leave.

"Ezaara will be assisting you," Lars said firmly.

"But she's no longer the Queen's Rider—"

"It's tradition that all females on the council dress a deceased female master, you know that. I've spoken with Ezaara and deemed her fit. It's only a matter of time until she's reinstated as Queen's Rider."

"Very well. My son will be pleased to welcome her back."

In a flash, Ezaara knew when she'd smelt that weird flavor—Simeon's relaxing tea. That's why she'd vomited—Simeon had poisoned her, keeping her away from Sofia to create more prejudice against her. But why? What did Simeon have to gain?

It didn't matter. Simeon and his family couldn't be trusted. Roberto had never trusted him—said he'd had good reason not to. She'd been a fool, thinking he was sweet when she'd first arrived.

Lars turned to leave.

"Lars, I need to talk to you."

"What is it, Ezaara?"

Ezaara couldn't help shooting a nervous gaze toward Fleur. "Sir, I think I know—"

Fire blinded Ezaara's vision. Flames licked along her skin, making her flesh sear and blister. The stench of her own burning flesh filled her nostrils. Flames rippled over her jerkin, smoke searing her eyes. Her brain jangled, making her want to scream. No, she would not, could not, give in to this illusion. No dragon's vision was going to beat her this time.

Gasping, Ezaara fixed her home in her mind, picturing their shutters, the fields, the Alps rising far beyond the forest toward the sky. Flames flickered, threatening to burst through the cobalt sky. She focused. The sky was blue. Blue. The clouds, white and fluffy. The flames were an illusion. The day was warm. Birds were singing. Tomaaz was outside in the garden, tilling the earth. Her father was planting beets. Her mother was kneading a second batch of bread in their cottage, the scent of baking loaves wafting through their home. She would not let an errant dragon force her into submission through mind-bending. Squeezing her eyes shut, Ezaara went over every detail, a summer breeze kissing her face.

She relaxed. She'd won the battle.

"Ezaara, what is it?" Lars asked. "Are you ill?"

She opened her mouth, about to speak, when Roberto melded. *"Careful, Ezaara. Everyone is watching you, and it's obvious you've been attacked mentally. Stay cool. Don't give anything away."*

Someone had prevented her from sharing vital information with Lars. A bead of sweat trickled into her eye. Either Alyssa or Fleur via one of their dragons. She coughed. "It doesn't matter, Lars. It was nothing."

Fleur, it had to be. Ezaara melded with Roberto, *"Shards! Fleur's the murderer, and her whole family are in on it."*

"Come on," said Fleur, "we need some privacy to prepare Shari for her death rites." She waved the men out of the room before Roberto could answer.

"I'm sending Adelina to help you," Roberto melded from the corridor. *"I don't want you to be in there without support, but we need to catch Fleur in the act."*

"Thank you." Although relief washed through Ezaara, she kept her face neutral.

Fleur opened one of Shari's drawers and pulled out a pristine white tunic and breeches edged with golden dragons. "This is fitting for her final passage." She shook her head. "Such a tragedy that she's died so young. So much vitality snuffed out."

She sounded so sincere. The woman was demented.

Adelina arrived, her usual perky attitude missing. "Please let me know how I can help."

Fleur laid the robe on the bed and then turned, as if she'd just spotted the bowl on Shari's bedside table. "Oh dear, we can't have food next to the deceased."

"Why not?" asked Ezaara.

"Fleur is from Montanara," Alyssa answered. "Montanarians never leave food near those who die. It's considered disrespectful. Here, Fleur, let me get rid of it for you."

"No, I'll do it myself," she replied. "Alyssa, please show Ezaara how to wash and dress Shari. I'll be back shortly."

A chill shivered down Ezaara's neck. Fleur was trying to destroy the evidence.

Adelina whisked the bowl away before Fleur could reach it. "Master Fleur, allow me to perform this menial task. The dressing of a master is of utmost importance and must be performed by our distinguished master healer." Before Fleur could utter a word, Adelina slipped out of the room with the food.

"Excellent," said Alyssa. "It is fitting that you dress Master Shari for her death rites, Fleur."

"It would've only taken a moment," Fleur said stiffly. "But it's kind of Adelina to help."

"Roberto, Adelina is bringing poisoned food. Save it for their trial."

"Will do."

They disrobed Shari and washed her. Adelina returned and helped Fleur and Alyssa fasten her tunic and arrange her hair.

A knock sounded at the door. Ezaara opened it and nearly leaped backward when Simeon gave her a dazzling smile.

"Ah, My Honored Queen's Rider, or soon to be again, I'm sure." He bent and tried to kiss her hand.

Ezaara snatched it back. This creep had attacked her. Mauled her. She'd never noticed how slimy Simeon was: getting her onside at the feast; poisoning her with that tea; and driving a wedge between her and Roberto. He'd probably broken her cane, too.

"I do wish I could welcome you back to Dragons' Hold under more pleasant circumstances," Simeon continued. He turned to Fleur. "Mother, you're needed urgently. Someone is gravely ill. Please come at once." Fleur hustled out the door after him, without a backward glance.

Simeon and Fleur were up to something. Was Alyssa in on it too? Would she believe them if they told her? Or would she stop them from following Fleur?

Ezaara stared at Adelina, stricken.

Adelina gave a subtle wink. "My Honored Queen's Rider, you look weary. You must've had a long journey with my brother. Why don't you take some time to freshen up? Alyssa and I will keep vigil here overnight."

"I can manage on my own." Alyssa commandeered Ezaara and Adelina toward the doorway. "Shari was my dearest colleague." She backhanded a tear from her eye. "It's a privilege for me to keep vigil until her death rites in the morning. Adelina, you must see your brother. Ezaara, you need to be reunited with Queen Zaarusha."

As she and Adelina rushed out the door, Ezaara melded with Roberto. *"Fleur and Simeon are up to something."*

"I've been called away to a tharuk attack." Roberto sounded torn.

"Have you got any idea where they've gone?" Ezaara asked Adelina.

"Along this way, but I've no idea where they're heading," Adelina answered as they ran past the guards, along the tunnel. "While you were away, I've been volunteering in the infirmary. Over the past few days, I've taken a sample of every substance stockpiled in that alcove we discovered." She patted the bag she always wore, slung over her shoulder. "They're all right here."

"Good work. I may be able to identify some of them," Ezaara replied.

"While you were away, a girl arrived from Lush Valley. You may know her—Lovina. She was poisoned, but I healed her."

"Lovina? Here?"

"Apparently your brother helped her get here," Adelina replied.

Tomaaz—the first news she had of her family. "It'll have to wait. We have to catch Fleur first. Have you any idea who she'll target next?"

"If it was me, I'd go for the queen."

"Zaarusha!" No answer. *"Roberto, I can't meld with Zaarusha, and Fleur is prowling around with Simeon."*

"Find the queen!" Tension rippled through his thoughts.

A hollow pit yawned in Ezaara's stomach as drumbeats thundered down the tunnel. Her heart lurched. "Is someone else dead?"

"No, these drums are ushering in Alyssa's overnight vigil, the first phase of the death rites for Shari." Adelina's bag of supplies jangled as she ran.

Ezaara thrust her cavern door open. She and Adelina dashed through the archway to Zaarusha's den.

Her nest was empty.

"Fangs! Where could she be?" Adelina smacked her palm against her thigh twitch.

"I don't know!" Ezaara had to do something. *"Erob, where's Zaarusha?"*

"Rumors say she's pining for you, but I can't meld with her, and that's highly unusual. Years ago, when she was missing Anakisha, Yanir, and her dead dragonet, she isolated herself at the imprinting grounds."

"How soon can you get there?"

"The tharuk attack was a false alarm. We're coming, but we're still far away."

Ezaara whirled. "Adelina, take me to the imprinting grounds."

Adelina swiped a torch off the wall. "We're going to need this," she said. "It's dark where we're going."

They ran through the tunnels, past the main cavern where the rise and fall of voices and slow beats of the drums marked Shari's death.

"We should be there for Shari," Adelina slowed, her face torn.

"Shari's already dead. We have to help Zaarusha, and stop more murders."

As they rounded a bend in the tunnel, Gret stepped from the shadows. "Ezaara, you're back? What's wrong? Where are you two going?" Before they could answer, her eyes flicked to the torch. "The imprinting grounds? I just followed Fleur and Simeon to the grounds' entrance tunnel ... but there are no hatchlings up there now. What's going on?"

"Zaarusha is missing. We believe Fleur may want to harm her."

"Oh, fangs! Let's go." Gret ran alongside them, yanking another torch from the wall.

"How long ago did you see them?" Ezaara asked.

"Not long."

"They must have run the whole way," Adelina panted as they passed the infirmary and sped along the tunnel to a cracked wooden door.

Hinges creaking, Adelina yanked it open, revealing a steeply ascending tunnel. They stumbled up half-hewn steps, the flickering torchlight shadowing pitfalls that were a nightmare to negotiate.

On and on they went. *Zaarusha.* There was no answer, not a glimmer from the queen.

"How long is this cursed tunnel?"

"We're about halfway." In front of her, Adelina's torch moved steadily upward.

A sharp cry rang out from behind. Ezaara spun, nearly losing her footing. Gret was on the ground, clutching her knee. Blood dripped from a deep gash that cut through her breeches into her knee. Gret's torch rolled down the slope, coming to rest in a hollow, then guttered and died.

Ezaara knelt beside her. "Did you trip? I'll go and find your torch."

"Go on. I'll catch up." Gret's eyes reflected the light from Adelina's torch above. "You have to go. *Now*."

"She's right, Ezaara. We can't delay. Come on," Adelina called.

Torn, Ezaara dashed upward, leaving Gret injured and alone in the dark. It was wrong, on so many levels, for a healer to ignore an injury and abandon a friend.

Soon, air grew fresher. They were nearing an exit.

Adelina doused the torch, and they crept up the tunnel using their hands against the walls to guide them through the dark. Ezaara barked her shin against a rock, biting her lip to stop herself from crying out.

The exit led to a huge plateau, stars glimmering above. Brightly burning torches on the rocky walls illuminated a blood-chilling scene. Simeon was stroking a gray dragon's head, while Fleur tipped the contents of a large bottle into its maw.

Zaarusha!

Her stomach dropped. The queen's scales were dull gray. There was no iridescence, not a flicker of color in the torchlight.

"The queen is dying," Adelina whispered.

Ezaara leaped across the plateau, her feet seeming to grind against the stone forever, as if she was pushing her body through syrup. A sickly green glow emanated from the queen, although Ezaara knew no one else could see it. *Sathir*.

Washed-out-gray, Zaarusha swallowed the substance. The queen's head slumped to the ground and her body seemed to deflate—as if the life breath was leaking out of her.

It was no use. She was too late. *"Zaarusha!"* Ezaara's mind screamed.

Hundreds of dragons roared mentally in reply.

Except the dragon she loved.

"No!" With a bellow, Ezaara barreled into Fleur, knocking her onto the rock. Fleur kneed her in the stomach. Clawed her face. Ezaara punched her, but Fleur was stronger than she'd thought. As they rolled and thrashed, she caught glimpses of Zaarusha's scales, turning an ever-darker gray. With a desperate thrust, she flipped Fleur under her and drove her knee into Fleur's groin, pressing her weight on Fleur's torso.

Cool metal kissed her neck. "Not so fast," Simeon said, behind her.

The sword's kiss bit, cutting her skin. Warmth trickled down her neck, wafting the metallic tang of blood. A dark drop hit Fleur's cheek.

Fleur grinned. "Bleed, wench."

"Unhand my mother or my sword will bite deeper." Typical Simeon, lyrical, even when threatening her.

"Scum," she spat, releasing her grip on Fleur. "I don't know what I ever saw in you."

He yanked her to her feet, his sword rasping against her skin. She'd be no use to Zaarusha dead. Behind Simeon, a shadow slipped along the rocky walls. Adelina. Then another slower shadow. Gret. Ezaara had to keep Fleur and Simeon talking, to distract them.

Simeon pulled her to his side, eyes roving over her body. "Well, I certainly know what I saw in you," he sneered.

"What have you done to the queen?"

"Pretty face, but pretty stupid," Simeon said.

"Simeon," Fleur warned, scrambling to her feet and dusting herself off. "Finish her off. We need to go. Ajeuria will be here soon."

So that *was* who the burning visions had come from.

"I don't know—maybe I'd like to *play with her* a little first, mother. Ajeuria can carry three."

If they took her, she'd have no chance of saving Zaarusha. "Why? Why did you do this, Simeon?" she asked, stalling. "I trusted you. You could've wooed me and ruled beside me."

"And lose the power Zens will give me?" Simeon scoffed. "His vision of the realm is far superior to anything dragons can offer."

Violence and hatred and an army of monsters? Superior to dragons and bonded riders protecting a realm? Simeon was far gone.

Fleur strode to Zaarusha and placed her hand on the dragon's forehead. "She's waning. It shouldn't take long now. Soon the realm will have no queen." She grinned.

Guilt knifed through Ezaara. She'd chosen Roberto instead of Zaarusha, and now the queen was dying. "What are Zens' superior plans? If they're really that good, maybe I should join you. I don't want to be on the losing side. I've always liked you, Simeon."

"You really think I'm that dumb? I'm not going to fall for—"

Adelina appeared behind Simeon, driving her knife up into his armpit. He released his blade, crying out.

Pulling her sword from its scabbard, Ezaara leaped toward Fleur, but she was too late. Gret was already there.

Fleur and Gret's blades clashed and scraped as they fought, the sounds grating on Ezaara's bones. Gret's blade work was as good as ever, but her blood-soaked leg slowed her.

With calculated moves, Fleur drove Gret past Zaarusha, pushing her ever closer to the cliff edge. Gret stumbled, but raised her sword to deflect Fleur's blow to her head.

Ezaara raced toward them.

Zaarusha! No one was saving Zaarusha.

"Ezaara," Adelina screamed.

Ezaara spun. Simeon was wrestling Adelina.

Flapping filled the air. She whirled again. Ajeuria dived at Gret, grasping talons outstretched.

With a desperate spurt, Ezaara shoved Fleur sideways, and dragged Gret back from the edge. Ajeuria roared, swooping down. Gripping her sword with both hands, Ezaara thrust it upward, aiming for the green dragon's soft belly.

A roar split the air. In a flash of midnight blue, barely visible against the dark sky, Ajeuria was yanked backward, screaming and twisting. Erob—with a death grip on Ajeuria's neck, Roberto flat against his back. The dragons writhed, plunging toward the valley below.

The air filled with the rumble of a rockslide. No, the flapping wings of a hundred dragons. Dragon cries ricocheted through her head.

"We're coming." Singlar.

"We heard your call." Septimor.

"Save the queen." Vino, Jaevin's dragon.

They were coming. All of the dragons of Dragons' Hold had heard her desperate cry that the queen was dying.

But only one person could save Zaarusha.

Ezaara raced over to Adelina's bag near the tunnel and snatched it up. Gret was still fighting Fleur. Adelina was battling Simeon. Roberto and Erob could be killed. Ignoring it all, she raced to Zaarusha.

Weak puffs of air issued from Zaarusha's nostrils. Ezaara laid her hands on the queen's skin. Nearly cold. Her scales were dark and flat.

Gods, gods. Please.

"Zaarusha."

Nothing, but she kept melding, talking to the queen. Focusing, Ezaara reached for *sathir*. A faint glimmering thread of life clung to Zaarusha—sickly green.

Hurry. Hurry. Her fingers fumbled as she opened the bag. No, she needed to see *sathir*. To be calm. Breathing deeply, Ezaara examined the bag's contents, pulling corks off jars and vials, and sniffing.

Woozy weed. Dragon's bane. Some foul-smelling green stuff. Clean herb. Rumble weed. More of that ghastly sleeping-draught poison. Clear-mind. The antidote to limplock. A little blue bottle of clear liquid. Bottles and jars of all shapes and sizes. How in the Egg's name could she know the correct cure?

Ithsar's lizard, Thika, came to mind.

Focusing on *sathir*, Ezaara held the bottle of the sleeping draught poison by Zaarusha's slumped head. A sickly green emanated from the bottle. The poison dimmed Zaarusha's life force. Good, hopefully the cure would show too.

She held up a vial of limplock remedy. Nothing.

The dragon's bane. Dimmer.

What about the woozy weed? Again, nothing.

Zaarusha's breathing was slowing, barely audible.

Around her, the sounds of fighting dimmed as she focused on the queen, willing her to consciousness.

Her hands shook as she held up item after item. The pale green thread faded until she could hardly see it. No, she was losing Zaarusha.

Wait, it was her. She'd just lost focus and couldn't sense *sathir*. She had to calm herself. There, the thread was back, but weak. There were now only three unidentified items left in Adelina's bag.

Ezaara held up a jar of Fleur's healing unguent. Dimmer and sickly green—so that was laced with weak poison too. She grabbed the next, a blue bottle, and held it near Zaarusha's head. A faint golden glow surrounded the bottle, connecting with Zaarusha's life thread, making it shimmer with gold light.

Just to be sure, Ezaara checked the last substance. Nothing.

Relief washed over her. She had the antidote. But how could this tiny bottle save such a massive queen?

Tooth & Talon

R oberto clung to Erob's back, his arms through the hand grips and legs cinched tight in the stirrups. His stomach somersaulted as Ajeuria bucked to free Erob's fangs from her neck.

Her tail lashed Erob's side, the tip slamming into Roberto's leg. He gritted his teeth, hanging on. Melded with Erob, Roberto felt Ajeuria's talons rake Erob's belly. The dragons snarled, twisting and thrashing.

Below, the pines were like an army brandishing lances at the sky.

"She can't hold out forever," Erob said.

"We don't have forever," Roberto melded. *"Any moment now, we'll be speared on those trees."*

Ajeuria blasted flame at Roberto as they plummeted earthward.

§

A hand grasped Ezaara's shoulder. "How can I help?" asked Lars.

"We need to feed this antidote to Zaarusha."

Nodding, Lars pushed Zaarusha's upper lips onto the sharp tips of her fangs, making the dragon open her maw reflexively.

Uncorking the bottle, Ezaara tipped clear liquid onto the queen's tongue.

"And now?"

"Now, we wait." Ezaara focused on Zaarusha's life thread. Lars paced. She was dimly aware that the noises behind them were quieting. Soon, Zaarusha's life thread glowed golden.

"What's happening?" Lars asked. "Is it enough?"

The gold was fading. "No, I don't think it is."

Lars ferreted through the jars and bottles. "Is that all we've got?"

"Adelina found it. Tell her to fetch all the antidote she can find." She passed Lars the tiny empty bottle.

He glanced at the collection of vessels on the ground around Ezaara's knees. "How will she know which one we're looking for?"

"It has a distinctive smell."

Lars sniffed it, wrinkling his nose. "Indeed. We'll be back soon."

Ezaara stayed, hands pressed against Zaarusha's side. *"Zaarusha."* No answer. The thread looked the same as it had a few moments ago. Her queen was still unconscious.

"I love you." Roberto's words blazed through her. Piercing pines grew ever closer in the moonlight. The rush of air and wind. Bucking writhing dragons. Him, holding on despite his leg searing. *"Ezaara, I—"*

"Roberto!"

Ripping her hands from Zaarusha, Ezaara rushed to the edge and gazed down. There was a burst of flame below. A roar. Then nothing but blackness.

§

Adelina watched helplessly as Erob latched onto Ajeuria and the dragons plunged through the sky. Roars ripped through the night, tearing at her heart, making her chest tight. Shards, her brother. With a surge of energy, she drove her knife upward, slashing Simeon's wrist.

He dropped his sword.

She leaped through the air, flinging out her foot and driving it into his chest. He stumbled backward. She leaped and kicked again. Simeon went down.

Adelina jumped on him, twisting his arm up his back, and pinned him to the ground.

Moments later, blue guards arrived, taking Simeon off her hands.

"I've been attacked!" Fleur pointed at Gret and Ezaara. "They attacked a master. Seize them!"

The guards ignored Fleur's outraged cries as they held her arms fast.

"You may think you're clever, Ezaara," Fleur's voice glittered with malice as she addressed the Queen's Rider. "But there's not enough antidote in the whole of Dragons' Realm to save your queen."

Adelina shuddered as the guards bound Fleur and swept her off on one of their dragons.

She helped Gret up. "Are you hurt badly?"

Gret smiled through gritted teeth. "Been better. With our master healer poisoning the council, I'm not sure who's going to heal me."

"Come on, Gret. There are others on duty in the infirmary." A blue guard helped Gret onto his dragon.

With shaking knees, Adelina stumbled past Ezaara and Lars, crouched by Zaarusha's dull-scaled head, toward the edge of the plateau.

Lars waved a bottle. "Adelina, we urgently need to get more antidote for the queen."

Who to save? Her brother? Or her queen? Her queen who'd helped banish her brother. No one had believed him innocent except herself and Erob. Now he was plunging to the valley, risking his life for his queen again.

It seemed like hours since she'd discovered Fleur's stash of hidden remedies—and poisons. Numbly, she nodded and climbed upon Singlar. She'd see Roberto from the air soon enough—if there was anything left to see.

Lars climbed on behind her and patted her shoulder. "He'll be all right. He's an experienced rider."

But Erob was falling, not flying.

Singlar leaped into the sky. Adelina scanned the basin below, searching through the patches of moonlight and shadows for—there, a burst of flame, a roar, then nothing.

Gods, no! He'd been beaten, turned traitor, imprinted and saved, only to be banished, then return—and now this? It was too much. Tears tracked down Adelina's face, bitterly cold in the night wind. She clung to Lars' back, burying her face in his jerkin.

His voice rumbled through his back. "Roberto will be all right."

But his words were hollow. How could Lars know? Hope caught, half-formed in her throat. "Has Singlar melded with Erob?"

"He's trying." Lars pressed a bottle into her hand. "We need more of this stuff. You'll know it by the scent."

He was deliberately keeping her busy. Adelina uncorked the bottle and sniffed. Ew, gross. "Lars, I don't know if there's any more. Fleur said—"

"Hurry," Lars said, leaping down as Singlar landed outside the infirmary. "Zaarusha is dying."

Inside the infirmary, Kierion and a young girl were bandaging Gret's leg. No one else was around.

"Thank the Egg, you're here, Kierion," Lars said to him. "We need the antidote to a poison that's killing Zaarusha. Help us find it."

Kierion sprang to his feet. "What am I looking for?"

Adelina shoved the empty bottle under his nose. "Anything that smells like this."

"Phew! At least it's distinctive."

"You search out here. Lars and I will look in Fleur's secret stash." Adelina rushed Lars into Fleur's alcove. "I found that bottle in here."

They frantically rummaged through the shelves, opening bottles and jars and smelling the contents.

"Not this one." Lars set the bottle aside and snatched up another.

It seemed to take forever. The whole time, Adelina fought the dark panic rising inside her. Still no word of Roberto. "We've looked everywhere," she finally said. "There isn't any more."

Lars flung his hands out. "We'll turn the whole infirmary upside down until we find it. Then search the whole of Dragons' Hold. We have to save our queen." He strode out of the alcove.

Adelina hurried after him.

"Whoa, Kierion," Lars called. "You've torn the place apart."

Drawers were yanked open, mattresses and sheets had been ripped off beds, and Kierion was sprawled on the floor with his head and arms inside a mattress, ferreting around. He emerged, triumphant, hair full of straw, with bottles in his hands. "Look what I found!"

"We've no time to waste." Lars slashed the pallet open with his knife, and yanked back the straw, revealing a cluster of jars, bottles and tubs, each carefully wrapped in sheep wool.

"I figured Fleur would be more likely to hide stuff in a spare mattress than in the ones patients use." Kierion gestured to some pallets stacked against the wall. "There are a few more to check yet."

Adelina undid the corks and test-sniffed the contents. "None are the antidote."

Where was Roberto?

Surely, if he was injured, he would've been brought to the infirmary by now. Was he dead? Dread filled her like an ominous tide. "Lars, have you heard from Singlar yet?"

Grim lines tugging at his mouth, Lars shook his head.

§

Zaarusha's glimmering thread was fading, her breathing slowing again. The antidote had helped, but it wasn't enough. Melding with the queen wasn't working. Or with Roberto. Or Erob. *"Singlar,"* Ezaara melded, *"Zaarusha's fading again. Are Erob and Roberto all right?"*

"We're nearly there." At least she could reach someone. Within moments, Singlar landed at the imprinting grounds.

Kierion jumped off Singlar, cradling a bottle as tall as an ear of corn. "We found the antidote," he announced. "And lots of it."

How should she administer the remedy? All at once? In smaller doses? Too little, and they could waste the whole bottle in dribs and drabs, and not combat the poison. Too much, and it could kill Zaarusha.

"Adelina's stayed in the infirmary with Gret. Kierion will keep vigil with you over Zaarusha," Lars said. "I have to get back to the dungeons to help Tonio interrogate Fleur, Bruno and Simeon."

"Of course. Any word of Erob, or Ajeuria?"

"Not yet. We're not sure where they fell, but riders have gone searching. None of our dragons can meld with them at the moment." His glance slid away.

He feared they were dead.

Her stomach lurched. No, not Roberto.

Time for that later. She had a queen to save. Swallowing, Ezaara cupped the bottle in her hands and closed her eyes. She breathed deeply, sensing Zaarusha's life thread. Pale gold—no longer glimmering. Kierion held up Zaarusha's top lip so she could jam the bottle in a gap between her fangs. Ezaara dribbled liquid into Zaarusha's maw. The queen swallowed.

And again.

Ezaara waited, then dribbled a little more. The gold of the queen's life thread started to glow a little more. Last time she'd deteriorated a while later. If only Ezaara knew what Zaarusha's life thread looked like when she was healthy. She'd only ever seen it tonight, while her queen was dying.

Surely, Zaarusha needed more. Ezaara gave her twice as much as before.

The gold grew stronger.

After a while, it faded again. She still had most of the bottle left.

She doubled the dose again, and waited.

"Trial and error," said Kierion lightly. "You're doing well." He shrugged a shoulder. "You can tell me I'm being nosy if you want, or you can refuse to answer. I mean, I'm just curious ..."

"What is it?" Ezaara met his gaze.

"Well, at the trial, you were accused of loving Master Roberto." Kierion paused, awkwardly. "Is it true? Are you in love?"

Was Kierion Tonio's spy, gathering information against them?

It came in a flash—she didn't care what anyone thought anymore. They'd been banished. Roberto had had his guts slit like a rabbit. She'd saved him from murder. And now he was ... what? Dead? Alive? The dragon masters' opinions weren't important anymore. "Yes, I love him. But I've never acted upon my feelings." Thank the Egg, Roberto had stopped her.

"What does it feel like? How do you know ...?" Kierion blushed.

So, he liked someone too. "I imagine it's different for each person. For me, love is sunlight shimmering on water, dancing into the darkest corners of my soul." Despite her missing connection with Roberto, and despite Zaarusha's state, the thought of Roberto's love made hope grow in Ezaara's heart. She paused as Kierion nodded to himself. "How does it feel for you?" she asked.

Kierion started. "Me?"

She let a faint smile touch her lips. "Yes, you."

Blushing beet red, Kierion stammered, "A-as b-bright as an eagle's eye, as soft as the clouds and as if I'm about to burst with joy."

"Does the person you like feel the same?"

"Um, ah, I ..."

"The one you love doesn't know?"

He grinned and ducked his head. "No, not yet."

Under Ezaara's hand, Zaarusha moved. She had to focus. As Ezaara tipped the bottle, Kierion shifted his weight and bumped her. A gush of fluid rushed into Zaarusha's mouth.

"Oh, I'm sorry." Kierion's face twisted with worry.

Ezaara bit her lip to stop herself from yelling. It was too late. He'd wasted half the huge bottle. The Egg only knew what the effect would be.

Suddenly, Ezaara's mind was bathed with colors swirling in golden light.

"Ezaara?" the queen melded.

"I'm here, Zaarusha." A hot tear slid down her cheek. Then another. "Thank you, Kierion. Don't be sorry. I never would have given her that much at once, but it was exactly what she needed."

Kierion's face lit up like a fistful of candles.

"Ezaara." Zaarusha raised her head, voice shaky. *"Why are my littlings fighting?"*

Littlings? Ezaara frowned. *"You mean the masters?"*

"No, my son and daughter."

Her son? And—

Erob! Ajeuria! *"They're alive?"*

"And that master you're so fond of—Roberto's alive too."

A wave of relief whooshed through Ezaara, so potent she was glad she was kneeling.

"Sorry, Ezaara. I shouldn't have doubted you and forfeited your right to ride me." Zaarusha nuzzled her hand. *"How can you forgive me?"*

More tears slid down Ezaara's cheeks. *"I already have."*

"You've always trusted me, right from the moment you saw me, but I let my heart be darkened by aspersions from others. They convinced me you'd fooled me, and were still fooling me, even though I found no malice in your heart."

Ezaara flung her arms around Zaarusha's neck. Her skin was warm and comforting, like soft leather.

"Singlar tells me Bruno, Fleur and Ajeuria double crossed me. They must have fed Ajeuria swayweed." Zaarusha's hurt knifed through Ezaara. *"I'm supposed to be a queen of steel, tough but wise, but I've made so many mistakes, lost so many loved ones. I've just had you two unfairly banished. I lost my rider Anakisha, and my mate Syan and his rider Yanir."* Again, Zaarusha shared Anakisha falling into a horde of tharuks and the glittering black dragon and his rider rushing to save her, only to be caught as well. *"Your mother killed my dragonet before it was born."* A dead purple dragonet floated in a translucent golden shell. Deep sorrow permeated Ezaara, so strong her bones ached. *"Not only did I lose my baby, but, in my wrath, I lost two of my best masters."* Younger versions of Ma and Pa swam before her. *"And now these two."* Shari and Jaevin.

"And before you and I imprinted, I'd just lost my other son." An orange dragon was trapped by tharuks in the midst of battle. They dragged him away in a net, tail and talons trussed up, snarling and roaring. *"Is it so wrong that I don't want to lose Ajeuria too?"*

§

Roberto hung on as Erob straddled Ajeuria, pinning her body to the earth. She thrashed, but Erob tightened his jaws around the back of her neck. His earlier fang marks around her throat were oozing blood. Ajeuria's head slumped on the ground. She held still, but kept snarling.

Roberto slid down Erob's side and leaped down. *"Hold her tight, Erob."*

"I've got her. You should be able to find something out now, without having your pretty fingers snapped off."

"Pretty?" Roberto snorted. His nails had half the Robandi desert stuck under them. He laid his hands on Ajeuria's head. It took every scrap of concentration for him to delve through Ajeuria's mind, discarding irrelevant memories and looking for clues to Ajeuria's behavior.

He found a memory laced with hurt.

Ajeuria nuzzled Fleur. "You're wrong. Zens doesn't want what's best for us at all. I'd usually do anything you ask, Fleur, but I can't go against my mother or the realm."

"Come with me, Ajeuria," *said her rider,* "and I'll show you what great things Zens has in store for us."

Eager to please Fleur, and keen to convince her Zens was evil, the green dragon followed her rider into a barn. As the doors closed behind them, Ajeuria scented tharuks. "Fleur, beware!"

A net flew over Ajeuria, pulled tight by a horde of tharuks. "Run, Fleur!" *Her wings were bent back, squashed against her body, her feet snared in the net's ropes. The beasts yanked, tightening the net.*

Fleur laughed.

Anguish ripped through Ajeuria. Her rider had betrayed her. The more she thrashed, the more tangled the net grew. She flamed the ropes, burning through those near her snout. A brute shoved a spear into the skin below her eye. "Move again and I'll blind you."

They muzzled her. Then the tharuks twisted her tail, sticking it with spears and drove more spear tips into her belly. They fastened metal shackles around her limbs, tying them together with chains so short she couldn't move. Reduced to huddling with her legs bunched under her and her snout and tail tied, Ajeuria was miserable.

Fleur visited her daily, watching Bruno lash Ajeuria with a metal-tipped whip until she cowered. They starved her for days, until she was thirsty enough to drink anything.

One morning, Fleur arrived with a bucket. "We're so sorry to have treated you this way, Ajeuria. I was being influenced by Zens, but now I've seen that he's a destroyer. He tricked me into believing him. Will you forgive me?" *Fleur started crying.* "You're one of the last of a long line of royal dragons. I never should have treated you this way."

Hobbled and aching all over from Bruno's whip, Ajeuria stretched her neck out to nudge Fleur. "I forgive you. I'm sorry Zens duped you and Bruno. Untie me so we can escape."

Fleur undid Ajeuria's muzzle. "First, drink. You must be thirsty."

Ajeuria thought nothing of the odd tang in the water.

"Quick," *said Fleur.* "Someone's coming, let me put your muzzle on so they can't tell." *Once she'd fastened the muzzle, Fleur laughed.* "Enjoy your swayweed, precious mummy's girl."

Starved and half-crazy from being tied up for days, Ajeuria was furious—until the swayweed took effect, filling her with hatred for the very dragons she loved. From that moment, she'd carried out Fleur's commands.

"Ajeuria," Roberto melded, hands still against her head. "I'm sorry for what Fleur and Bruno have done to you." He had to check her reactions, so he reactivated the memory. Ajeuria trembled, whimpering with each remembered strike of Bruno's whip.

Bitterness ricocheted through Roberto. Amato had whipped him too and whipped Razo, destroying all his love for his father. Bruno and Fleur had mistreated a royal dragon, twisting her love and loyalty into cruelty and deceit. They'd broken her.

"Please, Roberto, help my sister," Erob melded.

"Some dragons never recover from swayweed, Erob."

"I know." There was an ache in Erob's words that made Roberto's eyes sting. How would he feel if this was Adelina?

Shari

The drums beat softly as riders gathered beneath the dawn-kissed tips of Dragon's Teeth. Roberto approached the clearing with the other members of the council. Surprise rippled through the crowd. He didn't care what they thought; he'd been reinstated as master of imprinting and mental faculties early this morning, and cleared of attempted poisoning.

Shari, dressed in white and gold, was lying on top of a wooden platform, on a mat of woven river reeds with four long ropes at the corners. Her arms were crossed upon her chest, her face peaceful and her dark braids gleaming in the early morning sun. She looked serene.

Too serene for Shari. Her eyes were closed, not sparkling with laughter, or warm with understanding. Her lips were still, instead of smiling or encouraging. The only master aside from Lars who'd welcomed him here, Shari had brought light to his early days at Dragons' Hold. Amid whispers, stares and ugly rumors, she'd championed him and Adelina. He'd been hollowed out with the grief of losing Ma, bitter against his Pa, and angry at the world. Shari's trust had sown the kernel of his own self-belief and given him the motivation to train hard and become a dragon master. Despite his past, she'd won the council over, insisting they give him a chance to train here on Erob.

Without Shari and Adelina's love, he would've been a broken shell, stranded on a beach of grief.

The drums stopped. The only sounds were the soft breathing of the crowd and the birds warbling.

"It's time, Ezaara. Do you remember what to do?"

"Yes." Short and simple, but accompanied by a wash of warmth and a blaze of color that took his breath away. He'd done nothing to deserve this amazing woman in his life, yet she was here.

"You've let down your barriers," Erob said. *"You can finally be yourself with someone other than me."*

"It's her. She makes it easy."

"Maybe being an ignorant settler from Lush Valley was an advantage. She had no prejudices."

"But I did. And yet she won me over." Roberto stretched, trying to ease the ache in his shoulder. The fight with Ajeuria had been brutal, but she was safely in a holding pen. Within days, they'd know whether the swayweed had permanently affected her loyalty to her queen and the realm.

Above them, Zaarusha spread her massive wings and took flight. The sun caught her scales. A pale gray sheen dulled their usual iridescence.

"My mother isn't strong yet," Erob commented. *"She needs rest so she can recover."*

Roberto nodded. They all did.

Zaarusha landed on the far side of the clearing beneath her den, and Ezaara dismounted. Her emerald eyes met his, and his breath hitched. She was gorgeous. Her hair hung in a honey-blonde silken swathe, catching the dawn light as she moved with grace through the crowd, head high.

People watched her, some gazes curious, some welcoming, others openly hostile. A far cry from the warm welcome when she'd first arrived at Dragons' Hold.

Ezaara melded. *"Are you all right? Any injures from yesterday?"*

"None that you can't heal. Ezaara, you saved our queen."

"Thank the Egg."

"No, thank you."

"Well, actually, I couldn't have done it without what Ithsar taught me."

"I'm glad there was some purpose in us going to the Wastelands." His skin still prickled whenever he remembered his slit gut and the assassins' bizarre breeding plans.

"Good morning, Honored Council Leader." Ezaara stopped in front of Lars, bowing. "As rider of Zaarusha, Queen of Dragons' Realm, I, Ezaara, request that you begin the death rites for Shari, Honored Master of Livestock, who has recently died at the hand of a traitor."

Murmurs erupted as people realized Ezaara had been re-instated as Queen's Rider—and Shari had been murdered.

"I would be honored," Lars replied.

The crowd quieted as Lars plucked at his harp. Face careworn, he sang of Shari's ancestors across the Naobian Sea. Weaving a spell around the listeners, Lars sang of Shari's life, her journeys, her brief sojourn among mages, and then of her imprinting with Ariana and coming to Dragons' Hold to prove herself.

Ariana threw her head skyward and howled.

Roberto's throat ached. Would Erob howl for him when he died?

"Stop being so morose, or I'll howl right now," Erob said.

Roberto held back his tears as Lars sang of Shari's legendary gift with animals. But as Lars, gazing right at Roberto, sang about Shari's compassion for her fellow riders, tears ran freely down Roberto's cheeks, the sharp bite of salt on his lips.

§

Ezaara had never lost anyone she loved before, but it was obvious from Roberto and Adelina's reactions that they both had, and that Shari had been dear to them. Roberto's face was wet with tears as he cried unashamedly. To think this man had hidden everything behind a stone facade.

Shari's life-song danced among the crowd.

How would she die? Death had seemed so distant when she'd taken her vows as Queen's Rider. Would she plunge to her death amid a horde of bloodthirsty tharuks like Anakisha? Live her life enslaved to Zens like Roberto had been? Be murdered like Shari? Or killed in battle? Perhaps she'd die old, in Roberto's arms. Or would she, too, lose her life to a traitor?

For a moment, Handel's prophecy shot through her thoughts: Roberto's beautiful features twisted by hate, lunging at her. She shoved the image away. No, not Roberto. He would never harm her. He loved her.

Shari's life-song finished and the last quivering note of Lars' harp died.

"When you die, I will sing of your courage, fearlessness and willingness to give everything for the realm and for the man you love." Roberto's thoughts brought a faint smile to Ezaara's lips, even as she shed a tear for this woman she hadn't had the chance to know.

The dragons of Dragons' Hold joined Ariana in mourning for Shari. Their eerie howls reverberated off the mountainsides, making Ezaara's arms break out in goose bumps. Since she'd woken, she'd maintained her awareness of *sathir*, seeing the queen's vibrant connection wherever she went. Now, she opened her mind.

A rush of color enveloped her. The deep blue of Erob, the shimmering purple of Singlar, Vino's vibrant red, and the brown of Ariana. Hundreds of dragons' life threads were there, dancing across her vision, weaving from dragon to rider. Their loss surged through her and, for a moment, Ezaara faltered.

"This is why you're my rider. Feel them, understand them and honor them." Zaarusha strengthened her. Ezaara stood tall, letting their sorrow wash through her. *"You will lead the realm beside me with compassion, courage and strength."*

Ariana took one of the ropes at the corner of Shari's reed mat in her jaws. Erob, Vino and Singlar took up the other ropes. As one, they rose into the air, Shari suspended below them. The underside of Shari's mat was decorated with a breath-taking picture of Shari riding Ariana into a sunset. The dragons flew higher until they were nearly level with the peaks of Dragon's Teeth, then headed out over the forest.

In a seething mass of flapping wings and scraping talons, the rest of the dragons took flight, heading after Shari. To Ezaara's surprise, they hovered below Shari's mat, heads facing inward, forming layers of glinting rings as the early morning sun caught their scales.

"What's happening?" she asked Roberto.

"Something beautiful." As Roberto melded, his life thread became visible—a strong dark blue river flecked with silver, flowing between him, Erob and herself—accompanied by a rush of love.

Trumpeting, Ariana, Singlar, Vino and Erob released Shari's mat.

Ezaara gasped as Shari's limp form plummeted earthward toward the layers of waiting dragons. As her body fell between them, the dragons shot flames from their open maws, setting her body alight. Aflame, she fell, through more circles of flaming maws.

Within moments, the flames died and nothing but ash was left, scattering above the forest on the breeze.

TRAITORS

A surge of pride welled inside Roberto—Ezaara was seated at the head of the granite horseshoe, next to Lars. Finally, after all this time, she was in her rightful place as Queen's Rider.

Ezaara wiggled her feet under the table. *"Do you like my shoes?"*

Roberto smiled. *"Very nice."* She was wearing the shoes he'd given her on race day. Thank the Egg, *she* wasn't on trial today.

The council chamber was packed. Most people wore black armbands, to honor Jaevin and Shari, and brightly-colored ribbons to show support for Zaarusha.

Lars rapped his gavel. "Unfortunately, today's proceedings are no cause for celebration. First, I must apologize to Ezaara, Zaarusha and Master Roberto for our mistaken verdict. They have been cleared of all wrongdoing. Master Tonio expresses his heartfelt apologies." He nodded grimly. "Earlier this morning, after Shari's death rites, the Council of the Twelve Dragon Masters reinstated Roberto to his position as Master of Mental Faculties and Imprinting. We now also appoint our Honored Queen's Rider as a member of the council. Although she is not yet fully trained, she has proven her capability."

Cheers erupted, then clapping. Someone whistled—probably Kierion.

When the room quieted, Lars continued, "It's a tragedy that Master Shari and Master Jaevin, two of our finest dragon riders, have been murdered."

Around the chamber, people raised their fists to their hearts and murmured, "May their spirits soar with departed dragons."

"Thank you for your solidarity in protecting the queen last night. We expect Zaarusha to recover fully," Lars said. "No doubt, the praises of Ezaara, Master Roberto, Adelina, Gret and Kierion will be sung around hearths for years to come. But now, we must deal with the traitors."

The doors to the council chambers opened with an ominous thud. Blue guards led Bruno, Fleur and Simeon inside. The shackles on their wrists and ankles clanking, Fleur and Simeon sat in chairs facing the council. Simeon hung his head, pretending remorse. Fleur's nose was in the air, her lip curled in a faint sneer.

Roberto snorted. They were as guilty as rats crushing thrush eggs.

"Please sit, Bruno," Lars ordered.

Bruno objected. "Highly Honored Master Lars, may I *please* have a word with you?"

Lars sighed. "Make it quick."

Some people muttered as blue guards hustled Bruno forward. Others were deathly silent, staring daggers at the traitors.

Only one seat away from Lars, Roberto heard everything.

"My wife and son acted without my knowledge," Bruno whispered. "I'm horrified by their actions."

Bruno was trying to save his own skin—the coward.

Ezaara mind-melded, *"You took their crimes upon yourself to protect me, but he won't protect his own flesh and blood."*

"He's a gutter-swilling yellow belly."

"I'm worried, Roberto. Perhaps he knows we have no evidence against him, only against his wife and son."

There it was: his fear laid bare. *"Let's hope Lars has found something."*

"Hmm." Ezaara sounded as doubtful as he felt. As long as Bruno was at Dragons' Hold, no one was safe.

After ordering Bruno to his seat, Lars outlined the charges against Fleur and Simeon.

"He hasn't charged Bruno," Ezaara said.

"Not a good sign."

Walking out from behind the granite horseshoe, Lars addressed the assembly. "Last night, I inspected the infirmary. Fleur has stockpiled poisons and destroyed most of our healing remedies. The deadly cache she has amassed is enough to wipe out our dragons and riders several times over. She poisoned our queen, fought our Queen's Rider, and we suspect she has murdered two of our masters." The chill in Lars' voice sent frost down Roberto's spine. "I've said enough. Now, our Honored Queen's Rider will speak."

Ezaara's chair scraped as she stood, face grave. "I was too new and naive to detect the trap that Fleur and Simeon laid for me. They undermined my role and tried to banish me, knowing Zaarusha would be vulnerable. When Master Roberto was banished for their crimes, I discovered his innocence and left to rescue him. Although I am glad I did, I give my deepest apologies for not being here to protect our queen."

"Stop this. It's not your fault!"

Ignoring Roberto, Ezaara continued, "They poisoned Zaarusha. They attacked me, Gret and Adelina. Ajeuria nearly killed Erob and Master Roberto."

"She did not. I'm much stronger than Ajeuria," Erob interrupted, melding with them both.

Still facing her people, Ezaara ignored Erob too. "We were lucky, but Master Jaevin and Master Shari were not. As the evidence unfolds, listen carefully and learn. Zaarusha and I never want traitors at Dragons' Hold again."

"Lying swine!" Fleur scowled. "This is preposterous. We've done our best for Dragons' Hold. She's the traitor."

Not letting Fleur's outburst faze her, Ezaara sat, composed and looking … well, regal. Her speech was a far cry from her first one here, during the feast. Her whole demeanor had changed. Had it only been four and a half weeks ago? *Spoken like a true Queen's Rider.*

"Thank you."

Lars rapped his gavel. "I defer to our Dragon Corps Spymaster, Tonio, who will call our witnesses."

Tonio's dark eyes swept the chamber. "Our first witness is Adelina of Naobia." He nodded as Adelina stood. "Adelina, you came to me recently about something strange you'd found in the Queen's Rider's cavern. Please tell us."

"After Ezaara accidentally injured Sofia, Simeon gave her what he claimed was a restorative tea, but it contained a weak dose of skarkrak, a Robandi poison. It knocked her out, so she couldn't visit Sofia."

"How exactly did you recognize the skarkrak?"

"I smelt it as I emptied the Queen's Rider's vomit pail."

Amid a flurry of murmurs, Ezaara blushed bright pink. *"Great."*

"The scent of skarkrak was on Shari's soup bowl," said Adelina. "It was her last meal." Adelina produced Shari's dish from her bag, passing it to Tonio, who sniffed it and nodded.

Master Alyssa broke in. "When Jaevin died, Fleur disposed of his dishes, saying Montanarians didn't like food near corpses, but it was probably just an excuse to hide evidence."

Tonio gestured to a blue guard, who passed him a leather pouch. "This was found in the infirmary. Adelina, can you identify it?"

Adelina sniffed the contents of the package. "It's skarkrak."

"This is the same as the poison that was in Shari's soup. Thank you, Master Alyssa and Adelina." Tonio's predatory gaze swept over the traitors. "Most of you know the Queen's Rider had an accident at the knife-throwing range, but not many know that Ezaara injured Sofia because she was immersed in a violent mind-melded vision from Ajeuria. Ezaara, please explain exactly what happened."

Ezaara's voice shook as she spoke. Through her thoughts, Roberto saw flashes of fire and smelt the stench of burning flesh. Half way through explaining, she paled and gripped the table.

"Do you need fresh air?"

"No, I just need to get through this."

Sympathetic murmurs rippled through the crowd.

"She's lying," screamed Fleur. "Lying through her teeth."

Tonio shook his head. "Ajeuria was seen near the knife range. Our dragons witnessed the mental assault and have been on the alert since to find out who was responsible. When Ajeuria tried again last night, they recognized her."

"Fleur," Lars thundered, "we've mind-melded with Ajeuria, and she's revealed how you tortured her and fed her swayweed. You'd best stay silent until requested to speak."

Glaring, Fleur snapped her jaw shut.

"None of this has anything to do with me," Bruno whined.

Roberto's fists clenched. Bruno was right—it didn't.

"Silence, Bruno!" Tonio barked. "Kierion, you're our next witness."

At Tonio's taut nod, Kierion told everyone how Ezaara's cane had been snapped and hidden.

Fresh anger surged through Roberto. Simeon had ruined one of his mother's few remaining belongings.

Tonio continued, "Ajeuria's vision, the skarkrak and missing cane caused prejudice against our Queen's Rider, but she isn't the only one affected by Fleur's actions. Master Roberto has discovered another of Fleur's ploys."

Roberto pulled back his sleeve, revealing the wound that had never healed properly since the battle at River's Edge. "Fleur's famous healing unguent, used for years at Dragons' Hold, causes damage. Look." He walked through the chamber, showing the red lines webbing outward from his scar. "If you have a wound that Fleur's treated that hasn't healed properly, put your hand up."

Gasps ripped through the chamber as hands shot up.

"She's sabotaged our healing," someone cried.

Nodding, Roberto sat and Tonio started summarizing the evidence.

"Aren't you going to mention Shari's dragon?" Ezaara asked.

"You mean Ariana's belly gripe? No, we can't track it directly to Fleur." He sighed. *"It's been a tough day. How are you feeling?"*

"I should be asking you that after your fight with Ajeuria."

Revealing his feelings was strange after so many years of maintaining a tough facade. *"I'm good, but this is taking ages. I wish it was over."*

"Why? What's the hurry?"

"Then I can be with you."

Her surprise and pleasure rippled through him. *"Promise?"*

"A horde of tharuks couldn't keep me away." He stifled the urge to grin at her. Too many people were watching.

The doors burst open and Gret hobbled in, leaning on Ezaara's cane.

"Ah, I loaned it to her. Hope that's all right."

"Of course," Roberto replied.

Gret gazed at the packed room, her face reddening. "Sorry, I'm late! Master Lars and honored council members, I have evidence against Simeon, son of Fleur and Bruno."

Tonio paused, eyebrows raised.

Lars waved Gret forward. "Please proceed."

Gret limped through the onlookers to face the council. "I'm not sure if she told you, but the night our Queen's Rider left for the Wastelands, Simeon attacked her in the tunnels. His intent was to defile her. Our swords prevented him."

A chill ran through Roberto, and then the desire to drive his blade through Simeon's heart. *"Ezaara! When were you going to tell me this?"*

"I was too busy rescuing you," Ezaara snapped, a flash of Simeon's leering face and grasping hands shooting through him as she remembered. She paled. *"And it's not a memory I cherish reliving."*

Roberto seethed. That shrotty louse. *"Sorry, Ezaara, you need my understanding, not my anger."*

"Thank you." She bit her lip.

Shards, Roberto longed to shelter her in his arms—impossible with everyone watching.

"My Honored Queen's Rider, is Gret's accusation against Simeon true?" Lars' face was stormy. At Ezaara's nod, his piercing blue eyes cut Simeon to shreds on the spot.

Roberto rose. "If Simeon forced himself upon our Queen's Rider, then Trixia must've spoken the truth. He must've forced her, making her pregnant."

"Yes!" Gret exclaimed. "Trixia was innocent, but Simeon was not punished."

"You'd believe that whore, over the son of two dragon masters?" Simeon yelled.

"My daughter's not a whore!" Trixia's father rose from his seat, hands in fists.

"Yes, she is!" Fleur yelled back.

Lars rapped his gavel, but people were shouting, their outrage boiling over.

"Silence!" Lars bellowed, his icy gaze slicing through the crowd. "This is a trial, not a market place. Anyone who doesn't abide by the rules will be removed." As the crowd settled, he continued, "We have sufficient evidence against Simeon, son of Fleur and Bruno, and against Fleur, wife of Bruno, to banish them both. All dragon masters in accord, raise your hand."

One by one, the eight remaining dragon masters from the council of twelve raised their hands.

"Good, the voting is unanimous and complete. Simeon and Fleur shall be banished. Bruno, husband of Fleur and father of Simeon, please stand," Lars ordered.

Bruno's shackles clanked. He sneered at Simeon and Fleur as if they were dirt, then faced Lars. "I support my queen whole-heartedly, doing my best to protect her and Dragons' Realm. There's not a mark against me."

Fleur piped up. "It's true. My husband is innocent."

Roberto's heart raced and his hands curled into fists. Bruno was every bit as guilty as Simeon and Fleur. Surely they wouldn't get away with this?

Hendrik pounded the table with his meaty fist. "Bruno is my trusted and loyal friend. Not only my own, but also Jaevin's— may his spirit soar with departed dragons. I stand by Bruno and support him."

Lars gazed at Hendrik and Bruno intently.

Surely Lars didn't believe that? Roberto got up again. "Last night, Bruno sent Lars, myself and some blue guards away, to head off a so-called tharuk attack, while his wife and son were poisoning the queen. That was not a coincidence." He slammed his palms on the table. "Bruno is as guilty as Fleur and Simeon, and should be banished."

Tonio cut in, "To banish someone, we need evidence, not conjecture."

Roberto sat with a thud. That rankled. They'd wanted to convict Ezaara on less.

"Bruno is correct," Lars said. "In his entire six years at Dragons' Hold, there hasn't been a mark against him."

What? Couldn't Lars see how dangerous Bruno was? Ajeuria's memory of Bruno whipping her flashed to mind. He'd use that.

"But," Lars continued, "in his role as Master Seer, Bruno assured us all was in order. He caused us to doubt our own patrol leaders, while the tharuks made constant inroads into our realm, enslaving our folk, drugging them senseless, and starving them." He stabbed his finger toward Bruno. "You, Bruno, have not served us as master of prophecy. With the power vested in me as leader of this council, I demote you. You will no longer serve as a master on the Council of the Twelve Dragon Masters."

No! Lars had to banish him. Bruno was a snake lying in wait. He'd strike later. Hard, fast and venomous.

"Master Lars." Roberto rose. "I can test Bruno and discover any memories that betray his intent."

"That won't be necessary."

"But I also tested Ajeuria and—"

Lars cut in. "Roberto, you're obviously biased."

"With good reason," Erob interjected.

"I'm glad you *see through Bruno,"* Roberto melded.

The door slammed open. Seppi, leader of the blue guards, marched through the crowd. Taking a pouch from his belt, he tipped the contents on the table. Rough yellow gems glittered in the torchlight. "The blue guards searched Bruno's possessions and found these."

"No!" Bruno lunged, shackles crashing against the granite table, as he grasped at the gems. Blue guards yanked him back and held him at sword point.

"They're obviously yours," Lars stated. "What are they?"

Bruno clamped his lips shut, glaring.

Roberto's breath caught. He'd seen those gems before. "Zens mines those stones," he said. "They're only found in Death Valley."

"So Zens is your paymaster, Bruno." Lars scratched his beard. "What exactly has he been paying you to do?"

Her face weary and grief-stricken, Threcia stood. "I believe Bruno poisoned my husband." She spoke softly, everyone straining to hear. "Jaevin told me how kind Bruno had been. On his way to collect the ceremonial swords in Ezaara's cavern, Jaevin met Bruno in the tunnels. Jaevin was called away to a tharuk attack, so Bruno offered to collect the swords and take them to our cavern to be kept overnight for the Queen's Rider's test." She shook her head. "He had access to the swords. I'd forgotten all about it until now, because I thought Roberto was guilty. It never occurred to me that a close friend would—" Tears tracked down her face. "Excuse me."

"Thank you, Threcia," Lars said.

Wearing her grief with honor, Threcia made her way to the door.

Lars turned to Roberto. "Test Bruno, now."

Blue guards held Bruno fast while Roberto placed his hands on his temples.

Bruno had barred his thoughts behind a dark wall. The scar on Roberto's cheek twitched where his father had whipped him. Sweat beading his forehead, he peeled back Bruno's defensive layer, a scrap at a time, until his memories were stripped bare. "Bruno poisoned the ceremonial swords and encouraged Fleur and Simeon to kill as many dragon masters and their dragons as possible," Roberto announced.

"You lowlife, using me and Jaevin!" Hendrik drew his sword and leaped at Bruno. Blue guards grabbed him, dragging him out a side tunnel.

The room burst into an uproar, people yelling at Bruno and his family, waving their fists and spitting.

Zaarusha bellowed and the other dragons joined in.

Lars rapped his gavel on the table, but it was lost in the uproar.

Roberto scooped the yellow stones back into the pouch and passed them to Lars. "For shards' sake, keep these safe."

Lars tucked them away and dashed forward to help the blue guards restore order.

Had Lars even heard him? In the chaos, Roberto didn't have a chance to explain that, from examining Bruno's memories, he now understood why the yellow crystals were more dangerous than Fleur's poison.

River of Sathir

Simeon leered at Ezaara, his gaze crawling over her body like a cockroach. It made her want to brush herself off. Or, even better, punch him in the eye so he couldn't stare anymore. Seppi yanked Simeon's head around so he couldn't see her and dragged him off. Other blue guards manhandled Simeon's parents out the door.

"Shards, he's a creep," Roberto melded. *"Always has been. I'm glad he's leaving."*

"Did he really force himself upon that girl?"

Roberto's face was grim. *"They never proved it, but ask Gret. Trixia was her best friend."*

Lars dismissed the onlookers, who—some bandying insults about Simeon's family—trailed out the door.

Drumbeats boomed beneath Ezaara's feet. Banishment drums. She remembered Roberto's hateful expression and her horror at him murdering Jaevin.

"Oops, you shared that memory," he said.

"Sorry." Ezaara shuddered. *"Banishment drums are always going to remind me of you being sent away."*

"To save you, I'd do it again, in a heartbeat."

"Let's stay together instead."

"Sure, right after we're done here." A rush of heat accompanied Roberto's words, making her blush.

Tonio's keen gaze sharpened, flitting between her and Roberto.

When the crowd had dispersed and only the council were in the room, Lars spoke. "This has been a difficult time. I'm glad

Master Roberto and our Honored Queen's Rider have returned. We welcome Ezaara to our council. With two dead and two banished, we're now four masters short. Ezaara, would you mind overseeing the infirmary until we replace Fleur?"

"Yes, Lars, it would be my pleasure."

"Please urgently identify any poisons and antidotes. Fleur may have destroyed valuable remedies, so you'll need to build up supplies. I'll assign people to help." He glanced around. "Derek, as master of instruction, you'll take over Swordmaster Jaevin's duties until we have a replacement."

"Of course," Derek answered.

"Master Shari had several assistants, so I'll let them oversee her activities for now. Unfortunately, we have no one suitable to take the role of master of prophecy, so that post will have to remain empty." Lars' throat bobbed. "I am deeply saddened to lose two esteemed masters, as I'm sure we all are. Please comfort our riders and take care of our people."

Tonio nodded. "Zens has infiltrated our council once. He'll try to do it again. Report anything suspicious to me immediately."

"Any further questions?" Lars asked.

Everyone was too numb to say much, so Lars dismissed them.

Ezaara was bone-weary. *"Roberto, I'm so glad this is over. I could sleep for a week."*

"Later. Meet me in the orchard." Fire accompanied his words, leaping into her veins. Roberto's onyx eyes burned away her fatigue.

"See you there." Ezaara swept out the door upon the waves of drumbeats, Roberto at her side.

§

It'd been a long day, but there was more work to do. Lars put his gavel away and stood. He needed to see Shari's assistants. As the last of the masters drifted out of the room, Tonio sidled up to him.

"Come with me, there's something you need to see. Urgently."

Within a heartbeat, Lars was striding after Tonio to the landing outside. How could the sun shine so brightly over the basin when his heart was filled with sorrow? Two masters dead. Two more banished. And a royal dragon that might not recover from swayweed. "What is it, Tonio?"

"Look." He gestured toward Roberto on Erob, and Ezaara on Zaarusha, high above Dragon's Teeth. "Tell me what you see."

"Two highly skilled riders, but we knew that." Lars turned away.

"Look again."

Ezaara sat low on Zaarusha, Roberto mimicking her position on Erob. Simultaneously, both dragons swooped to the east, then spiraled down toward the orchard, replicating each other's movements with exact timing, as if attached by a giant piece of string.

"Have you seen dragons fly in such tight formation before?" The intensity of Tonio's voice made his spine prickle.

That's what he meant. Nodding, Lars replied. "Only two couples."

"*Couples.* Who?"

"Yanir and Anakisha, of course."

"And?" Tonio pressed.

Lars sighed. "Hans and Marlies. But that doesn't mean these two are mind-melding. Erob and Zaarusha are mother and son. Their bond is strong."

Tonio just arched an eyebrow.

"All right, so the riders might be melding, but that doesn't mean they're romantically involved."

"Blushing at each other in a council meeting isn't adequate evidence either, but the law is the law."

"Tonio, she's practically qualified," Lars warned. "We can't afford to lose another master, especially not the master of mental faculties and imprinting. Not when we need to perform mental tests on every newcomer to Dragons' Hold."

"Understood."

"This is one of those times when your suspicions must not result in action."

Tonio's gaze was stony. "Do I have to remind you of the only *other* couple that could mind-meld?"

Giddi and Mazyka—two of the most powerful mages the realm had ever seen.

"Mazyka was seventeen—like Ezaara," Tonio continued.

Impulsive and talented, Mazyka had quickly grown power-hungry and had encouraged her master to use his power in forbidden ways, nearly destroying Dragons' Realm.

Lars sighed. "Very well. Keep an eye on them, but do it yourself, not via one of your spies. Discuss your findings only with me."

"Will do."

"And Tonio," Lars cautioned, "Roberto is innocent of his father's crimes. This had better not be about you getting even with Amato."

Tonio's face tightened.

Lars shook his head and strode away.

§

Flying with Ezaara and Zaarusha was glorious. Every wing dip, each swoop and turn of their downward spiral were in harmony. Ezaara's laugh unfurled a coil inside Roberto that he'd held tight for years. Colors shot through him in a thousand tiny bursts.

He laughed too.

"*So, you've finally found someone you can meld with, who loves you for yourself,*" Erob said. "*Someone you can trust.*"

"*I had no idea I could feel so happy. It's amazing.*"

"*Caution, Roberto, you're both subject to the laws of the council.*"

"*As if I could forget.*"

They spiraled down among the trees, the air sweet with the scent of ripe peaches. Erob descended to the grass, his legs bunching to soften the impact. Within moments, Roberto was racing to meet Ezaara. When they were barely an arm's length apart, they stopped, staring at each other.

Her eyes were green sea foam at dawn, churning with power and emotion. Her face was awash with tenderness. What had he done to deserve her?

She smiled. "*You're you.*"

He swept her into his arms, burying his face in her hair and inhaling deeply. Light burst through him. This was so right.

§

Ezaara felt so alive. Every fiber of her being was singing. Roberto enfolded her in his arms, his onyx eyes full of wonder. The world shifted. This was where she belonged, right here.

"*I'm glad Zaarusha chose you,*" Roberto's breath caressed her neck, making her skin tingle. He traced her cheek with gentle fingers, and tilted her chin. "*I love you, Ezaara, and always will.*"

His lips brushed hers. Gods, they were so soft.

Ezaara slid her fingers into his hair and tugged him closer. "*And I love you too.*" And then, she was kissing him back, her lips against his, millions of stars exploding inside her, shimmering with liquid light.

And then a strange thing happened.

The *sathir,* dancing around them—a myriad of colors from her, and midnight blue shot with silver from him—merged. At first, her colors swirled around his, then the blue seemed to absorb them, lightening and pulsing until they formed one river of brilliant light.

Fire roared through Ezaara and images flitted through her—from him, from her—weaving in harmony, a life-song of their short time together.

Roberto's eyes shone. *"I never dreamed love would be like this."*

Ezaara touched his lips with her fingertips. She felt, more than heard, the sharp intake of his breath. His eyes smoldered, burning through her, making her tremble. He crushed her body against the firm planes of his chest, then his mouth was upon hers again.

Her heart raced as she melted against him, running her hands over his shoulders and into his hair, pulling him closer.

"I love you," she groaned against his lips. Never had she imagined a kiss could feel like this.

"Take care, Ezaara," Zaarusha melded. *"Dragon above."*

Ezaara broke off their kiss, and glanced up. Antonika was circling the orchard.

"Don't worry." Roberto stroked strands of her hair back from her face. *"Tonio's not riding her. She's alone."*

"If she tells him, we're in big trouble."

"After everything we've been through, I don't care. We'll face that if we have to, but one thing I know: we'll never be ripped apart again."

This time, when he kissed her, fire seared her lips, burning a trail to her core, setting her soul ablaze. Their kiss was urgent, ravenous. Ezaara was lost in a sea of sensation as tendrils spiraled deep inside her, awakening feelings she'd never known.

Roberto pulled back, his eyes swallowing hers. He ran a hand through her hair. "I've never felt this way before."

"Neither have I."

"One day, when you're qualified, I'll ask Lars if we can be hand-fasted."

She smiled against his lips, murmuring, "Yes, one day." For now, they had these forbidden, hidden kisses.

Roberto kissed her once more, gently. "We'd better get back before someone misses us."

They walked hand in hand through the orchard, toward their dragons, their river of *sathir* dancing around them. Birds flitted in and out of the trees, feasting on peaches in the summer sun. A deep warm glow suffused Ezaara.

"Do you realize, it's just over one moon since you arrived?" Roberto asked. "We should celebrate."

"We just did." Ezaara giggled. Four and a half short weeks. A whole different life.

She was Queen's Rider. She'd finally earned her rightful place on Zaarusha's back, leading Dragons' Realm. And Roberto had earned his place inside her heart.

"Help, Ezaara!" The voice was faint, as if it was far away, with a familiar deep timbre.

"Handel?"

"It's your father, Hans. He's dying."

Shock hollowed Ezaara's belly. No, not Pa. *"Where is he, Handel? What's wrong with him?"*

"I'm bringing him to the infirmary." Handel's voice was fading. *"Please, you need to—"*

"Handel?"

No answer.

Roberto touched her face. "What is it?"

"Handel melded. My father's dying." What about her brother? If Pa was dying, where was Tomaaz? And Zaarusha had said Ma was off finding Zaarusha's son. Was Ma in danger, too?

Roberto enveloped her in his arms. "It's all right, Ezaara. We'll face this together."

"They're on their way here. I have to get ready." Her hands grew slick with sweat and her pulse thundered. Pa. Dying. How could she prepare when she didn't know what was wrong with him? She only had a few healing remedies—and Fleur's questionable supplies. "Roberto, I don't know what … how …"

Roberto took her hands, squeezing them. "Ezaara, if anyone can do this, it's you. I'll be with you, every step of the way."

Breathing deeply, Ezaara nodded. "Let's go."

They ran to Erob and Zaarusha, and took to the sky, soaring above the trees, their dragons' wings flipping in perfect synchronicity.

More Riders of Fire Adventures

EZAARA—BOOK 1

DRAGON HERO—BOOK 2
Go on, turn the page for a sneak preview!

DRAGON RIFT—BOOK 3

DRAGON STRIKE—BOOK 4
(2019)

Coming Soon:
Riders of Fire Prequels

DRAGON HEALER—BOOK 5

DRAGON MAGE—BOOK 6

SEA DRAGON—BOOK 7

Free Novelette—Silver Dragon—Riders of Fire

Marlies is good at healing. But she wasn't good enough to save her friend. Now the Nightshader gang are after her.
They're fighters - strong, fast and mean. And they know where to find her. But when Giddi, the Dragon Mage, calls Marlies deep into Great Spanglewood Forest, she finds something she never expected...
What's waiting for Marlies in Spanglewood? And how will it change her life forever?

Find out what happens to Marlies, and how it shapes Ezaara's life, in *Silver Dragon*, exclusively on Eileen's site and only available for a limited time. EileenMuellerAuthor.com/Readers-Free-Books

Turn the page for a preview of *Dragon Hero*.
Don't miss out! Start reading today!

EILEEN MUELLER

DRAGON HERO

RIDERS OF FIRE

BOOK TWO

Dragon Hero
Riders of Fire 2

Prologue - Eighteen Years Ago

Marlies strode along the tunnel, torches flickering and shadows flitting across the stone walls. Although it'd been a long day in the infirmary, she had one more duty before she could sleep. Lifting her torch, she turned down the passage to the dragon queen's den.

Her footfalls echoed as she passed through Anakisha's empty sleeping chamber. Sadness washed through her. Had it only been two moons since they'd lost the Queen's Rider? It seemed longer. There'd been many people to mourn—and dragons. Marlies shook her head. Too many deaths in one battle; and more dead and wounded in skirmishes since. She walked under the archway into Zaarusha's den and placed the torch in a sconce.

Zaarusha, the dragon queen, was curled in her nest, her head tucked under a wing, and her tail snug around her body. She unfurled her wings, myriad colors flickering on her scales, like rainbows in an opal. A glint of gold under the dragon's haunches revealed her precious eggs. Zaarusha extended her neck, facing Marlies, her yellow eyes dull.

Marlies stretched out her hand to touch the dragon queen's snout, so they could mind-meld. She forced her thoughts to be cheery. The last thing Zaarusha needed was sadness.

"Thank you for coming," Zaarusha's voice thrummed in Marlies' mind.

"How are your dragonets doing today?"

"My babies are fine."

Babies. Marlies flinched.

"Only a few more weeks until they hatch." Zaarusha's sigh echoed like a rock clattering down a mountainside. *"Syan will never see our dragonets. I miss him: his companionship; flying together. Hunting."* The queen flicked her tongue out.

"Did anyone bring you food?"

"They did, but I had no appetite."

Marlies scratched the queen's eye ridges. *"Would you like to hunt tonight? A meal would do you good. It's been a while."*

"A week." The dragon's belly rumbled.

Marlies smiled. *"You are hungry. Sorry, I couldn't come sooner. Several of our wounded have infections and fevers, so I haven't left the infirmary for days."*

"I can always rely on you." Zaarusha gazed at her, eyes unblinking. *"You'll take care of my eggs?"*

"Of course. I'm not Syan, but I'll do my best."

"Remember not to touch them." Zaarusha butted Marlies' shoulder with her snout. *"I won't be long."*

"The fresh air will do you good."

Careful not to crush the eggs, the dragon queen rose to her feet and stepped out of her nest. She sprang to the open mouth of her den and, with a flash of her colorful wings, leapt off the mountainside and was swallowed by darkness.

Marlies turned back to the nest. Four golden eggs, as tall as a boy of ten summers, were nestled in the hay. The torch's flames made their translucent shells glow. Through the tough membrane of the eggs, dragonets were visible. The green flexed its wing nubs. Marlies held her breath, watching the magical creature.

"Zaarusha's babies." Unconsciously, her hand went to her belly. She swallowed. These were the last of the royal offspring. Syan, Zaarusha's mate, had been killed in battle. His rider, Yanir, too. Anakisha and Zaarusha had tried to save them, but Anakisha had fallen from dragonback, plunging into their enemies' hands. Zaarusha had still been carrying eggs, so, not wanting to risk the lives of her babies, she'd been forced to abandon her rider and her mate and return to Dragons' Hold.

For two moons, the Hold had been grieving—but no one as hard as Zaarusha. She whimpered when she slept, and keened by day. The only things keeping her clinging to life were her duty to the realm and the beautiful creatures moving within these fragile shells.

For Marlies, seeing the dragonets was like walking on glittering shards. Their beauty transfixed her but cut deeply. Married for three years now, she and Hans had no children. True, she was still young, only in her nineteenth year, but something was wrong.

Although she'd healed other barren women using herbal remedies, she couldn't heal herself. Only Hans knew the herbs she'd tried, the rituals by full moon and the tears she'd shed in his arms. And not even he knew of her bitter tears when she was alone. Every babe born at Dragons' Hold gave her reason to rejoice and cause for pain. Royal dragonets were no exception.

All gangly limbs and neck, the orange dragonet turned over. The deep blue dragon baby opened its jaws. The green wriggled. In the smallest shell, the purple dragonet was curled in a ball, its wings folded tight against its back. It was so delicate, so fragile, somehow endearing.

Her breath a whisper, Marlies watched it sleep.

It was still for a long time.

Perhaps it wasn't sleeping. Perhaps something was wrong.

Marlies moved closer, but recalled Zaarusha's warning. *"Remember not to touch them."*

As if it sensed her, the purple dragonet woke.

A faint humming came from the egg. Marlies' breath caught. She leaned closer, her nose a hand's breadth from the golden shell. If only she had her own babe to hold, to croon to. She caught herself humming back to Zaarusha's babe. Why not? She ached to have a baby. Why shouldn't she sing to Zaarusha's dragonet?

The dragonet pushed against the thin gold membrane, seeking her. First its snout, and then its body. Its crooning grew louder.

Was it calling her?

The dragonet's eyes pleaded with her.

Unable to help herself, Marlies sang a lullaby.

The baby dragon's music swelled, drawing Marlies closer, wrapping around her. The lonely, empty aching inside her eased. Her fingertips brushed the shell. She gasped in shock, but before she could draw her hand away, a heartbeat pulsed through the membrane, making her fingers tickle. Euphoria swept through her. Marlies laughed, like she hadn't in years.

The dragonet's humming rose in pitch then fell—it was laughing, as if they were sharing a joke.

Marlies lay her hands against the shell and closed her eyes, focusing on the voice and the pulse of the creature before her. Her hands filled with energy, her head with music. The stone floor swayed beneath her feet. Marlies felt as light as a petal drifting on a breeze, as radiant as a star.

The dragonet's pulse grew stronger, bounding against her hands. Energy ran up her arms to her core. Then it stopped.

Marlies' eyes flew open.

The dragonet was lying on its back, floating in the shell, its wings limp beneath it. She pressed her hands against the shell. No hum. No pulse.

"Please, please, no." Her voice caught. She rubbed her hands against the shell, willing the dragonet to move.

But there was only silence.

Stillness.

Nothing beneath her hands.

Marlies' mouth opened and shut. With a strangled sob, she fled.

LUSH VALLEY

Tomaaz adjusted the sack of potatoes on his shoulder and stepped over a wayward chicken. He frowned. What was Lofty up to? In a corner of the crowded marketplace, Lofty had his head together with Old Bill and the pair of them were grinning like thieves. Rather Lofty than him. He didn't want to go near Old Bill. The only decent thing about him was his cloth—bolts of bright turquoise seascapes, blazing-gold-and-orange birds and strange creatures and plants—transported into Lush Valley from far over the Grande Alps. From exotic places Tomaaz had never been, like Naobia on the southern coast, Montanara or Spanglewood Forest.

One day he and Lofty would leave this valley and explore those far-off places. It's not like he planned to lug Pa's vegetables around for the rest of his life.

Old Bill shook Lofty's hand, while beside them, Bill's drab daughter was lost among the bright cloth, staring at her feet. That was nothing new. Lovina was always staring at the floor. Tomaaz had never heard her mumble more than a word or two. Oh well, he had more exciting things to do than keep an eye on Lofty.

Like delivering potatoes.

Tomaaz dodged a bunch of children playing tag, and headed for the baker's stall, passing over the sack. "These should be good for your potato patties, Pieter," he said. "Pa's given you our best."

"As always." Pieter chuckled, and carried the potatoes to his cart.

"Thank you," said Beatrice, Pieter's daughter, flashing a smile, then ducking her head.

Inhaling the aroma of pastries and pies, Tomaaz smiled back at her. With Pieter distracted, it was now or never. He raked a hand through his unruly blond curls. "Beatrice, would you like to go for a walk? Later? I—I mean, after you've finished?"

"I'd love to. I can bring you an apricot pastry if you'd like." Beatrice gazed up at him through her red lashes. "I made them myself."

Red. Even her lashes were red. And her cheeks now, too. Tomaaz grinned. Asking her had been worth the gamble—she liked him. "Thanks. I'll come by after we've packed up."

Her smile lit her eyes, making his day.

Humming, Tomaaz strode through the marketplace past Klaus' leatherwear stand. The enticing aroma of cheese melted on slabs of bread made his stomach grumble.

Whistling nonchalantly, Lofty fell into step with him.

Tomaaz rolled his eyes. "Come on, Lofty. Tell me, what were you and Old Bill up to?"

"Nothing." Lofty gave him that innocent look of his. "Just ordering more silk for Ma's scarves."

"Of course you were." Tomaaz snorted. They skirted a goat pen and wandered past a weapon stand, stopping to admire a knife.

"Such a beauty," Lofty said, weighing the knife in his hand. "But way too expensive." Suddenly, Lofty dropped the knife, sucking in his breath. "There she is. Across the square."

Lofty had a sixth sense when it came to Tomaaz's sister. Like a homing pigeon, he always knew where she was. It'd been moons since Lofty had admitted to Tomaaz that he liked his twin sister. And Lofty had been trying to catch Ezaara's eye ever since—usually failing.

"You're not going to tease Ezaara again, are you?" Tomaaz asked, shaking his head.

"No, you are!" Lofty beamed. "I've hit upon the perfect plan. You challenge her to a sword fight, and I'll swoop in and save her. She'll finally see me as a hero."

"I doubt it."

"Go on, do it for me." Lofty was eager, like a bird bouncing on its perch. "I've got to try something."

Tomaaz hesitated. "Here in the square? Feathers will fly if Klaus catches us."

"Beatrice will be watching."

Tomaaz hesitated. Lofty had him. "All right, but if this doesn't work, promise me you won't cook up any more mad schemes."

"I promise." Lofty's solemn look didn't fool Tomaaz one bit. "Come on," he said, "it's just a bit of fun."

Tomaaz led Lofty further away from Klaus' stall—there was no point in asking for trouble. They trailed Ezaara as she examined plaited onions and garlic wreaths.

"Go on, now," Lofty urged, "before Ezaara notices us."

Beatrice had a good view from here. It was as good a time as any. Tomaaz slid his sword out of its scabbard. The scrape cut through the buzz in the market square.

Ezaara spun, dropping her basket. In a heartbeat, her sword was in her hand, her blade gleaming in the sun.

She'd always had good reactions. People backed out of the way, clearing a ring around Tomaaz and his sister. He lunged, striking fast. Ezaara parried, then feinted, but it didn't fool him. He pressed forward with a series of quick strokes, driving her back towards an apple cart.

"Take five to one for Tomaaz," Lofty yelled among the clink of coppers.

That idiot! Betting against Ezaara wasn't going to win her over. Tomaaz lunged again. That was close, he'd nearly scratched her face. That wouldn't impress Beatrice or Ezaara. He thrust again, but Ezaara danced out of reach, then lunged back at him.

She must've been practicing. Her counterattacks were coming hard and fast. Tomaaz blocked with power, driving his sword against hers. Dodging, Ezaara bumped Bill's table and bolts of cloth went flying. She leapt over them, fleeing.

Tomaaz chased her.

She whirled to face him, blade high. "Seen any pretty girls today? Look, there's one behind you."

If she'd seen him talking to Beatrice, he'd never hear the end of it. Ignoring her jibe, he deflected her sword and attacked again. When was Lofty going to jump in? This wasn't supposed to go on so long. And surely Beatrice had seen enough by now?

"Any more bets?" Lofty called to the onlookers. He seemed more interested in taking coin than rescuing Ezaara.

Ezaara was slowing, tiring. Maybe that's what Lofty was waiting for. Tomaaz slashed his blade at his sister's torso.

Ezaara stumbled, landing on her knee. "Ow!"

Oh gods, hopefully he hadn't hurt her. "Ezaara, are you all right?"

Driving her sword under his arm, Ezaara tapped his shirt. "I did it!" she cried, leaping to her feet. "I beat you."

Whistles and yells erupted around them. She'd fooled him, but it was a fair win.

"Go, Ezaara!" Lofty called.

She was beaming.

Maybe Lofty's strategy, whatever it was, would work today.

Tomaaz glanced towards the baker's stand. Beatrice wasn't there. All this for nothing. Oh well, at least they were going for a walk together, later. For now, he had to make Ezaara feel good about her win.

"Aagh, beaten," he groaned, sheathing his sword, and wiping sweat from his brow.

"You chose to fight me here." Ezaara's eyes blazed.

She'd fought well.

Grinning, she stepped back, sliding her sword into her scabbard.

Around them, coppers changed hands. He caught a glimpse of Beatrice on the edge of the crowd, smiling at him. Tomaaz's chest swelled with pride. She *had* seen him fight. And it looked as if she was glad for Ezaara's win, too. Not only was Beatrice beautiful, she was kind-hearted.

Lofty clapped Tomaaz on the back. Then he kissed Ezaara, right on the lips. What? That wasn't what they'd agreed. The crowd *oohed.*

Old Bill nudged his way forward and gave Lofty a handful of grimy coppers.

Lofty punched his fist in the air.

That's what they'd been up to! Rigging the fight to make money. And probably betting Lofty would kiss Ezaara. Lofty hadn't had a chance to rescue Ezaara because she'd won in her own right, but he'd still embarrassed her. Ezaara would never fall for Lofty like that. Why couldn't he see it?

Yep, Ezaara's cheeks were flaming. And not from passion. She was mortified—and as mad as a bear with a toothache.

People scattered as Klaus barreled through the crowd. "Is that those twins again?" With a bellow like an ox, a girth to match a draft horse, and even taller than Lofty, Klaus was the settlement's arbitrator. "What's going on?"

"I'm off to get that knife." Lofty thrust a handful of coppers at Tomaaz and slunk away. Typical—always the first to plan trouble and the last to get blamed for it. But Lofty's adventurous streak appealed to Tomaaz. No one else here was half as fun.

Beatrice gave Tomaaz a wave and headed back to her pastries.

"Tomaaz! Ezaara!" Klaus faced them off, hands on hips.

Tomaaz pocketed the coins and squared his shoulders. People were staring at them, but he didn't care. Beatrice had seen him fight. "It's my fault," he said. "I challenged Ezaara."

"In the middle of the marketplace?" Klaus snapped. "You could have taken out a littling's eye."

"Our tips were corked and the blades aren't sharpened," Ezaara defended. "See?" She passed him her sword.

Klaus ran his thumb and forefinger along Ezaara's blade. "It doesn't matter. You shouldn't—"

"She tricked Tomaaz," Old Bill called out. "Fighting sneaky, like a dragon rider."

Why was Bill bringing dragon riders into this? The fool. Any mention of dragons was bound to get Klaus riled up.

Klaus spun on Bill. "If I hear you mention those filthy winged reptiles and their stinking riders again, you'll be getting acquainted with our jail."

Bill glowered.

Klaus stabbed his finger on Tomaaz's chest. "No fighting in the marketplace."

"Sorry, sir, it won't happen again." Tomaaz inclined his head. One day, he'd be free from Klaus' silly restrictions. One day, he'd see dragons for himself.

"They knocked over my cloth," Old Bill protested.

"Help Bill tidy up." Flinging them a stern glare, Klaus strode off.

Old Bill rubbed his hands together. "So, kissed by Lofty, eh?"

Tomaaz stared at Bill in disgust. "I can't believe you put Lofty up to that. I mean, he's liked her for ages, and now he's blown it. There's no way my sister's going to like him back now."

Ezaara rolled her eyes. "Would you two stop talking about me as if I'm not here?"

They'd cheapened Ezaara with those filthy coppers—and she had enough problems with her self-confidence already. Tomaaz tried to make light of it. "Come on, Bill, you should've bet Lofty a silver."

It didn't work. Ezaara turned her back on him and dumped a roll of cloth on Old Bill's trestle table. Bill's daughter, Lovina, ignored them all, her filmy gray eyes examining the frayed stitching on her tattered boots. Boots so fascinating, she'd probably missed the whole sword fight. Tomaaz tossed the remaining bolts on the table and left.

Walking a little straighter as he approached Beatrice's stand, he winked at her. Despite Klaus' bollocking, today was shaping up nicely. He passed Beatrice a copper. "I'd like a potato patty, please." Tomaaz grinned at Beatrice, whose cheeks pinked. Now, that was the way to make a girl blush, not by embarrassing her in front of a crowd.

As he took the patty from Beatrice, their fingers brushed, sending a thrill through him. Tomaaz's heart thrummed. He was loathe to go, but didn't have a reason to stay. So, he turned away, biting into his patty, savoring the salty cheese and paprika.

Ezaara was still hanging around the cloth stall. Old Bill was leaning over his trestle table, shoving something into her hands. She glanced around furtively. Then, cradling her palms, she stared down, face full of wonder.

What was he showing her? Bill was very interested in Ezaara today. Tomaaz ground the now tasteless patty between his teeth. One of Bill's customers bumped Ezaara and she shoved the object back at Bill and hurried away.

Scoffing the last of his patty, Tomaaz rushed after her, but the next moment, Lofty was there.

"Hey, Maaz, look at my knife. It's a real beauty."

The handle was bone, carved with interwoven vines. Tomaaz let out a low whistle. "Nice."

Lofty weighed it in his palm. "And it's beautifully weighted. Here, try." Lofty held the knife as if he was about to throw it.

"Watch it," said Tomaaz. "I don't want Klaus over here again." He took the blade. "Feels good. That should improve your aim."

Lofty nudged him, crowing. "At least, that's one thing I can do better than you!"

"True." Tomaaz passed the blade back, and Lofty rushed off to show someone else as Ezaara came out from behind the cooper's stall.

"There you are." Tomaaz approached her. "I was looking for you."

"Marco got a bleeding nose from Paolo."

Tomaaz rolled his eyes. "Those two again." The boys were always getting into scrapes.

"Now you sound like Klaus." Ezaara grinned. "They don't know the sharp end of a sword from a hilt, and Paolo swings way too hard. We should teach them."

"Good idea," Tomaaz said, tugging Ezaara toward their parents' produce stall. "Now, what was Bill showing you, on the quiet?"

Glancing around again, Ezaara whispered, "Cloth—speckled with dragons of gold and bronze."

"Contraband cloth? Lucky Klaus didn't catch you." What was Bill's game? "Be careful. Old Bill's bad news."

Ezaara's face was filled with longing. "Even if dragons are evil, the fabric was beautiful."

Tomaaz wrinkled his nose as they passed a pen of piglets. "Lofty says dragons are honored beyond the Grande Alps." Dare he tell her? Might as well. "One day, I'm going to look for myself."

She elbowed him, hard. "Someone will hear you."

"So what? I'm not going to live here forever, you know."

Her eyes flew wide. "You'd leave us?"

Tomaaz blew out his cheeks. "Don't know. Maybe."

Ezaara frowned. "That's why Lofty's ma wanted owl-wort—you and Lofty are planning to go tonight, right?"

Tomaaz laughed. "If only!"

"If you ever leave, take me with you." Ezaara's voice was fierce.

"All right." Tomaaz cuffed her arm. "But no running off without me, either."

"Never," Ezaara swore. They bumped knuckles, sealing their vow.

When they reached their family stall, Ma sent Ezaara off to gather more herbs in the forest. "I'll duck home and get some flatbread on the hearth before the fire's dead," she said.

Pa brushed his dark curls back from his forehead. "We've sold out sooner than I thought. How about a dip, Tomaaz?"

"Sounds great," Tomaaz replied. Good thing too: the coating of dust and grime he was wearing would ruin the impression he'd made on Beatrice. She was the prettiest girl in Lush Valley. For many moons, he'd been working up the courage to ask her out. Thank the gods, Lofty had dared him earlier, otherwise he'd still be wondering whether she'd say yes.

"Not so fast," Pa said. "First, take this last sack of carrots to the smithy."

Tomaaz wasn't in a hurry—Beatrice and Pieter always took their leftovers to the bedridden and widows after the market. And he didn't want to seem too eager to get clean—his family would tease the hair from his head if he told them he was seeing a girl.

"Sure, Pa." He shouldered the carrots and headed to the smithy. How many sacks would he haul and how many carrots would he harvest before he had a real adventure? Probably hundreds. Thousands. Tomaaz sighed, trudging away.

§

Hans floated on his back in the warm water. He and Marlies had discovered this swimming hole years ago, when they'd first arrived in Lush Valley and settled on their farm near the forest. It was his favorite place to bathe.

His son was scrubbing at his curls with more vigor than usual.

Hans raised an eyebrow at Tomaaz. "Going somewhere special later?"

"Just off for a walk."

Hans couldn't help grinning. Did Tomaaz think he was a fool? He'd taken so long delivering those potatoes, and it hadn't only been that sword fight with Ezaara that had delayed him. And he'd been as jaunty as a songbird when he'd returned. "I know market day's a welcome break, but tomorrow, we'll need to get back to harvest, Son."

"I know." Tomaaz dived under, then popped up, floating on his back, too.

Laughing, Hans waded ashore and dried himself. "Come on, we've got stock to feed before you go off on your *walk*." He pursed his lips, blowing Tomaaz a kiss.

"Hey!" Tomaaz swept his arm across the river's surface, spraying him. "You can feed the stock yourself, just for that!"

Hans laughed and tugged his clothes on. Marlies' flatbread and soup might be ready by the time they returned. He bent to tie his boots.

Was that a tingle in his chest? After all these years?

He'd never had *that* feeling since living *here*. He scanned the sky—as he had done every day since they'd settled in Lush Valley.

The tingling grew stronger, pulsing across his ribs. The range and focus of his vision extended.

There, a flash in the distant sky. Moments later, he saw another.

Keeping his voice casual, Hans addressed his son, "Want a race through the forest to the clearing?"

Still in the river, Tomaaz grinned. "The loser cleans the dinner bowls?"

"You're on." Hans took off.

"Hey," Tomaaz called, splashing out of the water behind him. "Not fair!"

Hans threw caution to the wind, racing ahead. The power in his chest intensified and he sped forward, leaping logs, charging through the forest. Liquid fire sang in his veins.

With his enhanced dragon-sight, Hans recognized the mighty multi-hued dragon approaching from the north. The dragon was circling down towards ... there, through the trees ... his daughter! Shards! Zaarusha, the dragon queen, was coming for Ezaara! No! An eye for an eye, but this was crazy. If he could get there in time, perhaps he could reason with the dragon queen. He raced through the forest to the sacred clearing.

"No! Ezaara!" he cried out, as she jumped. Hans gathered his strength and leapt into the air. His fingertips grazed the tip of her boot as she shot skyward. He fell to the earth.

The dragon was too fast. She already had Ezaara.

Energy ebbed from Hans' body as Zaarusha winged her way towards the distant ranges. The dragon queen had found them. And Ezaara was gone.

What a price for an innocent mistake. His breath whooshed from his chest.

Several clear stones were scattered on the grass. He grabbed them, rubbing their smooth oval surfaces and pointed ends. Zaarusha had left him calling stones.

Twigs cracked and leaves rustled. *Someone* was coming.

Hastily, Hans pocketed the stones, mentally cursing the silly tales of dragons carrying off young maidens, made up years ago to keep young girls close to home. Such stupid tales might help folk guess what had happened.

Marlies broke into the clearing, breathing hard. "Hans! Where are the children? Tomaaz? Ezaara? Are they all right?"

"Zaarusha came. Ezaara's gone."

"No!" Marlies whispered, her face hollow. "My baby!"

Nearly seventeen, Ezaara was hardly a baby, but Hans felt the same—Zaarusha had raided their nest. "There may be hope yet. Zaarusha wants us to contact her." He showed Marlies a calling stone.

Marlies recoiled. "Contact her?"

Hans gripped her arm. "It may be our only chance of seeing Ezaara again."

Her breath shuddered. "Oh, Hans, what have I done? It's my fault. If only I hadn't touched her dragonet's egg …" She sagged against him.

Hans cocooned her in his arms. "You didn't know. It was an innocent mistake."

Marlies' turquoise eyes were heavy with tears. "I'll fix this. I have to. Please, pass me the stone."

"Don't be afraid." Hans tried to comfort her, in vain. If only he could stop his own heart from hammering like a battle drum.

§

READ
DRAGON HERO
RIDERS OF FIRE, BOOK TWO

ATTACK on DRAGONS REALM

EILEEN MUELLER

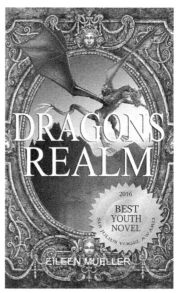

DRAGONS REALM

2016 BEST YOUTH NOVEL

SIR JULIUS VOGEL AWARD

EILEEN MUELLER

FANGTASTIC DRAGON JOKES

AND

CLAWSOME LIMERICKS

Compiled By
EILEEN MUELLER

DRAGON TALES

EILEEN MUELLER

HERBAL LORE IN DRAGONS' REALM

Arnica—Small yellow flower with hairy leaves. Reduces pain, swelling and inflammation. The flower and root are used in Marlies' healing salve.

Bear's bane—Pungent oniony numbing salve with bear leek as the primary ingredient.

Bergamot—Citrus fruit with a refreshing scent.

Clean herb—Tangy, pale green leaves with antibacterial properties.

Clear-mind—Orange berries, used to combat numlock. Stronger when dried, but effective when fresh.

Dragon's bane—Clear poison that, when it enters the blood, makes wounds bleed excessively, and then slowly shuts down circulation and breathing.

Dragon's breath—A rare mountain flower, that when shaken, produces a soft glow.

Freshweed—Chewing freshweed masks the user's scent.

Healing salve—Contains arnica, piaua juice, peppermint, and clean herb, and promotes healing.

Jasmine—Highly-scented white tubular flowers. Promotes relaxation.

Koromiko—Thin green leaves that, when brewed as a tea, prevent belly gripe.

Lavender—Highly-scented lilac whorled flowers. Relaxant, refreshing.

Limplock—Green sticky paste with an acrid scent, used to coat tharuk weapons. Acts on the victim's nervous system, causing slow paralysis, starting with peripheries and making its way to the vital organs.

Limplock remedy—Fine yellow granules that reverse the effect of limplock. Dose: one vial for an adult; three vials for a dragon.

Numlock—Thin gray leaves, ground into a tangy powder. Saps victim's will, determination and coherent thought. Used by Zens and tharuks to keep slaves in submission. Creates a gray sheen over the eyes and fingernails.

Owl-wort—Small leaves that enable sight in the dark.

Peppermint—Dark green leaves with aromatic scent. Good for circulation, headaches and as a relaxant.

Piaua juice—Pale green juice from succulent piaua leaves. Heals wounds and knits flesh back together in moments.

Rubaka—Crushed leaves produce a pale green powder used as a remedy against dragon's bane.

Skarkrak—Bitter gray leaves. A Robandi poison. In mild doses causes sleepiness and vomiting; in strong doses, death.

Swayweed—Fine green tea. Reverses loyalties and allegiances.

Woozy weed—Causes sleepiness and forgetfulness.

Acknowledgements

I t takes a village to birth a book, and *Ezaara* is no exception. My heartfelt thanks to Mandi Ellsworth, Deb Jensen, Erika Butters, Neil Mueller and Karen Brookes—you championed *Ezaara* and *Riders of Fire*, back in 2009. The manuscript won the SpecFicNZ 2013 Going Global contest, but the story still wasn't how I envisaged it.

Thank you to my fantastic colleagues Michelle Child, Peter Friend, Charlotte Kieft, Simon Fogarty, Lee Murray, A.J. Ponder and Kevin Berry—you were generous with your talents and advice. *Ezaara* is now how I truly want it to be.

And my young adult readers? I'm lucky to have the best teen advisors: thank you Ash Rachel and Lisa Artmann for loving Ezaara's story as much as I do.

John Turner, hey, you're my expert—forensics, battle techniques, medieval weaponry—you're my man! Ava Fairhall, your map of Dragons' Realm rocks. Christian Bentulan, your cover art brings my dragons and riders of fire to life. It really does—and I know my readers agree! Mandi Murphy, your animation of Ezaara's cover is awesome.

My readers and reviewers make this writing gig worthwhile. I love your reviews and enthusiasm for my stories. Thank you for your feedback.

Finally, all my love to my family. Kurt, you have been generous beyond measure in helping me pursue my dreams. Jan, Neil, Raphael and Mia, thanks for putting up with a mum who is well and truly dragon-mad!

About Eileen

Eileen Mueller is a double SJV award-winning author of heart-pounding fantasy novels that will keep you turning the page. Dive into her worlds, full of magic, love, adventure and dragons! Eileen lives in New Zealand, in a cave, with four dragonets and a shape shifter, writing for young adults, children and everyone who loves adventure.

Visit her website at EileenMuellerAuthor.com for Eileen's FREE books and new releases or to become a Rider of Fire!

Please place a review

People will find my books and enjoy these adventures if you leave a review. Readers are my lifeblood, so I'd love you to pop a line or two on Amazon or Goodreads. Thank you

BECOME A RIDER OF FIRE

Every author needs a team on their side to help them fight tharuks, imprint with dragons, and keep the realm safe. Being a Rider of Fire gives you early copies of my books, the chance to name characters, dragons and villages, and other special glimpses into Dragons' Realm, the world of Riders of Fire.

I would be grateful for reviews, social media shares and recommendations. If you're keen, please sign up on my site www.EileenMuellerAuthor.com

Made in United States
North Haven, CT
15 December 2021